THE
Magical
BOOKSHOP
Volumes 1–3

EVERY TRICK IN THE BOOK
BROUGHT TO BOOK
DOUBLE BOOKED

LIZ HEDGECOCK

WHITE
RHINO
BOOKS

For Stephen, bookworm and proud
For Paula, my book bestie
For John, who keeps me on the right lines

THE MAGICAL BOOKSHOP: 1

Every
TRICK
in the
BOOK

LIZ HEDGECOCK

WHITE
RHINO
BOOKS

'It's nothing personal, Jemma.'

Jemma sat clutching the edge of the chair, taking it very personally.

'I can't say this enough,' said Phoebe, her boss. 'It isn't about the person, it's about the job. And unfortunately, your job is no longer required.'

'That's exactly it,' said Wendy from HR. 'It's a business decision.' Her expression softened a little. 'I know that doesn't make it any easier for you.'

Jemma suspected that she was meant to speak at this point, but she couldn't. All her words had hardened into a tight lump in her throat, and she had a feeling that if she tried to talk, something entirely inappropriate would come out. Not that it mattered now, really.

'Now, of course we have a redundancy package,' said Wendy, and Jemma winced. Wendy had explained her presence at the beginning of the meeting, but Jemma had been so shocked that she had barely taken a word in. The R-word made it final.

That morning she had at last finished the report she'd been

working on for most of the week, sent it to her boss, then popped out to Pret for her Friday treat: a chicken and avocado sandwich, a slice of carrot cake, and a flat white. Then she re-entered the open-plan office, and all talk ceased.

'Phoebe asked me to let you know that she'd like to see you,' said Yvonne, Phoebe's PA.

'Oh. OK.' Jemma changed course and began to walk towards Phoebe's office.

'She's up in Meeting Room Four,' said Yvonne.

Jemma's skin prickled. Yvonne was looking at her in a sympathetic sort of way. 'Is it about the report? I didn't think she'd have had time to read it yet—'

'She didn't say what it was about,' said Yvonne, though her expression indicated that she knew.

Jemma walked to her desk, put her lunch down, then took the lift to the meeting-room floor. When she saw Yvonne's expression repeated on her boss's face, *she* knew. Wendy's presence was the icing on the cake. Although suddenly she seemed to have lost her appetite.

Wendy was still talking, and Jemma hastily tuned back in. 'Now, we've decided to let the two years you spent in our graduate scheme count towards your service. That makes four years' service, so we have calculated your redundancy payment as *this*.' She pushed a printout across the glass-topped table. There were various numbers on it, all doing a little dance. Jemma nodded, numb, and pushed the piece of paper towards Wendy.

'Normally you would have a notice period of one month. However, given that we have sprung this on you rather, we shall put you on gardening leave for that month to enable you to look for alternative employment.' She smiled. 'Which I'm sure won't be long in coming.'

'No,' said Phoebe. 'I shall give you an excellent reference. Your conscientiousness and your diligence have been an asset to the company. I am truly sorry to lose you.'

Jemma's thoughts were a blur. No more early mornings in the office with an espresso, saying hello to the others as they came in. No more quick drinks after work with Em, which often turned into staying for happy hour, then going for a pizza, then finding herself tumbling into bed happily drunk at a ridiculously early hour. And no time to organise a leaving do.

'So if I could have your badge, and your door pass?' Wendy held her hand out expectantly. 'Oh, and if any of your files aren't saved on the network drive, could you move those over.'

Jemma bent her head and removed her lanyard. 'The door pass is behind the badge,' she said.

Wendy slid it out to check. 'Excellent,' she said brightly, and ticked two boxes on the sheet of paper in front of her. 'Now, I think we've covered everything. Would you mind signing here to confirm?' She pushed the sheet of paper across the desk to Jemma, with a pen.

Jemma signed the paper without reading it. Odd that her signature was just the same as usual. The same neat loops, the same flourish at the end which she had added when she was fourteen, and kept ever since. What now? She looked at her boss for a cue.

'Would you like me to take you back to the office, Jemma?' Phoebe asked, still with that same sympathetic expression on her face. 'I'm sure you'll want to say goodbye to everyone.'

No, I don't, thought Jemma. 'I'll be OK,' she said, with a brave smile.

When Jemma returned to the main office, every head was down. 'Hi,' she said, wondering if she had become invisible.

There were a few mutters of 'Hi' in response, but all heads remained resolutely bent. Em would have said hi, would have smiled; but Em was on leave today, celebrating her boyfriend's new job.

3

Jemma felt like shouting at them, asking 'Why did none of you warn me? You obviously all knew.' But that would be mean, and she wasn't a mean person. Just ambitious.

The company's clean-desk policy meant Jemma had little to pack up. A pen pot, a business-card holder, a small fake cactus. It all fitted, along with her lunch, in a canvas tote bag emblazoned with the company name. The irony of becoming a walking advertisement for the company just now wasn't lost on her.

'Bye, everyone,' she said as she opened the door. She didn't bother waiting for a reply.

She had to ask Dawn on reception to buzz her out. 'It's my last day,' she said, as explanation.

'You kept that quiet,' said Dawn, as Jemma wrote her leaving time in the book. 'Off to bigger and better things?'

'Yes,' said Jemma, and smiled.

***

The city bustled past her as she stood outside the building. *I don't want to go home yet*, she thought. *If I go home, I'll probably sit in front of the TV and cry.* Besides, the thought of packing into a tube, a sardine like any other, repelled her. *I have to do something*, she thought, and started walking. She wasn't entirely sure which direction she was heading in; but she was going west.

Jemma walked past office blocks, and shops, and churches. Gradually the City of London became less and less citified, and she found herself in Covent Garden. But today she wasn't in the mood for boutiques or quirky little speciality shops, so she carried on to Charing Cross Road. Here everything seemed slower. People flicked through boxes of books on the pavement, or pointed at window displays. People didn't hurry; they sauntered, or just stood. So far on her journey Jemma had felt like a slow person in a fast world. Here, it was the other way round. She wandered down the street, ready to stop for anything that took her fancy. But the people loitering in front of shops and in doorways made it hard to see, and she moved on.

Then she noticed a little shop set back from the rest, like a shy person at a party. She looked up at the sign. *Burns Books*, it said, in faded gold on navy. *Secondhand Booksellers.*

'Burns Books?' Jemma said, and laughed. 'What a silly name for a bookshop!' In the window were a box set of *The Lord of the Rings,* a dusty collection of Dickens, and a row of Poldark novels, labelled *Two missing.* It wasn't so much a display as an apology. Jemma opened the door, and went in.

A bell above her head jangled, and a man reading *2000 AD* jumped and hastily put it down on the counter. 'Hello,' he said, frowning. 'What do you want? You're not from the council, are you?' He pushed a hand through his sandy hair.

'No,' said Jemma. 'Would it matter if I was?'

'Sometimes they try and sneak in undercover,' said the man. 'It's to do with business rates.' His eyes narrowed. 'Don't tell me you're from the retail association.'

'Still a no,' said Jemma. 'I just wanted to come in and look at books.' She took a step towards the shelves, but the man unfolded himself from behind the counter and intercepted her.

'Why are you dressed like that, then?' he asked, eyeing her suit and heels.

Jemma eyed him back. 'I could ask you the same question.' He was wearing blue and green tartan trousers, a thick bottle-green velvet waistcoat incredibly unsuitable for the weather, a dress shirt with a pleated front, and a gold lamé bow tie.

'I'll dress how I like, thank you very much,' the man replied, with dignity. 'Which books do you wish to look at?' He said this as if expecting her to back down and admit defeat.

'Novels,' declared Jemma, nose in the air. 'I like novels.'

'The fiction section starts there,' he said, jerking a thumb at it, and retreated behind the counter.

Jemma approached the shelves, trying to remember the last

book she'd read. She liked reading – loved reading, in fact – but somehow those evenings working late or getting merry with Em, and the weekends doing a little bit of extra work to stay ahead, really cut into her reading time.

She scanned the shelves for something impressive. Something which would show this snooty bookseller that she wasn't an illiterate fool who had stumbled into a bookshop by accident. Tolstoy. That should do it.

Her hand stretched towards *Anna Karenina* on the bottom shelf, but before she could grasp it the book was obscured by a blur of marmalade fur. Yellow eyes glared at her. The cat sat down right in front of the book, then without ceremony began to clean its bottom.

'Um, excuse me?' Jemma called.

There was no response, and she had to call again.

'Yes?' the man enquired.

'There's a cat in the way of a book I want to buy.'

'Oh yes, that will be Folio.' And the man returned to his comic.

'I don't think you understand,' said Jemma. 'I need you to move the cat.'

The man stared at her over the top of his comic. 'I don't think Folio would like that.'

'He's a cat,' said Jemma. 'I'm a customer. Or at least, I'd like to be a customer, but I'm finding it difficult.'

'I know!' the man cried, looking as pleased as if he had made an important discovery. 'I can make a note of the book you want, and your name. When Folio moves, I'll put the book in a safe place and you can come back for it!'

Jemma stared at him. 'Or I could go to another bookshop.'

An unpleasant shiver ran down her spine. Really, the bookshop was remarkably cold. And it smelt a bit damp. She straightened up, and looked around her. *It's like going back in time.* The counter was dark wood, probably mahogany, and on it stood a huge brass cash register. The shelves were sagging pine, and the floor was wood in a herringbone pattern, like in an old-fashioned school. There were no posters, no promotional materials, no recommendations… The only attractive thing in the bookshop was a red leather button-back armchair with a tapestry cushion. That looked warm and inviting. She took a step towards it, and the cat – Folio, was it? – dashed past her, leapt into the armchair, and settled himself down. *What a miserable dump.*

Jemma bent, retrieved the book, and took it to the counter. 'I'd like this, please,' she said.

The man inspected it, and shrugged. 'Never read it myself.' He opened the front cover. 'Two pounds fifty, please.'

Jemma held out her phone, and the man looked at it. 'That's worth more than two pounds fifty,' he said.

Jemma put it back in her bag and took a card from her purse. The man shook his head again.

'Good grief,' said Jemma, staring. 'You actually want money?'

'That's how it works,' said the man. He pushed buttons on the cash register and with a great clanking and ringing, figures pinged up in the top window.

Jemma opened her purse and handed over a two-pound coin and a fifty-pence piece. 'I'm afraid I'm fresh out of shillings,' she said.

'Very funny,' said the man. 'I can write you a receipt, if you wish.'

'Don't worry about it,' said Jemma.

'Would you like a bag, then?' He indicated a nail driven into the shelf behind him, from which hung plain brown-paper bags on a string.

'I'll put it in my own bag, thanks,' said Jemma. She felt something pushing at her ankles. It was the cat, Folio. 'Oh, he likes me,' she said, bending to stroke the cat.

'I wouldn't do that,' said the man. 'He isn't very friendly.'

Folio looked up at her, then put his head against her leg and butted. Jemma took a step back, and he advanced and butted her again. *He's trying to push me out of the shop*, she thought. *Well, that's fine by me. I don't think I'll be returning here in a hurry.* 'Bye,' she said, and walked briskly towards the door.

As she reached for the handle Jemma noticed a small white card stuck into the wood with a drawing pin. *Help Wanted*, it said, in elegant copperplate script. *It certainly is*, thought Jemma, with a smile. *I don't think I've ever seen such a sorry excuse for a bookshop in my whole life.* And with that comforting thought, she closed the door firmly behind her.

Chapter 2

Jemma felt unaccountably nervous as she walked down Charing Cross Road on Monday morning. *It's only a bookshop*, she told herself. *I could work anywhere I like.*

She had spent the weekend trying to decide what she wanted to do with the rest of her life. She had made lists. She had read articles about how self-made millionaires under thirty got their start. She had updated her CV. But still, when she closed her eyes, the scruffy bookshop with so much potential kept reappearing. *I could make something of that*, she thought. *I really could.*

She hadn't said anything to Em when she rang on Saturday afternoon. 'How are you, Jemma,' Em had enquired, with a wheelbarrow-full of concern in her voice. 'I'm sorry I couldn't be there yesterday. I'd have rung earlier, but I've just got up. Damon had tickets for the races, you see, as a leaving present from the agency, and then there was a boat trip, and it got a bit messy—'

'You knew, then,' said Jemma, feeling like a flat glass of lemonade.

'I didn't exactly know,' said Em. 'I mean, I'd heard talk. But you know I don't spread rumours.'

Em had been in the same intake of the graduate scheme as Jemma. Despite cheerfully admitting that she didn't know one end of a spreadsheet from the other, she had risen in the company through what she called a series of happy accidents. If Jemma hadn't been her friend, she would have envied Em tremendously. She had shiny dark hair that never seemed to need washing or cutting, and looked good in whatever she wore.

'I'm going to regard it as an opportunity,' said Jemma. 'A chance to do something different. The company wasn't right for me; that was the problem. Our values weren't aligned.'

'That's exactly what I think,' said Em. 'Do you fancy going for a quick drink?'

Jemma wrinkled her nose at her pyjama bottoms and T-shirt, and examined the split ends in her reddish-brown hair. 'Maybe not today,' she said. 'I'm taking some downtime to consider my new direction.' Plus she didn't feel ready to face Damon, whom she found hard going at the best of times. With a new job, he'd be insufferable.

'Oh, OK,' said Em. 'Well, Damon and I will be in the Grapes if you change your mind. I expect we'll be there for some time.'

And so, after considerable research, Jemma found herself striding down Charing Cross Road wearing ballerina flats, wide-legged black trousers, a smart-casual top, and her second-best work jacket, ready to make an impression.

The shop was closed.

Jemma looked at her watch, and tutted. The door had a brass knocker in the shape of a mythical creature; she wasn't sure quite what. Jemma lifted it, and brought it down sharply three times.

After two minutes, she knocked again. This time she was greeted with a yowl. Then she heard a muttered word which sounded rude, and someone fumbling with the lock.

The man who had been in the shop on Friday opened the door. He was wearing a mustard-coloured dressing gown over sky-blue silk pyjamas. 'Not today, thank you,' he said sharply.

Jemma put a foot in the door. 'I'm here to help,' she said.

'What, at this time of the morning?' The man looked incredulous. 'I don't need my soul saving, thank you very much.'

'I meant in the bookshop,' said Jemma. 'Help wanted?'

The man stared at her. 'I never expected anyone to answer,' he said. Then, grudgingly, 'I suppose you'd better come in.' He opened the door wider. 'Here, take a seat.' He indicated the armchair. 'I'll go and, um, get dressed.'

Jemma did as she was told and gazed around the shop. It was as dilapidated as she remembered. *Good. That means I can make more of a difference.* She opened her large work handbag, took out a folder, and put it on her knee, ready. At least that cat didn't seem to be around.

'Sorry about that,' said the man's voice. He reappeared, now dressed in a navy velvet suit with a crisp white shirt and a floppy black bow at his neck. Jemma wondered how on earth he had managed to get changed in such a short time. 'So.' He stood in front of Jemma, hands clasped, rocking gently on the balls of his feet.

'Aren't you going to interview me?' asked Jemma.

'Oh,' said the man. 'Um, yes, I suppose I am.'

'I'm Jemma James,' said Jemma, standing up and extending a hand. She had to look up quite a long way, as the man was at least a foot taller than she was.

He shook her hand firmly. 'Raphael Burns, owner and proprietor of Burns Books. Pleased to meet you.' He nodded, and Jemma sat down.

'About that,' she said. 'Do you really think Burns Books is a good name for a bookshop?'

The man seemed rather offended. 'The shop has been called Burns Books ever since it opened,' he said. 'It's been in the family for a long time.'

Jemma took that as a no. 'Would you like to see my qualifications?' she said, opening her folder. 'I've brought my GCSE, A-level and degree certificates, and my management diploma.' She held out a sheaf of papers, which the man took and paged through – possibly, she suspected, more from good manners than anything else.

'All most satisfactory,' he said, handing them back. 'When can you start?'

'Aren't you going to ask me any questions?' said Jemma. 'My previous experience, or why I want the job, or what I could bring to it?' Then she reflected that her lack of retail experience might count against her. 'Actually,' she said, 'I've put together a short-term action plan. Would you like me to present it to you?'

Raphael shuddered. 'Would you like a cup of tea?' he said.

'Yes please,' said Jemma. *While he's gone*, she thought, *I'll get my bullet points in order.*

She was fully prepared when Raphael Burns returned, bearing a tray with a cloth, two china cups and saucers, and a large teapot with a Space Invaders tea cosy over the top. 'I thought of some questions while the tea was brewing,' he said.

'Oh good,' said Jemma, composing herself. She hoped that his previous absentmindedness hadn't been an act, and he wasn't about to skewer her with something she hadn't thought of.

Raphael put the tray on the counter, poured out, and delivered a cup of tea with milk and one sugar, as Jemma had requested. Then he brought the chair from behind the counter, placed it facing her, and sat down. It was slightly too small for him, and he inhabited it like a wooden artist's figure arranged to show discomfort. 'This is my first question,' he said grandly. 'Do you like cats?'

As if on cue, Folio sauntered into the room, meowed at Jemma, then jumped into her lap, sitting on her papers and kneading them with his paws.

'Um, yes,' she said. 'Yes, I do like cats.'

Folio looked round at her and his golden eyes narrowed. The sound of tearing paper grew slightly louder.

'Excellent!' exclaimed Raphael. 'Now for my second question. Do you mind being bored?'

'Did you say bored?' asked Jemma, wondering if this was a trap.

'Yes, I did. Do you mind being bored, sometimes for hours at a time?'

'I don't think that question applies to me, really,' said Jemma. 'I find I'm hardly ever bored, as I can always think of something to do. For example, if business was slow in the shop, I could spend time writing and scheduling posts on the shop's social media feeds.'

'But we don't have any social media feeds,' said Raphael.

'I know,' said Jemma, triumphantly. 'I checked. And that, if I may say so, is one of your problems. Social media would give you additional shop windows onto the world. With the right targeted content, you could bring people here from far and wide.'

Raphael picked up his cup and drained it. He was clearly impressed.

'Another thing I could do during downtime in the shop,' said Jemma, 'would be to create eye-catching themed displays of books which we have in the shop. For example, you have *The Lord of the Rings* in the window, and I'm sure you must have Harry Potter books knocking around. We could make a display with a starry backcloth, and pointy hats, and maybe a flying broomstick or two.'

'Good heavens,' said Raphael.

'And I'm sure I could organise a way for the shop to take credit and debit cards,' said Jemma. 'You know, bring you into the twenty-first century.'

'I'm really not sure that's necessary,' said Raphael. He looked down his nose at her. 'All right, I shall employ you.'

'Wait a minute,' said Jemma. 'Aren't you going to ask me if I have any questions?'

'Do I have to?' asked Raphael.

'Yes, you do,' said Jemma, who had been on a recruitment course. She tried to remember what she had written, since Folio showed no sign of moving. 'What is the salary?'

Raphael looked nonplussed, then rather cunning. 'What did you earn in your previous job?'

Jemma wondered whether her answer would give him a heart attack, then decided to be truthful. Perhaps he was an eccentric millionaire who kept the shop as a hobby.

From Raphael's reaction, he was not an eccentric millionaire. He goggled at her. 'What on earth are you doing here, then?'

Jemma was prepared for this. 'I decided it was time for a change of focus,' she said grandly. 'I enjoyed my previous job, but it was taking up too much of my life. I want to shift down a gear and engage in a role I can give my heart to.' She remembered all the nights she had worked late, polishing reports for Phoebe, and crossed her fingers. 'I would be prepared to take a pay cut' – she named a figure which was approximately half of her previous salary – 'with the understanding that I would be rewarded appropriately for improving the bottom line of the shop.'

'The bottom line?' said Raphael, leaning down to look at the skirting board.

'The profits,' said Jemma, wondering if this man had ever read a business book in his life. Actually, she was pretty confident that he hadn't.

'All right, so that's salary,' said Raphael. 'What other questions do you have?'

'How many weeks' holiday will I have per year?' asked Jemma. 'What will my working hours be? Do you open on Sundays? Do you ever open in the evenings?'

Raphael held up his hands to ward her off. 'The shop hours are nine till five, Monday to Friday,' he said.

Jemma couldn't believe her ears. 'Not Saturdays? Not the busiest shopping day?'

'Not Saturdays,' Raphael said firmly.

Jemma shrugged. 'Fair enough. What about holidays?'

The cunning look came over his face again. 'What did you get in your previous job?'

Jemma told him.

'The same, then,' he said.

Jemma gave him a mental tick. 'Do you have a benefits package? Discounts, pension scheme, luncheon vouchers?'

'I could give you ten per cent off the books,' said Raphael. 'But to be honest, you can read those for free when it's quiet. Which it generally is. And I expect I'll buy you a coffee occasionally.'

Jemma sighed. 'That'll do,' she said. In any case, when more branches of Burns Books opened, she would be able to pay into her pension.

Raphael waited. 'Do you have any more questions?' he asked, as if opening the door to a tiger's cage.

Jemma considered, then decided she had probably put him through enough. 'Not just now,' she said.

'Well, in that case,' said Raphael, 'I suppose you can start.' He extended a hand carefully over Folio, and Jemma shook it again. 'I'll go and find you an apron.' He eyed her. 'It might be a bit big for you. The previous assistant was taller.'

'Oh, that's a question I should ask,' said Jemma. 'Why did the previous assistant leave?'

Raphael looked extremely uncomfortable. 'He found that the post didn't agree with him.' His eye fell on Folio.

'Oh,' said Jemma, 'was he allergic to cats?'

'Yes,' said Raphael. 'Or something like that. It was more that Folio was allergic to him. He was a nice chap, too. But not everyone is suited to a bookshop.' He regarded Jemma thoughtfully. 'In fact, I think we should begin with a week's trial.

To see how you get on with the shop, and how the shop gets on with you.'

'That's a good idea,' said Jemma. *After all*, she thought, *if it's as boring as he says, a week might be plenty*. 'So, until Friday?'

Raphael looked as if he were solving a complicated sum in his head. 'Yes,' he declared, eventually. 'Until Friday. I'll go and find that apron.' He uncurled himself from the chair and disappeared into the back room.

Jemma gazed down at Folio, who had fallen asleep in her lap, bits of paper caught between his claws. *I'm in*, she thought. *I've done it. I've landed a new job. And if I have anything to do with it, there will be changes around here.*

Folio purred in his sleep, stretched out a lazy paw, and sank his claws into her thigh.

Chapter 3

'Do I have to wear that?' asked Jemma, eyeing the brown apron which Raphael was holding up. It would probably cover her from neck to ankles, not to mention twice round.

'Well no, you don't have to,' said Raphael. 'But you might get a bit dusty otherwise.'

'Clothes are washable,' said Jemma. 'I mean, you don't see the assistants in Waterstones wearing—'

'Perhaps I should take this opportunity to mention,' said Raphael, 'that we'd rather you didn't talk about…' He lowered his voice. '*Other bookshops.*'

Jemma stared at him. 'Why ever not? They're our competitors.'

'Yes, yes, competitors is fine,' said Raphael. 'Rivals, also good. But don't name names.'

He probably finds it embarrassing, thought Jemma. 'Is it a sensitive point?' she asked, with a sympathetic smile. Then she wondered if her sympathetic smile looked the same as Phoebe's, and put it away.

'It is,' said Raphael. 'Thank you for understanding.'

'That's quite all right,' said Jemma. 'But I'd rather not wear the apron, if you don't mind.'

The letterbox rattled. 'Aha, the post!' cried Raphael, and dived for the doormat. He gathered up five or six envelopes and leafed through them. 'Bill . . . bill . . . junk mail . . . bill...' Jemma noticed that several of the envelopes had red ink on them. He opened a plain white envelope, unfolded the sheet within, scowled at it, then crumpled it into a ball and stuffed it in his pocket. 'And that was the post,' he said, going behind the counter, opening a drawer, and dropping the rest of the envelopes in unopened. 'Now the day can begin.'

'Shouldn't you open the bills?' Jemma wondered when, or if, she would be paid.

'Don't worry,' said Raphael. 'I have a special time put aside for dealing with things like that.'

'Oh, good,' said Jemma, pleased to learn there was some sort of organisation to this enterprise. 'When is that?'

'When the man arrives to cut it off, usually,' said Raphael. 'No sense in dealing with these things before you have to.'

Jemma opened her mouth to argue, then thought better of it. This felt like a battle for another time. Besides, she was curious to learn how the bookshop worked. If it did.

'When opening up,' said Raphael, 'the first job is to unlock the door. Which we've already done today, so we're ahead of ourselves.' He looked rather impressed with himself. 'Then, we turn the sign around.' He demonstrated. 'Next, we raise the blind in the shop window, like so.' He moved to the window, tugged on the cord, and the blind shot up. 'Voilà. Finally, we switch on the lights. One at a time, please. You never know.' He moved to a brass panel of toggle switches by the door, tensed himself, and pushed one down.

A dim light flickered on.

Raphael exhaled. 'And so on.' Gradually the shop became slightly brighter than it had been before. 'Do you need to make any notes?'

'I think I've got it so far,' said Jemma.

'Next, we check the till. You press this button to open it.' The drawer shot out with a ping. 'Now, I usually write down how much is in the till at the end of each day, so that we know where we're at. If it's a bit empty in the morning, there are some bank bags of change in this drawer.' He opened it, then closed it again. 'But I think we'll do.'

'So you don't cash up properly at the end of each day?' asked Jemma.

Raphael looked blank. 'Do you think I should?'

'Aren't you bothered about getting burgled?'

Raphael stared at her, then his face crumpled into a laugh. 'Burgled? Us? I don't think that's likely. We have good security, and Folio is an excellent guard cat.'

'I'm sure he is,' said Jemma, studying Folio, who was washing himself in the middle of the Science section.

'As a rule of thumb,' said Raphael, 'I tend to visit the bank when the till money gets above fifty pounds. That's a nice round number.'

Jemma's eyebrows shot into her fringe. She wanted to say many things at this point, but settled for 'I see.'

'Now, working the till,' said Raphael. 'When a customer buys a book, you check the price, then press the appropriate buttons so that the right amount comes up in the little window at the top. Then you press the *Sale* button, and the drawer opens. I'll show you properly if we get a customer.'

'What if they buy, say, two books?' asked Jemma. 'Do you add the number up first, then put it in? Or do you put the two numbers in separately?'

Raphael's brow furrowed. 'I don't think we'll worry about that just yet,' he said. 'That's all you need to know.'

'But what about dealing with customers?'

The blank look came over Raphael's face again. 'Um, I say hello to them, and then I generally let them get on with it. Obviously, if they ask me a direct question I answer them. After all, I wouldn't wish to be rude—'

The shop bell jangled.

'I'll watch and learn, shall I?' said Jemma, and took a step back. She unbuttoned her jacket and hung it on the old-fashioned coat stand next to the counter, ready for action.

'Good morning,' Raphael said politely to the somewhat frazzled woman who entered the shop.

'Good morning,' she said, looking about her. 'I wonder if you could help me. My sister is in hospital, and her TV doesn't work, and she's bored out of her brain.'

'Oh,' said Raphael. 'I'm afraid I'm not good with machinery. Especially not when electricity is involved.'

Jemma took a decisive step forward. 'What does she like to read?'

'Well, I took her my daughter's copy of *Jane Eyre*, and she was enjoying that, but I had to get it back because my daughter has to write an essay on it by Thursday.'

'Right, *Jane Eyre*. Charlotte Brontë.' Jemma went to General Fiction and found the Bs. 'We have two copies of that, and one copy of *Villette* by the same author. Oh, and one copy each of *Agnes Grey* and *The Tenant of Wildfell Hall*.' She thought. 'Would she like Jane Austen, do you think?'

The woman laughed. 'I know she liked *Pride and Prejudice* when it was on TV. Especially the bit where Mr Darcy dived into the lake.'

Jemma moved along to the As. 'We've got three of those and two copies of *Emma*. Oh, and a *Mansfield Park*.' She put her chin on the pile to keep it stable, took them to the counter, and spread them out.

The woman looked at the books. 'That's a lot,' she said.

'Of course you don't have to take them all,' said Jemma, 'but I could probably do you a deal if you buy a few.' She glanced across at Raphael, who was watching the transaction rather as one would watch a cobra emerging from a snake charmer's basket. 'I take it we can do a deal?'

'Yes,' said Raphael, as if hypnotised. 'We can do a deal.'

The woman brightened. 'Oh well, in that case...' Her hand hovered over the books. 'That one . . . and those two . . . and that one. And that *Pride and Prejudice.*' Her finger landed decisively on Colin Firth's chest.

'So that's five books.' Jemma checked the prices. 'At two pounds fifty each...' She glanced at Raphael. 'Can we do ten pounds? That's one book free.'

Raphael jumped. 'I'm sorry, what did you say?'

'Ten pounds for these five books,' Jemma said patiently. 'That's fair, isn't it?'

'I'll take them,' said the woman, digging out her purse. 'And I have a ten-pound note, which is lucky.'

'Isn't it,' said Jemma. She moved behind the counter and pushed the *10* button on the cash register, then the *00* button. The numbers appeared in the window. 'What do I do now?' she muttered to Raphael.

'Press the *Sale* button,' said Raphael, pointing.

'Oh yes, that's it,' said Jemma. 'Sorry, it's my first day.'

'Are you enjoying it?' asked the woman, handing over the note.

'Yes,' said Jemma. 'I am. Oh, and if you need any more books for your sister, you know where we are.'

'Indeed I do,' the woman replied. 'It's funny, but I hadn't noticed the shop before today. I think it's because you're set back.'

'Maybe that's it,' said Jemma, vowing to establish the shop's social media presence at the first opportunity. 'Would you like a bag? Or a receipt?'

'Oh yes, a bag would be good.'

Jemma pulled a paper bag off the string, then wrote *Burns Books* on it, and copied the telephone number from the dial of the black Bakelite phone next to her. 'There,' she said, slipping the paperbacks inside. 'If you want to check if we have a book, you can phone us and ask.'

'What a good idea,' said the woman. 'Must go, I was meant to be at work ten minutes ago.' She picked up the bag and scurried off.

'That was fun,' said Jemma, as the shop door closed behind her. 'Do you have any feedback for me?'

'Er, feedback?' said Raphael.

'Yes, on my handling of the retailer-customer interface,' said Jemma.

Raphael flinched. 'You did very well,' he said. 'In fact, I think you're ready for one of the more advanced aspects of working in a bookshop.'

Jemma could feel herself puffing up with pride. 'What's that?' she asked.

Raphael beamed. 'Now, don't be too disappointed if you don't get it right first time. Most people don't.'

'I'll give it my best shot,' said Jemma. 'What is it?'

Raphael looked very serious. 'Do you think you could possibly make us both a cup of tea?'

Chapter 4

No, Jemma told herself sternly. *You are going to avoid the takeaway, go home, and cook yourself a proper meal.*

But I have to stand up to do that. I've been on my feet all day —

Then you'll have to get used to it. Jemma took a deep breath, looked straight ahead, and marched past the takeaway. Enticing smells of grease and pepperoni assaulted her nostrils. *I am strong. I can do this. Anyway, I had pizza for lunch.*

She had been surprised when Raphael announced that he was nipping out for lunch at twelve thirty, then returned with a pizza box emblazoned with the logo of the takeaway next door, Snacking Cross Road. 'I hope you like anchovies,' he said, lifting the lid and revealing a pizza Napoli.

'Ooh, thanks,' said Jemma. She salivated at the aroma. Breakfast had been light, as she had been too nervous to eat much, and had happened what seemed like a very long time ago.

Raphael lifted a slice in his long fingers and took a hefty bite. 'Well, go on then,' he said, through the pizza.

Jemma glanced at the door. 'Should I wait?' she asked. 'A

customer might come in.'

'And the pizza *will* get cold,' said Raphael, giving her a severe look.

'Fair point,' said Jemma, and dived in.

No, there was definitely no excuse to stop by the takeaway tonight. The shop had closed at five o'clock precisely, and they had cashed up and found £152.50 in the till, which Raphael pronounced a record for a Monday. He locked it in the safe, then glanced at his watch, cried 'Good heavens, it's almost half past!', and shooed her out of the shop.

I'll wear more comfortable shoes tomorrow, she thought as she walked down her road, wincing as her heel rubbed yet again. *Are Converse acceptable?* She decided that if dress suits and gold bow ties were OK, then baseball boots would be fine. Especially since she would be behind the counter a lot of the time.

She arrived at the slightly dilapidated Victorian townhouse where she had a studio flat, let herself in, and wished, not for the first time, that her landlord would put in a lift. *I can probably cancel my gym membership*, she thought. *It isn't as if I went anyway, and the shop will keep me fit.* She climbed up the grand staircase to the third floor. As usual, the slightly wonky B on the door of the flat irked her. *Not much I can do about it*, she thought, and opened the door.

Jemma kicked off her shoes, resisted the call of the sofa, and went to investigate the cupboards in the kitchenette. She found pasta, a tin of tomatoes, a tin of beans, and in the fridge, a heel of cheese and some dried-out ham. She checked in the bread bin, but the three slices of bread left had green speckles blooming on them, and she put them in the bin. 'Pasta it is,' she said, and filled a pan with water.

Even after filling a bowl with the resultant cheese and tomato gloop, there was still plenty left. *I can have it again tomorrow*, she thought. She flopped on the sofa, switched on the TV, and was puzzled for a moment when she didn't see what she expected. *Of course, it's still early*, she thought, channel-surfing until she found something suitable to accompany forking pasta into her face.

She had just put a particularly cheesy, tomatoey forkful into her mouth when her mobile rang. 'Mmff,' she said, reached for her phone, and looked at the display.

Em.

Jemma pressed *Accept*. 'Hi, Em,' she said, after swallowing.

'I called to see how you were doing,' said Em. 'I hope you're all right.'

Jemma smiled to herself. 'I'm fine, thanks. I haven't long got in from work. I've been cooking.'

'Work?' said Em. 'What are you doing?' Suddenly a loud metallic-sounding voice boomed unintelligibly. 'Sorry, just waiting for my train. You did say work, didn't you?'

'Yes, I found a job,' said Jemma, feeling exceptionally perky. 'I'm working in a bookshop.'

'Oh,' said Em. 'That's a bit different.' A pause. 'Are you enjoying it?'

'Yes,' said Jemma. 'It's an independent one, on Charing Cross Road.'

'Oh, right,' said Em. 'Doesn't that have loads of bookshops?'

'That's right,' said Jemma. 'My one is called Burns Books.'

The tannoy boomed out again, and Jemma waited patiently for Em's congratulations. The noise ceased, but Em was still silent. 'Em? Are you still there?'

'Yes, I'm still here.' Em sounded faint, but down in the tube the signal was always poor. 'Was that Burns Books you said? Only —'

'Have you heard of it?' asked Jemma, eagerly. 'It isn't a big shop, but it's got lots of potential. I think I can make a real difference.'

'Um,' said Em. 'It's just that – My train's here, but I read

25

something. I'll send it to you. You haven't signed a contract or anything, have you?'

Jemma laughed. 'Raphael isn't that kind of boss,' she said. 'But what did you—'

'Got to go, bye, bye.'

Jemma looked at the phone for a moment, then put it down and scooped up more pasta. *Maybe she's jealous of my new start*, she thought to herself, chewing.

She had just finished the bowl when her phone pinged with a message. *You might want to read this. Sorry.*

Jemma clicked on the attachment. It was an article: *The Ten Worst Bookshops in Britain*. It was from a website that specialised in listicles, and beneath the title it said, in smaller letters: *Information taken from The Bookseller's Companion and social media*. And at number two – not even the top spot – was Burns Books.

Looking for a satisfying shopping experience? Then don't come here. The owner dresses like a failed Doctor Who who's found a bookshop from the bad old days and brought it kicking and screaming into the present. He couldn't care less about the customers, the shop is a death trap, and if the shop doesn't get you, the cat will. How the shop keeps running is a complete mystery, but I wouldn't advise you to try and solve it by going there.

Jemma's mouth twitched. She had to admit that, as descriptions went, it wasn't entirely inaccurate. She closed the article and hit *Reply. That was an interesting read*, she texted. *Thanks for sending it. The shop does have a lot of potential.*

She yawned widely, and covered her mouth. *I shall read in bed*, she decided, and opened out the sofa-bed. *If I'm going to turn the shop around, I'll need to be well rested.*

Folio, now the size of a tiger, roared at Jemma, and she had to build a barricade of books to keep herself safe. She had just put the last book into place when Folio leapt on top of it and books rained down on her. 'No!' she cried, flinging up her hands. Then she blinked, removed *Anna Karenina* from her face, and realised that the roaring was a loud rock number which, in her view, was completely inappropriate for breakfast radio.

She got ready, had a large bowl of cornflakes, and set off for the tube. As before, she had to knock for admission, but at least this time Raphael was dressed. Today's outfit was a tweed suit with elbow patches, a pink shirt, and a navy cravat with stars on. Jemma remembered the article, and tried not to smirk.

'You're early again,' said Raphael, with a yawn. 'Perhaps I should sort you out with a set of keys, and then you can open up when you arrive.'

'Oh, could I?' said Jemma, beaming.

He stared at her, nonplussed. 'If you like,' he said slowly.

A yowl came from behind him. Jemma peeped and saw Folio, now normal-sized, yawning. 'Hello, Folio,' she said, extending a hand.

Folio put his head on one side, considered her hand, then walked off.

'Right, important business,' said Raphael, rubbing his hands. 'Tea!'

'But aren't we going to refill the shelves?' said Jemma. 'We sold quite a few books yesterday. Shouldn't we put more stock out? Where is the stock?'

'In the stockroom,' said Raphael. 'Where else would it be?'

'OK,' said Jemma. 'Do we know what's in there?'

'Broadly, yes,' said Raphael. 'Specifically, not really. I just open a box when I feel the urge, and see what's inside.'

'Would you mind if I had a look?' asked Jemma.

Raphael shrugged. 'Be my guest. If you go into the back room, it's the door on the right.'

'Do I need a key?'

His only response was a laugh.

Jemma went into the back room and faced the door. What would she find behind it? She imagined a broom-cupboard-like space, with boxes stacked one on top of the other and barely room to turn round. She took a deep breath, and opened the door.

'The light switch is on the left,' called Raphael. 'One at a time, remember.'

Jemma snapped on the light. 'Woah.'

It was like the warehouse at the end of *Raiders of the Lost Ark*. OK, maybe not that big, but *big*.

'How does this room fit into the shop?' Jemma muttered to herself. 'It's like the Tardis. But stop with the Doctor Who comparisons, it's getting weird.' She walked down the middle aisle of the three. Boxes squatted on metal shelves, seven rows high, which reached to the ceiling. She lifted a box out carefully, and saw at least two more behind. As far as she could tell, not one box was labelled. 'How on earth does he find anything?' she said, aloud.

The answer came to her immediately. *He doesn't.*

Jemma's sense of order, of how things ought to be, bristled. *He needs a spreadsheet,* she thought. *A big spreadsheet. No, he doesn't need it. The shop needs it.* She resolved to bring her laptop in the next day and start cataloguing this fearful mess. *Well,* she conceded, *not exactly a mess.* After all, the books were in boxes. It was a mess made to look as if it wasn't a mess, which was even worse.

She took the box she had selected through to the shop, then returned to switch off the light and close the door. She found Raphael regarding the box with curiosity. 'I wonder what's inside,' he said.

'If you labelled the boxes,' said Jemma, 'you'd know.'

'Where's the fun in that?' said Raphael. 'This is like Christmas.'

'Let's hope it's a good Christmas,' said Jemma, grimly. 'Do you have any scissors?'

The lid of the box was taped down. Jemma cut into it carefully, opened the flaps, and revealed a stack of Mills and Boon romances and, sitting next to them, what looked like a complete set of CS Forester's Hornblower novels.

'Strange bedfellows,' she murmured. 'Oh well, I might as well put them out, seeing as the box is open.'

'Pass me one, would you,' said Raphael.

Jemma picked up *Mr Midshipman Hornblower*.

'No, from the other side.'

Jemma shrugged, and passed him *A Debutante in Disguise*.

'I've always wanted to read one of these,' Raphael said, opening it. 'Never got round to it.' He sat in the armchair, took out a pair of reading glasses, and settled them on his long nose. Folio hopped onto his lap, and was peacefully asleep within seconds.

'Guess I'd better restock the shelves, then,' said Jemma, but there was no response.

Jemma put out the books, turned the sign, raised the blind, switched on the lights, and checked the till, but not a customer appeared. In the end she took out her copy of *Anna Karenina* and attempted to read the first chapter. But somehow images of a roaring Folio, a bookshop travelling through space, and an empty till kept getting between her and the pages. She glanced across at Raphael, still reading, and the words of the article echoed in her head. How *does* the bookshop keep running?

Chapter 5

Jemma was no wiser on that subject by Friday. It had been a whirlwind of a week. She had sold, in her estimation, hundreds of books to a range of people, from harried office workers looking for 'something on emotional intelligence' to bewildered and often bedraggled tourists in Harry Potter scarves, who arrived in the shop asking if she could direct them to the Leaky Cauldron.

At first she had told them, rather shortly, that while the Leaky Cauldron was on Charing Cross Road in the books, it was filmed elsewhere in London. Then she wised up, gathered Harry Potter books, and displayed them in the window, along with a straw broom she had found at a hardware shop down the road and a witch's hat from a fancy-dress shop. She had assumed that they would burn through their entire Harry Potter stock in one day. Somehow, though, every time she went to the stockroom, she struck lucky and found yet another box of Harry Potters in her random selection.

'It's a bit odd,' she said to Raphael, one day.

'What's odd?' he asked, looking wary.

'Well, because of the shop display we have lots of people

wanting Harry Potter books, and somehow, those are what I'm finding in the stockroom.'

'Mmm,' said Raphael. 'Probably just coincidence.' And sure enough, the next box Jemma opened turned out to contain a mixture of books by Zadie Smith, China Miéville, and Gabriel Garcia Marquez.

But the shop was definitely making more money; of that Jemma was certain. She made sure to always be present at cashing-up time, and on some days they took as much as three hundred pounds. 'I don't know what the bank manager will make of this,' said Raphael.

'They'll probably be very pleased,' said Jemma.

'They'll probably think I'm up to something,' said Raphael.

'I told you that getting the shop on social media was a good idea,' said Jemma. So far the shop had a Facebook page, a Twitter feed, and an Instagram account. She liked the idea of TikTok, but suspected that making videos with Raphael in the shop would be difficult.

She had even attempted to catalogue the books, but that hadn't gone to plan. It ought to have been perfectly straightforward, if laborious. But somehow her laptop kept saving the spreadsheet to weird locations, and when she found and reopened it the data was corrupt, or one of the columns had vanished. In the end she gave it up as a bad job. *There's probably professional software I could get to do this*, she thought. *Maybe I could persuade Raphael that it's an investment.* And she left it at that.

And now it was Friday, and the end of her trial week. Her clock radio woke her with 'Don't Leave Me This Way'. She tried to read that as a positive sign that the shop couldn't cope without her, but didn't even manage to convince herself. She hunkered under the duvet and stared at the ceiling, where a crack was creeping towards the light fitting. *Come on Jemma, best foot forward*, she told herself. But she waited until the Pet Shop Boys' 'Opportunity' was playing before getting up. You never knew.

Ridiculous, she thought, throwing off her duvet. *As if I've ever been superstitious. Superstition gets you nowhere.* But she felt better as she got ready, humming along.

That's probably because you're eating better, she thought. *Although Kris from the takeaway probably thinks I've died.*

On Wednesday, after the previous night's palatial supper of leftover pasta, and realising that if she didn't do something she would be having a bowl of baked beans for tea, she had borrowed a book called *Easy Suppers* from the cookery section and visited Nafisa's Mini-Market two doors down. It had taken her an hour and a half to cook a meal which allegedly took twenty-five minutes, but while it looked nothing like the photograph, it tasted nice. And she couldn't feel her arteries closing up as they did when she wolfed down one of Kris's offerings…

Jemma realised the time, and dashed to the tube station. The first train was already full so she waited for the next, which took ten minutes to come and was full again. By the time she managed to squeeze onto a train then dash to the shop, it was five to nine. 'Sorry I'm late,' she panted, as Raphael opened the door in his usual unhurried manner. 'It was the trains. They were awful, and I had to wait ages.'

'Never mind,' said Raphael, absently. 'You're here now. I was just about to open.'

There was no hint of reproof in either his voice or his face, but Jemma still felt it. *Nice one, Jemma,* she thought to herself as she scurried to the window and pulled up the blind. *Stellar move, being almost late on the day when your boss decides if he's keeping you or not.* She remembered a day, perhaps a year ago, when the tube had let her down, and she had arrived in the office at her actual start time instead of her usual hour earlier. The office had given her a round of applause and raucous cheers, with cries of 'Here she is at last!' and 'We were going to call the police!'

Even Phoebe had come out of her office to comment. Jemma had taken it with a smile; but she had never been so late, as she thought of it, again.

The shop was quiet that morning and Jemma kept her head down, getting stock on the shelves (today's boxes held travel guides, books on hobbies, and manuals about budgeting). 'I thought it would be busier on a Friday,' she ventured at eleven o'clock, when their only customer so far, a man looking for books on the Indian railways, had departed with three large hardbacks under his arm.

'It goes in waves,' said Raphael. 'I'd like to tell you that it varies with the weather, or the season, or what's on television, but really, in my many years running this bookshop, I've learnt that there is no rhyme or reason to it.'

'But surely there are trends,' said Jemma. 'Lots of new books are released in September, and then there's the run-up to Christmas—'

'Not in this bookshop,' said Raphael. 'I think it's time for elevenses. Would you mind doing the honours?'

Jemma went through to the back room, switched on the kettle, and found that they were out of Raphael's favourite Earl Grey teabags. 'I don't believe it,' she muttered. 'I swear the shop is out to get me.' She remembered the article that Em had sent her, and shivered. 'He'll have to make do with ordinary,' she told herself, dropping three teabags into the pot. She felt somewhat less sanguine when she saw Raphael's face as he took the first sip of his tea.

She could bear it no longer. 'About the trial period—'

'Oh yes,' said Raphael, putting his cup down precisely in the saucer. 'It's been very nice having you here.' Then he returned to his newspaper.

Oh, thought Jemma. *I guess that's it then.* She felt as if she had had a rug pulled from under her but nothing else had changed. 'I

33

suppose you want your cookbook back, then.'

'Only when you've finished with it,' said Raphael, filling in a clue on the crossword.

'I don't have it with me today,' said Jemma. 'I'll – I'll bring it in next week.'

'Oh yes, you do that,' said Raphael, not looking up.

'I'm just going into the stockroom,' said Jemma. Receiving no response, she bolted, and presently found herself staring at the aisles of boxes. *What do I do now?*

The blank boxes stared back at her.

Jemma searched through her memories of all the courses she had attended and all the blog posts she had read for some nuggets of wisdom. 'What can I learn from this experience?' she whispered.

'You could ask for feedback,' said a helpful little voice which sounded rather like Em's.

Oh God, I'll have to tell Em that I only lasted a week. I'll ask for feedback on what I did wrong, and promise to do better, and ask for another week's trial. Jemma took several deep breaths, then went back into the main shop. 'Could I ask for your feedback, please?'

She spoke louder than she had intended, and Raphael almost jumped out of the armchair. Folio, who was sitting on his lap, rearranged himself with a baleful glare at Jemma. She was getting used to Folio's baleful glare, though, so that didn't worry her too much.

'Feedback?' said Raphael. 'About what?'

'About my performance this week,' said Jemma. 'Because if there are things I've done that you weren't happy with, or that I could have done better, I'd welcome the opportunity to learn from you, and perhaps we could do another week's trial?' She gave him her best enthusiastic smile.

Raphael stared at her in disbelief, then started laughing. 'You haven't done anything wrong,' he choked out eventually. 'The shop hasn't burnt down, and we still have all the books, and there haven't been any riots so far this week.'

'That's a fairly low bar,' said Jemma.

'You haven't met some of my assistants,' said Raphael darkly. 'There was one time when I had to escape in a kayak. And no, I don't want to talk about it.'

'So . . . does that mean I can stay?' said Jemma.

'I don't see why not,' said Raphael. 'Folio seems to like you.'

Jemma looked at Folio, whose glare had softened to topaz inscrutability.

'Do you still have all your fingers?' Jemma held them up. 'Exactly,' said Raphael. 'And the shop seems to like you. Most of the time.'

It was on the tip of Jemma's tongue to ask how a shop could possibly have feelings; but she sensed that now was not the right time to voice such a thought. 'That's good, then,' she said, rather weakly. 'If you like, I could show you some projections I've put together, based on the recommendations in the action plan I drew up—'

'That won't be necessary,' said Raphael. 'Just keep doing what you're doing. And perhaps not too much of that.'

'Too much of what?' asked Jemma.

'You know,' said Raphael. He waved a hand. 'The spreadsheety, projectiony, computery thing.'

'The computery thing,' said Jemma. 'All right, I'll do less of the computery thing.' She resolved to do computery things when he wasn't watching, as they seemed to be working. 'But I can stay?'

'Of course you may stay,' said Raphael, sounding surprised. 'You're the first assistant I've had since – well, I can't remember – who has lasted till Friday.'

Jemma felt a slight prickle of unease. 'Why is that, do you

think?'

Raphael considered, gazing into the middle distance, or possibly at the Self Help section. 'Oh, there are many reasons which I won't bother you with just yet. I really don't think it will be relevant. Now, would you like to ask me again if you can stay, or may I get on with my crossword?'

Jemma opened and closed her mouth like a fish out of water.

'We can sign something, if it would make you feel better,' said Raphael. He got up, went to the counter, and pulled a brown-paper bag off the string. Then he took a fountain pen out of his jacket pocket and wrote rapidly on the paper. 'Here.' He held it out to Jemma.

Jemma read what he had written in his beautiful copperplate.

I, Raphael Burns, promise to employ Jemma James at Burns Books for as long as it is mutually convenient to us both.

I, Jemma James, agree to work in said bookshop until I am bored or for other reasons.

Raphael had already signed it. 'Will that do?' he said.

Jemma thought of early mornings clutching a cup of grainy coffee from the kiosk by the tube, hurrying home in the evening via Kris's Takeaway, and waking up in the middle of the night convinced she had left something vital out of her latest report.

'It'll do,' she said. Raphael passed her his fountain pen, she signed with her little flourish, and the deed was done.

Chapter 6

Jemma's clock radio woke her with 'Fame' on Monday morning, which she took as an exceptionally good omen. Not that she wanted to be famous – good heavens, no – except perhaps as some sort of shop turnaround-er, like Mary Portas. Yes, that would be good. Maybe she could have her own series, going into unprofitable businesses and, with a wave of her magic wand, transforming them into happy places where the money poured in. She decided to have wholemeal toast with organic strawberry jam for breakfast. After all, it was an important day.

Today the tube didn't misbehave, and Jemma arrived at Burns Books at a quarter past eight. It was a lovely bright spring day, but with a fresh breeze and a slight chill in the air which she hoped would induce chilly tourists to pop in for a browse. *A day to blow the cobwebs away*, she thought. *Oh, what a good idea.* She delved into her bag and brought out her new prized possession: the keys to the shop.

Raphael had given them to her after closing on Friday. 'Would you mind opening up on Monday?' he asked. 'I always find Mondays rather difficult.'

'Yes, of course,' Jemma said, watching the keys as they swung gently back and forth on Raphael's finger.

'Now, the big iron key is for the lock which is under the handle,' said Raphael. 'It's a bit stiff. And the other lock is at eye level.' He studied Jemma. 'Actually, you might need to look up.'

'I'm sure I can manage,' said Jemma, taking the keys off his finger. *I'll get a keyring for them*, she thought. *Something bookish. I wonder if we could sell keyrings in the shop?* She resolved to follow that up at the weekend.

And she had, as well as planning the bookshop's social media content for the next three months, and producing a set of graphs showing which genres had sold best over the previous week. She had also bought herself another pair of baseball boots, an extra pair of smartish trousers, this time in navy, and, on impulse, a T-shirt which said *Bookworm And Proud* in curved rainbow lettering. It was a bit children's TV presenter, but she figured that sending a clear message was part of her communication strategy.

She had also found time to send a quick text to Em. *Had my review yesterday and I'm permanent in the shop. Can't wait to get properly started.*

And she couldn't. Not even when Em replied: *Are you sure you're doing the right thing? I just don't see how this can be a career X.*

I can, and that's what matters. And with that Jemma put her phone out of reach, and carried on with her trend analysis.

But I have to get back to basics first, she thought, as she jiggled the huge iron key in the lock. *I have to get into the shop, and open it up.*

The lock finally gave in, and admitted her. The Yale lock, by comparison, was a doddle, though she did have to stand on tiptoe to get a good view of it. The door swung open, and the bright, merciless light revealed the state of the shop.

'I'm here!' she called, but there was no response. Not even a meow.

Oh my, she thought, as cobwebs wafted gently in the breeze. *The shop looks as if it's been asleep for a thousand years. And it's only been a weekend.* She heaved a sigh, then winced as a cobweb settled on her face. She batted it away, then frowned. *If there are this many cobwebs, then how many spiders must there be? And how many flies?* She shuddered, and pulled up the blind to reveal a decidedly grimy shop window.

'You need cleaning, and no mistake,' she said, nodding at it. 'I'll open up, and then I shall deal with you.' She ran a fingertip over the window, and grimaced at the result.

There was plenty of change in the till, even though Jemma had made Raphael go to the bank with a large bundle of cash on Friday afternoon, and she switched the lights on without any untoward incidents. *In some ways*, she thought, surveying the premises, *it might be better to leave them switched off*. The additional light emphasised the dust which rose every time Jemma moved around, and gave the cobwebs shadows which made them seem twice as thick. *Right*, she thought, *I'd better get to it. I've got about half an hour before the shop is supposed to be ready for customers.*

Jemma looked for a bucket, but drew a blank. *How does he clean this place?* Then she tried the cupboard under the sink in the back room for cleaning materials, but found nothing. She decided to assume that Raphael kept such things in his own flat above the shop. The alternative was too depressing to imagine. In the end she commandeered the washing-up bowl, which she filled with hot water and a squirt of washing-up liquid in the absence of anything better, and grabbed a J-cloth from the side of the sink. She made a mental note to research natural cleaning products, and carried the bowl through to the front of the shop.

I'd better start at the top, she thought, and fetched the small step which she used for restocking the middle shelves. Then she

39

cleared out the window display, which needed redoing anyway, and set to work.

She was stretching into the top right-hand corner of the window when a cough nearly sent her into space. 'What are you doing?' enquired Raphael.

'What do you think I'm doing?' Jemma replied.

Raphael said nothing for a moment, but gazed at the window. 'I heard squeaking,' he said.

'That,' said Jemma, wringing her cloth out, 'is the sound of clean.' She gestured at the bowl. 'Look at the state of that water.'

Raphael frowned. 'Why are you using dirty water to wash the window?'

'It wasn't dirty when I started,' said Jemma, between gritted teeth. 'Where do you keep your cleaning stuff?'

'I need a coffee,' said Raphael. 'And it needs to be an espresso.'

'Not like that, I hope,' said Jemma, eyeing his dressing gown.

Raphael looked down at himself, and seemed surprised. 'Good point,' he said, and disappeared, returning a very short time later in a surprisingly normal combination of cream linen trousers and a white shirt. 'Back soon,' he said, and loped off. As he opened the door the bell rang, and a fine mist of dust floated down.

'I give up,' said Jemma. 'No, I don't. I am going to get this filthy shop clean if it kills me.'

Outside, the sun went behind a cloud.

'That's actually an improvement,' said Jemma, and faced the window again.

A few minutes later the window was, if not sparkling, not noticeably dirty. On the inside, at least. Jemma looked at her watch. Fifteen minutes until opening time. *I can nip out and do the outside as well*, she thought. *With fresh water.* Whistling, she went to refill her bowl, and found that, without knowing it, she had managed to use all the washing-up liquid. *Well, hot water is better than nothing.*

Ten minutes later Jemma re-entered the shop, reasonably pleased with the state of the window, and found Folio chewing the broom which had been part of her Harry Potter window display.

'That's a good idea, Folio,' she said. 'If I can't wash the floor, at least I can sweep it.' She knelt and attempted to take the broom from Folio, but he responded by leaping on top of the bristles and digging his claws into the wooden handle.

'If you won't let go,' said Jemma, 'then I'll have to sweep the floor with you as well.' She picked up the broom by the end of the handle, since she didn't like the look of Folio's claws, and took it to the back of the shop.

'I think Raphael is overfeeding you,' she said to Folio as she wielded the broom. 'You really are a bit heavy for a cat.'

Folio hissed, and attempted to swipe at her.

She had swept most of the dust to the front of the shop when Raphael returned. 'If you hold the door for me,' said Jemma, breathlessly, 'I'll just sweep all this outside, and then we can open.'

Raphael raised his eyebrows. 'Aren't you going to clean the window first?'

Jemma followed his pointing finger and saw that within the last few minutes, the entire local bird population had used the shop window for target practice. Her jaw dropped, and the breeze from the open shop door blew a long thread of cobweb into her mouth. 'Ugh!' she exclaimed, trying to spit it out.

'I'll deal with the window,' said Raphael soothingly. 'You go and get a drink of water.'

'I need something stronger than water,' muttered Jemma.

When she returned from the back room, having taken several deep breaths to calm herself, the window was clean again, and somehow the shop seemed considerably less dirty. Raphael had procured a feather duster from somewhere, and was winding cobwebs around it like candy floss. Folio had abandoned the broom, and was sitting in the shop window between copies of *Catwatching* and *The Unadulterated Cat.* A couple stopped, pointed at Folio, then entered the shop.

Jemma's fists clenched automatically, and she uncurled them with an effort. 'Good morning, how can I help you?' she said, stepping forward. *Don't think you've won,* she told the shop, in her head. *I'm not going to be beaten by a shop with a mind of its own. And if you think this is over, you are so wrong.*

She felt something drop on the back of her neck and scuttle under her top, but her smile, now rather forced, never left her face.

Chapter 7

The rest of the morning passed without incident, possibly because Jemma confined herself to normal duties such as restocking the bookshelves and serving the customers. *Perhaps I tried to do too much*, she thought. *It was a bit ambitious for a Monday morning.* The sun came back out, and Folio spent his morning reclining in the shop window, shifting himself along every so often to stay in the sunshine. Jemma found a box of books on pet care in the stockroom, put them in the window, and sold half the box within an hour.

'Have you trained him to do that?' asked a woman in cycling gear, nodding at Folio.

'Do what?' said Jemma.

'Stay in the window like that.'

Raphael came to join them. 'Folio is very much his own cat,' he said. 'He does as he pleases.'

Folio opened a lazy yellow eye, regarded them all, and closed it again with a contented whiffle.

It was a pleasant morning, but truth be told, Jemma found it dull. *What about my action plan? How will I implement it if the shop is determined to thwart me at every turn?* Then she laughed. *Listen to yourself, Jemma James. This is a shop. An inanimate object. It's all just – coincidence.* She went to get more books from the stockroom, tripped over the broom which definitely hadn't been there before, and almost went flying.

'Steady now,' said Raphael, grabbing her arm. 'I don't want to have to use the first-aid kit.'

'I'm glad to hear you've got one,' Jemma said grumpily, as she had stubbed her toe.

'I think we have,' said Raphael. 'It sounds like the sort of thing a shop ought to have.'

'Yes, it does,' said Jemma, hoping that her stern expression would prompt Raphael to go and look for said kit and thereby prove that it existed. Given that morning's experience in the shop, she had a feeling that a well-stocked first-aid kit was an essential item.

Raphael opened the cupboard under the sink and pulled out a square green box with a white cross on the lid. 'Here we are,' he said. 'I knew we had one somewhere.'

'But that wasn't—' Jemma stopped. Certainly she hadn't noticed a first-aid kit when she had searched for cleaning materials that morning, but that didn't mean it hadn't been there. It was just that she hadn't been looking for it. Of course, that was it. There was no other explanation. None at all.

Raphael gave the lid of the box a pat and put it back into the cupboard. 'Good to know it's there,' he said. 'One never knows, does one.' He gave Jemma a stern look of his own. 'But it still pays to be careful. Health and safety, you know.'

'That's a point,' said Jemma. 'Is there a course I should go on?'

Raphael shivered, though the temperature in the shop must have been at least twenty degrees. 'I hardly think that's necessary,' he said. 'Really, it's a matter of common sense, isn't it. Staying out of trouble. Avoiding temptation. Not – not overdoing things.' From his serious expression, Jemma gathered that she was supposed to be deriving wisdom from these vague comments.

'That is true,' she said. 'But nothing ventured, nothing gained.' She went into the stockroom, and closed the door behind her.

I can't believe he's lecturing me, she thought. *Raphael, who barely knows one end of the till from the other! The shop's profits have gone up by . . . a lot since I started working here.* She pulled out the first box she saw, reopened the door with difficulty, and carried it through to the counter. When she opened the box, the book on top was *Accidents at Work: A survey of the most common workplace injuries, with notes on how to avoid them.*

Jemma dropped it on the counter. 'Very funny,' she muttered. Beneath it was a copy of *Howards End.* Jemma reached into the box, lifted out a stack of books, and moved around the shop shelving them.

As she slid the last book into the Biography section, Raphael wandered through. 'I might go for lunch,' he said vaguely. 'Would you mind if I left you alone in the shop for an hour or so?'

Jemma folded her arms, mainly to stop herself rubbing her hands with glee. Until now, Raphael had never left her alone in the shop for more than twenty minutes or so. 'Oh, sure,' she said casually. 'That'll be fine. I'll pick something up when you get back.'

'Excellent,' said Raphael. 'I'll be in Rolando's if you need me. You know, the deli?'

Jemma knew. After all, she passed it every day when she came to work, and again when she left. It was always busy, and a delicious aroma of coffee and baking seeped out every time the door opened. As yet she hadn't ventured in, suspecting that acquiring a deli habit would eat into her slim salary and expand her waistline. She could get an egg mayonnaise sandwich from the mini-market for a pound, anyway.

'Jemma...'

She came to and saw Raphael looking at her curiously. 'Yes, what is it?' she asked, cross at being caught daydreaming.

'You aren't planning to do anything while I'm out, are you?'

'Who, me?' Jemma laughed. 'The thought hadn't even entered my head.'

'Good,' said Raphael. He smiled. 'I find, with the shop, that it's best to introduce things gradually. Nothing too . . . surprising.'

'Oh yes,' said Jemma. 'Incremental steps. Continuous improvement. Kaizen.'

'Bless you,' said Raphael, and left.

Once the shop door had closed behind him Jemma went into the back room, stretched out her arms, and spun around. She wasn't sure why being alone in the shop gave her such joy, especially after this morning's shenanigans, but it did. *Perhaps one day I shall have a shop of my own*, she thought, *and I'll arrange it just as I like.* Then the shop bell rang, and she hurried into the shop to assist the next customer.

A stream of customers came into the shop over the next hour. Some wanted travel guides to plan for their holidays. Some were thinking of getting a kitten or a puppy, and were researching different breeds. One even asked whether marmalade cats like Folio were easy to live with. Jemma, now in an excellent mood, replied, 'We get along fine. But he isn't my cat, he's the bookshop cat.'

Folio leapt onto the counter and sat with his paws together, looking extremely pleased with himself. The customer asked if she could take his picture.

At one point there was even a queue. *Imagine that*, thought Jemma. She wondered if it would be rude to ask whether she could take a picture of the line, to show Raphael, and decided regretfully that it would. *He'll be stunned when I tell him*, she thought, putting two twenty-pound notes into the right

46

compartment in the till, and getting change. *Maybe we can set a new record for takings today. That would be something.* She saw herself putting today's number into her spreadsheet, and watching the trend line adjust itself upwards.

Eventually the rush died down, and the shop bell was quiet. Jemma checked her watch. It was a quarter to two. *Raphael's having a long lunch*, she thought, and tried not to feel resentful. Her stomach growled in agreement, and she patted it. 'Don't worry, you'll be fed,' she said. 'Given what a profitable morning it's been, I might treat you to lunch from the deli today. I think it's time for a change from egg mayo.'

She surveyed the shop from her vantage point behind the counter. Despite all the customers, everything was spick and span. She needed to get more stock out, of course, but—

Her eye fell on an envelope which was sitting on the doormat.

Funny time for the post, thought Jemma. Then again, she hadn't taken notice of what time it usually came. She went over and picked the envelope up.

It was a long white envelope, unstamped, with *BURNS BOOKS* written on it in block capitals.

How odd, thought Jemma. She slid her thumb under the flap, then stopped. *Should I open it?* But why not? It wasn't addressed specifically to Raphael, but to the bookshop. It didn't say *Private*, and it didn't look official.

Maybe it's a fan letter, she thought, letting her imagination run wild. *Maybe it's a thank-you letter from one of our customers. Or it could be someone searching for a special book, like Helene Hanff.* She imagined a handsome stranger writing from somewhere she'd like to visit; Barcelona, or Lisbon, or Paris. He would be seeking a specific edition of… She looked at the shelves for inspiration. *Great Expectations.* And she would reply, enclosing the book, and they would court each other by letter—

Folio yowled, and Jemma jumped. She ripped open the

envelope, displeased to be brought back to stone-cold reality.

Inside was a sheet of A4 paper, folded in three. Jemma opened it out, and stared.

It wasn't a fan letter.

It wasn't a thank-you letter.

And it wasn't a request for a specific edition of *Great Expectations*, or any other of Dickens's works.

The text had been cut from newspapers and magazines.

I kNOw WhAt yOu'Re uP To, AND i'M gOiNg tO StOP yOu. fOr GooD.

Chapter 8

Jemma blinked, then read the letter again. If anything, it made even less sense the second time. *What the—*

She let the letter fall on the counter, and shivered. Suddenly the shop seemed cold, and there was a strange, musty, heavy smell in the air.

The bell jangled. Jemma snatched up the note and put it behind her back before realising that it was Raphael. He looked concerned. 'Is everything all right?' he asked. 'I – I felt I should pop in and check.'

Jemma replaced the letter on the counter and shook her head. 'No,' she said. 'The shop has had a letter. We've had a letter. An anonymous letter.'

Raphael dived for the letter, scanned it, then screwed it up in a ball and put it in his pocket. 'Just someone being silly,' he said. 'Don't worry about it.'

Jemma frowned. *When have I seen him do that before?* Then she remembered him sifting through the post on her first day in the shop. 'This isn't the first, is it?'

Raphael said nothing, but jammed his hands into his pockets

and shifted from foot to foot.

'So it isn't,' said Jemma, folding her arms.

'No, it isn't,' said Raphael. 'But it really isn't anything to worry about.'

'Have you phoned the police?' asked Jemma. 'What did the first note say?'

'No, I haven't phoned the police,' said Raphael. 'I don't think it would do any good to have the police round here asking questions. And I can't remember what the first note even said. I threw it in the bin.' His brow furrowed. 'To my recollection, it was pretty much like this one.'

'But someone's threatening you!' cried Jemma. 'That's serious.'

'People can threaten all they like,' said Raphael. 'They can't do anything. What could they do?'

Jemma shrugged. 'I don't know,' she said.

'Exactly,' said Raphael, and the atmosphere in the shop lightened a bit. 'Just empty threats.' He reached into his coat pocket and held out a paper bag. 'I brought you a panini. Cheese and ham.'

'Oh. Thank you,' said Jemma as she took it. She managed a wavering smile. 'Who do you think sent the letter?'

'Not a clue,' said Raphael. 'And what's more, I don't care. Now, why don't you make a nice cup of tea to go with that panini.'

Jemma went through to the back room and put the kettle on. She tried to think of nice things like serving customers and putting money into the till, but the note, with its cut-out lettering and its vague threat, kept getting in the way. *He clearly doesn't want to talk about it*, she thought, putting teabags into the pot. *And he won't call the police.* She sighed. *So there's nothing I can do.*

She felt pressure against her legs, and looked down to find Folio rubbing his head on her ankle. 'Good cat,' she said absentmindedly, and reached down to stroke him. When her hand was within clawing range she wondered if that was a good idea, but Folio accepted the fuss readily enough, and even managed a throaty purr.

'Gooooood cat,' Jemma purred back, feeling much less troubled. Raphael was right. It was an empty threat. She could barely remember what the letter had said.

She made the tea, took it through, and enjoyed the luxury of eating her panini in the armchair while Raphael counted the morning's takings. 'Excellent,' he said. 'The shop *is* doing well,' and Jemma felt a little ember of pride warm her through. The sun had come back, lending a pleasing glow to the mahogany counter and the parquet floor, and the shop did look very nice indeed.

Everything went swimmingly, in fact, until Raphael let out a groan. Then he jumped up and strode into the back room, calling over his shoulder, 'If he asks to see me, tell him I'm dead. Or travelling the world. Or otherwise engaged.'

'If who asks to see you?' said Jemma.

'I don't know who you're talking to,' Raphael shouted. 'I'm not here.'

The door opened, and a smiley man in a short-sleeved shirt, beige chinos and a tie came in. He was holding a clipboard. 'Could you spare me a moment?' he asked.

'Um, probably,' said Jemma. He seemed harmless enough.

'First of all, I don't suppose your boss happens to be about, does he?' He consulted his clipboard. 'Mr, ah, Burns.'

'I'm afraid he's busy in the stockroom,' said Jemma, crossing her fingers under the counter. Raphael might well be in the stockroom, and possibly busy.

'Oh, I see.' The smile became even more open and friendly. 'Could you pop through and ask if he's got time for a word?'

Jemma shook her head. 'I can't leave the shop unattended.'

The man nodded. 'Quite right too. In that case, I'll introduce myself. My name is Richard Tennant, and I'm from the

Westminster Retailers' Association, Charing Cross Branch.' He extended a large hand.

Before Jemma could shake it, Raphael erupted from the back room. 'Don't waste your breath, Tennant,' he said, taking up position behind the counter next to Jemma. 'I'm not joining your stupid association. Not now, not ever.'

Mr Tennant looked rather hurt. 'That's a real shame, Mr Burns. Our membership on Charing Cross Road is higher than ever, and we're getting to the point where the association has a real voice. Strength in numbers, and all that.'

Raphael looked down his long nose at him. 'To paraphrase Groucho Marx,' he said, 'I wouldn't join any association that wanted me for a member.'

Mr Tennant chuckled. 'Very droll, Mr Burns, very droll. Well, I see I won't be able to convince you today, so I'll leave you our latest newsletter and be on my way.' He unclipped a colourful pamphlet from his board and laid it on the counter. 'Perhaps I should add that many of the bookshops in this area are finding it beneficial. Anyway, if you do change your mind, you know where to find me.'

'Thank you so much,' said Raphael coldly. And as Mr Tennant turned to go, Raphael picked up the newsletter and, very deliberately, tore it in half. Mr Tennant's shoulders stiffened slightly, but he kept walking, and left without another word.

'What was all that about?' asked Jemma, once the door had closed behind him. 'Why don't you like him? And why wouldn't we want to join a retail association? Surely that would be good for us.'

'Not if they start telling me what to do,' muttered Raphael, tearing the newsletter into long strips. 'Not if they start saying the shop has to conform to this or that regulation. I'll – I'll sell the shop before I let some chirpy chap with a clipboard tell me what's what.' He picked up the wastepaper basket and swept the strips of paper into it, scowling. 'I need pastry,' he said, and stalked out.

Back to Rolando's, I presume, thought Jemma, with a sigh. She eyed the shelves, which looked distinctly gappy, and hurried to the stockroom for more books. When she opened the boxes, she found an assortment of novels by Len Deighton and Robert Ludlum. Yet they hadn't sold any spy thrillers that morning, as far as she remembered.

I wonder why he is so against the retail association, she thought, as she began to shelve the books. *I mean, I can see it would be a good thing. He could learn from the other booksellers. And I doubt they would tell him what to do.*

Then a sneaky little thought almost made her drop *The Bourne Identity*. *Maybe Raphael doesn't want to join because he doesn't want anyone to know what he's doing. And that note said he was up to something.*

She slid the book into place, and reached for another. *But what, exactly, is he up to?*

Chapter 9

Jemma mused as she shelved books. What could Raphael be up to? She was half tempted to nip to Rolando's and peek in at the window to see if he really was there.

But he was there earlier, her rational brain said. *He brought you a panini, remember?*

It takes, what, three minutes to buy a panini? He could have popped in after he'd been doing – whatever he had been doing.

It could be something perfectly innocent, she told herself. *Raphael might have some sort of side hustle.*

Or he could be – I don't know – smuggling, or money-laundering? On impulse, Jemma opened the till and looked inside. While the shop's takings were definitely up from the heady heights of the fifty pounds that Raphael had mentioned, there definitely wasn't enough cash in there to fuel anyone's suspicions of money laundering. Jemma closed the till drawer, which snapped shut with its usual satisfying chime. Yet she remained unsatisfied.

'The stockroom,' she muttered. 'All those unlabelled boxes. Anything could be in them.' On impulse she went into the stockroom and picked up a few boxes to test their weight. To be perfectly honest, they all felt about the right weight to be boxes of books, and with some gentle shaking, they sounded like books, too.

Whatever he's doing, thought Jemma as she closed the stockroom door, *I don't think it relates to the shop.* Then she remembered how the shop had chilled when she read the anonymous letter. She tried to dismiss it as a coincidence. But frankly, there had been a lot of similar coincidences. Including the way that the air had thinned and the musty smell had vanished when Raphael dismissed the letter as nonsense.

'You'll start reading your horoscope next,' she said aloud, and snorted. Actually... The newspaper was folded on the counter where Raphael had left it. Jemma opened it and found the horoscope section.

TAURUS: Today will be a day of ups and downs, but beware of jumping to conclusions. A mysterious stranger will bring you something of value.

Jemma harrumphed, refolded the paper, and put it back. *That was probably Raphael bringing me a panini. I bet they're expensive.* Or could it mean Mr Tennant from the Charing Cross Retail Association, who had brought that newsletter? She rummaged in the bin, and began to piece it together.

She was reading the newsletter when Raphael returned, looking much happier. 'Any customers?' he enquired.

'None, actually,' said Jemma. 'I'm just reading that newsletter you ripped up.'

A pained expression passed over Raphael's face. 'What rare gems have you discovered?' he asked.

'They're talking to landlords about lowering shop rents,' said Jemma. 'That's good, isn't it?'

'It would be,' said Raphael. 'But I happen to own the shop, so that doesn't apply to me.'

'Oh yes,' said Jemma. 'I forgot.' She eyed Raphael. 'So, how long have you been in charge of the shop?'

'Oh, years,' said Raphael. 'Ages.'

'Like, in the last century?' asked Jemma. She studied him. There wasn't any grey in his sandy hair, but he didn't seem young. And she couldn't get any clues from the way he dressed. She suspected Raphael was one of those people who had always looked middle-aged, and always would.

Raphael laughed. 'Are you trying to work out how old I am?'

'No,' said Jemma. 'OK, maybe.'

'That's a bit cheeky,' said Raphael, but he didn't seem annoyed.

'Sorry,' said Jemma. 'I suppose I'm curious because I don't know anything about you.'

Raphael raised his eyebrows. 'I've told you my name, and you know that this is my shop, and I live above it. What else is there?'

'All sorts of things,' said Jemma. 'What music you listen to, what you like to do in your spare time. What you did before you inherited the shop.'

'Oh, I see,' said Raphael. 'What do you like to do in your spare time?'

'Oh, well...' Jemma thought for a while. 'I suppose I don't really have any.'

'How come?' Jemma wondered briefly if Raphael was attempting to distract her, but he appeared genuinely interested.

'Well, in my last job I got into the habit of working long hours, and...' She tried to think of a way to put a positive spin on her lack of a private life. 'I'm very driven, you see,' she said. 'Even when I'm not in the shop, I'm thinking of ways to improve the shop. New initiatives, exciting window displays. That sort of thing.'

The pained expression returned. 'You don't have to try so hard, Jemma,' Raphael said gently.

'But what's the point of having a shop if it isn't successful?' Jemma asked. 'I mean, look how your sales have increased! Look how much money there is in the till! When I first came, you weren't even making fifty pounds a day.' She opened the till, took out a wad of notes, and shook them at him.

Raphael didn't quite recoil from the money, but he regarded it with a troubled air. 'How much have you got there, do you think?'

Jemma began counting the notes. When she got to four hundred Raphael said quietly, 'That will do.'

'See?' said Jemma, putting the money into the till. 'You won't even let me implement my plan fully, but it's working. The shop is doing better than – probably than it ever has. But I feel that I have to make the effort, because *you* won't.' *There*, she thought triumphantly. *I've said it. If that doesn't get him on board, I don't know what will.*

'But before you came, the shop had been here for generations,' said Raphael. 'The shop existed before Charing Cross Road was built. That's how old it is. In living memory, there has always been a Burns Books. So we must have been doing something right.'

'Oh, I didn't mean you've been doing things wrong,' Jemma said kindly. 'I didn't mean that at all. But—'

'The shop has been here so long,' said Raphael, 'because it knows its place. Among the other shops, and particularly the bookshops. Every shop has its own character, its own specialism, and its own particular set of customers. It's a delicate balance, and upsetting it might have consequences.'

'Like a sort of business ecosystem, you mean?' said Jemma. 'I read a blog about that last year.' She frowned. 'So what is our specialism? I thought we sold all types of books.'

'Oh, we do,' said Raphael. 'The distinction is subtler than that. When you've worked here a bit longer, you'll be able to identify it for yourself.' He smiled. 'Tea?' And without waiting for an answer, he went through to the back room.

Jemma gathered up the torn strips of newsletter and dropped them into the bin. It seemed pretty clear that, whatever the benefits, Raphael wasn't ever going to join the Charing Cross Retail Association. She remembered his plea to her not to do the spreadsheety computery things. Her brow furrowed. 'But if I don't do those,' she murmured, 'then why am I here? Anyone could put books on the shelves, then put them into bags for the customers and take the money. If I can't bring my own particular skill set to the job, then what's the point?'

Folio leapt onto the counter and nuzzled into her elbow.

'That's very kind,' said Jemma, stroking his head. 'I appreciate it.' She let out a heavy sigh. 'Perhaps I should take up a hobby. Civil War battle re-enactments, or crochet, or something.' She considered checking the Hobbies section, but Folio flopped down and lifted his chin for a tickle, and it would have been rude to ignore him.

'Here we are,' said Raphael, coming through with a tray. 'The cup that cheers but not inebriates.' He looked at Folio, who looked back at him upside down. 'Good heavens.'

'Maybe he does like me,' said Jemma, and felt a little bit better. But as Raphael busied himself pouring out, two quite different thoughts popped into her head.

The first thought was that he hadn't answered any of her questions. Not with anything you could call detail, or specifics.

And the second thought was that, even though she wasn't happy with the idea of just being a normal shop assistant, and of course she *could* walk out and get a role more suitable to her talents whenever she liked, the thought of looking for another job hadn't crossed her mind. Not once.

Chapter 10

Jemma was quiet for the rest of the day; so much so that Raphael asked if she was feeling all right.

'What?' she said. 'Oh yes, just thinking.'

And Jemma was thinking. She thought as she walked down Charing Cross Road at five minutes past five, as she touched in at Embankment tube station, as she swayed from a strap in the train, and as she let herself into her flat.

Nebulous thoughts swirled around her brain.

What do I do if I can't improve the shop?

What do I do if I don't want a different job?

What can I do?

She had no answers to the questions yet. They just continued to echo in her head in a disquieting manner. And that was the main problem. She had absolutely no idea what to do.

I don't understand, she thought. *I always know what to do. I apply the lessons I've learned through training, or I do research, or I work harder. But I've tried that with Raphael. I've tried every trick in the book, and none of them seem to work.*

She thought of Phoebe, her former boss, with affection. Even when things hadn't gone to plan Phoebe always had a suggestion, or would agree with what Jemma proposed. The second was what she generally did, and Jemma appreciated it. It showed that Phoebe valued her opinion.

But Phoebe had let her go. She had said it was a business decision and not a personal one; but she had still let her go.

Jemma sighed, went through to the kitchen, and looked through the *Easy Suppers* cookbook for something which would challenge her. If she couldn't achieve her potential in the workplace, she'd darn well hone her skills somewhere else.

An hour and a half later Jemma sat down to four ramekins, each containing a cheese soufflé at a different stage of deflation. If anything, she felt slightly more frustrated than she had when she started cooking.

'But what do I do?' she said, through a mouthful of soggy soufflé.

Two soufflés in, Jemma decided her need for clarity was stronger than her need for further cheese-based sustenance. In a fit of desperation she fetched the tote bag she had brought home from her previous job, hung up on the back of the door, and forgotten about. She couldn't even remember what was in there, but perhaps there was something that could help. She rummaged within, and found a pen and two packs of company-branded Post-it notes. 'Why on earth did I put those in?' she said, staring at them. Never mind; they would do.

Jemma sat down at the little drop-leaf table she used for eating and working, clicked her pen, and began to write.

Problem: Raphael won't let me do things. After some thought, she added: *Why?*

'Of course! The Five Whys technique!' she cried. 'Why didn't I think of that before?' She almost started writing that before she realised it wasn't a relevant Why. She pulled off the first Post-it note and stuck it on the table.

He doesn't want to upset the balance of the business ecosystem, she wrote on the next note. She stuck it on the table and regarded it for some time. 'Do you really believe that?' she asked herself.

On the next note she wrote: *Maybe he doesn't trust me. Why?* The next notes were much easier.

Maybe because I'm new.

Maybe because he's worried I'll mess up.

Maybe because he's worried I'll take over the shop. She considered that final point; she had to admit that it was an attractive prospect. 'OK, fair enough,' she said. 'You've got me on that one, Raphael.'

On the next note, she wrote simply: *What can I do?* She stretched and stuck that on the far side of the table. Underneath it she placed the following:

Continue to implement small-scale quick wins to build R's trust in me.

Wait until I've been there longer before suggesting more improvements.

Focus on something else to lull his suspicions.

Jemma sat back, folded her arms, and regarded the last note. It didn't convey the message that she wanted, which was one of mild diversion rather than all-out subterfuge, but she had a feeling that it might work.

'I'll persuade him,' she said slowly, 'that finding out who's behind the anonymous letters is a good idea. That will help me to learn more about the shop, more about the people who come in, and possibly more about Raphael.' *And what he's up to,* she thought to herself.

Pleased with her proposed course of action, Jemma wrote another note, *Find the anonymous letter-writer,* and stuck it at the head of the table, then rearranged the other Post-it notes into a hierarchy. She considered starting a spreadsheet, then thought that might be overkill, seeing as she needed to win Raphael over first.

She sighed with satisfaction and dug her spoon into the last cheese soufflé, which was now cold and tasted like a cheese puff that had been dropped into a bucket of water. *Rome wasn't built in a day*, she thought.

***

The next day, Jemma dressed in what she thought of as her least professional and most unthreatening outfit: a pair of faded jeans, her baseball boots, and a plain pale-blue T-shirt. 'The psychology of dress is very important,' she said, nodding to her reflection in the mirror and slouching a little.

She didn't get her usual tube train, setting off twenty minutes later than she normally would, and arriving at the shop at an unprecedented five minutes past nine. 'Sorry I'm late,' she said cheerily. 'Rush-hour. You know.'

'I'm not sure I do,' said Raphael, but he appeared rather relieved. 'If you get the kettle on, I'll open up.'

'Righto,' said Jemma, and made sure that she brewed Raphael's Earl Grey to the required strength.

They had a couple of customers first thing; two smartly dressed women in late middle age who weren't together, but were both looking for Golden Age crime. Jemma packed up a selection of Agatha Christie, Ngaio Marsh, and Gladys Mitchell for them, and wrote the shop's phone number on their bags. The two customers also swapped their phone numbers and left together, chatting.

'That was nice,' said Raphael. 'I like to think that we're bringing readers together.'

It was on the tip of Jemma's tongue to suggest that they start genre-specific book clubs, and perhaps a customer network, but she bit it back. Instead she took in the atmosphere of the shop. It was pleasantly warm and bright today, and the sometimes harsh spring sunshine had mellowed to a comforting glow.

'If you don't mind,' she said, 'I might polish the counter.'

Raphael stared at her. 'I suppose you could,' he said doubtfully.

'You'll find polish and a duster under the sink.'

Jemma smiled to herself as she went into the back room. The polish and duster were right at the front of the cupboard. She went through, sprayed polish on the counter and rubbed it in, working with light, smooth strokes, and following the grain of the wood.

Folio, who was sitting on the chair arm, rolled onto his back, presenting Raphael with his tummy.

'I was wondering,' said Jemma, continuing to rub. 'You know the letter that came?'

Raphael looked across at her, one hand poised above Folio's belly. 'Yes?'

'Would you mind,' said Jemma, 'if I made some discreet enquiries?'

Raphael said nothing. Folio was motionless. The shop seemed to be waiting.

'You see,' said Jemma, 'I think stuff like that brings bad vibes to the shop. And we don't want that, do we?'

'No,' said Raphael warily. 'We definitely don't want that.'

'So if I could put my brain to work and ensure that the letters stopped,' said Jemma, 'that would be a good thing, wouldn't it?' She paused, sprayed more polish, and worked on.

Folio stretched out a foreleg and began to wash it. Raphael tickled his tummy.

The light outside grew a little brighter and a sunbeam shone golden light on the counter, illuminating the rich red grain.

'And it would keep me busy,' said Jemma. 'Along with restocking the shelves, and serving the customers, and keeping the shop tidy, of course.'

'Of course,' agreed Raphael. 'I must admit that it isn't a pleasant situation, and if we could see them off that would be wonderful.'

'I'm not promising anything,' said Jemma, applying slightly more pressure to the shop counter. 'It could be too difficult for me

63

to solve. But I'll try.'

'That would be very kind of you,' said Raphael. Folio rumbled out a purr.

'OK, then,' said Jemma, addressing the counter. 'I'll see what I can do.' It took all her strength not to punch the air, or exclaim 'Yes! Did it!', or to dismiss the counter with a final brisk rub. Somehow she managed it, polishing the whole counter with the same careful attention. She allowed herself one quiet round of applause when she went to put the polish away, and that was all.

When she came back in, Raphael regarded her curiously. 'How do you think you'll go about it?' he asked.

'I'm not exactly sure,' said Jemma, grinning inwardly. 'Let me have a think, and maybe I can get started after lunch.'

'Oh. Very well,' said Raphael, and returned to his newspaper.

It's working, thought Jemma. *My plan is actually working.* She felt pleasingly smug that she had managed to get round Raphael, Folio, *and* the shop with her clever side-swerve. She went to the stockroom and brought out another box, which yielded a stack of Miss Marple novels and a complete set of Sherlock Holmes. *The game is afoot*, she thought, and she couldn't stop herself from smiling.

Chapter 11

Jemma had said she would start her investigation after lunch; however, in reality she planned to begin a little earlier. 'Is it all right if I pop out for a sandwich?' she asked, at around twelve o'clock. 'If I go now, I can probably miss the rush.'

Raphael looked up from *Devil in a Blue Dress*. 'Yes, of course,' he said. 'I'll nip out when you get back.'

'I won't be too long,' said Jemma, edging towards the door. 'See you later.'

Her first stop was at Rolando's. Despite going early there was still a queue, and she had to wait a few minutes to place her order. However, this gave her time to watch the barista, who was a graceful young man with rich brown skin. 'It's my first time in here,' she remarked, when her turn came. Unfortunately the roar of the coffee machine completely drowned her out.

'I'm sorry, what was that?' Could he be Rolando? Surely he was too young. She peered at the name badge on his chest: *Carl*.

'I said this is my first time,' she shouted. All the noise stopped part-way through her announcement, and someone giggled. 'In here, I mean,' she said, conscious that her cheeks were burning.

'I've just started working in Burns Books. Um, can I have a cappuccino, please?'

'Coming up,' said the barista. He turned away, poured milk into a metal jug and began frothing it. At the same time, he made an espresso. Jemma kept her eyes on his shoulder blades.

'Have you been into the bookshop?' she asked.

'Not yet, no,' said the barista. 'I haven't worked here long.' He poured milk into the cup and dusted the top with cocoa powder. 'There you go.'

'Maybe you could drop in some time,' said Jemma, determined to salvage something from her failed mission. 'We've got lots of books.'

Carl looked slightly puzzled. 'Yes, I suppose you would have.'

'I'm Jemma, by the way,' said Jemma, and felt the person behind her in the queue shuffle closer. She sighed, and moved to the till to pay for her drink. While the cappuccino would no doubt be lovely, she didn't think the intelligence she had received was a fair swap for three pounds. *Never mind*, she thought, *I have a contact.*

Her next port of call was the mini-market. 'Plenty of egg mayo,' called Nafisa.

'I might have a change today,' said Jemma. 'What would you recommend?'

Nafisa came out from behind the counter and scrutinised the selection of sandwiches and wraps. Her nose wrinkled. 'Home cooking,' she said.

'I work in Burns Books,' said Jemma, apropos of nothing.

Nafisa laughed. 'For now,' she said.

Jemma frowned. 'What do you mean?'

Nafisa's dark eyes sparkled. 'That shop's had more assistants than a bad magician.'

Jemma continued to regard the display, her heart thumping. 'Why do you think that is?' she asked, as casually as she knew how.

'No idea,' said Nafisa. 'I don't know what he does with them.'

'Maybe they don't get on,' said Jemma. After some thought, she selected tuna and cucumber on wholemeal bread.

Nafisa shrugged. 'Maybe. He's always perfectly polite when he comes in here. He looks a bit down if I haven't got his teabags in, but he's never rude. Are you taking that?' She stretched out her hand for the sandwich. 'Anything else?'

On an impulse, Jemma moved to the biscuit selection. 'And these,' she said, picking up a packet of custard creams. She wasn't entirely sure what biscuits Raphael liked, but she felt you couldn't go wrong with a custard cream.

'OK, that's two pounds ten,' said Nafisa. She rang up the items, and Jemma paid with her phone. 'Good luck!' She flashed a broad grin at Jemma, then went back to pricing up a tray of tinned tomatoes.

Jemma considered trying more shops in the parade; but her hands were full, and she was conscious that she had already been out for twenty minutes. *Besides*, she thought, *I must write all this up while it's fresh in my mind.*

She returned to the shop, and was surprised to find Raphael dealing with a customer. A customer he knew, from his level of alertness. He was a tall, stooped man with a fierce white moustache, wearing baggy corduroy trousers of indeterminate colour, a burnt-orange waistcoat, and a cheesecloth shirt. 'So if you happen to have that elusive third volume, Raphael, I'll give you a good price for it.'

A crafty gleam came into Raphael's eye. 'What's a good price, Brian?'

Brian drew himself up and gazed at the cash register, then at Raphael. 'We've done a lot of business together, Raphael,' he said briskly. 'And as we're in the same trade, I know there's no cheating you. So I'll err on the side of generosity and say fifty.'

67

Raphael straightened up too, so that he was slightly taller than Brian. 'You'll lose the sale without that volume,' he said. 'I can let you have it for eighty.'

Brian laughed. 'What use is one volume to you? I'm doing you a favour by taking it off your hands. If you don't grab this opportunity, you'll probably still have that book in twenty years' time.' He paused. 'I'll go up to sixty, then.'

'If I don't grab this opportunity,' said Raphael, his words dripping with sarcasm, 'I'm prepared to wait. Seventy-five, and not a penny less.'

The two men's eyes met. They stared at each other for perhaps a minute and a half before Brian's gaze dropped to the shop counter. 'I'll remember this next time you need a favour,' he said. 'Go on, show me the book. I'll pay your price if it's in good condition. Otherwise, you can whistle.'

'Jemma, would you mind fetching the book for me?' said Raphael, still looking at Brian. 'Volume three of Geeling's *Metaphysical Studies*. You'll find it in the Science section, in the middle of the top row.'

'You've got it on display?' Jemma heard Brian say as she retreated towards the back of the shop. She fetched the ladder, climbed up, and found a leather-bound chestnut-brown book with its title stamped in gold. She slid it out carefully, descended the ladder, and hurried to lay it on the counter.

'Hmmm,' said Brian, bending over the book until his nose nearly touched it. 'May I?' He motioned with a hand towards the cover.

'Be my guest,' said Raphael, all affability.

Brian opened the book in a few different places, letting the leaves slip through his fingers. The volume was closely printed in two columns, with several intricate diagrams.

'Righto,' he said, closing the book. He reached into his waistcoat pocket and extracted a slim wallet. 'I suppose you're still a troglodyte when it comes to money.' He counted out four twenties. 'Got a fiver?'

Raphael opened the till and handed him a five-pound note without looking down. 'Need a receipt?'

'If you don't mind,' said Brian. 'Always helpful to keep things square.'

Raphael took a receipt book from the drawer and filled in the details. Jemma watched the intricate loops and swirls of his elegant hand, and wondered where on earth he had learnt to write like that. 'There you are,' he said, handing it over. 'Pleasure doing business with you, Brian. Would you like a bag?'

'I think I can manage,' Brian said heavily. He tucked the book under his arm, nodded to them both, and left the shop.

Jemma exhaled, then took the lid off her cappuccino. It was still fairly warm. 'Who was he?' she asked.

'That was Brian,' said Raphael. 'Weren't you listening?'

'Well, yes,' said Jemma, 'but he obviously wasn't a normal customer.'

'I'm not sure we have such a thing as a normal customer,' said Raphael. 'He's a bookseller. Antiquarian.'

'Oh, right,' said Jemma. 'But we're not, are we?'

'Good grief, no,' said Raphael, and laughed as if the very idea were absurd.

Jemma took another sip of her cappuccino, then regarded him over the top of her disposable cup with what she felt to be a steely gaze. 'Then how did he know to come here?' she said, setting her drink down with an unimpressive tap on the counter. 'How did he know you might have the book he wanted?'

'Word gets around,' said Raphael. 'Besides, Brian and I go back a long way.'

'Oh.' Jemma imagined Brian perhaps twenty-five years ago, with a slightly less ferocious moustache and newer corduroys, showing Raphael the ropes of the bookselling business. 'Did he

69

teach you everything you know?' she asked, with a smile.

'Oh no, I was here first,' said Raphael. 'Are those biscuits?' He pointed at the custard creams.

'Yes, they are,' said Jemma. 'Why don't you open them?'

Raphael's hand stretched towards the packet, then hesitated. 'Actually, I might go for my lunch,' he said, eyeing Jemma's tuna sandwich with curiosity. 'Is that all right? It's been quiet, Brian's been the only customer since you went out.'

'That's absolutely fine,' said Jemma, though she would have liked to continue their conversation about Brian, and perhaps extend it to other booksellers with whom he had a similar relationship. Had they been hostile towards each other? Not really. And friendly wasn't right either, although they had seemed reasonably cordial. Ambivalent, perhaps? Then she remembered watching two stags fight on a wildlife program. This hadn't been anything like as alarming, but she had a definite sense they were vying for the upper hand. While Raphael had got it this time, she suspected Brian would bear that in mind for the next encounter. *I must write all this down*, she thought.

She didn't have long to wait, for Raphael was already buttoning his jacket. 'You'll be fine, won't you?' he said, which Jemma took to be his way of telling her that it would be a long lunch. 'Negotiating with Brian does take it out of me, rather.'

'You surprised me,' said Jemma. 'I didn't think you'd be so . . . businesslike.' She had almost said *ruthless*.

'I let him off lightly,' said Raphael. 'That book is easily worth a hundred pounds, and Brian knows it.'

'Is that because it's old and rare?' asked Jemma.

Raphael's eyes gleamed, but he hesitated before replying. 'Yes, it's old and reasonably rare,' he said. 'And of course when someone needs a book to complete their set, that allows you to add a bit on. Anyway, I'd better go.' He strode to the door and left without looking back.

Jemma watched him hurry past the window, and shrugged. Then she opened her bag and pulled out the notebook and pen she had packed that morning. She opened it at the first page, wrote *Investigation*, and underlined it. Then she wrote the date, and *Initial Findings*.

- *Visited Rolando's. Spoke to Carl, barista. Doesn't know R, hasn't been in the shop, is new. Cappuccino very nice. Also Carl.*
- *Called in at mini-market for sandwich and biscuits. Nafisa says R's assistants don't stay long, but he's always polite.*
- *Returned to find antiquarian bookseller Brian and R negotiating over book. R was ruthless. Sounds as if this behaviour is long-standing. Could letters come from angry bookseller who doesn't like R's methods?*

Jemma underlined the last sentence, feeling pleased with herself. Her stomach rumbled. *Detective work does make one rather hungry.* She peeled the film back from the sandwich box, smiling in anticipation, lifted a sandwich out, and took a large bite. Then she grimaced as her palate adjusted to dry tuna, slimy cucumber, and damp, thin bread. She looked at her notebook and added another sentence: *Don't buy the tuna and cucumber sandwich again.* However relevant or otherwise Nafisa's other observations had been, perhaps she was right about home cooking.

71

Chapter 12

The afternoon passed quickly. Jemma was kept busy dealing with customers in the shop. They seemed more demanding than usual; maybe Brian had left some sort of pernickety residue behind which had influenced them.

Raphael, as predicted, had taken an extremely long lunch break indeed, returning to the shop at about two thirty. Jemma wondered how on earth he had managed before she came along. Had he been tied to the shop? If anything, she suspected he had merely turned the shop sign from open to closed, and kept the hours he currently did.

When he returned, he did lend a hand with the customers, though. Jemma hurried back and forth, fetching books and laying them on the counter for inspection, and replenishing the stock whenever she got a minute. She noted that the boxes she opened contained more Golden Age crime, Brother Cadfael novels, and some slightly dogeared Nancy Drew books. *Don't lose sight of your mission, Jemma*, she told herself, as she unpacked yet another box.

In the end they didn't close the shop until a quarter past five, and then there was cashing-up to be done, accompanied by a cup of tea, as there had not been time to make a brew since lunch. 'Look at the time,' said Raphael, as he picked up bundles of notes and bank bags full of coins, ready for the safe. 'At this rate I shall have to consider paying overtime.'

'Oh, don't worry about it,' said Jemma, without thinking. 'I used to work much later in my last job. I'll take a long lunch one day, or come in later.'

Raphael eyed her doubtfully. 'If you're sure,' he said. 'But get yourself off home now, and I'll see you tomorrow.'

Jemma slung her bag over her shoulder, and left. She had intended to visit more shops in the parade, but most were closed. There was the takeaway, but she didn't want to risk temptation, and the only other one still open was an estate agent called Ransome's, whose window bore the slogan *NO ONE DOES IT CHEAPER!* Jemma glanced at the properties on display; lots of flats to rent, and shops too.

A young man in a shiny suit came out of the shop and accosted her. 'What sort of thing are you looking for?'

'Oh, I'm not, not really,' said Jemma. *Then again,* she thought, *it might be worth seeing if there are any nice flats in the area.* Perhaps she could cut out the tube and save money.

'Come on, people are always after something,' said the man.

'Well, I could look, I suppose,' said Jemma. 'I work in the bookshop. Burns Books.'

The young man frowned. 'Burns Books, you say?'

'I know, it's a funny name,' said Jemma. 'I've just started there, and I'm trying to find out a little more about the neighbourhood.'

'Ah, property around here, you see, it looks nice – or some of it does – but you want to watch out,' said the man, licking his lips. 'Unfortunately, being in a nice bit of London doesn't always count for much.'

'Really?' said Jemma. 'What about location, location, location?'

'You don't want to listen to that rubbish,' said the man gloomily. 'They don't know what it's like at the sharp end. A shop with an upstairs and everything, you'd think it would be worth a tidy packet, wouldn't you? But given the state of it, and that it's in the wrong part of Charing Cross Road, well, you'd have to pay me to take it off your hands.'

Jemma frowned. 'I was actually wondering about flats for rent nearby,' she said.

'Oh, right,' said the young man, without much more enthusiasm. 'Bit dangerous at night. Wouldn't recommend this area for a young lady.'

Once Jemma had insisted that she could look after herself, stalked into the estate agent's, and demanded to be shown some flats, the young man brought her a selection of five depressing properties, all smaller and more expensive than the studio flat she currently inhabited. 'I see what you mean,' said Jemma. 'Thank you for your time.'

'Been a pleasure,' said the young man, shuffling the information sheets into a pile.

It was half past six by the time Jemma got home. She dropped her bag on the sofa and considered going back out for a takeaway, or even breaking her own rule and getting one delivered. *No*, she told herself. *You've done so well. Don't spoil it now.* She perused the recipe book, and decided that pasta primavera would be healthy yet also comforting. It had been a long day. She took the book to the kitchenette, and began assembling ingredients.

As she chopped, on the worktop which was perhaps four inches higher than she would have liked it, she idly thought that it was a shame all the flats near Charing Cross Road had been so disappointing. It came to something when even an estate agent couldn't recommend anything.

Then her knife was arrested, mid-chop. The estate agent had said Raphael's shop wasn't worth a great deal. That meant whoever had written the letters hadn't done it because they wanted to get their hands on the shop. Jemma put her knife down and ran to fetch her notebook. *Getting hold of shop not a motive*, she scribbled. *Not worth a lot. Estate agent said wrong part of Charing Cross Road.* She thought for a moment, then added: *Perhaps R aware of this and therefore unwilling to invest money or time in shop?*

She was considering this nugget of information when her phone rang. The display said *Em*.

'Hi, Jemma,' said Em. 'Fancy meeting up for a drink? We're heading to the Marquis in a minute.'

Jemma looked at the half-chopped vegetables in front of her. 'Thanks, Em, but I've only just got in. We closed late, you see.'

'You stayed late?' said Em, with an odd note in her voice. 'I hope you're getting overtime for that.'

Jemma laughed. 'I'll take a long lunch tomorrow. Actually, no, Wednesdays tend to be busy.'

Em huffed out a sigh, and Jemma could imagine her rolling her eyes. 'Don't let the owner take advantage of you, Jemma. Before you know where you are you'll be working through your lunch hour and staying late, and for what?' She paused, and when she spoke again her voice was bright. 'Anyway, that doesn't stop you coming for a quick one, does it?'

Jemma eyed her notebook. 'I've got something to do after I've had dinner. But I can come out another time,' she added hurriedly.

Another pause. 'Jemma, you're a sweet person, and very trusting, and I love that about you,' said Em. 'But I have to admit that I think this bookshop job is a bad move. I bet you're working for almost nothing and wearing yourself into the ground.'

'I like it,' Jemma began, but Em wasn't finished.

'I mean, are you using your skills? Really? You'll end up just as unappreciated as you were before. I hate to say it, but Phoebe walked all over you, and this bookshop person will do exactly the same thing if you're not careful. Now I'm heading out, and if you have any sense you'll join me. I hope I'll see you later.' And the call ended.

Jemma stared at her phone. It was completely unlike Em to get annoyed. She looked at the vegetables, then at her notebook, then her watch. It was getting on for seven. Slowly, she resumed chopping, but Em's words made her feel a little queasy. *Is Raphael taking advantage of me?* she thought. *After all, he won't let me do what I'm good at, and now I'm running around investigating. Mostly in my own time.*

'Ow!' She looked down; she had nicked her thumb with the knife. 'For heaven's sake!' She threw the knife down in disgust, washed her hands at the sink, and went in search of a plaster. Then she scooped the vegetables into a container, slammed it into the fridge, found the takeaway menu, and rang for a pizza. She didn't trust herself to go for a drink with Em; she suspected that if she did, she would end up rambling loudly and incoherently, and possibly being put into a taxi. Instead, she went to the wine rack and opened a bottle of Chilean red.

***

'Morning,' said Raphael, when Jemma arrived at the shop the next morning. 'Well, more or less.'

'Morning,' muttered Jemma. *I'm clearly out of practice*, she thought. Last night's wine and pepperoni pizza were proving uneasy bedfellows. To make it worse, the bright morning light pierced her brain like a laser. She wished she had been able to find her sunglasses, but even after standing under the shower for twenty minutes, getting dressed and out of the flat had taken all her capability.

'Tea?' said Raphael, in an irritatingly jaunty voice. 'I mean, I've had a cup already, but I can always put the kettle on again.'

'Coffee. Black,' said Jemma. 'I'll do it.' She went into the back room, where at least there were no windows to torture her, and flicked the kettle on. While she waited she leaned on the worktop, her head in her hands. She tried to remember exactly what Em had said, but it was jumbled up in a resentful haze. Maybe Raphael was taking advantage of her. He'd said himself that she could take the time back, and now he was teasing her about it. *Em's right, I'm being played for a fool,* Jemma thought bitterly, and put two heaped teaspoons of coffee into her mug.

She heard a small, low-pitched meow, and Folio jumped onto the worktop, his tail a question mark. 'You're not supposed to be on there,' said Jemma, scooping him up and setting him on the floor.

Folio purred, rubbed his head against her shin, and gazed up at her with amber eyes.

'I'm not cross with you,' she said, rather crossly. 'I'm cross with him, and – and *things.*'

'Would you like some toast?' called Raphael. 'You look a bit, um, hungry.'

Typical, thought Jemma, as she dropped two slices of white into the toaster and rammed the catch down. *He's worked out that I'm on to him, and he's buttering me up.*

But there was no denying that after half a mug of black coffee and a slice of toast, Jemma felt considerably better. By the time she went back into the shop the sun had had the decency to retreat behind a cloud, which made things much more bearable.

'I was a bit later than I intended,' said Jemma. 'Sorry.'

'That's quite all right,' said Raphael. 'I'm sure you've worked extra, anyway. Now, do you mind if I nip out for twenty minutes or so?'

Here we go, thought Jemma.

Raphael gestured to a small stack of books on the counter. 'I had a call earlier from an acquaintance of mine who owns a shop down the road. He needs a few books to complete an order, and as it happens, I've got them. He's single-handed and can't leave the shop, so I said I'd pop round with them when I could get away.'

Jemma felt heat creeping up her neck. 'Oh, absolutely,' she said. 'Sorry I kept you waiting.'

'No need to apologise,' said Raphael. 'Are you sure you can manage?' He did actually appear concerned.

'I'm fine,' said Jemma. 'Had a glass of wine too many last night,' she confessed.

Raphael laughed. 'Oh, we've all done that. I'll be as quick as I can.'

Once he had gone Jemma looked around the shop for things to do, but everything appeared in good order. There weren't obvious gaps on the shelves, the till had a float, and Raphael had replaced their stock of paper bags. *I could sit and read.* She opened her bag, pulled out the copy of *Anna Karenina* which had been there for some time, then put it back and found *Lucy Sullivan Is Getting Married* instead. *I bet a customer will come in before I finish the first page*, she thought, and sat in the armchair. Folio settled next to her, his furry bulk pressing against her elbow.

Jemma was about thirty pages in when the shop bell rang. She sighed, and looked up.

'Um, hello?' said a nervous youth in an army-surplus coat, holding a sheet of paper covered in scribble. 'I've got a reading list for my dissertation topic, and I wondered if you had any of the books.'

Jemma hunted for a bookmark, and finding none, used a paper bag instead. 'I can check,' she said, holding her hand out for the list.

Fifteen minutes later her customer, balancing a teetering pile of books, headed for the door. 'Oh, you've got a letter,' he said. 'I'd pick it up, but…'

Jemma saw a square, pale-blue envelope face down on the

doormat. 'I'll get it in a minute,' she said, and went to hold the door open for him.

When he had gone, she didn't pick the envelope up immediately. *It's nothing like the first one. It's probably a card.* On turning it over, she saw that the envelope was addressed to Burns Books in neat, forward-slanting writing. It was unstamped.

It won't be another anonymous letter. And if it is, I can analyse it properly. It won't be like last time, when Raphael took the note away before I'd had a chance to look at it. Before she could change her mind, she ripped it open.

Inside was a piece of pale-blue notepaper, folded in half, but Jemma could feel unevenness through the paper. She took a deep breath, and opened it out.

kEEp YOuR nOSe OuT, uNdERLiNg, oR wE'll cOmE fOR yOu TOo

Chapter 13

Jemma felt her knees wobble. She hurried to the armchair and sat down, still staring at the note. She was conscious of a strangeness about the air, as if a thunderstorm approached.

Who's sending these? And why are they coming after me?

Because they know you want to track them down. They're scared of you.

Jemma closed her eyes and visualised Raphael saying 'empty threats'. She repeated the words like a mantra, and as she did so the oppressive atmosphere seemed to lift. She smelt vanilla, and cinnamon, though she couldn't work out where it was coming from. Surely not the note? She sniffed it, but it smelt of paper, and faintly of glue.

The shop bell jangled and she looked up, guiltily. Raphael came through the door smiling, a paper bag in his hand. 'Most satisfactory,' he announced. 'I got cinnamon rolls from Rolando's to celebrate. Is it too early for elevenses, do you think?' Then he took in her expression. 'What's wrong, Jemma?'

Jemma looked at the note in her hands. 'The anonymous letter-writer strikes again,' she said, trying to keep her voice light.

'Oh no, not again.' Raphael walked over and held his hand out for the letter. 'Don't pay any attention. Here, I'll get rid of it.'

'No, I'll do it,' said Jemma, screwing the letter up into a ball. 'And I'll make tea to go with the cinnamon rolls.'

'Oh yes, good idea,' said Raphael, but he still seemed worried. 'Are you sure you're all right?'

'Yes, fine,' said Jemma, already on her way to the back room. 'All in a day's work. We had a customer while you were out. He bought lots of music theory books.'

'Oh good,' said Raphael. 'I did wonder, when I unpacked that box, how long we'd have them for. Not as long as I thought.'

In the back room, Jemma smoothed out the letter and replaced it in its envelope. *No one threatens me*, she thought, grimly. *The more they try to put me off, the more determined I am to catch them.*

When she took the tea through, Raphael was ensconced in the armchair. 'So which books did you take round to your colleague?' she asked.

'Works about the Knights Templar,' said Raphael. 'A historian friend of his is working on a new book, and looking for research materials.'

'The Knights Templar?' asked Jemma. 'Who or what are they?'

Raphael's eye-roll was subtle, but still discernible. 'I'd tell you to go and read a book about them, Jemma,' he said. 'But at the moment, we don't have any. Ah, tea. Thank you.' He took a sip, then set his cup down with a sigh of pleasure. 'Jemma, I've been thinking. Maybe you shouldn't seek out this letter-writing chump. Perhaps you're right, and it is a police matter.'

'But I thought you didn't want the police round here asking questions?' said Jemma. Her cup trembled in her hand, and she put it on the counter. Suddenly she felt as if she were at the top of a mountain; it was hard to breathe. 'Like you said, it's a load of silly notes.'

'I know,' said Raphael. 'But just because something's silly, that doesn't mean it can't be dangerous. Look at bungee jumping.'

'What has bungee jumping got to do with anything?' said Jemma. 'The police will probably laugh at you, anyway. I don't think we should get the police involved, not at all.'

'Is that your honest opinion?' said Raphael, frowning.

'Yes,' said Jemma. 'I think we should get on with the day-to-day business of running the shop and ignore it, like you said.' As she said it, her lightheadedness began to fade.

'Yes, I did say that, didn't I?' Folio jumped on Raphael's lap, purred, and butted his head against Raphael's hand. 'And the shop does take a fair bit of running. Particularly now that we're so busy.'

As if they had heard this, two women came in. 'My, what a lovely little bookshop!' exclaimed the shorter one, in a southern American accent. 'I simply must have a look around!'

Twenty minutes later, they left. The enthusiastic woman had bought nothing, but her silent companion had bought all the Charlaine Harris in stock. 'I'll go and get more books,' said Jemma, wondering what a random box selection would turn up.

'Don't forget your cinnamon roll,' said Raphael. 'They're very good.'

'I'll have it when I've restocked,' said Jemma. It did look tempting; but she felt she needed a breathing space more than sugar.

Jemma took her time in the stockroom, wandering down the aisles and trailing her hand along the boxes. *I'll have to do this undercover*, she thought. *Raphael can't catch me with the note. I'll go out for lunch, and see what I can accomplish.* She could feel her heart thumping, and took a few deep breaths before selecting a box and going back to the main shop. When she opened it, she found that the box was full of Hercule Poirot mysteries, all vintage.

'Those will do well,' said Raphael. 'There are a lot of Agatha fans and collectors out there.'

'Yes, there are,' Jemma replied, smiling. She was sure that there were; but she was happier that her choice of box appeared to indicate that she was doing the right thing. It was almost as if the shop approved, although of course that was ridiculous.

Raphael went for his lunch first, and as soon as he was safely away, Jemma spread the note on the shop counter and retrieved her notebook. She wrote the date, then *New Development*.

A second note arrived between 9.30 and around 10.15. Note apparently for me. She copied it out, including the capital letters. *Sender addressed me as 'underling' so we can assume they don't know my name.* She pursed her lips, and read what she had written. *Or do they?*

She examined the note. *The envelope and the paper don't match*, she wrote. *The envelope is a slightly different blue, and the wrong size for the notepaper. The previous note was on standard A4 paper, and was in a long white envelope. It looked like office stationery, while this looks like an envelope from a greetings card, and notepaper from a pad.* She held it up to the light, peered at it, and noted: *Basildon Bond*.

Next she examined the text. *The note is composed of letters cut from newspapers and/or magazines.* On impulse, she fetched Raphael's newspaper and studied the headlines. The letters looked similar, but not exactly the same. She sighed, and picked up her pen again.

At lunchtime, check a selection of publications for a match.

She took a picture of the note with her phone, focusing as closely as she could on the letters, then put it in her bag. *It would be just my luck for Raphael to walk in on me at the mini-market,* she thought. *This way I can lock my phone, and he'll never know.*

The time dragged until Raphael returned. Jemma made a list of all the shops in the parade, then all the people who might bear a grudge against Raphael. This included rival bookshop owners, booksellers with whom he had driven a hard bargain, former assistants (she wrote *'who are still alive'* next to this entry), and Mr Tennant from the Retail Association. However you looked at it, it really wasn't a detailed list. *I must find out more about him.* She unlocked her phone and typed *Raphael Burns* into Google.

Nothing came up; or at least, nothing that was related to Raphael. She tried *Raphael Burns bookseller*, and got the same result. 'That's weird,' she said. 'How can there be nothing on the internet about someone?' She Googled her own name for comparison and three pages of information came up, including her neglected Twitter feed, her Instagram, which was mainly photos of beverages, and her company profile. *They haven't even bothered to delete me,* she thought, and blinked.

Then she typed in *Burns Books Charing Cross Road.* The first entry was from TripAdvisor: *Read 54 unbiased reviews of Burns Books.* Remembering the article she had read, Jemma held her breath as she clicked the link.

It was even worse than she had thought. The shop had an average rating of 1.5.

I had to have a tetanus jab after the shop cat attacked me.

I couldn't pay for my book for 15 minutes because the owner was building a house of cards on the counter.

I shall never set foot in this bookshop again. I'd like to tell you why, but children might read this.

'Oh dear,' murmured Jemma. At the bottom of her list of people she added: *Almost anyone who has visited the shop. See*

TripAdvisor for more details. 'Careful what you wish for, Jemma,' she said to herself. 'You wanted more suspects, and now you have plenty.'

Raphael came in, and Jemma pretended to be reading the newspaper. 'Nice and quiet, then?' he asked.

'Yes, pretty much,' Jemma replied. 'I'll head out for my lunch, if that's OK.'

'Yes, go ahead,' said Raphael, walking to the crime shelves and selecting *Murder On The Orient Express*.

'Good choice,' said Jemma. She frowned. What if – what if a group of disgruntled customers were taking it upon themselves to drive Raphael out of business?

Don't be daft, she told herself. *It would make much more sense for them to go to a different bookshop. And that would be a lot less trouble.* She got her jacket, and set off for the mini-market. *Time for more research.* But even in the half a minute that it took her to get there, her other internet discovery – or rather, lack of discovery – nagged at her. *How is it possible for a normal human being to have absolutely no presence on social media whatsoever?*

You shouldn't be surprised, she told herself. *He doesn't even have a card machine in the shop. Modern technology's completely beyond him.* She pushed open the door of the mini-market with a pleasing sense of superiority. *Time for me to drag him into the modern world.*

Chapter 14

'Afternoon,' said Nafisa as Jemma entered the shop. 'Will you be browsing our sandwich selection again today?'

'I think I'll stick to egg mayo,' said Jemma. She got a sandwich from the cabinet, and after some thought, added a can of Diet Coke and a Twix. She put those on the counter, then went to the newspaper section and took out her phone. Opening the picture, she compared the typefaces on the photo with those in front of her.

'I suppose at least you're not reading them,' said Nafisa. 'What are you doing?'

'I'm, er, looking for something,' said Jemma.

'I can see that,' Nafisa replied. Shaking her head, she carried on reading her magazine.

Jemma glanced across, and her eye snagged on the headline. 'What magazine is that, please?'

'*Take a Break*,' said Nafisa.

'Right. Thanks,' said Jemma, and added a *Take a Break* to the pile. Then she peered at her phone again, and put a *Daily Mail* on top of it. She scanned the other newspapers and magazines, but nothing was quite right. 'That'll do,' she said.

Nafisa rang up her purchases. 'Slow day today?' she asked.

'Oh no, Raphael says it's much busier since I've come,' said Jemma. 'I'm getting these for, um, later.'

'No need to explain to me,' said Nafisa, laughing.

She passed the card machine over and Jemma touched her phone to it. 'How much do these cost?' she asked, pointing at it.

'Oh, not much,' said Nafisa. 'Got this one a few years ago, but now you can pick up a card reader for about twenty quid if you shop around.'

'That's good to know,' said Jemma. 'I'm thinking of setting the bookshop up to take electronic payments.'

'Really?' Nafisa's eyes were as round and bright as new pennies. She snorted. 'Good luck with that.'

Jemma looked at her curiously. 'Why do you say that?'

'Oh, no reason,' said Nafisa, waving a casual hand. 'He just doesn't seem the type. I mean, he wears those waistcoats.'

'Lots of people wear waistcoats,' said Jemma.

'Waistcoats, yes,' said Nafisa. 'But not those waistcoats.' She nodded with an air of ineffable wisdom.

'Right, well, thanks,' said Jemma, gathering up her purchases. 'See you tomorrow, I guess.'

'See you tomorrow,' said Nafisa, already absorbed in her magazine.

Jemma considered calling in at a few more shops to try and glean more information about Raphael, but she had already used ten minutes of her lunch hour. So she decamped to the Phoenix Garden, found a bench in the sunshine, and spread out her picnic, publications, and the fateful letter.

She ate half her sandwich without realising, so intent was she on matching the letters in her note. *Take a Break*, as it turned out, was a valuable source of different typographical styles and colours. Fifteen minutes later, Jemma had identified perhaps two-thirds of the letters. Then she studied the *Daily Mail*, which was particularly useful for the capitals.

Jemma ate the second half of her sandwich while considering the last two unidentified letters: a Y with a curious flourish on its right-hand arm, and an intricate g whose lower loop was narrow and slanted. Both were black, on a cream background, and Jemma didn't recall seeing anything like them in either a magazine or a newspaper.

'Still pretty good work, though,' she said to herself. She unwrapped her Twix and ate half before realising that she was already full. *I'll save the other half for the tube*, she thought, and put it back in its wrapper. 'Back to it, I suppose,' she said, brushing her hands together, and headed towards the bustle of Charing Cross Road.

But as she came to the parade of shops in which Burns Books was located, she hesitated. Was it worth another look in the mini-market to track down the elusive last two letters? Could she even, perhaps, show the letters to Nafisa – in close-up, of course – and see if she recognised them? After all, she handled dozens of publications every day. Surely the chances were good.

'Is it tomorrow already?' said Nafisa as Jemma hurried in. Jemma detected distinct testiness in Nafisa's tone. Now was clearly not a good time for special requests.

'It's OK,' she said, edging towards the door, but scanning the magazine shelves as she did so. 'To be honest, I've forgotten what I came in for.'

'At your age? That's bad,' said Nafisa. 'Are you going back to the shop?'

'Yes, that's right,' said Jemma. She reached for the door handle.

'In that case, can you tell Raphael that his *Bookseller's Companion* has come in? I'd give it to you to pass on, but if I do he'll never remember to pay me.' She reached under the counter and brought out an odd-looking publication, printed on cream-coloured paper with bold black typography.

Jemma stared at it. 'I can take that for him,' she said. 'Don't worry, I'll pay you.' She fumbled for her phone and held it to the card machine, her eyes never leaving the magazine in Nafisa's hand.

Nafisa laughed. 'Are you going to read it before you give it to him? You're keen.'

'Yes I am, rather,' said Jemma. 'I'd better get back. Bye, Nafisa.'

But Jemma did not return to the bookshop. She stood outside the mini-market and leafed through the magazine until she had found the letters she wanted, in articles headed *Your Book Care Tips* and *Reading Recommendations: Friend or Foe*? Only then did she allow anger to wash over her.

'Him all along!' she said, her voice as bitter as strong black coffee. She imagined Raphael upstairs in his flat, which was probably an absolute tip filled with unwashed mugs and smelling of cat. He would lounge on a battered old chesterfield sofa which had probably been worth a lot of money before he mistreated it, and which would have horsehair leaking from the cushions. A pot of paste and a pile of old magazines would sit on the stained low table in front of him, and he'd arrange the letters on a sheet of paper and chuckle to himself at how stupid she was.

'I should have realised,' she muttered. 'No wonder he was always out when the letters came. He was the one delivering them! All this to stop me from turning that shop around!'

Jemma had worked herself up into a storm of fury by the time she pushed open the door of Burns Books. Luckily for Raphael, he was actually dealing with a customer, and while Jemma was tempted to denounce him then and there, she told herself that she was far too professional to do that sort of thing.

At length the customer departed, clutching a copy of *The*

Accused. The moment the door closed behind him, Jemma stalked over and threw the *Bookseller's Companion* onto the counter. 'I know what you've been doing,' she said.

Raphael immediately looked very guilty indeed. 'Oh,' he said. He bit his bottom lip. 'Do you?'

'Yes,' said Jemma, 'I do.'

'Oh dear,' said Raphael. He grimaced. 'That's awkward.'

'Yes, it is,' snapped Jemma. 'Maybe I should be flattered that you went to so much trouble to stop me doing my job.'

Raphael frowned. 'Your job?'

'Yes, my job,' spat Jemma. 'Or what should be my job; dragging this bookshop into the twenty-first century and making it a going concern instead of the shambles it currently is. Look at it!' She swept a hand round the interior, which appeared particularly grey and dismal. 'Nothing on the walls, no extras or accessories for customers to buy, no recommendations, nowhere for customers to sit except an armchair which you and that cat hog all the time.' One of the lights above Jemma's head flickered, buzzed, and went out, but she kept going. 'I've read the reviews on TripAdvisor. I know what people are saying about this shop. You ought to be grateful that I work here at all. And now you've pulled a stunt like this!'

She took a breath and focused on Raphael, who seemed utterly bemused. 'Jemma, I have absolutely no idea what you mean,' he said.

'This shop is a pigsty!' she cried. 'Most of your customers hate you! And instead of doing anything about it, you spend your time faking stupid anonymous letters to distract me!'

'Me?' said Raphael. 'You think I sent them?'

'You did it all right,' said Jemma. She took the letter out of her bag, unfolded it, and stabbed an accusing finger at the Y and the g. 'Those letters come from this magazine, and I know Nafisa orders it in for you, because she told me. Letters from this, and the *Daily*

Mail, and *Take a Break*, all of which you can buy from her. All your flannel about business ecosystems and balance is just that; a load of old flannel. You can't face the fact that you, Raphael Burns, are a failure, and so is this crappy excuse for a bookshop.' The door rattled, and cold air blasted Jemma's ankles. 'You've got a motive and plenty of opportunity, and all the evidence points to you.' She folded her arms and glared at him. 'So as far as I'm concerned, it's up to you to prove me wrong.'

Chapter 15

'I admit that it doesn't look good,' said Raphael. 'But it really wasn't me.'

'Prove it,' said Jemma.

Folio jumped onto the counter and yowled at her, but she ignored him. 'It stinks, and you know it.'

'I'm rather hurt that you'd think such a thing of me,' said Raphael. 'I mean, as if I'd read the *Daily Mail*.'

Jemma's mouth twitched in spite of herself. Then she banged the counter with her fist. 'It isn't funny! How dare you send me off on a wild-goose chase! But the joke's on you, Raphael. I could have made something of the shop, if you'd let me, but why should I bother now?'

'The shop,' said Raphael, with dignity, 'is already something, thank you very much.'

'Yes, it is,' sneered Jemma. 'It's an example of how not to run a bookshop.'

'I think you're forgetting yourself,' Raphael observed, calmly.

Jemma opened her mouth to reply, then pulled her jacket round her and shivered. The weather was ridiculously changeable today.

As if in agreement, she heard a rumble. *I was right*, she thought. *There's a storm coming.* And another low, bad-tempered rumble would have confirmed that, if she could have been sure that it came from outside the shop. Something fizzed overhead, followed by a tinkle of broken glass as another lightbulb smashed.

Raphael lifted both hands into the air, as if calming an invisible opponent. 'I suggest you go for a walk, Jemma. I think you need time out of the shop. But before you go, I shall reiterate that I did not send any of those anonymous letters, and I don't know where they came from. You may believe what you like, but that is the truth.' He held her gaze a moment longer, then looked away as if that were the end of the matter.

Jemma was taken aback. She had expected Raphael to mount an indignant defence, at the very least. She had been prepared to counteract any argument he made with damning circumstantial evidence. His refusal to engage irked her. 'Right,' she said. 'Fine. If that's how it is.'

Raphael didn't reply, and didn't look up. So Jemma wrenched the shop door open and slammed it behind her without a backward glance.

She hadn't walked more than a few feet before it started to rain. Not a light drizzle, oh no. Big, fat raindrops that meant business. Jemma pulled up the collar of her jacket and huddled into it, but drops still found their way down her neck, into her pockets, and through her shoulder seams, until she was thoroughly damp. She thought about sheltering in a doorway till the rain had stopped; but the rain didn't look as if it would ever stop. The world was dissolving into a grey mist of rain, losing both colour and definition. The only real thing was Jemma herself: wet, clammy, and indignant.

She had stalked away from the bookshop full of self-righteous purpose. *He'll be lucky if I ever set foot in that shop again.* But the rain, and the accompanying gusts of wind, made striding rather difficult. Jemma's pace slowed even as people scurried past her, holding umbrellas and coats and magazines over their heads. Really, once you were wet through, you couldn't get any wetter, so there wasn't any point in trying to keep dry. Jemma took her hands out of her pockets and turned her face up to the rain. A large cold raindrop splashed into her eye, and she bit back a swearword.

After fifteen minutes of wandering, Jemma wasn't sure where she was, or why. *Raphael*, she thought. *He made a fool of me.* Then she remembered his quiet denial, and frowned. 'But it was him,' she muttered. 'It must have been. Who else would bother?'

She thought about getting her notebook out of her bag, but decided the rain would do it no good. She shivered, and pulled her useless jacket around her.

And now that she had left the shop, of course, there was no rumbling at all. 'Stupid weather,' she muttered, scowling at the rain. It had seemed so very storm-like with the rumbling, and the electricity in the air, and the lights blowing.

'It must have been a storm,' she said aloud. 'There isn't anything else it could be.' Nothing rumbled like that. Unless it had been a tube train going under the shop. But firstly, she was fairly sure that no tube line was near enough, and secondly, she had never heard a rumble like that in all the time she had spent at Burns Books.

Jemma's pace quickened until she was the one scurrying past other pedestrians. She couldn't say why, but she wanted to put as much distance between herself and the shop, and Raphael, as she could. She wanted to be doing normal things, not hurrying through the streets of London in the pouring rain, or dealing with customers' strange requests and finding that yes, actually, they did happen to have that unusual book in stock, or opening boxes of books which seemed determined to tell her something—

'What's the most normal thing I can think of?' she muttered as she sped along, cheeks flushed, arms pumping. 'Who is the most normal person I know?'

A bus shelter reared up at her through the rain, and she flung her hands out to ward it off. 'Watch where you're going, love!' a voice said, and laughed.

Jemma took a step back, and looked. The bus shelter had a huge poster advertising ice cream, of all the ridiculous, inappropriate things on a day like today. Magnum ice cream, with a big gold *M*.

Em.

Of course! Jemma ducked into the bus shelter and rang Em's mobile. She hoped that she wasn't in a meeting.

The phone rang five times. Jemma sighed out her disappointment, and her warm breath added to the mist.

'Hello, Jemma!' Em sang out. 'You missed a good night last night. There was karaoke and everything.'

'Oh,' said Jemma. Her teeth began to chatter, and she clamped her jaw shut.

'I can't talk for long,' said Em. 'I have to go into a meeting in ten minutes, and I haven't read the stuff yet.' She laughed. 'Same old, same old.' Then a pause. 'Are you all right? You're very quiet.'

'I don't know,' said Jemma. 'I'm soaking wet.'

'Oh dear,' said Em, in the casual manner of someone who has never been absolutely soaked through. 'Did you get caught in the rain?'

'I'm out in it now,' said Jemma. 'My boss told me to go for a walk.'

'In this?' said Em. 'Oh, actually it's stopped raining over here.' Another pause. 'So did you ring me up to tell me that you're soaking wet?'

'I should have listened to you, Em,' said Jemma. 'I tried my best, I really did, and for nothing.' She stared at the rain lashing down all around her.

'Oh,' said Em. 'Is this about that bookshop?'

'Yes,' said Jemma. 'It is. I could have made a success of it, but he wouldn't let me. And now this.'

'Oh dear,' said Em. 'That doesn't sound good. Look, I have to do work stuff, but I'll be thinking about you. In a way I'm glad that it's happened now, and you didn't get hurt worse later on. Men, eh?'

'Yeah,' said Jemma. For no particular reason she thought of Carl the barista, whom she might never see again.

'You can do better than that smelly little bookshop,' said Em, in an encouraging tone. 'I know you can. You just need the right opportunity. When I get out of this meeting I'll ask if anyone knows of an opening. That idiot in the bookshop is taking advantage of you, and I'm glad that you've seen through it. Honestly, Jemma, you'll look back at this in a year's time and laugh. You really will. I have to go, but I'll call you later if I can. Bye, Jemma, bye.' And the call ended.

Jemma gazed at the phone, then put it in her bag. *I knew Em would agree with me.* She imagined herself, nice and dry, returning to the shop to tell Raphael that she had got herself a lovely shiny new job that paid twice what the bookshop did, so he could shove his job where the sun didn't shine. But somehow, as she visualised it, she couldn't see Raphael being angry, or devastated, or even slightly upset. He just listened, and said that that was a shame. She sighed a huge sigh, and pushed sopping rat's-tails of hair away from her face.

It would be nice, though, to go and tell Raphael exactly what she thought of him.

And then she remembered reading in the armchair, and writing the shop's phone number on the customers' bags, and tickling Folio under his chin, and polishing the shop counter, and the tingly feeling she had when she opened a box of books with no idea what she might find inside.

Jemma swallowed, and felt something warm trickle down her cheek. Absentmindedly, she rubbed it away.

I should listen to Em. Em is sensible. Em knows what's what. Em has a boyfriend, and they have a lovely flat together, and a mortgage, and she doesn't get hangovers. And I could get another job, I know I could.

She stared at the rain. Perhaps she was getting used to it, or perhaps it was a little less misty and blurred than before.

'I can get another job,' she said, and the other ten people in the bus shelter looked at her, then shuffled further off. 'But I don't want to. I want to find out what's going on.'

She peered at the map on the inside of the bus shelter. Somehow, in her wandering, she had managed to travel almost in a complete circle. She was about two minutes' walk from the bookshop. She sighed and stepped out into the rain, which slowed to a drizzle, then stopped entirely.

Chapter 16

Jemma had rehearsed a short, pithy speech in the time it took her to walk back to the bookshop, but the words fled when she pushed open the door. The shop was dark; only one light was on. She wasn't sure whether Raphael had switched the others off, or they had blown. Raphael himself was shelving books, his back to her. It looked as if a bunch of unruly customers had come in and wrecked the place. Books lay randomly on the floor, everything in the window display had been knocked over, and somehow the paper bags had come off the string, and lay around the counter like fallen leaves.

'What happened?' she asked, stepping in carefully.

Raphael turned round, and Jemma braced herself to be shouted at, or worse, disapproved of. 'Oh, it's you,' he said. He didn't look annoyed, or disapproving. But he did look very, very tired. Her heart went out to him, and at the same time her anger dissolved.

'Shall I make tea?' she asked.

Raphael considered her question. 'That would be nice, but best not,' he said. 'I've put Folio in the back room.' As he slid another book onto the shelf Jemma noticed he had a large plaster on his right hand.

'Oh dear,' she said. 'That isn't like Folio.'

'It isn't, usually,' said Raphael, shelving another book. 'I mean, he does occasionally go for a customer or two, when they're being troublesome, but that's different.' He moved along the shelf, bending every so often to pick up more books and replace them. 'That's why I sent you for a walk. I was a bit worried about what might happen if you stayed.'

'I'm sorry I shouted at you and – said what I did,' Jemma said, all in a rush.

'I thought that was the problem, you see,' said Raphael, almost as if she hadn't spoken. 'I thought you were causing the disturbance. But it wasn't just you. It was me, too.'

Jemma opened her mouth, but could think of nothing to say, so she closed it again.

'I thought that once you'd left the shop everything would go back to normal.' Raphael peered at a book, then lifted his long arm and fitted it on a shelf above his head. 'Or what passes for normal, in here. I told myself that without you the shop would calm down. But it got worse. As you can see.' He glanced at Jemma. 'Do you know that you're soaking wet?' he asked.

'It had come to my attention,' said Jemma.

'Well, you can't stay here like that, you'll catch a cold. Wait there.' He put down his pile of books and strode to the door which led to his rooms upstairs. Two minutes later he was back, with a pair of blue and white striped flannel pyjamas and a purple silk dressing gown.

A despairing feline wail sounded from the back room.

'Are you going to behave yourself, Folio?' Raphael demanded.

There was a pause, then a conciliatory meow.

'Good,' said Raphael. He opened the door and Folio sauntered out, tail flicking. He walked over to Jemma and gazed up at her, his eyes brilliant golden spheres. Jemma stretched out a timid hand, and he rubbed it with his cheek. She heard a gentle sigh. When she looked up, Raphael was watching her.

'I'll go and get changed,' she said, and hurried to the toilet. The pyjamas were, of course, far too long for her, and both the trousers and the sleeves had to be rolled up, but at least she was warm. And the silk dressing gown made her feel rather exotic. She dried her hair with the hand towel, and draped her soaked garments over the radiators in the back of the shop. Then she put the kettle on. If there was ever a time for a large pot of tea, it was now.

'We should probably close the shop,' she called. 'I'm not sure I ought to serve customers wearing your pyjamas.'

Raphael appeared in the doorway. 'I closed it when you left,' he said. 'I couldn't have the customers coming to any harm. After all, it isn't their fault.'

Jemma gave him a curious look. 'What isn't their fault?'

Raphael appeared to be searching for the right word. 'The . . . *atmosphere.*'

The kettle boiled, and Jemma warmed the pot. 'I don't understand anything,' she said. 'I don't understand why someone's sending anonymous letters. I don't understand why you don't want the shop to do well. And I really don't understand why things – things *happen* in here.'

Raphael sighed. 'I'm not sure I can answer all of those questions,' he said. 'But I presume that whoever is sending the anonymous letters wants me, and Burns Books, to disappear. They're trying to frighten us away.' He managed a thin smile. 'It won't happen, but that's what they want.'

Jemma eyed the copy of the *Bookseller's Companion* which was still lying on the counter where she had thrown it. 'They wanted me to think you were sending them, so that I'd leave too.' She frowned. 'But do they want us to leave, or do they want to get hold of the shop? The estate agent said it wasn't worth much.'

'Oh, the estate agent,' Raphael said, with scorn. 'They'll tell you anything.' Then he gave her a quizzical glance. 'Why were you talking to an estate agent about the shop?'

'I wasn't!' exclaimed Jemma. 'Well, I was, but I didn't start it. I was looking in the window when I left the other day, and someone came outside to entice me in, and I said I worked here, and he began talking about the shop. I was thinking of looking at flats, but he kept saying that the area was expensive and dangerous.'

'I see,' said Raphael, grimly.

'Do you think they're involved?' asked Jemma.

Raphael considered. 'To be completely honest, I've no idea how much the shop is worth. For all I know flats round here are expensive. But it seems a bit odd, given the letters.'

Jemma made the tea and fitted the Space Invaders tea cosy over the pot. 'Maybe it's them; maybe it's a rival bookshop owner.' She sighed. 'But let's leave that one aside for now,' she said. 'Why don't you want the shop to do well? I mean, I haven't changed much since I started working here, apart from doing a couple of window displays and talking to the customers, and it's so obvious that with a little bit of love and care, the shop could do really well. Yet the reviews on TripAdvisor are terrible.'

'Love and care isn't the issue,' said Raphael, sounding ruffled.

Jemma got the best cups and saucers out of the cupboard. The occasion seemed to demand it. Then she faced him. 'So what is?' she asked, as gently as she could.

Raphael looked extremely uncomfortable. 'I do care about the shop,' he said. 'Of course I do. It's been in my family for years and years.'

'Yes, I know,' said Jemma. 'You told me. But if you care about the shop, then why is it so tired and shabby?'

'Careful,' warned Raphael.

Jemma looked around nervously, half expecting one of the wall cupboards to fall on her, or at least to be showered with crockery, but apart from a slight momentary heaviness in the air, nothing happened. She lifted down the biscuit barrel and put the last of the custard creams on a plate.

'Don't you start,' muttered Raphael. Jemma glanced at him, surprised, then realised that he wasn't talking to her. 'All right. I haven't done all the things I could for the shop because I need to protect it. I don't want busloads of tourists taking pictures of it, and tagging it on Facebook, and journalists writing it up as a top London destination. The more interest the bookshop gets, the more likely it is that people will ask questions. And I don't want that.'

Jemma poured tea into the cups, thinking all the while. 'A few days ago,' she said, 'you talked about balance, and the shop's niche, and you said that when I'd worked here longer, then I would understand.'

Raphael darted a look at her. 'I did, didn't I?'

Jemma took a deep breath. 'When you said that, I thought you were using it as an excuse for being lazy. I found it frustrating. I wanted to do things to improve the shop, and you wouldn't let me. It was like pushing against a brick wall. When Nafisa gave me the *Bookseller's Companion* I wanted to believe that you had sent the letters, because that made everything your fault. So I jumped to the wrong conclusion. And I'm really sorry.'

Raphael cleared his throat noisily. 'Thank you for your apology. Now shall we get on and drink this tea?'

'I've only worked here a few more days since then,' said Jemma, 'and I don't understand the shop yet. But I'm beginning to, if that makes sense. I think we can make changes in the shop, very gradually, and still maintain a balance. And I think the shop would appreciate that.' She squeezed her eyes shut and braced herself for some sort of catastrophe.

After a few seconds, nothing had happened. Then she heard a chuckle, and felt a vibration on her left ankle. She looked down to find Folio's chubby body pressed against her leg.

'I think you're right,' said Raphael quietly. 'Perhaps the shop has been attracting the wrong sort of attention all this time, and I never realised. I was so busy making sure it didn't become successful that I went too far the other way.'

'But that isn't everything,' said Jemma. 'We have to find out who is sending the letters, and why. And then we have to stop them.'

She waited for a sign. But the cupboard stayed on the wall, Folio continued to purr, and the books remained on the shelves.

'I agree,' said Raphael. 'We have to stop them.' And the sun broke through the clouds outside, and made the shop bright again.

Chapter 17

They basked in the pleasant warmth of the shop, until Raphael spoilt it by asking 'But how?'

'I don't know,' said Jemma. 'We need answers, but I'm not entirely sure what the questions are.' She bit into a biscuit reflectively.

Ping!

'Was that an answer?' asked Raphael with a smile.

'Unfortunately, it was a text message,' said Jemma. She walked over to the coat stand, unhooked her bag, and delved inside for her phone. 'Oh.'

The message was from Em. *Can't talk right now but friend of a friend sent me this. Analyst job, Highgate. Going on job websites next week, but you can get in early.*

Jemma clicked the attachment. The job was at a company she'd heard of, paid roughly what she had earned before, and was well within her capabilities.

'Is it good news?' asked Raphael.

It took Jemma a while to look up from her phone. 'I'm not sure,' she said. She thought about closing the message and telling him that it was just a normal text. But that didn't feel right. 'It's from a friend. She's sent me details of a job in Highgate.'

'That's quite a long way away,' said Raphael.

'Yes, it is,' said Jemma. 'It would be a long commute.' *And a long way from here*, she thought. *In more ways than one.*

'Is it a good job?' asked Raphael. 'I mean, obviously I'd like you to continue working in the shop, but I can't stand in your way.' The words were conventional enough, but Raphael appeared genuinely crestfallen.

'It is a good job,' she said. 'But I didn't ask her to go job-hunting for me.' She pressed *Reply*, and texted *Thanks, I'll have a look X.* 'More tea? I think we can get another cup each out of the pot.'

Jemma was mid-pour when her phone rang. She set the teapot down carefully. 'Em must have finished her meeting,' she said, and pressed *Accept.*

'What do you mean, you'll have a look?' Em demanded. 'I thought you were desperate for another job, after the way that man treated you!'

'Um, hello Em,' said Jemma. 'Thank you for sending me the job, I appreciate it.'

'But you won't follow it up, will you?' said Em. 'In fact, I bet you're in that shop right now. You've gone crawling back, after everything I said. Why do you have to be so stubborn, Jemma? Why won't you listen to me? I'm only trying to do the best for you, believe me. You ought to thank me, and instead you disregard me completely. Well, that's it. That's the last time I help you. I'm through. You're on your own.' She paused, but Jemma felt too battered by her words to venture a reply. 'Goodbye, Jemma.' *Click.*

'Do you need to sit down?' asked Raphael. Jemma nodded, and allowed him to lead her to the armchair and plump up the cushion.

'I don't understand,' she said. 'I suppose that's another one for the list. Sorry. I feel very stupid today.'

'Oh, I wouldn't worry about that,' said Raphael. 'In fact, often it's when we are at our most stupid that we are on the brink of understanding.'

'I hope you're right,' said Jemma. 'Could you pass me my tea?' Raphael obliged, and she sipped thoughtfully. 'She sounded really angry,' she said, in a puzzled tone. 'That's so unlike Em. She's never liked the idea of me working here, though. I remember when I told her I'd got this job. Almost immediately she sent me an article about the worst bookshops, and we were number two.'

'At least we weren't number one,' said Raphael, with a wry smile. 'Who was, if you don't mind me asking?'

'Can't remember,' said Jemma. 'Hang on a minute, I'll look.' She opened her messages, then scrolled up Em's feed. 'Here we are.' But when she clicked on the article, the worst bookshop in Britain wasn't the thing that caught her eye. 'The *Bookseller's Companion*!'

'Yes, it's over there on the counter,' said Raphael.

'No, this is taken from the *Bookseller's Companion*!' cried Jemma. 'Or at least, the information is.'

'That could be a coincidence, though,' said Raphael.

'It could,' said Jemma. 'But that means Em knows about it. And why is she so keen for me not to work in this particular bookshop? She must know something.' She frowned as she recalled Em's attempt to get her out to the pub the evening before. 'She's been trying to convince me that I'm doing the wrong thing working here. She tried to get me to go drinking with her yesterday, and I didn't because I was going to – do things.' She grimaced as she remembered her hangover. 'She probably wanted to pump me for information. And today another letter came! For me this time, telling me to keep my nose out. And they used – *she* used the *Bookseller's Companion* so I'd think it was you! Or another bookseller, at least. But I bet she wanted to pin it on you.'

'But how would she know you were looking into the letters?'

said Raphael. 'Had you told her about it?'

'No, I haven't said a word. But I got home late yesterday partly because I popped into the estate agent. The moment I mentioned the shop, he started telling me that it wasn't worth anything and I shouldn't move into the area.'

'I could be wrong,' said Raphael, 'but it sounds as if she's warning you off.'

'You're right,' said Jemma. 'From what, though? What's going to happen?'

Raphael shrugged. 'Search me. Your friend isn't an estate agent, is she?'

'Oh gosh, no,' said Jemma. 'She was a colleague of mine until two weeks ago.' Then she gasped. 'But her boyfriend is. And the day I left work she wasn't there, because she had a day off. They were celebrating Damon's new job.'

'Hmm,' said Raphael. 'This sounds suspicious. I don't suppose you know which estate agency he's with?'

'No idea,' said Jemma. 'But I bet I can find out.' She opened Google and typed *Damon Foskett estate agent*.

A page of results came up, and images of Damon smiling in black tie at various industry bashes. In one he was even clutching an award. But the one that caught Jemma's eye was an announcement from Ransome's. 'We are delighted to welcome Damon Foskett as Commercial Manager of our two Westminster branches.' She showed Raphael. 'That's good enough for me,' she said grimly. 'I imagine that if you'd gone into the branch and asked for a valuation, they'd have spun you the same tale as they did me: that the shop wasn't worth a great deal.'

'I'd expect nothing less from an estate agent,' said Raphael. 'But while you think your friend sent the letter to warn you off, the letters to me were designed to make me sell up and leave.' He mused for a moment. 'This Damon, would you say he is a particularly evil chap?'

'Not particularly,' said Jemma. 'Very focused on his job, but so am I.'

'Do you know,' said Raphael, 'I might recognise that young man. Can you show me the pictures again?'

Jemma passed Raphael her phone. She noted that he knew how to enlarge the images with his thumb and forefinger. *He knows more about technology than he lets on.*

Raphael held the phone at arm's-length, and looked over his glasses at it. 'Yes, I'm almost sure,' he said. 'Obviously he's a lot smarter there, but I had an assistant called Dave, for a short time, and I'm sure that's him.'

'Really?' said Jemma. 'When was this?'

'Oh, maybe a year ago,' said Raphael. 'He was a funny one, Dave. I mean, funnier than most of my assistants. Very keen on his first day, then kept disappearing into the stockroom. By Wednesday, I had to fetch him out of there at the end of the day. Then he disappeared completely. Never saw him again. I couldn't work out if he'd left of his own accord, or if the shop had been up to mischief. But as no one came asking, I thought least said, soonest mended.' He examined the photo. 'Yes, Dave had big black-rimmed glasses, and stubble, and he normally wore a baseball cap, but I'm pretty sure that's him.'

'He must have been looking for something,' said Jemma. 'I wonder what it was? And did he find it?'

'You could interpret the situation two ways,' said Raphael. 'Either he did find it, but couldn't get it out of the shop, or else he didn't find it but he knows it's here, and he wants to keep searching.' His fists clenched. 'I was rather sorry when Dave disappeared, but now I wish that the shop had done its worst.'

'What do you think he's looking for?' said Jemma.

'If he's an estate agent, I assume he wants money,' said Raphael.

Jemma gave him a significant look. 'Raphael, would you mind

answering a question?'

Raphael looked deeply guilty. 'It depends what it is,' he said.

'Do you know of anything about the shop which would make an estate agent keen to get hold of it?'

Raphael's expression lightened immediately. 'Not in the slightest,' he said. 'Several windows need repairing, the bathroom upstairs is cramped, and the central heating is temperamental. Not to mention the decor.'

'Hmm,' said Jemma. 'Bear with me a moment.' She unlocked her phone, made use of Google, and typed in a phone number. 'This might not work,' she said, 'but I found the number for Westminster Council's planning department. Can you ask them about any enquiries for this address?'

'I'll give it a try,' said Raphael. He pressed the dial button, and when someone answered, slipped into a near-perfect imitation of Damon's voice. 'Hello? Just calling to follow up 139A Charing Cross Road? Yeah, I'll hold.' He covered the mouthpiece and grinned at Jemma, who was gaping at him. 'Yeah, yeah, still here. Oh yeah, haha, fab. Right then. Yeah, that's cool. Bye.'

He ended the call. 'The cheeky monkey!' he exclaimed. 'The council official kindly informed me that they would welcome a change of use for this premises from a bookshop to a wine bar, provided that the proposed alterations were made.'

'*What?*' said Jemma.

'I haven't finished,' said Raphael. 'She also said that no, I wouldn't need planning permission to carry out works in an existing basement.' Then he frowned. 'But the shop doesn't have a basement.'

'Damon thinks it does,' said Jemma. 'And Damon appears to have plans for the shop.' She reached for a custard cream and snapped it in two. 'I think we should put Damon straight, don't you?'

Chapter 18

The next day, Raphael opened up the shop and they carried on in the usual way. Customers came, they sold them books and made a reasonable profit, and everyone was happy.

Everyone, that is, except Raphael. 'Can't we just get this over with?' he grumbled, almost before one customer had left the shop.

'Not yet,' said Jemma. 'We have to be patient. We have to wait for them to make the next move.' She opened up her phone and read Em's message again. 'Em said this job will be advertised next week, and today's Thursday. I don't think they'll leave it much longer.' She smiled. 'Why don't you take a nice long lunch break?'

Raphael glanced around furtively. 'Do you think they'll suspect anything if I do that?'

'I doubt it,' said Jemma, laughing. She went to fetch more books from the stockroom, and when she opened the box, found it full of John le Carré novels. 'There,' she said, holding up *Tinker Tailor Soldier Spy*. 'That settles it.'

Raphael rubbed his hands. 'Much as I dislike the idea of acting on the questionable messages of a random selection of books, on this occasion I'll humour you.'

Jemma stared at him. 'Do you mean to say that your actions are based on logic and reasoning?'

'Now I never said that,' said Raphael, and left before she could question him further.

Jemma tried her best not to watch the door. She shelved books, she went into the back room and made tea, she even popped into the stockroom. But nothing happened. She was beginning to despair when two men wearing deerstalkers, claiming to be from the Baker Street Irregulars, came in looking for what they described as Sherlockiana. Jemma was kept busy pulling out monographs about cigar ash, suggested chronologies of the stories, and theories of what Dr Watson had really done in the war. When they left, grasping two dusty volumes each, she was gratified to see that her patience had paid off. There, on the mat, lay a long white envelope.

Jemma hurried over and picked it up. It was addressed in wobbly capitals as if the person had been in a hurry. Or disguising their handwriting. Her thumb moved instinctively to the flap, then stopped. *I'll wait. We should open it together.*

She didn't have long to wait. Raphael came in, looked enquiringly at her, then exclaimed as Jemma pointed to the counter, where the envelope lay neatly squared up.

'It worked!' he cried. 'I knew it!'

Jemma cleared her throat noisily. 'Shall we open it?' she asked.

Raphael glanced at her, and she saw a mischievous spark in his blue eyes. 'Yes,' he said, smiling. 'Let's.' And he picked the envelope up, and handed it to her.

Jemma ripped the envelope open and withdrew the letter. It was on white A4 paper again, folded into thirds. She unfolded it, laid it on the counter, then came round to Raphael's side.

gAMe's Up. WE've gOT pRooF. BeSt QuiT wHiLe You'Re aHEaD

Raphael recoiled from the letter and put a hand to his brow. 'Oh no!' he cried. 'I am ruined!'

Jemma stared at him. 'What are you talking about?'

Raphael clutched at his sandy hair, then put his face in his hands. 'I'm putting on a show in case anyone's watching,' he murmured.

'Oh no!' exclaimed Jemma. She put her hands to her mouth, and opened her eyes as wide as she could.

Raphael snatched up the letter and strode off to the back room. 'I shall make tea,' he said, out of the side of his mouth.

'All done,' said Raphael, sauntering into the shop twenty minutes later. 'I've done some very conspicuous packing in my front room, and I have phoned Ransome's and asked for someone to come and do a valuation of the shop. They are coming at two.'

'That's quick,' said Jemma.

'It is rather, isn't it?' said Raphael, his expression deadpan.

'Shall I text Em, then?' Jemma found it hard not to grin as she said this.

'Why not,' said Raphael. 'Actually, pop into the back. You wouldn't want me to know you were a rat leaving the sinking ship, would you?'

'True,' said Jemma, and scurried off. She opened her messages, and texted.

I'm so sorry about yesterday. My emotions were all over the place. Now I've slept on it, you're right. Things here are too unstable. I'll polish my CV when I get in tonight. Thank you for being a true friend, Jemma X

She read it through. In some ways, she thought, the message was true. She was sorry that Em had chosen Damon's nasty plan over their friendship. Her emotions had been all over the place. And things at the shop, it had to be said, were frequently unstable. *But somehow, that's how I like it.* And she pressed *Send*.

They closed the shop at a quarter to two, to give themselves breathing space before things kicked off. Jemma had popped round to the mini-market for a sandwich, but when she unwrapped it, she found herself unable to eat more than a couple of bites.

'Are you all right?' asked Raphael, as she put her unfinished sandwich back into the packaging.

Jemma grimaced. 'A bit nervous, I guess.'

Raphael grinned. 'Haven't you been on a training course to deal with that sort of thing?'

Jemma raised her eyebrows. 'What, a training course on managing your emotions when your best friend and her scummy boyfriend are trying to cheat your employer and take away your job?' She laughed.

'You know what I mean,' said Raphael. 'Emotional intelligence, or resilience, or one of those sorts of things.'

Jemma stared at him. 'How do you know about those sorts of things? I didn't think you paid attention to management jargon.'

'I don't,' said Raphael. 'But as a business owner, I know all about resilience.'

Folio, who had been mysteriously absent for most of the morning, made his entrance with a bloodcurdling yowl, then leapt onto the counter and followed up with a purr.

'Don't peak too early, Folio,' said Raphael, rubbing his cheek. 'You must have your company manners ready for the nice man.'

'Have I seen Folio's company manners?' asked Jemma.

'Let's hope you don't,' said Raphael darkly.

At one minute past two they heard three sharp knocks at the door. 'Here we go,' said Raphael. Jemma retreated to the fiction shelves and picked up a pile of books she had left there, and Raphael opened the door.

In walked Damon, in a new-looking navy suit. 'Good afternoon, Mr . . . Burns, is it?'

'That's right,' said Raphael, pumping Damon's hand up and

down till Damon winced. 'I take it you're the estate agent.'

'Yes. Commercial manager, actually. Damon Foskett, at your service.' Raphael released his hand and Damon flexed it for a moment, then massaged it gently.

'Excellent. I am Raphael Burns, and this is my assistant Jemma.'

Damon followed Raphael's gaze, and a slow smile spread over his face. 'Well, well! I didn't know you worked here! I mean, Em said something about you having a new job, and I think she mentioned books...'

Jemma nodded. She didn't trust herself to speak.

'So, shall we get on?' asked Raphael, rubbing his hands.

'By all means,' said Damon. He pulled out a laser measuring device and started pointing it at the walls of the shop. 'Hmm.' He took out a notebook and pen, and scribbled numbers. 'Mind if I go into the back?'

'Be my guest,' said Raphael. He followed Damon and Jemma waited, her heart in her mouth.

They returned a few minutes later, and Damon looked glum. 'I'm afraid it isn't brilliant news, Mr Burns.'

'Oh, but don't you want to see upstairs?' asked Raphael.

'I'm assuming it's the usual over-the-shop kind of thing,' said Damon. 'Bedroom, living room, small kitchen, small bathroom, box room? Maybe a balcony, if you're lucky.'

Raphael nodded, the corners of his mouth turned down.

'Then I don't need to see it,' said Damon, and snapped his notebook shut. 'It isn't a great time to sell, truth be told. Very slow at this time of year. Obviously I'll give you the best price I can, because I know your delightful assistant.' He winked at Jemma, who managed a smile in return. 'So this is what I think it's worth. And that's at the top end, mind.' He opened his notebook again, scribbled a number, and showed it to them both.

Raphael whistled. 'Gosh, that's rather low.'

114

'That's the market at the moment, you see,' said Damon, with a sigh.

'Oh, I'm sure it is,' said Raphael. 'But I was hoping for more. The other estate agents' valuations were higher than yours.'

'Other estate agents?' said Damon, frowning.

'They do exist,' said Raphael. 'I thought it best to get a few quotes, you see. Sound business practice, and all that.'

Jemma hid a smile. It had been her idea to book two valuations the evening before, when she judged that Damon would probably be at home with Em, a pile of newspapers, and a pot of glue.

'Oh, I see,' said Damon. 'They were probably trying to reel you in, mind. Some of the less scrupulous estate agencies do that. They get you on their books, then once the place has failed to sell they drop the price to exactly my figure. If you want a quick sale, we're the company to go with.'

Raphael looked thoughtful. 'I do see your point,' he said. 'And I am interested in a quick sale. You see, my assistant and I have been subject to a hate campaign recently. Anonymous letters.'

Damon assumed a concerned expression. 'Oh dear,' he said. 'I am sorry to hear that.'

'Don't worry,' said Raphael. 'It's in the hands of the police. We got another letter this morning, if you can believe that. Actually, Jemma, would you mind taking it round to the station? The detective inspector did say we ought to submit any further evidence promptly.'

'I'm sure that can wait until I've finished,' said Damon. A hopeful, slightly nervous smile appeared on his face. 'Actually, could I take another peek at the back premises? I don't think I appreciated the full extent of the stockroom.'

'I don't know what you mean,' said Raphael. 'I thought you took measurements.'

'Oh yes, so I did,' said Damon. 'Perhaps I was a little hasty in my calculations. Let me look again.' He opened his notebook, and inspected the page. 'I could push the valuation maybe fifty thousand higher.'

'That's promising,' said Raphael, 'but I don't think it's enough. After all, if you're planning to make this place into a wine bar, I'm sure you'll get a much better return on it.'

Damon stared at him. 'A – a wine bar?' he faltered.

'Yes, a wine bar,' said Jemma. 'I suggested we check in with the planning department at the council. Strangely, they thought Raphael was a Mr Foskett, who had enquired about this very premises, the possibility of turning it into a wine bar, and doing work on the basement.'

Damon ran a hand round the back of his collar. 'Very common name, Foskett. And London's a big place.'

'That it is,' said Raphael. 'I suppose I ought to thank you for uncovering something I never knew about my own shop.'

Damon opened his mouth to speak, but Raphael held up a hand. 'Jemma is an expert in finding things out. We were puzzled because, as far as we knew, the shop didn't have a basement. But after a bit of Googling, and investigation of lost buildings of London, and plenty of staring at maps and plans, we found evidence. I imagine you know what I'm referring to.'

Damon swallowed again. 'Yes,' he squeaked.

'I thought you would,' said Raphael. 'When you worked here briefly as my assistant, you spent an awful lot of time in that stockroom. I did wonder if it would eat you alive at one point.'

Damon tried to look innocent. 'Assistant? What do you mean?'

'You know exactly what he means, *Dave*,' said Jemma, and Damon had the grace to blush.

'All right,' he said, 'so I have a particular interest in this property. An affection for it, even. What's wrong with that? It's normal for an estate agent to have an interest in property. That's why we do the job.' He sighed. 'How about a joint venture, Mr Burns? I'll make you a handsome offer for half the property, I'll get our team to develop it, and fit out the basement, and get it set up as a wine bar, and we'll split the profits. You won't have to do a day's work ever again.'

Raphael's brow furrowed. 'Half the profits, you say? What would you estimate that at, per annum?'

Damon turned to a new page in his notebook. 'Well, I'd say the fit-out will cost about *this*, and obviously that's an upfront cost which I'd want to recoup from the business, but I would estimate that once that's paid off, you could be looking at this much.' He scribbled a figure, and held it up.

'Mmm,' said Raphael, with a gleam in his eye. 'That *is* interesting. And I'd never have to do a day's work again, you say?'

Jemma's jaw dropped. Damon the slime-ball had found Raphael's weak spot, and she had a horrible feeling that he had won. She eyed his smug smile, and her heart plummeted into her baseball boots.

Chapter 19

'No!' cried Jemma. 'Raphael, you can't! What about the history of the shop? What about the customers? What will they do if we're not here?'

Raphael shrugged. 'They'll find another bookshop,' he said. 'After all, there are plenty on this road.'

Damon laughed. 'I'm surprised at you, Jemma,' he said. 'What about that business brain? What about that ambition?' He looked at her, and his lip curled. 'Em was right. This shop's done something to you.'

Jemma drew herself up. 'Yes, it has,' she said, her eyes flashing fire. 'It's given me something to aim for besides success. It's given me a purpose. It's given me satisfaction. And it makes people happy. If that's wrong, then *I'm* wrong, and I don't care.' She felt tears prickling at the back of her eyes, and fled to the bathroom. *I'm not going to cry in front of Damon Foskett*, she thought, as she washed her face in cold water and scrubbed it dry with the scratchy towel. Whatever else he told Em when they were celebrating their success tonight, he couldn't tell her that.

Raphael cleared his throat. 'So, this mysterious basement.

We've looked at plans and maps and whatnot, and we're sure it's there, but we haven't actually found a way into it yet. Have you had any luck, Mr Foskett?'

Jemma emerged from the bathroom, dry-eyed and shamefaced. She couldn't run away. She had to see how things played out, however bad it was. And she was most definitely a spectator, as the men stood close together.

The corner of Damon's mouth turned up in a slow, cunning smile. 'It's not easy to find, Mr Burns. As you now know, I tried when I worked here, and I had no luck. But after a bit more investigation on the internet, I'm pretty sure I can uncover it now. Come this way.' And he opened the door of the stockroom, and invited Raphael in. Jemma followed, her heart in her mouth.

Damon switched on the lights, pulled out his phone, and opened an app. 'Compass,' he said, in explanation. 'Now if I'm right, it's ten steps north, five steps east.' He began to pace. 'Course, I might not be exactly spot on. Depends how long a pace is, doesn't it?' He took ten steps down one of the aisles and stopped at a break in the shelving. 'That's convenient,' he said, in a pleased tone, and turned right, counting under his breath. 'Should be about here,' he said, pointing to his feet. 'Any chance we can get this carpeting rolled back?'

'I should think so,' said Raphael, rolling up his sleeves. 'Come on, Jemma.'

Jemma sighed, and followed suit. They rolled up the carpet, and the underlay, and some ancient, stiff linoleum, until they arrived at wooden floorboards and a trapdoor with an iron ring set into it.

'Looks like I was right,' said Damon, smiling.

'It does,' replied Raphael. 'Would you like to open it?'

Damon grasped the iron ring, and pulled. The trapdoor swung open, revealing a flight of stone steps which were worn in the middle.

'Twelfth century, they say,' breathed Damon. 'The crypt of a lost cathedral. It'll be the talk of London.' He switched on the torch app on his phone. 'Mind if I...? I mean, it's your shop, but it might not be safe, and I'm insured for this sort of thing.'

'Oh no, absolutely,' said Raphael. 'Please, go ahead.'

Damon didn't need telling twice. A second later he was heading down the steps. He disappeared, then the light from his torch faded too.

Raphael nudged Jemma and gave her an enormous wink.

'Woah,' Damon exclaimed, and the cellar echoed it. 'This is amazing.'

Jemma clutched Raphael's arm, and strained her ears to hear more. There was nothing for a few seconds, then a muttered 'Hang on a minute—'

The next sound was a rush of water. A shriek followed, then the whoosh of a giant wave breaking against a wall. 'Help!' cried Damon. Then 'Shit! Pike!' His exclamation was followed by frenzied splashing. Then another cry, followed by 'What the heck? Get off me!' More splashing. 'Since when have there been octopuses in London?'

Jemma looked at Raphael, who was shaking with silent laughter. 'He won't die, will he?' she whispered.

Raphael glanced at her, and shook his head. Folio trotted up, peered into the hole, and gave a small meow.

They heard more splashing, then a murmured 'Thank God for that,' and the sound of feet squelching up the steps. Damon appeared out of the darkness. His hair was plastered to his head, the navy suit, now black, clung to him, and he clutched a dripping phone.

'I take it the cellar requires extensive work, then?' said Raphael, and laughed.

Damon fixed him with a look of pure hatred. 'Get out of my way,' he said.

120

'Now, now,' said Raphael. 'No need to be rude.' But he didn't step aside. 'Don't ever come back here, Mr Foskett,' he said, quietly. 'And if you know what's good for you, you will go far, far away. Because if you bother me again…' He leaned closer, until he was almost touching Damon's dripping nose. 'There will be consequences.'

Damon swallowed, and nodded. Raphael stepped aside, and the estate agent squidged off, leaving only a trail of water.

'That was rather fun,' said Raphael, closing the trapdoor. 'I propose a cup of tea while you finish your sandwich, and then we can open up the shop.' He kicked the floor coverings into place.

'But – but—' Jemma pointed at the floor. 'None of the documents said the entrance was there!'

'No, they didn't, did they?' said Raphael. 'And I don't think it is. I think that poor young man imagined it. Look.' He rolled everything back again, and Jemma stared at the place where the trapdoor had been, and where the floorboards were now as solid and uniform as their neighbours.

Then she stared at Raphael. 'So where is it?'

'Where do you think it is?' he asked.

'The maps and plans say there is a staircase in the back room,' said Jemma. 'There isn't room, though. It can't be there.'

'No such word as can't,' said Raphael. 'You'll be telling me next that there isn't a bloodthirsty octopus living in our cellar.'

Jemma frowned. 'There isn't, is there?'

Raphael shrugged. 'Might be.'

They went into the back room, and Jemma pointed at the wall. 'It's supposed to be about two feet past there. But there's nothing. I even sneaked into the yard the other day, and there's no sign of any staircase whatsoever.'

'I see,' said Raphael. 'I wonder…' He pointed at the floor. 'Isn't that his little gadget thingy?'

Jemma switched the laser measure on, moved back to the

121

doorway, and pointed the little red dot at the wall. Then she read the display. 'See? Two feet short.'

Raphael advanced to the wall and knocked on it. 'Sounds hollow,' he said. 'If that was an outside wall, it would be made of brick. Jemma, can you fetch the sledgehammer? You'll find it under the sink.'

Jemma did as she was told, and Raphael hefted the sledgehammer. 'Stand clear, please. Apart from anything else, if I'm wrong then the whole shop might collapse.' He drew his arms back, and swung.

Plaster and wood splintered, and stale air rushed out. Jemma switched her phone into torch mode, and shone it through the hole. 'I can see steps!' she said. 'Keep swinging, Raphael, keep swinging.'

Raphael obliged, until there was a hole big enough to step through. Then he turned to Jemma. 'Do you want to go first, or shall I?'

'We'll go together,' said Jemma.

Carefully they stepped into the space, and Jemma illuminated the stairs with her phone. The steps, oddly, looked less worn than the ones Damon had descended. She made to take a step, then paused. 'There won't be a killer octopus down there, will there? Or an underground river?'

'I can't promise anything,' said Raphael. 'But I doubt it. Let's go and see.'

The staircase was wide enough for them to walk side by side, and handholds had been left in the brickwork. Their footsteps were quiet on the stone. Jemma listened for water, but heard nothing.

The steps went down a long way. As they descended, a large wooden door with iron hinges came into view. Jemma clutched Raphael's arm. 'It's your shop,' she said. 'You should open it.' She glanced up at him, and he looked as nervous as she felt.

'To think,' he said quietly, 'that my own shop can still surprise me.' He grasped the latch, and lifted it.

The door swung open.

'Woah,' they said, together.

Chapter 20

Jemma looked at her watch as she strolled down Charing Cross Road. She had plenty of time, even though Rolando's didn't open until eight thirty. Or at least, not for most people. She did her special knock on the window, and Carl made a face at her through the glass, then opened the door. 'Usual?' he asked.

'Yes please,' said Jemma.

'Better come in, then,' he said. 'Before you attract the attention of the coffee-drinking zombies.'

'Can't have that.' Jemma grinned, then stepped inside and fished her reusable cup out of her bag.

The coffee machine was already on, and Carl set to work. 'Getting ready for a busy day at the bookshop, then?'

'Something like that,' said Jemma. 'It's window-display day, and we've got someone coming to quote for building work.'

'Extending your evil empire, huh?' Carl set the milk frothing.

'Absolutely,' said Jemma. 'You'll have to come and see when it's finished.'

'I will,' said Carl. 'So long as you don't expect me to make any literary comments.' He sprinkled cocoa powder on the top of her cappuccino. 'That's two pounds seventy-five, with the reusable cup.' Jemma paid with her phone, then handed him her loyalty card. 'And the next one is free,' said Carl, stamping it and handing it back.

'Excellent,' said Jemma. 'Thanks, Carl. See you tomorrow.'

'Yes,' said Carl. He ran a hand over his twists, as if checking they were still there. 'Unless you pop in for lunch? We've got quiche Lorraine on the specials board today.'

Jemma looked regretful, and patted her bag. 'And I've got a homemade pasta salad that I can't cheat on,' she replied. 'Maybe tomorrow.' She took her coffee, and pulled the door to behind her. Two passers-by stopped at the shop, read the *Closed* sign, and murmured in a discontented manner.

Jemma glanced up at the bookshop sign as she approached. It was much clearer now that Raphael had got it repainted. He'd been cagey at first when she asked, worried that she would want him to accept a new design, or worse, call in an agency to present a range of options. Once Jemma had said that the sign was fine, but so faded that nobody could read it, he'd been happy to agree. *Next up, frontage*, thought Jemma. But she was picking her battles at the moment, and she felt that one could wait. After all, she had got her way on Saturday opening.

She fished in her bag for the keys, and opened up the shop. Everything was in order. The counter shone with polishing, the shelves were crammed with books waiting to be read, and the armchair invited customers to sit down and do just that. 'Hello,' she called. 'Morning, Folio.'

Folio walked into the shop, stretched out his right paw in salute, and executed a big stretch. 'No sign of Raphael yet, then,' she said, and Folio purred. 'I'll take that as a no.'

Jemma wandered through to the back room and eyed the large hole in the wall. Raphael had neatened it up a little since they had smashed through a few weeks ago, but its edges were still ragged.

He had resisted any further entreaties from Jemma to do something with it, saying that that was what the builders would be paid to do. Once they had decided what the space was for.

'Raphael! I'm just going downstairs,' called Jemma, and climbed carefully through the gap. Folio put his front paws on the bottom edge of the hole, then leapt gracefully through and ran down the stairs ahead of her.

On that first day the cat had lurked at the top of the stairs, looking more apprehensive than Jemma had ever seen him, but Raphael had beckoned him, then scooped him up into his arms and carried him through the door. Folio's eyes grew as wide and dark as saucers as he took it in; the high vaulted ceiling with decorated bosses, the carved stone columns, the sheer size of it all. Jemma had expected to find it scary, or at least creepy, but actually, once she had adjusted her mind to the scale of it, the crypt didn't worry her in the slightest. *It's been here for eight hundred years*, she thought, *and it's survived. Frankly, it's probably in a better state than the rest of the shop.* Folio, once he had explored it thoroughly, seemed to agree with her.

They were still debating what to do with it. Jemma could absolutely see it as a reading area and café, but she didn't want to compete with Rolando's, so she had suggested extending their book stock, perhaps moving the fiction section downstairs, and introducing sofas, armchairs, side tables, and desk lamps. 'It could be a cathedral of reading,' she said.

'Or it could be my basement den,' said Raphael.

Jemma goggled at him. 'A basement den? This? Seriously?'

'Why not?' said Raphael. 'I'd have room for my hobbies then.'

Jemma's eyes narrowed. 'Do you have any hobbies?'

'Not really,' said Raphael. 'I've never had the space, you see. But now…' He rubbed his hands, then caught Jemma's disgusted look and burst out laughing. 'You're far too easy to wind up, Jemma James.'

And that was where they had left it. Jemma hoped that getting a builder round would focus Raphael on the task in hand. Structurally, everything appeared sound to her. And they had already invited over a couple of people from the planning department, who had hummed and hawed over tea in the bookshop, and then, having descended the staircase with them, gasped and raved about the space and the potential.

Of course, whatever Raphael decided to do would require at least some money to fit out. When she had explained that to him, he had sighed as if the world were on his shoulders. But Jemma had, very gently, shown him the daily takings of the bookshop, introduced him to a simple projection of what the shop could reasonably expect to earn in a month, then set that against the figures she had coaxed out of him for the utility bills, Folio's food, and her wages (now a slightly larger sum than before). 'So the shop is making a profit,' she said. 'But if we could get that number higher…' She pointed at the income line. 'Then our profit would be higher too, and we could get the shop sorted more quickly. Once we do that, we'll have much more space for customers. We could even put another till in downstairs.'

'I'm not sure I like the sound of that,' said Raphael. 'That would mean we'd have to be on different floors all the time. I wouldn't be able to go out and – see to things.'

'Maybe,' said Jemma. 'Or we could hire another assistant, perhaps.' She had wondered briefly whether she could tempt Carl away from Rolando's, then realised that might mean no more early cappuccinos. But that was a discussion for the future.

Jemma picked up the camping lantern they'd left at the top of the stairs, switched it on, descended carefully, and opened the great door for Folio, who thanked her with a sharp meow. She drank her cappuccino gazing around the vast, shadowy space, then put her arms out and spun round and round until she was lightheaded. *We could hold events. Book readings, or even theatre.*

127

She imagined rows and rows of chairs, and a rapt audience gazing at Hamlet declaiming to a skull.

A cough almost made Jemma fall over her own feet. She came to a stop just in time and frowned at Raphael, who was leaning on the door frame and smiling at her. 'Getting a feel for the space, are we?'

'Before I was interrupted, yes,' said Jemma. 'We could have events down here.'

Raphael ambled in and gazed around him. 'We could, yes. We could do all sorts of things. Not a wine bar, though,' he added hastily. 'I don't think Rolando would be too happy about that.' He eyed Jemma's cup. 'Is that another cappucino?'

'Maybe,' said Jemma. 'Speaking of not too happy, did you ever go into the estate agent's and tell them what Damon had been up to?'

Raphael shook his head. 'It didn't seem worth it,' he said. 'I don't think Mr Foskett will ever bother us again, and hopefully he's learnt his lesson.' He looked at Jemma. 'Did you hear anything from your friend?'

'Not directly,' said Jemma. 'But I did see a post on her Instagram feed about London being for losers, with a photograph of fields and blue sky. She'd tagged it RuralWins.'

'I see,' said Raphael. He regarded Jemma for a while without speaking. 'Do you miss her?'

Jemma shrugged. 'In a way. She was trying to protect me,' she replied. 'I think I was supposed to be grateful. But if I'd listened to her I would have walked out of here on my first day, and we'd never have found this, and I'd never have learned the things I have.'

Raphael gave her a pained glance. 'I do hope you haven't been at the management literature again, Jemma.'

'Will you be quiet?' said Jemma, and grinned. 'Why don't you accept the compliment, and put the kettle on. It's half an hour to opening time.'

'Good heavens, is it really?' said Raphael. 'And it's window-display day.'

'It is,' said Jemma, 'but I won't be doing that until twelve o'clock. The regulars get ever so disappointed if I move it.'

'What is it today?' asked Raphael.

'Beach reads,' said Jemma. 'I've got a sandpit, some inflatable beachballs, buckets and spades, several plastic starfish, and a striped windbreaker ready to deploy.'

'Do you think that will work?' said Raphael.

'I don't see why not,' said Jemma. 'Window-display day's always our best sales day. If it doesn't bring people in, I'll change it.'

'I've said it before, and I'll say it again,' said Raphael, bending to stroke Folio. 'People are strange.'

'Whereas this bookshop is perfectly normal, I suppose,' said Jemma.

Raphael chuckled. 'I wouldn't go that far.' He gazed at the dramatic space before him; the arches in sharp relief, the pillars with their lurking shadows. 'It's certainly been an interesting few weeks since you came, Jemma.' He smiled. 'And at least that chump of an estate agent never found out what I was really up to.'

'What do you mean, up to?' demanded Jemma. '*Are* you up to something?'

Raphael straightened his face hastily. 'Who, me? Up to something? Not a sausage. I'm not, am I, Folio?'

Jemma crouched down and looked into the cat's face for a sign, but Folio's amber eyes were as inscrutable as ever.

129

THE MAGICAL BOOKSHOP: 2

BROUGHT
to
BOOK

LIZ HEDGECOCK

WHITE
RHINO
BOOKS

132

'Lights!' called Jemma.

Raphael approached the bank of switches, screwed up his face, and remaining at arm's-length, flicked one on. Overhead, the iron chandelier lit up without a flicker.

Jemma laughed. 'It's perfectly safe.'

'Then why are you standing all the way over there?' asked Raphael.

'Fine.' Jemma rolled her eyes, walked across to the light panel and switched on the remaining eleven lamps in one go. The huge lower floor of the bookshop was bathed in warm light, and the sinister shadows Jemma remembered from their first foray down the stone steps were a thing of the past. Now the huge room looked grand; majestic, even.

'Wow,' breathed Carl. 'It's something when you see it all put together, isn't it?' He shot Jemma an admiring glance, and she tried not to preen.

'It is, rather,' she said, and smiled.

In some ways it had been much easier than she thought to get the space renovated. The cathedral crypt, as it had been, was sound, watertight and pest free, which had spoiled the fun of their tradespeople considerably. Apart from getting electricity and water put in, most of their time was focused on buying furniture and fittings, and giving what was already there a good clean.

And that was where Carl had got involved.

It had begun when Jemma, exhausted after a morning downstairs removing centuries of grime from the stone floor, had called into Rolando's for a panini and a double espresso. Carl had done a double-take when she presented herself at the counter and gave her order.

'Not a cappuccino?' he asked.

'Not today,' said Jemma.

He continued to gaze at her, and she realised from his expression that she possibly should have checked her appearance before venturing out. She felt sweat in the small of her back, and suspected that the dirt on her clothes, while possibly antique, was not a look favoured by the majority of Rolando's customers. 'Don't worry, I'm taking it away,' she said, blushing.

'Never mind that,' said Carl, putting the panini in to warm. 'What have you been doing?'

'Cleaning,' said Jemma. 'Raphael and I are taking turns.'

To give Raphael credit, he was putting in some work. Admittedly, if ever Jemma went downstairs during one of his cleaning shifts, she often found him leaning on his mop and reading a book. But when he came upstairs and she took over, he had always managed to get a lot done.

Carl put a disposable cup under the coffee machine. Then he turned back to her, and leaned forward. 'Do you need any help?' he muttered.

'Oh heck, yes,' said Jemma. 'You've seen it.' She had invited Carl to pop round one day when he had finished his shift, and he had marvelled at the high ceilings, the pillars, and the intricate stone carvings. Taken as a whole, it was an amazing room. Up close, though, it was decidedly dirty. *Then again*, Jemma thought, *if I hadn't had a shower for five hundred years or so, I probably wouldn't look my best either.*

'I can ask Raphael, if you like,' she said. 'Aren't you busy here?'

Carl eyed the queue and grinned. 'Yeah, but extra money is always handy. The theatre I was ushering at closed.'

'Oh, I see,' said Jemma. Carl always appeared so contented when she saw him that she had never really thought about him outside the café.

'Yeah,' said Carl. 'And I took that on because I was resting between acting jobs. Anyway, better get on or I'll be out of this one as well.' He gave her a tight little smile, and put her panini on the counter.

So Carl had come to do three hours' cleaning downstairs when he finished at Rolando's. Jemma always took him downstairs, made sure he had everything he needed, and brought him tea and biscuits halfway through his shift. She had hoped that they would get chatting, and she would get to know him better. But he was focused on the job, and disinclined to be communicative. She longed to ask him about the acting jobs he had had, and whether she might have seen him in anything, but she sensed that would be an awkward question. Anyway, she had things to do upstairs.

But now the crypt was irreproachably clean, and fitted out with light-oak bookshelves and comfortable old armchairs. That accounted for two-thirds of the room. The rest, following negotiations, had become a café.

Jemma had always imagined having a café as part of the space, though she realised it would be in direct competition with Rolando's. It had been Raphael, surprisingly, who suggested discussing it with Rolando. 'I don't want to tread on any toes,' he said, 'but it strikes me that there could be advantage on both sides.'

Jemma had gaped at him. 'Will you be all ruthless again, like you were with Brian?'

Raphael laughed. 'Not at all,' he said. 'And Rolando is rather a different proposition from Brian, although not necessarily easier to deal with. I'll pop in when the lunchtime rush is over, and see if I can get an audience.'

He had returned fifteen minutes later with the news that Rolando would call round at about four.

Jemma had waited with bated breath. Even though she was busy in the shop, the hands of the clock still crawled round. Then at four o'clock precisely, as she was putting *Men Are From Mars, Women Are From Venus* into a bag, a small dark-haired woman erupted into the shop, fixed beady black eyes on her, and demanded 'Where is Raphael?'

'Oh, I think he's in the back somewhere,' said Jemma. 'Shall I call him?'

The woman walked straight into the back room as if it were the obvious thing to do, and called out 'Raphael? Dove sei?'

'Ciao, Giulia,' Raphael replied from the stockroom, and came out. 'We're just popping downstairs, Jemma,' he called, and she heard footsteps which were quickly drowned by a stream of rapid Italian. Jemma looked after them for several seconds, even though she could see nothing and hear little more, and only a discreet cough from her customer recalled her to what she was meant to be doing.

Half an hour later the footsteps travelled the other way, again accompanied by voluble Italian, but this time Raphael was saying at least as much as Giulia was. The meeting ended in the back room, where Giulia gave Raphael a firm handshake, then scurried out.

Jemma didn't get a chance to ask about the outcome until they closed at five. 'Go on, then,' she said, as Raphael turned the sign from *Open* to *Closed*. 'What happened?'

136

'Oh, but don't you want to cash up first, Jemma?' Raphael's eyes twinkled with evil mischief.

Jemma drew herself up to her full five feet two. 'No, I do not, and you know it. Come on, Raphael, spill.'

'Oh, very well.' Raphael sat down in the armchair, and Folio jumped into his lap. 'So, what Rolando and I have agreed—'

Jemma's eyes narrowed. 'But that wasn't Rolando. I heard you call her Giulia.'

'Yes,' said Raphael. 'It's complicated, and I'll explain in a minute. Anyway, what Rolando has agreed is that they will rent the café space from me for an agreed amount, paid monthly, and that they will offer drinks and hot and cold snacks, prepared in the main shop. Oh, and cake, of course. They will provide a coffee machine and the heating and serving equipment, and I shall provide tables and chairs. One of their staff will run the café, and they will remain an employee of Rolando's.'

'That sounds sensible,' said Jemma. 'Do we get to choose who they send?'

Raphael smiled. 'I did suggest that, as we know Carl best, and he has helped us out already, he would be a good fit. Providing he is receptive to the idea, of course. And Rolando seems happy with that.'

Jemma couldn't help executing a little round of applause.

'I'm glad you approve,' said Raphael, drily.

'Oh, I do,' said Jemma. 'But tell me about Rolando. Or Giulia.'

'There isn't much to tell,' said Raphael. 'Rolando's opened in, what, the nineties. The bookshop was going through a difficult time, so I didn't really pay much attention. There might have been a Rolando, there might not. In any case, Giulia has always insisted that the café is called Rolando's, and that Rolando makes the business decisions. Behind closed doors, where it doesn't matter, she answers to Giulia. Everywhere else, she is representing Rolando.'

'What happened, do you think?' asked Jemma.

'I used to wonder about that,' said Raphael. 'Then I realised it was none of my business, and it was up to Giulia to decide how she did things.'

Jemma bit her lip at the implied rebuke. 'Well, I'm glad it's sorted,' she said. 'Let's get on and cash up.'

After that, time had flown; working with Jim from James's Antique Emporium, who had found them classic bentwood tables and chairs, moving the fiction section downstairs, and restocking a shop at least twice its previous size, at the same time as continuing to serve their ever-increasing customer base. There were days when Jemma found herself putting the key into the front door of her flat, unsure how she had got there, or woke up on the sofa as light crept through the gap in the curtains. *But it was all worth it,* she thought, gazing around her at the beautiful room, the gleaming café counter, and of course, the books.

Today was the grand reopening. They had closed the shop for the morning to put the finishing touches to it all, and the hands of the huge railway clock on the wall showed one minute to twelve. She ticked *Lights* on her list, and looked up at Raphael. 'Are you ready?' she asked.

Raphael raised his eyebrows. 'We open the shop every morning, Jemma.'

Jemma sighed. 'Are you ready, Carl?'

Carl adjusted the bib of his apron, and grinned. 'I'm ready,' he said.

Jemma took a deep breath. 'In that case,' she said, 'it's showtime.' She ran upstairs and into the main shop, and grinned at the crowd peering through the shop window. Then she turned the shop sign around, and flung the door wide open.

Chapter 2

As Jemma had expected, she saw familiar faces in the stream of people who rushed through the doors of the shop. The two Golden Age crime fans were there, and the man with an inexhaustible appetite for books about railways, and the woman, now out of hospital, whose sister had come in search of *Jane Eyre* on Jemma's first day, and who was working through Mrs Gaskell. 'Where is the fiction section?' she asked, stopping dead and staring at the place where it had been, now occupied by Cookery, Craft, and Travel.

'Don't worry,' said Jemma, smiling. 'It's moved downstairs and expanded.'

And expanded it had. When the new oak bookshelves arrived, Raphael had gasped in horror, convinced that Jemma had ordered double what was needed. But once the van men had got them all downstairs, he wondered audibly whether they had quite enough.

'We can always order more,' said Jemma. 'Anyway, better to have too many books for the shelves than too many shelves for the books.'

But it felt like a close-run thing at times. They had packed up and brought down the fiction books on the shelves upstairs, and using the calculation that one full box of books equalled one shelf of a bookcase, Jemma had worked out that they would fill about a third of the space. 'We need more fiction!' she had cried, and rushed upstairs to the stockroom.

Luckily the bookshop agreed with her, delivering box after box of novels, mostly in complete sets. 'Thank you,' whispered Jemma, time after time, as she unpacked boxes of Stephen King, Terry Pratchett, and Nora Roberts. Quite apart from the time saved in sorting and alphabetising, she was relieved that the shop seemed content with their plans, and even inclined to encourage them.

Once or twice, as she unpacked boxes, Jemma had caught Carl looking first puzzled, then suspicious. 'Jemma,' he said, as she unpacked a complete *Forsyte Saga*, 'how do you know what's in the boxes?'

'I don't,' said Jemma.

'Oh,' said Carl. 'Isn't that a bit . . . odd?'

'What, that we don't label the boxes when they go into the stockroom?' said Jemma.

Carl's face lit up. 'Exactly! I mean, imagine if I opened a box expecting it to be chocolate chips, and it turned out to be sun-dried tomatoes?'

'You're absolutely right,' said Jemma, and opened a box which was full of Anne McCaffreys. She looked up, and saw Carl watching her.

'You weren't expecting that, were you?' he said, accusingly.

'I wasn't expecting anything, really,' said Jemma. 'I just have faith that we've got enough fiction books in our stockroom to fill up the shelves.'

Carl sighed, and carried on filling the cupboard behind the counter with boxes of sugar lumps, individually wrapped coffee biscuits, and reams of paper napkins. Jemma could tell that he wasn't satisfied with her explanation, but what else could she say?

How could she explain the vagaries of the bookshop? *You'll get used to it, just as I did*, she said to herself, and carried on shelving.

Customers continued to stream past her, all following the arrows through the back room to the stairs. Jemma had kept a tally in her head as people passed her, and she reckoned that she was up to about a hundred and eighty. The council had recommended that they limit numbers downstairs to two hundred, which at the time she had thought ridiculously unachievable. She shook her head in disbelief. *Twenty more, then people will have to wait*, she told herself. The stream was beginning to slow as she counted another ten, then another five. At last, a pause of perhaps ten seconds, then a couple came hurrying through the door. 'Is it today?' they asked. 'The opening?'

'Yes, it is,' said Jemma. 'We're almost full, so you're just in time. If you follow the others, you can see the new room downstairs.'

They hurried off, closely followed by an elderly man with a string shopping bag.

'Um, Jemma.' Raphael was standing in the Science section, looking perturbed.

'Hi, Raphael,' she said. 'How's it going down there?'

'It's busy,' he said.

'Good busy?' said Jemma, as a man in a suit strode by in a purposeful manner.

'Yes, good busy,' said Raphael. 'But *busy*. You should go down and see.'

'I thought you'd never ask,' said Jemma, grinning.

'Er, excuse me?' said a timid voice behind her.

A pale, thin young man stood on the step, dressed in a black raincoat, black beanie hat, black jeans and sunglasses. 'Hello!' she cried. 'Are you coming in?'

'I wasn't sure if I could,' said the young man, shifting from foot to foot. 'I thought it might be invitation-only.'

'Everyone's invited,' said Jemma. 'Well, until we're full, at any rate. And you're the last customer we can allow in, so you'd better hurry.'

'Yes, do come in,' said Raphael. He looked at Jemma hopefully. 'So does that mean that I can't let anyone else into the shop?'

'That's exactly it,' said Jemma. 'Not till people start leaving. One out, one in.'

'That makes things considerably easier,' said Raphael. He dashed behind the counter, pulled a sheet of paper from one of the drawers, wrote *Currently Full – Please Wait To Be Admitted* in his flowing copperplate, and stuck it in the middle of the shop window with sticky tape. 'There,' he said, picked up his newspaper, and collapsed into the armchair.

'Don't get too comfortable,' warned Jemma. 'If the queue gets too big at the downstairs till, I may send them up to you.'

Raphael lowered the newspaper until his eyes were visible, then rolled them at her. 'If you could give me five minutes first, I'd appreciate that.'

'See you later,' said Jemma. The young man was still standing there, watching them. Jemma noticed that he now had a copy of *Databases for Beginners* in his hand. 'Would you like to come downstairs and see the new book room?' she asked.

'Oh, um, yes please,' said the young man.

'Come along, then,' said Jemma. She led the way downstairs, reflecting that it was nice to have a customer who waited to be asked, rather than plunging among the books and luxuriating in them in the messy manner that so many people did. She had a feeling that this customer, if he took a book from the shelf then decided against it, would replace it exactly where he had found it.

'Watch out,' she warned him, as they approached the large oak door. 'It may be a little crowded.' She felt as if she were warning herself, too.

But nothing prepared her for the swarm of people downstairs. Some customers were doing what she had expected; sitting or standing in the café area chatting and enjoying the range of canapés which had come from Rolando's that morning. Other customers seeking a proper lunch queued up nicely at the café counter, where Carl seemed his usual unflappable self.

But the bookshop area was in a state of polite chaos. Customers were wandering from shelf to shelf, or standing in the middle of aisles, reading. Several already carried piles of books. And most of them were chatting, or calling friends over to look at what they had found. The effect was of a hive of companionable bees.

'I'd better get to the till,' said Jemma. She excuse-med her way through the knots of people, having to stop several times and accept compliments, and eventually slipped behind the shop counter with a sigh of relief. 'Till's open!' she called, and a couple of the more suggestible customers actually wandered across, eyes slightly glazed, chins on their piles of books.

Jemma was kept busy ringing up purchases for the next few minutes. A couple of customers did leave; but most of them wandered back towards the café area. The rest seemed in no hurry to finish browsing, or chatting. In a rare lull she looked past the queue to the shelves. Some of them already had considerable gaps showing.

Briefly, she panicked. *How do we keep up?* Then she remembered Raphael, with his own till upstairs, and relief broke over her like day. She served her next customer, then climbed on the wooden chair they had put behind the counter for slack periods and waved her arms for attention.

'Customers!' she shouted. 'If you wish to make a purchase, and you're not currently in the queue, please go to the till upstairs. I'm closing this till in a few minutes so that I can fetch more books.'

She heard muttering, but it remained low-level.

'Bit busier than you expected?' said Mohammed, putting two RK Narayan novels on the counter.

'Just a bit,' said Jemma. She had persuaded Raphael to let her order a box of a hundred large paper bags with handles, and their level was already diminishing. 'That's five pounds, please. Cash or card?'

Mohammed grinned. 'Phone,' he said. He paid, then wandered towards the café.

Jemma had a sudden vision of herself trapped in the crypt for eternity, with customers who never left but merely moved to different parts of the room; browsing the books, buying the books, going to the café, then wandering back to the shelves.

'I need a big bag if you've got one,' said the next customer, a harassed-looking woman in a floral dress, putting a stack of eight books on the counter.

'That's fine,' said Jemma, pulling a large paper bag from the box and checking each book as she slipped it inside. 'That will be twenty pounds, please.'

It'll be fine, she told herself, as the customer rooted through her handbag, pulled out her purse, put a ten and a five-pound note on the counter, and began counting out coins. *Of course it's busy on the first day. That's what you wanted. That's why you did the window display, and ran a countdown on social media, and made sure that all our regulars knew. It won't be like this every day. Apart from anything else, this lot are buying enough books to keep them going for a good month, if not more.*

'And that makes twenty,' said the customer, putting down a five-pence piece, two tuppences and a penny and closing her purse with a snap.

'Lovely, thank you,' said Jemma, counting the bits of change into the right compartments of the till. Not that that would do much good when Raphael had put everything everywhere, but still. She had standards. 'Next please,' she said, and counted three more customers behind the man who stepped up with an armful of Robert Harris.

Four more to serve, then she could scurry upstairs to the stockroom and begin refilling the shelves. And once the canapés and complimentary drinks ran out, people would leave. They must have places to be, after all. *You can handle this, Jemma,* she told herself, and beamed a confident, happy smile at her customer, who looked, if anything, rather taken aback.

Chapter 3

Despite keeping up a stream of positive internal self-talk as she dealt with the remainder of the queue, Jemma was still very glad to serve the last person. 'Back in five minutes!' she shouted, and dashed out from behind the counter.

'Jemma!' She turned to see Carl, coffee pot in one hand, cloth in the other, looking terrified.

She hurried over. 'What is it?'

'Don't leave me!'

'I have to,' she said quietly. 'We need more books.'

'What if they start coming to me with them?'

'Then send them to Raphael. If they have book questions, send them to Raphael. I'll be gone for five minutes, I promise.' But as she weaved her way through the customers Jemma didn't see all the boxes of lovely books which she would bring down and open, but Carl's agonised face.

Upstairs, she almost collided with the back of the queue for the till. She thought briefly about asking Raphael how it was going, then decided that would be unwise, at best. Instead she wrenched open the door to the stockroom, closed it behind her, and leaned against it, panting.

What have we unleashed? Then she told herself that she was being silly, grabbed the first box she saw, took it to the top of the stairs, and went back for another. She had to go further into the room this time, because more and more of the shelves were growing bare. 'We have to get more stock,' she said, out loud. *But when?* She brushed the thought aside for now, and took another box outside. When she did, she found that the first box had vanished.

'Has anyone seen my box?' she asked the queue.

'I think it went thataway,' said a cheery red-faced man, pointing towards the main shop.

Jemma sighed, and walked in to find the box open on the counter and three customers adding books to their piles. 'Leave some for the rest of us,' said a woman further down the queue.

'Those are supposed to be for downstairs,' said Jemma, but nobody took any notice. Raphael was busy with the cash register, and had co-opted Mohammed to pack books for him. Mohammed looked very cheerful; Raphael decidedly less so.

'Should I ask?' asked Jemma.

Raphael, tight-lipped, shook his head. 'Later,' he said.

So Jemma returned to the stockroom, and this time carried each box individually to the lower floor and put it behind the café counter. 'Don't let anyone get at them,' she told Carl.

On her way upstairs she almost fell over a group of customers crouching on the floor and worshipping Folio, who was purring and waving his tail as if this was perfectly normal. He did look particularly large and sleek today, and his orange fur glowed in the lamplight as if he had been polished for the occasion. 'Be good, Folio,' she called as she passed, and he flicked his tail as if to say that she didn't need to remind a cat with such impeccable manners. Still, he appeared happy enough, so off Jemma went.

One more box, she told herself, *and that's it. And if we run out*

147

of books, we'll just have to close early.

She carried the last box down, put it on the shop counter, and got out her scissors. Within she found a stack of Isaac Asimov books, and heaved a sigh of relief. She took the box to the right section, began shelving, and soon found herself surrounded by a group of people clearly waiting for her to finish so that they could undo her good work. After a minute or two, feeling eyes on the back of her neck, she asked, 'Would it be easier if I left the box for you?'

Multiple nods.

Jemma sighed. 'Fine. I'll come back in a few minutes and shelve anything you don't want, then.'

She took her scissors to the café counter and attacked the next box. 'I've never seen anything like it,' said Carl, staring at the masses buzzing around the shelves. 'It's like the January sales.'

'I guess this is what success looks like,' said Jemma. But as she said it, she felt strangely flat.

Carl shrugged, poured out two Americanos, and slid them across the counter. 'Maybe. Whatever it is, it's exhausting.'

Jemma opened the next box. 'Oh gosh,' she said. Inside were rows and rows of Chalet School stories. 'I remember these! They spoke a different language every day, and they never did any work.' She grinned. 'I have a feeling these won't last long.' She carried the box to Children's Fiction, put it on the floor, yelled 'Chalet School!', and took a step back as women hurried from all around.

Then she heard raised voices from the Science Fiction shelves. 'I think you'll find that this is mine now,' said a bald-headed man in a black T-shirt.

'You've already got five,' said a woman with tortoiseshell-framed glasses and bright-red hair. 'I really want this one. You're just picking them up.'

The man's nose wrinkled. 'I don't see how you've reached that conclusion,' he said. 'Speed doesn't necessarily equate to lack of discrimination. In other words: you snooze, you lose.' And he added the book to his pile with a smug smile.

'Is everything all right here?' said Jemma.

The red-haired woman flung out an accusing finger. 'He took my book! I was reaching for it, and he snatched it from right under my nose!'

Jemma looked at the book, then at the shelves. 'There's another copy,' she said, pointing.

'But I wanted that edition!' wailed the woman. 'With that cover!'

The bald-headed man sighed, took the other book off the shelf, and gave her his copy. 'If it's that important,' he said wearily. 'Honestly, Felicity, what a fuss over nothing.'

'Wait a minute,' said Jemma. 'Do you two know each other?'

The woman sniffed. 'In a manner of speaking.' She paused. 'But thank you, Jerome,' she said, and gave him a shy little smile.

Jemma walked off, shaking her head at the absurdity of people. But she hadn't walked far when she heard an '*Ow!*'

Potential catastrophes flashed before her eyes. A heavy book on the head? A hot coffee scald? She hurried to the source of the noise, and found the pale young man sucking his forefinger and staring at a hissing Folio. 'What happened?'

'He scratched me,' said the young man. At least, Jemma thought that was what he said, as he hadn't removed his finger from his mouth.

'Is that right?' she asked Folio, who had fluffed up in rage and now appeared twice his normal size.

Folio glared at her with eyes that were almost all black pupil, but was silent.

'Oh dear,' said Jemma. 'May I see?'

The young man took his finger from his mouth and held it out to Jemma, looking resolutely away.

Jemma, knowing Folio as well as she did, had expected a wound of some magnitude; what she was presented with resembled a paper cut. 'That doesn't seem too bad,' she said. 'It isn't bleeding—'

The young man shuddered. 'Good,' he said.

'I bet it hurts, though,' she said, to save his dignity. 'And of course, Folio shouldn't have done it.' She glared at Folio, who blinked. 'Were you stroking him at the time?'

'No,' said the young man, looking anywhere but at Folio. 'That is, I was going to, and I reached down, and – then it happened.'

'I'm afraid he's probably a bit over-excited today, what with all the people,' said Jemma. 'He's normally a very nice cat. Aren't you, Folio?'

Folio gazed up at her with innocent eyes, his paws placed neatly together.

'I'll get this cleaned, just in case, and put a plaster on, then you'll be fine.' She gave his arm a reassuring pat. 'Come upstairs and I'll get the first-aid kit. Folio, if you're going to be grumpy, take a time out.'

Folio interpreted this as an instruction to jump on the shop counter. Jemma sighed, and led the way upstairs.

She might have been imagining it, but the queue in the shop seemed a little shorter. Jemma retrieved the first-aid kit from under the sink, opened the stockroom door, and beckoned the young man in. 'This is probably the quietest place in the shop at the moment,' she said.

'Wow,' he replied. 'I mean, I thought you had a lot of books. I didn't realise there was this, as well.'

'It is quite something,' said Jemma proudly.

'And this is all books?' He took off his sunglasses. His eyes were pale green, like sea-glass.

'Yes,' said Jemma, 'all books. Now, do you think we should wash this?' She examined the finger in question.

'No, it'll be fine,' said the young man. 'I think it was the shock.'

'Mmm,' said Jemma. 'Well, keep an eye on it.' She squeezed antiseptic cream on the place where Folio had broken the skin, and rubbed it in. 'Would you like a plaster? I'm afraid we've only got Mr Bump ones.'

The young man nodded, and Jemma carefully wrapped a plaster around his finger. 'There you go,' she said, 'all done.'

'Thank you,' said the young man. Jemma noticed that he looked slightly less pale than he had before. Perhaps he really had been suffering from shock.

'Would you like a cup of tea?' she asked. 'Or a biscuit?'

'Oh no, I'd better go,' he said, heading for the door. 'I need to be somewhere, that is, I mean—' He glanced at the book in his hand.

'Don't worry about that,' said Jemma. 'You can have that for free, as an apology from Folio. And me.'

'Can I?' He smiled. 'Thank you.' He had an unexpectedly nice smile, if a little toothy.

'Don't mention it,' said Jemma, and held the door open for him. 'Folio-related injury,' she muttered in Raphael's direction, as she escorted the young man from the shop.

Downstairs things were still busy, but less frantic than before. The customers were more inclined to sit in the café with a drink, or settle in an armchair and read a book. But they were still coming to the counter with purchases, of course, and Jemma was kept very busy. She used all the big paper bags; she ran dangerously low on the normal-sized bags, and had to send Carl to the stockroom for another box. At least he looked less hunted and more cheerful, now that the earlier rush had died down.

At half past four Jemma had just finished serving a customer when an ostentatious throat-clearing behind her made her stub her toe on the counter. 'I think we should close early today,' said

151

Raphael. 'I suggest a quarter to.'

Jemma eyed the scene before her. Apart from the queue, they were down to about ten customers who wandered aimlessly around the bookshelves, as if they were lost in a labyrinth of books and had forgotten their ball of string. 'You're right,' she said. 'Fifteen minutes till closing, everyone!' she shouted.

Raphael winced. 'I do wish you'd warn me, Jemma.'

'Sorry, forgot,' said Jemma, cheerfully. Actually, she had forgotten that she *could* shout like that. Four years of careful corporate self-presentation had almost taken it out of her.

At length the last customer was served, the last book bagged, and the last money placed in the till. Jemma saw the last two customers upstairs and out of the shop, and turned the sign to *Closed* with a feeling of great relief. 'Well,' she said, 'what did you think of our reopening?'

Raphael sagged like a puppet whose master had gone on holiday. Carl was in slightly better condition; but his shoulders sagged, and the corners of his mouth did too.

'I know it was tiring, but it's opening day,' she said. 'Of course it was going to be busy—'

'How do we know it won't always be this busy?' said Carl, and Raphael gave him a grateful look.

'He's right,' he said. 'We only opened at midday, and we're exhausted. Imagine if it's like this again tomorrow.'

'It won't be,' said Jemma. 'And we can put systems in place to manage capacity. I could bring down more stock before we open, and then it will be much easier to fill the shelves. And maybe Carl could help in the shop when the café's quiet.'

Carl's eyes widened in a way that suggested that he was not on board with this idea.

'Anyway,' said Jemma, 'it will all be much easier when the lift is put in.'

Raphael was silent for a moment, thinking. A meow from the

152

back room made them turn. Folio strolled in, hopped into the armchair, flopped down, and closed his eyes.

'That might help,' said Raphael. 'I agree that we can't predict how busy the shop will be every day. But we *will* be busier. We *will* need more books, which means that someone – me – must go out and find them. And if we couldn't keep on top of things with you, me and Carl in the shop today, what will it be like if I'm out on a book-buying expedition? Or one of you has a day off, or rings in sick? No, I've decided.' He drew himself up and looked at them both. 'We must hire another member of staff, and the sooner the better.'

Chapter 4

Jemma told herself, as she stood on the tube with her nose millimetres away from someone's back, that she only felt defeated because she was tired. It was probably true. She hadn't slept well the night before, it had certainly been a stressful day, and they had had no breaks from the grand opening until the shop was closed.

And that hadn't been a break, as such. Admittedly, Carl had made tea, and they had shared the last two cakes from the café, which had been delicious. But all the time, an air of oppression had hung over them.

Cashing up ought to have been a triumphant occasion. They reviewed the transactions on the card machines, then counted up and bagged the money in the three tills. The shop had never known a day like it. Raphael was actually nervous about leaving so much money in the safe overnight. 'I'll take Rolando's share round first thing tomorrow, then I'm heading to the bank,' he said, slamming the door of the safe and turning the dial quickly, as if it might bite him. And again, the joy that they should have felt became fear, and mistrust.

Jemma had to admit, glancing around the near-empty shelves,

the books left on the floor, and the cake crumbs and occasional teaspoons which littered the café, that it had come at a cost. 'We'll get you cleaned up,' she said, to no one in particular, and got the broom out of the small cupboard near the equally diminutive customer toilets. *Raphael is right. We need help.*

So why don't I like the idea? She swayed gently with the motion of the train and bumped against a man in a leather jacket whose large headphones rendered him oblivious. *Why does it bother me?* She closed her eyes, tuned out the faint thumping coming from the leather-jacketed man, and tried to concentrate.

You failed, said a chirpy little voice. *You couldn't manage it all. You fell short.*

Jemma frowned. *How could I have known it would go so well? No one could have predicted it would be so busy.*

But you wanted it to be, said the annoying little voice. *You set things up to make sure that it was. And then you couldn't follow through.*

Jemma squeezed her eyes shut. *It was mostly fine,* she insisted, feeling injured. *OK, so Folio scratched that man, but it was only a little scratch, and I sorted it out.*

Two customers nearly came to blows over a book. Raphael actually had to grab one of the customers to pack books for him. The voice paused. Jemma wouldn't have thought it was possible to pause in a smug manner, but the voice managed it. *Rather unprofessional, don't you think?*

Jemma was about to reply in her head when the train forestalled her by announcing her stop. She opened her eyes, squeezed through the press of commuters, and popped onto the platform, surprised, as usual, by the fresh September air.

She was sorely tempted to stop in at the takeaway. *Stay strong, Jemma,* she told herself, turning her head away from the bright lights, the neon, and the enticing smells. Besides, she had picked up the ingredients for spaghetti carbonara from the mini-market, as well as a two-glass bottle of wine. A hard day was no reason to lose one's self control.

She let herself into the townhouse, walked slowly up all the flights of stairs – there seemed at least twice as many as usual after the day she'd had – and gazed at the front door of her flat. One day she would get a screwdriver, and put that *B* on straight. It irritated her beyond words every time she saw it, but somehow there was never time. Or a screwdriver.

Jemma hung her bag on the back of the door, changed her boots for the padded slippers she had treated herself to a month before, and took the food into the kitchenette. The cupboards were still a bit too far up on the wall, and the worktop was too high, but at least she could afford nice olive oil now, and Parmesan cheese. Jemma switched on the radio, got herself a glass of squash (wine was to go with dinner), opened *Italian Food for Beginners*, and set to work.

Over the last month or so, cooking her own meals had gone from being a laborious exercise with often surprising and atypical results to something which, usually, tasted quite nice. She had even come to find it therapeutic at the end of a long day. A chance to turn events over in her mind, and think about how she should have responded, or what she could have done better. But this evening, as she sweated garlic in a pan and chopped bacon into little pieces, she was too tired to beat herself up. *I'll leave that to my inner critic.* Instead, she thought how nice it would be to cook for somebody. Well, not *for* somebody, exactly, but to share a meal with them. Of course, there were occasions when she ate her ham salad sandwich or her Friday splurge of crayfish and rocket pasta in the same room as Raphael read his newspaper, but that wasn't precisely what she had in mind. *In any case*, she thought with a wry smile, moving the pan's contents around with a spatula, *given that Raphael can speak fluent Italian, I doubt he'd be impressed by my carbonara.*

Would Carl be?

The pan sizzled unexpectedly and Jemma took it off the heat before anything bad happened. Maybe she should open the window. The kitchen was rather warm. She sipped her squash, leaning against the worktop.

No point thinking about that, said the smug little voice which Jemma had really hoped was finished for the day. *You were so busy running round after the customers and barking orders at him that I doubt he thinks of you in that way at all.*

'Thanks for your feedback,' said Jemma, and looked longingly at the wine.

Then again... If we did have another member of staff – a new member of staff – then I'd be senior. Of course I would. Jemma's mouth dropped open. *Why didn't I think of this before? Here was I, thinking I'd failed, and actually the shop has grown to the point where we need to expand! It's twice as big, it makes a lot more money, and we need staff!* 'Hah!' She executed an overhand stroke with her spatula and smashed the irritating little voice in mid-air. 'Take that, self-doubt!'

The spaghetti carbonara which emerged at the end of the cooking process perhaps wasn't the best ever, since Jemma had had to rouse herself several times from dreams of saying to the faceless new assistant, 'Would you mind fetching five boxes of books from the stockroom and shelving them for me, please?', 'Could you mind the till upstairs while Raphael is out?', and her personal favourite, 'Do you think it's time for a cup of tea?' But what she had made was creamy, cheesy, and satisfying, even if the spaghetti had stuck together a bit, and she ate it at her little table without regret, accompanied by a glass of wine.

When her bowl was clean she looked at the second half of the bottle. She deserved another glass, certainly.

Must keep a clear head, she thought, screwing the top on and taking the bottle through to the fridge. *Work to do.* She pulled out the sofa-bed in anticipation, fetched her laptop and put it on the table, and made herself a strong coffee.

***

The next morning, Jemma was at the shop for eight o'clock sharp. She had stock to move, tills to manage, and most importantly, Raphael to convince.

'Morning!' she called, as she let herself in. She hadn't expected a response, and was surprised when Raphael wandered into the back room a few minutes later, pyjama-clad and bleary-eyed.

'I thought it was my turn to open up,' he murmured.

'It is,' said Jemma. 'Tea?'

Raphael nodded. 'You seem very . . . cheerful,' he ventured, after a minute or so.

'I suppose I am,' said Jemma. 'I was thinking of what you said yesterday, about getting more help in the shop, and you're right.'

Raphael stared at her. 'Oh.' Another pause. 'So you . . . agree?'

'Yes, I do,' said Jemma, getting the best china from the cupboard. 'Now that the shop is so much bigger and more profitable, it's absolutely right that we expand. I'll be able to manage the new person just fine.'

Raphael squeezed his eyes shut, rubbed the right one, then looked at her as if it would help him to see her better. 'Did you say manage?'

'Well, yes,' said Jemma. 'I mean, I'll be senior, obviously, and if you're out hunting down books a lot of the time, then someone should have oversight of the shop. And it makes sense that that person should be me.' The kettle boiled, and she warmed the pot. 'I worked out an appropriate division of duties last night, and drew up a sample job description and person specification. Oh, and I drafted an advert.'

'An advert,' Raphael repeated faintly, like an echo that had grown bored with its job.

'Yes, of course,' said Jemma. 'Obviously we'll aim to attract a wide range of suitable applicants, then cherry-pick the best ones to invite for interview. I mean, we wouldn't want to employ just anyone who walks in off the street.'

'Wouldn't we?' Raphael asked with a sly grin, and Jemma remembered belatedly that she herself had done just that not so long ago.

'That was different,' she said. 'Anyway, I was qualified.' *I was*, she told herself. *Wasn't I?*

'I never said you weren't,' said Raphael. 'But don't you think this is all a bit much? I mean, I've found plenty of good assistants by sticking a notice on the door.'

'I bet you've had some stinkers, too,' retorted Jemma, throwing teabags into the pot and drowning them. 'Didn't you say that most of them didn't last a week?'

'True,' said Raphael, 'but that doesn't mean they were necessarily bad. Just – temporary.'

'I don't want temporary,' said Jemma. 'I want committed, and conscientious, and – and—'

'Comatose? Canonical? Cantankerous?' Raphael laughed. 'I'm sorry, Jemma, but you take these things so seriously that it's hard not to poke a bit of fun occasionally.' He assumed a contrite expression as she scowled at him. 'I'll take a look at your – stuff – and we'll agree an advert to go out in an appropriate publication. I shall also follow my usual procedure, and put the Help Wanted sign on the door. I've still got it in a drawer somewhere. Between us, I'm sure we'll find someone suitable.'

Jemma drew herself up. She wasn't about to let herself be outsmarted by a man in green paisley pyjamas. 'I'm sure we shall,' she said, and picked up the teapot. The tea was perhaps a little stronger than her preference, but that was what milk was for. 'Here's to our new assistant,' she said, raising her cup. 'Cheers.'

'Yes, indeed. Cheers,' said Raphael, and they clinked cups. And that, as far as Jemma was concerned, was that.

'We did say a quarter past five, didn't we?' Jemma glanced at her watch yet again, then at the door.

'We did,' said Raphael. 'At least, I assume you did.'

It was interview day for the new bookshop assistant, and so far, it wasn't going exactly to plan. Jemma had managed to get tomato sauce on her top, thanks to an incautious bite into a fortifying bacon roll earlier, and had had to nip out and find a substitute. In the end she had bought a nice blouse from a local charity shop, but when she put it on, it was a fraction too tight and too short. She had been wriggling all afternoon. And now their first candidate was late.

Jemma had written a lovely advert, packed with keywords and phrases which ought to attract any aspiring bookshop assistant. Then she checked the rate per word in the local paper, and had to draw a line through it and start again. She had wanted to place an ad in a prestigious booksellers' publication, but Raphael managed to convince her that people looking for a job at that salary probably weren't scouring its glossy pages. Applications trickled in over the week: some typed (although the ones in Comic Sans or

Papyrus went straight in the bin), some handwritten (ditto any written in green or violet ink). They ranged from the frighteningly professional to the frankly delusional. In the end they were left with three applications. The first demonstrated a lack of experience but a great deal of enthusiasm; the second Jemma almost wished she had written herself, so accomplished was the applicant, and the third was short, to the point, and ticked all the boxes. Jemma had high hopes of the second; but she felt it only fair to give the other two a chance.

Raphael cupped a hand to his ear. 'Did I hear a knock?' They both strained their ears and sure enough, Jemma detected a gentle but persistent tapping. 'Hopefully that's our first interviewee,' she said, going to the door.

She opened it to reveal a breathless, flustered young woman in the act of buttoning her jacket. 'Oh, hello,' she said, 'I do hope I'm not too late. I got lost, you see. I went the wrong way. On the tube.'

'That's quite all right,' said Jemma, though she felt that it wasn't. Knowing where one was going was the first rule of a successful interview. 'Do come in – is it Dora?'

'Yes, that's right,' said Dora, looking worried.

Jemma admitted her to the bookshop and introduced her to Raphael, who seemed to unnerve her even more. After Jemma performed the preliminaries of enquiring about her journey, getting her a glass of water, and taking her downstairs, Dora perched on the edge of one of the armchairs Jemma had arranged to make things less formal, gripping it as if it might turn into a fairground ride at any moment.

'So, Dora,' said Jemma, smiling at her encouragingly, 'why would you like to come and work for us?'

Dora appeared stricken. 'Well, I like . . . I like . . . books?'

Jemma and Raphael tried to ease her along as best they could, but Dora was only too willing to talk about her lack of experience

161

working in a shop, admitted freely that she had trouble adding numbers up in her head, and said firmly that she hated confrontation or unpleasantness of any kind. Knowing the bookshop and Folio as she did, Jemma decided that it would be kinder not to consider her. So she ended the interview as quickly as she could, and presently Dora was on her way. Where she would end up was anyone's guess.

Raphael sighed and stretched his legs out once the door had closed behind her. 'On the bright side,' he said, 'we have time for a cup of tea before our next arrival.'

But he was mistaken. No sooner had Jemma poured out than they heard three no-nonsense knocks on the door. 'He's early,' said Jemma. 'Darn.'

On the doorstep stood a well-groomed young man in a dark suit and conservative tie. 'You must be Jemma,' he said, extending a hand. 'I'm Marcus. Here for the job interview?'

'Oh yes, indeed,' said Jemma, feeling as if *she* was. 'You're a little early.'

'Yes, I am,' said Marcus. 'I always make a point of leaving extra time in case an unexpected event occurs. One never knows, does one?'

'No, one never does,' said Jemma, and stood aside to let him in.

Marcus refused a cup of tea, and merely asked for a glass for the water which he had brought with him. Within one minute he was sitting composedly in the armchair, a folder on his lap, waiting for Jemma and Raphael to get themselves organised.

Over the next half hour they were treated to a potted history of Marcus's employment career, from working in his parents' bookshop as a teenager, through his degree and subsequent postgraduate work in business studies and library science, and ending triumphantly with his position as manager of the leading bookshop in Tamworth. He discoursed eloquently on different

162

book-classification systems, the historical legacy from the collapse of the Net Book Agreement, the psychology of bookselling, and the importance of A/B testing one's window displays.

Jemma hated him. Particularly when he said he would be more than happy to deputise as manager if she were ever on leave or engaged in other business. He didn't seem to be saying it with any malign intent, but, as he himself had said, one never knows.

They managed to dispatch Marcus one minute before the next candidate was due to arrive. 'I do hope he's late,' said Jemma.

'Ah well, it probably doesn't matter now,' said Raphael. 'Marcus is quite a find.'

Jemma gaped at him. 'You have to be kidding me. Him? He'd have us tied in knots by the end of the first day.'

'Don't you think he'd be good in the bookshop?' said Raphael. 'I imagine we can both learn from him. He's so professional.'

'Are you saying that I'm not professional?' demanded Jemma.

'No, not at all,' said Raphael. 'That isn't what I meant. But you have to admit that he knows an awful lot.'

'Too much,' said Jemma darkly.

Raphael looked at her curiously. 'Do I detect a note of jealousy, Jemma James?'

'Of course not,' said Jemma. 'As if.' But she found herself hoping against hope that the final candidate would turn out to be the one.

A decisive, yet unintrusive knock sounded upon the door at exactly the appointed time. Jemma leapt up. 'I'll get it,' she said.

'I had a feeling you might,' said Raphael, and sniggered.

At first when Jemma opened the door she couldn't see anyone. Then a figure stepped out of the shadow of the shop next door, wearing a black suit, shirt and tie. 'Good evening,' she said. 'Are you here for the interview – oh, it's you!'

It was the pale young man whom Folio had attacked only a few days before.

'Good evening,' he said, smiling. 'Yes, I am.'

Jemma consulted a piece of paper. 'Luke Varney?'

'That's right.'

He settled himself, looking much more at home than he had on his previous visit to the shop, and refused a drink, saying that he had just had one. At first Jemma had her fingers crossed under her notepad, and willed him to provide half-reasonable answers to their questions. But after a tentative beginning, his confidence grew and Jemma relaxed. He liked books; he had read widely and could talk about his favourite authors and why he liked them; he was methodical; he had an A in GCSE Maths. And, wonderful to relate, he had worked in a secondhand bookshop before, and seemed in no doubt that his previous employer would give him a good reference. Jemma made sure to take down the name and contact details of his previous employer. If she had her way, she would be sending them an email as soon as they had shown Luke out.

'Do you have any questions for us?' she enquired, leaning forward in her chair and remembering just in time not to smile too broadly in case she frightened him.

Luke considered. 'Let me think. You've outlined the salary and the benefits, you've talked about the possibility of overtime... Oh, there were a couple of things.'

'Oh yes?' enquired Raphael.

'Yes, about the overtime,' said Luke. 'If possible, could I do any extra work in the evenings? It's a bit difficult for me to get here before eight thirty in the morning. I don't mind working late, not at all.'

'I don't think that would be a problem,' said Jemma. 'To be honest, it would be good to have someone around in the evenings to help with cashing up. And if we do start doing events, that would work really well. Wouldn't it, Raphael?'

'It would,' said Raphael. 'Was there anything else?'

'Just – if you don't mind, I'd prefer to work in the fiction section.' Luke waved a hand at the shelves. 'Certainly at first.' Then he looked a little embarrassed. 'As I mostly read fiction, I feel I'd be best placed to advise people there.'

'That seems reasonable,' said Raphael. 'What do you think, Jemma?'

Jemma thought for a moment. She much preferred working downstairs. Partly because, like Luke, she felt more knowledgeable about novels than non-fiction; but also because she liked being able to chat to Carl and sneak a cheeky cappuccino when it was quiet. Then again, if the alternative was Marcus, she was prepared to make allowances.

'I'm sure we can work something out,' she said. It didn't have to be for ever. Part of Luke's training could involve familiarising himself with the various types of books upstairs, and then everything would be back the way she wanted it.

'Oh yes, and one more thing,' said Raphael. 'Will you be able to get along with our cat, Folio? After all, you two didn't get off to a very good start.'

Luke swallowed. At that moment Folio chose to saunter into the room. He looked at the luckless interviewee, then strolled to a position between Raphael and Jemma, sat down facing Luke, and stared at him.

'I'm sure we'll manage just fine,' said Luke. 'I shouldn't have attempted to stroke him when the shop was so busy. I'll wait until he makes a move towards friendship before I attempt it again.'

'Very wise,' said Raphael. 'Now, we have your telephone number and there isn't anything else I need to ask. You'll hear from us soon, either way.'

'Thank you for the opportunity,' said Luke, with a nervous smile. 'I do hope I can come and work with you.' He shook hands with them both – Jemma noticed the Mr Bump plaster had disappeared – and left without further ado. He had already vanished into the darkening street by the time Jemma closed the front door.

'Kettle on,' said Raphael. 'Decision time.'

'There is no doubt in my mind,' said Jemma. 'Luke all the way. I suspect training Dora to become a competent employee would be a full-time job. As for Marcus, I couldn't bear him for more than a day. He's so annoying, with his suit, and his folder, and those little nuggets of information about Dewey Decimal versus whatever the other one was.'

Raphael laughed. 'He'd do very well,' he said. 'But if I did hire him, I'd have to find myself a new bookshop manager within days. Or possibly break you out of jail.'

'I'm not murderous,' said Jemma. 'He just rubs me up the wrong way.'

'I had observed,' said Raphael. 'All right, for the sake of a quiet life, neither of those two. What about Luke? Can you work with him?'

'I don't see why not,' said Jemma. 'He's polite, he knows his stuff, he's qualified. And possibly most important of all, he won't tell me how to do my job, or try and swipe it from under my nose.'

'Most territorial of you,' said Raphael. 'Very well, subject to a decent reference and the customary checks, Luke it is.'

A sharp meow sounded from below, and he looked down in surprise. 'Are you expressing an opinion, Folio?'

'He's probably peckish,' said Jemma. 'Wasn't he supposed to be fed half an hour ago?'

'Good heavens, you're right,' said Raphael. 'I'll do that now, and make a pot of tea, if you phone Luke and tell him the good news. Knowing you, you'll email his previous employer too.'

'Might do,' said Jemma, grinning. 'Although we've still got to cash up this afternoon's takings. To be honest, I'd rather email from my laptop. Typing on the phone is so fiddly.'

Raphael nodded in agreement, though Jemma was fairly sure

that he had never done such a thing, and disappeared, followed by an eager Folio.

Jemma retrieved her phone from her bag and typed in Luke's number. It went to voicemail after a couple of rings. *He probably hasn't taken it off silent mode*, she thought, and left him a brief positive message asking him to return her call at his earliest convenience. *There.* Things were in motion, and she, for one, was pleased with the way it had all worked out.

Chapter 6

'You're absolutely sure you can manage?' asked Raphael, for perhaps the third time.

'Yes,' said Jemma, again. 'All I'm doing is showing Luke the ropes, then setting him to do some easy stuff. If that's too much for him, we can always close the downstairs till and I'll keep him with me. Monday mornings are generally fairly quiet, anyway.'

'I know,' said Raphael. 'That's why I agreed to go and view this book collection.' He glanced at Jemma. 'I could still cancel it —'

'There's really no need,' said Jemma.

'No,' said Raphael. 'And we do need more books.'

They certainly did. While the few days following the opening had been considerably less hectic, they were still ploughing through their book stock at an alarming rate. 'What would happen,' Jemma said one evening, as they stood together and gazed at the depleted shelves, 'if we ran out of stock altogether?'

'That will never happen,' said Raphael.

'It could,' said Jemma. 'If we have a very busy day.'

Raphael shook his head. 'Even then, it wouldn't.' And he

seemed so certain of the fact that Jemma felt pushing the matter further would be rude.

'Ah,' Raphael said, as a tap on the door was followed by its tentative opening and Luke's dead-white face in the gap. 'The man himself.'

'Good morning,' said Luke, although he didn't look as if it was. If anything, he looked as if he might be sick.

'Are you all right?' said Jemma. He wore sunglasses, and she imagined his eyes behind them, bleary and red-rimmed.

Luke swallowed. 'Yes, fine.' He managed a weak smile. 'I'm not a morning person. But I'm sure I'll get used to it in a day or two.'

'Of course you will,' said Jemma. 'Good thing you're a little early; Raphael will have time to say goodbye before he leaves.' She shot Raphael a significant glance.

'Yes, I'm off to acquire books,' said Raphael, holding up a set of keys. 'My carriage awaits. I should be back sometime after lunch.'

'Wow,' said Luke. 'Are you travelling a long way?'

Jemma snorted. 'I believe he is venturing as far south as Bromley,' she said. 'But I suspect lunch, and possibly elevenses, will form a key part of the expedition.'

'You know me so well,' said Raphael, and strode to the door.

He was arrested before he reached it by a querulous meow, as Folio galloped through the shop and skidded to a halt on the parquet floor beside him.

'I wondered where you'd got to,' said Raphael, stroking his head.

Folio meowed again, then rubbed his cheek against Raphael's hand. 'Marking your territory, eh?' Raphael chuckled. 'Back soon, Folio.'

Folio jumped into the window display and watched as Raphael passed out of sight.

'And he's off,' said Jemma, putting the latch on the door. 'Now, we don't open until nine o'clock, and I'm not expecting Carl till at least then, as the café opens at nine thirty, so it's the perfect opportunity to show you around the shop.' She glanced at Luke, who was still wearing his sunglasses and a heavy coat. 'Are you absolutely sure you're all right? Would you like a cup of tea?'

Was she imagining it, or did Luke shudder? 'No, thanks,' he said. 'I don't – that is, caffeine has a bad effect on me, so I tend to stay away from it.' He rummaged in his black rucksack and brought out an enamelled metal drinks bottle. 'I'll stick to this.'

'OK,' said Jemma. 'Mind if I make myself one?'

'No, go ahead,' said Luke.

Mug in hand, Jemma began the tour. 'As you'll be downstairs mostly – at least at first – we won't spend too long in the main shop,' she said. She demonstrated the workings of the till, enquired whether he knew how the card reader worked (he did), and pointed out the various categories of books. 'Right, let's head to the stockroom.'

On the way, she indicated the cupboard under the sink. 'You'll find anything you need in there. First-aid kit, cleaning materials, household stuff in general. That sort of thing. I'm sure you can work out the fridge and the kettle.'

She opened the door to the stockroom, switched on the light, and ushered Luke in. 'As you can see, we're running a bit low at the moment, but hopefully Raphael will fix that this morning.'

'There must still be an awful lot of books,' said Luke, going halfway down the middle aisle and revolving slowly. 'How do you keep track of them all?'

'We don't,' said Jemma. She caught sight of Luke's horrified expression, and her grin disappeared.

'What do you mean?' he asked, looking very serious.

'Oh, well, obviously we've got a broad idea of what goes where,' Jemma gabbled. 'But given all the books passing through, it would be counterproductive to maintain detailed records when a book could come in and go out on the same day.'

Luke took off his sunglasses, as if to see her more clearly. 'So how do I find anything?'

Jemma smiled in what she hoped was a reassuring manner. 'You probably won't at first, but Raphael and I can direct you.'

'Oh, all right.' He wandered further down the aisle, trailing his hand along the shelf, and Jemma exhaled slowly.

Crisis averted. She had been so looking forward to having an extra pair of hands in the shop that she hadn't given any consideration to how she would explain away its peculiarities. And to be honest, the shop was almost all peculiarities. *We'll have to muddle on for now,* she thought. *When Luke's been here a while, it will probably seem quite normal.*

She composed her face as he came towards her. 'Have you considered labelling the shelves?'

'I suppose we could,' said Jemma. 'But at the moment we don't have time for any extra work. Just getting the books on the shelves and selling them is about all we can do. Oh, and posting on social media when we remember.'

Jemma had felt rather aggrieved when she realised at the end of the grand reopening day that she had not had time to take photos or update the shop's status. In the end she had had to compose a quick post when she got home, and illustrate it with a stock photo of books. Now, that would change. 'Are you good with social media?' she asked.

'Not bad,' said Luke cautiously. 'I tend to interact in closed groups, mostly.'

'But you could take a photo every so often, and write a post, and maybe add a hashtag or two?' she persisted.

Luke looked relieved. 'Oh yes, I could do that.'

'Excellent.' *Delegation accomplished,* thought Jemma. 'Let's head downstairs.'

'So when did you discover this?' asked Luke, as they gazed around the huge, silent lower floor.

'Just a few months ago,' said Jemma. 'We found stuff on the internet which suggested there might be something down here, and when we investigated, there was!'

'It's incredible,' said Luke, craning his neck and staring at the ceiling. 'Would you mind if I took a look round? I mean, obviously I saw some of it when I came for the opening, but – it was busy, and I didn't know I would be working here.'

'Of course,' said Jemma. 'Go right ahead.' She leaned on the counter and watched Luke wander round. He pulled out a notebook, and seemed to be drawing himself a little map of the different sections. *Sensible and methodical*, thought Jemma. *Just what I want.*

'So everything is arranged by section, then alphabetically by author surname?' he asked.

'Everything except the children's picture books,' said Jemma. 'Those get picked up and put back so many times that we've given up keeping them in order.'

He laughed. Already he looked happier, and a bit less unhealthy. *I do hope he stays.*

Luke returned to the counter, pressed a button on the till, and the drawer opened with a ping. 'Is Mr Burns out of the shop often?'

'Call him Raphael; I do. And it depends,' said Jemma. 'He hasn't been able to get out much since the opening, because of all the customers. But now there are two of us I suspect he'll be out and about more. Even when he's in, he disappears to Rolando's fairly often in search of coffee and pastry.'

Luke's eyes widened. 'But you have a café.'

'Raphael claims that the coffee in the main shop tastes slightly different,' said Jemma, straight-faced.

'I see,' said Luke gravely. 'So he isn't hands-on, then?'

Jemma laughed. 'Well, he owns the shop, so he has final say on everything, of course. But I run the place, mostly. With help from Folio, of course. And Carl providing the refreshments.' She studied Luke. 'So a lot of the time you'll be down here in charge of the fiction section while Carl runs the café, and I'll be upstairs in non-fiction.'

'Oh, OK,' said Luke. 'So in bookshop terms, it's just you and me.'

'Yes,' said Jemma. 'Just you and me. Is that all right with you?'

She wondered if she had perhaps stressed the responsibility of the job a little too early, but Luke seemed unfazed.

'Yes,' he said, running his hand along the shop counter as if he were stroking Folio. 'That's absolutely fine.' He took his coat off, hung it on the row of pegs by the customer toilets, and came back rolling up his sleeves. 'What do I have to do before we open?'

Jemma thought. 'Make sure the toilets are clean, check the float in the cash register, like I told you upstairs, and you're good to go. I'll bring down more stock, and then you're all set.'

'I guess I am.' Luke's brows knitted slightly with determination. 'I'll do my very best,' he said quietly.

'I know you will,' said Jemma. 'And if there's anything you can't handle, come and tell me.' But somehow, she suspected it wouldn't come to that. He might have looked ill at ease when he arrived in the shop, but now Luke appeared completely at home.

Chapter 7

It was Friday morning, half an hour before opening time. Luke had just arrived and was happily shelving books downstairs. Meanwhile, Jemma was pouring tea into two large mugs. Fridays tended to be busy, so this brew might have to last her until lunchtime.

'So what do you think?' asked Raphael.

Jemma looked as innocent as she could. 'About what?'

Raphael rolled his eyes. 'You know what. Today is Friday.'

'Is it?' said Jemma. 'Thanks for letting me know.'

'And you do know,' said Raphael, adding milk. 'It's the end of Luke's trial period today. What do you think?'

'I think he's great,' said Jemma. 'He comes in on time, he does what I need him to, the customers like him—' She grimaced. 'Sometimes they even ask for him.'

'Do they, now?' asked Raphael, smiling. 'How do you feel about that?'

Jemma considered. 'All right, actually. I mean, it's good to have someone who knows what they're doing, and to feel that it doesn't all depend on me.'

Raphael raised his eyebrows.

'Don't look at me like that,' said Jemma. 'And he's organising the stock.'

One day, when the shop had just closed and they were alone together, Luke had sidled over and asked if he might have a word. 'Of course,' said Jemma, though his nervous expression alarmed her slightly. *What has he got in mind?*

Luke fidgeted with a pen on the counter. 'It's... I've been meaning to ask you pretty much since I came,' he said. 'It might not be appropriate, seeing as you're my boss...'

'Go on,' said Jemma, bracing herself.

'I wondered if we could, um, start scanning the books.'

Jemma stared. 'Scanning the books?'

'Yes,' said Luke. 'We don't know exactly what's where in the stockroom – well, I don't – but what we could do is scan the books when we put them out on the shelves, import the information into a database, then scan them again when we sell them. We'd be able to see what sells quickly, and over time, we'd get a much better idea of the stock in the shop.'

'Ooh, that's interesting,' said Jemma, forgetting her initial mild disappointment that Luke's question was related to books. 'Can we do that?'

'I don't see why not,' said Luke. 'I mean, it's easy enough to scan a book barcode with a mobile phone and get the data. The question is how we then move the data so that we can analyse it. Would you mind if I looked into it?'

'Not at all,' said Jemma. 'Fill your boots, in fact.'

And the experiment had begun. They had only been scanning books for two days, but already Luke was building up an impressive picture of what was selling in the bookshop, and what was going on the shelves. He had made graphs, and everything. Jemma gave Raphael a summary version of this information, resisting the temptation to batter him with bullet points. However, he didn't look as pleased as she had expected.

'I'm not sure I like the idea of all this – information gathering,' he said. 'What will you do with it all?'

'Analyse it,' said Jemma, unable to stop herself. 'Look at trends. Make forecasts. Plan.'

'I do wish you wouldn't use words like that,' said Raphael.

'What, *plan*?' said Jemma, grinning. 'I suppose it does have four letters.'

Raphael winced as he sipped his tea. 'Anyway, you're happy with him.'

'Yes,' said Jemma. 'He's exactly what the shop needs.'

Raphael studied her. 'You don't find him a little . . . quiet?'

Jemma considered the question. 'He does keep himself to himself,' she said. 'And I sometimes think it would do him good to get out of the shop at lunchtime, rather than eating on his own in the stockroom. Then again, better he does that than taking a long lunch or skiving off all the time. And his references were glowing.'

'True,' said Raphael. 'And it's hardly up to us to tell an employee how they should spend their lunch hour. Well, in that case I'll let Luke know he is a permanent fixture. Unless you want to do it?'

'I really don't mind,' said Jemma. 'To be honest, I'd rather you did. We have a visitor coming today, and I must make sure the shop is looking its best.'

'A visitor?' said Raphael, frowning. 'What sort of visitor?'

'A book blogger,' said Jemma. 'Now we've got time, we've been posting regularly on social media, and Stella sent me a message to ask if she could visit the bookshop today. You probably won't have heard of her, but she's very influential. Hopefully she'll feature us on her blog.'

Raphael looked mystified, but not hostile. 'Do you need me to be around? I was planning to go and see a man about some books —'

Jemma waved a dismissive hand. 'We'll be fine. You go and do what you do best.'

'All right then,' Raphael said, with a quizzical glance, 'I shall do that. But I'll go and speak to Luke first.' Mug in hand, he wandered downstairs.

Jemma went into the main shop and made her customary checks. The shelves were full of books. There was plenty of cash in the till, and the window display hadn't collapsed overnight. Yet something niggled her. What was it?

Is it me, she thought, *or was Raphael a bit doubtful about Luke?*

There's no reason for him to be, she argued. *Luke's good at his job, he's settled in well, and he's got over his nervousness. I don't see how we could have picked a better assistant.*

She regarded the shop counter critically, and fetched a cloth and some polish. *What you mean, Jemma, is that you're worried about this blogger coming, and you're transferring that to Luke. Really, you'd do much better to take it out on the counter.*

She sighed, sprayed polish on, and began buffing.

***

'Wow,' said Stella, or Stella the Bookworm as she was more commonly known. 'It's incredible.' She revolved slowly, her eyes like saucers.

'It is rather nice, isn't it?' said Jemma, trying not to preen too obviously.

Stella had been due to arrive sometime between ten and eleven, but at a quarter to twelve, just as Jemma had given up hope, she saw a pink-haired woman outside the window and her heart leapt.

'Sorry I'm a bit late,' said Stella, as soon as she entered the shop. 'I got held up coming in, then I spotted some amazing things while I was walking over and I *had* to get pics.'

'That's quite all right,' said Jemma, wishing evil on the amazing things, and hoping the photos were underwhelming. 'It

177

isn't as if we're going anywhere. I'll finish serving this customer, and then I'll take you downstairs and give you a tour.'

She dealt with her customer, then picked up the walkie-talkie which lay beside the cash register. 'Luke, can you come up? Stella has arrived. Over.'

Nothing. She glanced at Stella, who was meandering among the shelves and weaving round the other customers, occasionally stopping to read a book title.

'Luke, I need you upstairs. Over.'

The walkie-talkie crackled into life. 'It's really busy. Over.'

Jemma frowned at it. 'Don't worry, I can deal with that. But I do need you here now. Over.'

Two minutes later, Luke appeared. 'Is it a bit chilly down there?' Jemma asked, as he was wearing his big coat.

'I'm feeling the cold today,' he said. He blinked, then took his sunglasses from his coat pocket and put them on.

'Everything's in order,' said Jemma. 'I'll show you around, Stella, then you can have a bit of a wander about if you like. Stairs, or lift?'

'Oh, stairs please,' said Stella. She took several pictures with her phone as they descended. 'What an amazing door. It looks like the entry to a magic kingdom. Oh yes, that's good.' She opened an app on her phone, and said into it: *The imposing oak door reminds me of the entrance to a magic kingdom, full stop. And in a way, comma, of course it is, full stop. A kingdom of books.'* She pressed a button and grinned at Jemma. 'I always find it helps to capture ideas as soon as I get them.'

'You really have a way with words,' said Jemma. She opened the door and waved Stella through. *Please be good*, she implored the shop, silently. *Just until Stella's gone.* And she followed Stella in, her fingers crossed behind her back.

Chapter 8

Jemma was aggrieved to find that the shop wasn't particularly busy for a Friday lunchtime. *What was Luke talking about?*, she thought crossly. However, from her point of view, it was much easier to escort Stella around a shop that wasn't packed full to the brim, and without fielding enquiries from several eager shoppers along the way. She fed Stella as many soundbites as she could, including the long history of the shop, the discovery of the original cathedral crypt, and the quantity and variety of books that they could offer. Stella said 'Wow' to most of these, and also recorded several of them on her phone, which gratified Jemma immensely.

She was just talking about their new book-scanning system when she heard a loud cough behind her. She turned to find Brian the antiquarian bookseller fixing her with a stern look as he rocked backwards and forwards on his heels. 'Any chance you can get hold of Raphael for me?' he asked.

'Do excuse me,' Jemma murmured to the blogger. 'I'm sorry, Brian, he's out at the moment.'

'Well, do you know when he'll be back? Your assistant had no idea, and sent me down here.' He gazed about him. 'So this is the new floor, eh? Bet this takes some running.'

'Yes, it does,' said Jemma. 'Raphael is out sourcing stock for it now.'

'Books by the yard, I expect,' said Brian. 'Pile 'em high, sell 'em cheap.' He laughed, and nudged Stella.

'Raphael chooses his stock with great care,' Jemma said, in her most withering tone. 'We are a general bookshop, and we stock a wide range of books.'

'Excuse me?' Jemma felt a light touch on her arm. A tense woman was at her elbow, clutching a large handbag. 'I do wonder if you can help. I'm looking for Agatha Christie, and I can't find her at all.'

'We definitely have some,' said Jemma. 'She'll be in the Crime section.'

'Oh,' said the woman. 'I might have been in the wrong place. Could you tell me where the Crime section is?'

'Yes, it's over there.' Jemma pointed and the woman peered.

'I can't see, with all the people,' she said. Certainly they had acquired several more visitors in the last couple of minutes.

'OK, do you see that man in the blue T-shirt? If you go to where he is, then turn right, it's just down there.'

'Oh, I see.' She mulled this over for a few seconds. 'I'll try, but I may have to come back.'

'So can you give me any idea of when Raphael might deign to return to the shop?' asked Brian.

'He didn't say,' said Jemma. 'So I suppose sometime today is the best I can offer you.'

He sighed heavily. 'I'll hang around for a few minutes. Take a look at what you've got. I'm sure he'll be interested to hear my opinion, if he ever returns.' He strolled towards General Fiction with a face like a thundercloud.

'Sorry about that,' Jemma said to Stella, who was taking it all in with an expression of extreme interest.

'You do have to do an awful lot, don't you?' Stella replied.

'Friday's a busy day, and lunch is a busy time.' Jemma glanced at Carl, who was dealing competently with a queue of customers. 'Our local café and deli, Rolando's, have opened a sort of junior branch, and it's very popular. I'll try and introduce you to Carl when the rush has died down.'

'Ooh, yes please,' said Stella.

'You can go back up now.' Luke, slightly breathless, arrived at her side.

She raised her eyebrows. 'Er, who's looking after upstairs?'

'Raphael's just got back,' said Luke. 'He's minding things. Although he did mention nipping out.'

'OK,' said Jemma, with what she felt was great forbearance. 'Would you mind the till? I want to make sure Stella has everything she needs.'

'Oh, don't you worry about me,' said Stella. 'I'm always at home in a bookshop.' She jabbed at her phone and intoned '*I'm always at home in a bookshop,*' then beamed at Jemma. 'Do you mind if I take photos?'

'Oh no, please do,' said Jemma, waving a hand around the shop. 'Would you like a drink? I'll see if I can jump the queue.'

'A milky coffee would be wonderful,' said Stella, already eyeing potential scenes to photograph.

'I'll see what I can do,' said Jemma, and sped off.

She ducked behind the café counter. 'Milky coffee, disposable cup, soon as you can,' she said, out of the side of her mouth.

Carl made a face. 'There's a queue for a reason.'

'Just this once. Please?'

The corner of his mouth curled up. 'All right, seeing as it's you.' He made the coffee quickly and efficiently and fitted the lid on. 'Freebie?'

'I'll settle up with you later,' said Jemma. She took the cup and headed into the bookshelves, looking for Stella.

It was surprising how easy it was to lose sight of a pink-haired woman. *Where did she go?* thought Jemma, cruising among the shelves, cup in hand.

'Excuse me?' The Agatha Christie hunter appeared in front of her holding two books, with a slightly forced smile on her face.

'Oh good, you found them!' said Jemma.

'Yes, I did,' said the woman. 'But they weren't where they should have been. I did find the Crime section, but these books were in Science Fiction and Fantasy. That doesn't seem right at all.'

'No, it doesn't,' said Jemma. 'Why don't you take them to the till and let our assistant know.'

'Yes... Rather odd, don't you think?' The woman stood for a couple of seconds, meditating the oddness of it, then as if she had resolved an inner battle, made for the till.

As Jemma watched her go, her eye was caught by a flash of pink at the shelves near the till, and she set off in hot pursuit. 'Here's your coffee,' she said, handing it over.

'Oh, thank you,' said Stella, taking the top off and sipping. 'Lovely.' She put it on the shop counter, took a couple of steps back, and focused her phone. 'Say cheese!' she called.

Luke looked up just as the flash went off. His neutral expression transformed into a mask of terror, and with a yell, he flung himself behind the counter. The customer he was serving recoiled in horror, and her flailing arm knocked the coffee cup onto the floor.

'Oh, sorry,' called Stella. 'Did I startle you?' She hurried up to the counter and peered over it. 'Are you all right down there?'

Slowly, Luke's head, then his top half came into view. 'A warning would have been nice,' he snapped.

'Luke!' cried Jemma. Then she regretted her cross tone, for as well as looking furious he was deathly pale, and his hands trembled. 'Go and have your lunch break,' she said. 'I'll take over.'

'Sorry,' Luke mumbled in Stella's direction, and walked slowly away, brushing himself down as he went.

Jemma heard a rumbling laugh behind her, and turned to see Brian, arms folded, chuckling. 'Bit camera-shy, is he?' he asked.

'Just a bit surprised,' said Jemma. 'And Raphael's back, so if you'd still like a word, now's the time.'

He strolled off, his shoulders shaking with mirth.

'I'm so sorry about that, Stella,' she said. 'Did you get the shot you wanted?'

'Yes, I did,' said Stella. 'I might take another one with you, if that's all right.'

'Oh yes, that's absolutely fine,' said Jemma, and plastered a cheery smile on her face.

'Marvellous,' said Stella. 'I'll take a few more of the shop and the shelves. Don't worry about the coffee.' She nodded at the floor, where the coffee cup lay in a small puddle, then wandered off.

'Oh darn,' said Jemma. 'I'll get that cleared up.' She hurried off for equipment, mopped and dried the stone floor, disposed of the cup, then scurried back behind the counter. The Agatha Christie hunter was waiting patiently.

'I'd like to buy these, please,' she said. 'And the lady over there said I should tell you that I found them in the Science Fiction and Fantasy section.'

Jemma raised an eyebrow. 'I see. I'll make sure I let her know that you told me. That will be five pounds, please.'

The woman gave her a five-pound note. 'Thank you so much,' she said, taking the books, and tripped away with an air of having accomplished her mission.

Jemma sighed, then smiled at the next customer, who put three Terry Pratchett books on the counter. 'Should I tell you that I found these in Crime?' he said, grinning.

Jemma fixed him with a horrified stare. 'You didn't, did you?'

'No!' he bellowed, and started laughing.

'Ha ha, very good,' said Jemma, and rang up the sale. But all the time she served the customers, her mind was whirring. *What's been going on down here? Why did Luke say the shop was busy when it wasn't? Did he mis-shelve the books, or has it happened some other way? And most importantly, why on earth did he react like that when Stella took a photo of him?* And not even the sale of the whole *Forsyte Saga* in one go could distract her from her thoughts.

Chapter 9

A quarter of an hour later, Luke was back on the shop floor. 'I'll take over,' he said, not meeting Jemma's eyes. 'Sorry about earlier.'

Jemma studied him. He certainly looked better than he had when he left. The colour had returned to his face, and he stood taller, seemed more self-assured. 'If you're sure,' she said, stepping away from the counter.

'I'm sure,' he said, moving smoothly into place. 'Besides, Raphael probably wants a break.' He grinned, and Jemma grinned back before realising that Luke's smile was for the next customer, not for her.

She looked at Carl, who was still busy with his queue. 'OK, I'll go and see how Raphael's getting on,' she said to Luke's back, and headed upstairs.

She found Raphael sitting in the armchair, reading a book about paint effects and stencilling. 'Oh, hello,' he said. 'The rush is over up here.' He closed the book. 'If it's all right with you, I might—'

Jemma checked for customers, and saw none. 'Could I have a

quick word?' she said. 'It's about Luke.'

Raphael eyed her. 'It doesn't look like a good word,' he observed.

'It's a worried word,' said Jemma. 'He's been a bit odd today.'

Raphael gave the book a regretful glance. 'In what respect?'

'Well, when Stella the blogger came he didn't want to come upstairs; he kept making excuses. Then he came down again as soon as you got back, and some books downstairs were mis-shelved, and when Stella took a photo of him he dived behind the counter and freaked a customer out.'

Raphael considered. 'Maybe he's a bit camera-shy.'

'That's what Brian said,' Jemma replied. 'What did he want, anyway?'

'He asked my advice about the restoration of a volume he's recently acquired,' said Raphael. 'But I reckon he fancied a snoop round the shop. He'd never admit that, of course.'

'Oh,' said Jemma. 'But what do you think about Luke?'

'I think he prefers working downstairs,' said Raphael. 'Putting books in the wrong place doesn't sound like him, though.'

'It doesn't,' said Jemma. 'I even wondered if he'd done it on purpose, but what would be the point?'

'Exactly,' said Raphael. 'I suspect the shop has something to do with it. It doesn't always react well to new employees, as you know.'

Jemma recalled her own first week in the shop; the hazards that had appeared, the cobwebs that had materialised from nowhere, and the strange incident of the window display. 'I suppose you could be right,' she said.

Raphael laughed. 'I've spent enough time in the shop to know its little tricks. The other thing is—' He paused, as if thinking how to phrase his next sentence. 'The shop has been very busy lately. I mean, there's been fitting out downstairs, moving things round, and bringing new stock in. Add two new members of staff and it's not surprising that things are a little chaotic. And even if the shop were a little more like most shops—'

'You mean normal,' said Jemma.

Raphael winced. 'Everyone's normal is different, Jemma. Any shop would be bound to have a few mishaps if it suddenly doubled in size and had twice as many staff.' He eyed her. 'And you've been doing an awful lot, Jemma. When was the last time you had a proper lunch hour? Out of the shop, I mean; not just eating your sandwich or whatever, then getting back behind the till.'

Jemma thought. 'I have been eating properly,' she said, as a beginning.

'Yes, I've seen your quinoa salads and your apples and bananas,' said Raphael. 'But when was the last time you left the shop for a whole hour?'

Jemma didn't even need to think. 'About a month ago,' she said. 'The shop's been so busy, and you've had to go out and buy books, and there was the building work to oversee—'

'I'm not saying those aren't good reasons,' said Raphael. 'But today Luke is downstairs, I'm upstairs, and everything is in hand. So go and get whatever virtuous thing is in your lunchbox, buy yourself a treat to go with it, then take yourself out for an hour. I don't mind where you go, so long as you don't go sneaking into any other you-know-what shops to do research, or check out their displays, or look at the shelving arrangements. It'll do you good.' He paused. 'I don't want you to burn out. I do value you very highly, you know.' He nodded briskly. 'Now, be off with you.'

Jemma managed a smile, collected her quinoa and bean salad from the fridge, and unhooked her bag from the coat stand. 'See you in an hour then, I suppose,' she said, and headed for the door.

She had just reached it when Folio streaked into view and flung himself down in front of her. 'Oh, really,' she said, and bent to stroke him. Folio chirruped, and rolled onto his back for her to scratch his tummy. 'Where have you been all morning, anyway?'

she said as she rubbed. 'I've hardly seen you.'

'Probably asleep, knowing him,' said Raphael. Folio gave him an indignant glare, then rolled onto his feet, lifted his chin for a last fuss from Jemma, strolled to the armchair and jumped on top of Raphael's book. Raphael sighed, scooped Folio up with one hand, and moved the book away. Folio sank into Raphael's lap and put his head on his paws.

Jemma laughed. 'I'll leave you two to it, then,' she said, and left.

'Hello, stranger,' said Nafisa, as she pushed open the door of the mini-market. 'What can I interest you in today?'

'Chocolate,' said Jemma firmly. She could have had her pick of any number of tempting Italian pastries and desserts from Rolando's; but sometimes what you needed was a sugary chocolate bar filled with a flavour not found in nature. She selected a Peppermint Aero and a Diet Coke.

'Interesting combination,' observed Nafisa, ringing them up. 'How's the shop doing?'

'We're very busy,' said Jemma. 'That's why I haven't been in much. We've got a new downstairs, you see.'

'A new downstairs, eh?' said Nafisa. 'With more books?'

'Yes, and an extra Rolando's.'

'You *have* been busy,' said Nafisa. 'That throws my new pie display into the shade.' She indicated a cabinet next to the counter, where a selection of pastry items glistened beigely.

'I'll try one sometime,' said Jemma, 'but I've brought my lunch today.'

'Up to you,' said Nafisa. 'I'm vegetarian.'

Jemma strolled along Charing Cross Road feeling aimless. Perhaps Raphael was right. A great deal had changed in a fairly short time. Not just for the shop, but for her. All of a sudden she had a much bigger space to manage, not to mention two new staff, and Raphael was hardly ever there to help. *Not that Carl needs*

188

looking after, exactly, she added hastily to herself. *He can manage himself perfectly well.* But her vision of chatting to Carl in quiet moments, perhaps sharing a joke, or taking a coffee break together, had never materialised. Their breaks were never at the same time. And on the shop floor, one or the other of them was always too busy to talk. When the bookshop was beginning to quieten, at four o'clock or so, Carl was often still busy serving drinks. She sighed. *So much for getting to know him better.*

And then there was Luke, whom she had regarded as almost the perfect employee until about an hour ago. *Why did he dive behind the counter like that? If he didn't want Stella to photograph him, he could have blocked the shot with his hand.* She sighed. *But it probably was the shop playing tricks with the books*, she told herself. *Although it never did that with me.*

It couldn't afford to, she thought. *Remember how desperate things were when you first arrived? Fifty pounds on a good day? And you wondered how Raphael was going to pay you?*

She laughed at the magnitude of the change. Nowadays it wasn't unknown for Raphael to take money to the bank in thousand-pound instalments. If they could get a clear idea of what was in the stockroom, and set up the online shop she wanted, then it would become even more profitable...

Jemma's heart beat faster, and suddenly she felt rather breathless. She looked at her watch; forty minutes left of her hour. *Raphael's right*, she thought. *An hour to myself and I spend it thinking about the bookshop. I need to go somewhere quiet and zone out.*

Soho Square Gardens was nearby. She made her way there, sat on an unoccupied bench, admired the trees in their autumn clothes for a moment, then unpacked her lunch. She couldn't remember packing cutlery that morning, but sure enough, she had a spoon and fork wrapped in a paper towel. 'Autopilot,' she said, and winced. 'If you're not careful, Jemma, you'll grind yourself down

189

like you did at—' She stopped before she got to the name of her last employer. 'And you don't want that,' she told herself severely. She unclipped the lid of her salad, opened the Diet Coke, and began her lunch.

If anything, I should work out how to slow things down, she thought, chewing. *I'll park the online shop idea, at least until we know how busy the actual shop will be. If we sell many more books, I'm not sure any will be left for the other bookshops.* She looked around guiltily at the mention of other bookshops, then remembered that as she wasn't in the bookshop, it didn't matter.

Then she recalled something Raphael had said months ago, when she was new and keen to get things moving. What had it been, exactly? Something about the shop having to balance with the other bookshops. *Would he explain what he meant if I asked him now? After all, I'm much more experienced.*

'He's had the bookshop for what, thirty years?' A teasing little voice laughed in her ear.

But I'm more experienced than I was, argued Jemma. *And I care about the bookshop, and I don't want to hurt it.*

She ate the last mouthful of quinoa, put her spoon and fork inside the box, and snapped the lid on. Time for chocolate. She popped a segment into her mouth, closed her eyes, and leaned against the bench. Questions could wait until she got back. Some things were too important to rush, and a Peppermint Aero was one of them.

Chapter 10

Jemma returned to Burns Books feeling considerably calmer than she had done when she left. That said, as she approached the shop she felt a little frisson of nerves. Would everything be all right?

Raphael laughed as she pushed open the door. 'Nothing's happened,' he said, smiling. 'Apart from selling books, of course. You may find this hard to believe, Jemma, but there was a time when the shop had to manage without you.'

Jemma smiled back. 'I know,' she said. 'And you're right; I should ease up a bit.' She glanced around her. The upstairs of the shop, at least, was quiet. Even Folio had gone off somewhere. 'I was thinking about what you said,' she ventured. 'About keeping in balance with other bookshops.'

Raphael frowned. 'Did I? When?'

'Oh, ages ago,' said Jemma. 'When I first started, and I was trying to get you to let me do things in the shop. You talked about the shop's niche, remember?'

Raphael gazed at the books behind Jemma for inspiration. 'Oh yes, so I did. I'm afraid that was partly intended to calm you down a bit.' He grimaced. 'Sorry.'

'That's OK,' said Jemma, and reflected on how angry she would have been at the time, had she known that. 'You said *partly*. What was the rest?'

Raphael looked wary. 'I didn't want the shop to be too busy. You've seen now what can happen when it gets a little . . . over-excited.'

'I see,' said Jemma. And she waited. Perhaps she was mistaken, but she had a distinct feeling that there was something Raphael hadn't said.

Raphael shifted nervously in the armchair. 'I may nip out for a coffee in a minute—'

'How did the book buying go this morning?' asked Jemma. 'I did mean to ask, but somehow with everything else it slipped my mind.'

A casual observer would have said that Raphael's face remained impassive, but Jemma noted a slight furrowing of his brow. 'Quite well, thank you. A couple of rare books, and fifteen boxes of general stock.'

'Oh, like what?' asked Jemma. 'We could do with more science fiction; we had a run on Asimovs.'

'I'm afraid it's all still sitting in Gertrude,' said Raphael. 'I haven't had a chance to unload her yet.'

Jemma had originally imagined Raphael going on his book expeditions in a car either grand but dilapidated or completely impractical. When she was introduced to Gertrude, she had to bite her lip and turn away for a good few seconds. Gertrude was an ancient bright-orange VW camper van who looked as if she had escaped from a children's movie. She had a rakish air, as if she might at any moment come round the corner on two wheels, pursued by an old-style police car or the sleek, low-slung vehicle of a villain. Somehow being Raphael's book van seemed a placid retirement for her, and Jemma hoped that Gertrude had had a full and interesting former life.

'Well, if I mind the till up here and it's quiet downstairs,' she said, 'you and Luke could go and unload. Or maybe Carl could help, if the café is quiet. Three of you could get it done really quickly. Not that I'm saying I can't help unload the van, but—'

'But you're the manager, and I know what's in the boxes,' finished Raphael. He picked up the walkie-talkie and pressed the button. 'Raphael to Luke. What's it like down there? Over.'

A tinny reply came back. 'It's pretty quiet, two people at the till. Why, what's up?' A pause. 'Oh, over.'

Raphael chuckled. 'You young people, always expecting the worst,' he said to Jemma, and pressed the button again. 'Nothing's up, just wondered if you could help me unload some books.' He peered out of the window. 'If we hurry, we can get them in before it starts raining. Looks a bit dark outside. Over.'

'OK, coming up. Do you want Carl as well? The café's empty. Over.'

'Yes please,' replied Raphael, and put down the walkie-talkie. 'Operation Restock can commence,' he said, and wedged the front door open with the owl doorstop they kept for such occasions.

Luke and Carl arrived upstairs together. Luke peered outside, pulled his beanie hat from his coat pocket, and put it on.

'You probably won't be out long enough to get wet,' said Jemma.

Luke looked at the sky and pulled a face. 'You never know.' The three of them left, and Jemma took up position behind the counter in case a random customer walked in.

Boxes of books began to enter the premises a few minutes later, two at a time. 'How on earth can you see?' Jemma asked Luke, who carried his boxes high, with his forehead pressed against the top one.

Luke didn't answer, but took them through to the stockroom. When he returned, he seemed almost a different person. 'I've had a thought,' he said.

'I thought you might have,' said Jemma. 'What is it?'

'This is the first time that we've been able to bring books into a quiet shop,' said Luke. 'We could open the boxes and scan them right away.'

'Do what right away?' said Raphael, entering the shop weighed down by two more boxes.

'Scan the books,' said Jemma. 'For our stock database.'

'Oh,' said Raphael. He set the boxes on the counter. 'Right now, you mean?'

'There's no reason why not,' said Jemma. 'I mean, I could do it here—'

'Or I could,' said Luke. 'We could take the boxes to the stockroom and I could scan them, and as I know exactly what we need downstairs, I could sort those ones into separate boxes and have them ready to take down.'

'Good heavens,' said Raphael. 'Very efficient.'

Luke picked up Raphael's boxes and walked through to the stockroom.

Carl arrived next, carrying three boxes and looking as if he had decided that was a bad idea at least a minute ago. 'Where do you want them?' he gasped out.

'Stockroom, please,' said Jemma, and watched him go, his shoulders back and his jaw clenched. She realised she was frowning. Yet she wasn't sure why, exactly.

Ten minutes later all the boxes were in, and Raphael disappeared to take Gertrude to her garage, wherever that was. 'I might go for that coffee on the way back,' he said. 'I feel as if I've been in the shop a very long time.'

'You have, for you,' said Jemma, and grinned. 'See you for cashing up.'

She leaned on the counter and doodled on the notepad. A flower, with two leaves at the bottom of its stem. A heart with an arrow through it. A pile of books. A sketch of a cat who might be

Folio—

I haven't seen much of Folio lately, she thought. *I wonder where he's been. And I haven't seen him go downstairs, either.*

She shrugged. *He's probably out catching mice or birds, or something.*

But what's bugging me? She returned to the notepad. It wasn't the flower, that was for sure. The heart – well, she was too busy for that sort of thing. Although maybe that ought to change. *I should stop fretting whenever I'm at a loose end, and learn to enjoy it.* Her pen pointed to the pile of books. *That's it. I was going to scan them, but Luke cut in and took over. While he has a point, it still means that I'm stuck up here doing nothing, and no one's downstairs.*

Downstairs... Due to the current working arrangements, she hadn't been downstairs during a busy spell for about a week before this morning's adventure. *Was it different? And if so, how?*

Her brow furrowed in thought. It had been busy, though not as busy as it had on opening day. And the shop had misbehaved in a way that it had never done with her. The shop's tricks at her expense were generally designed to make her uncomfortable. But moving books into the wrong places was different. Could it be that the shop wanted to send customers away? But it was easy to move books back to the right places, and she doubted that any of their customers would worry over where books were shelved, so long as they could find them eventually. Browsing, after all, was one of the great pleasures of a bookshop.

The other option was that Luke had mis-shelved the books, either accidentally or deliberately. Again, it seemed unlikely. He was too careful, too meticulous.

Jemma sighed, and was on the point of drawing a line through the books when her pen stopped, and hovered above the paper.

What if – what if the shop wanted to get Luke into trouble?

But why? He seemed harmless enough. *He's a nice person,*

Jemma thought to herself. Then she remembered him on that first day, when Folio had scratched him. It had been a tiny wound, but still… Folio was much more placid these days, possibly because the shop was larger and tidier and he had more space to roam around. All the same, it was odd.

The stockroom door creaked, and she glanced up as Luke appeared. 'One for the shop so far, three on the shelves,' he said, smiling.

'How's it going?' Jemma asked, hoping that her thoughts weren't visible in her face.

'Fine,' said Luke. 'I feel as if I'm finally settling in, now I'm starting to sort things out in there.' He pushed his dark hair out of his eyes, and his smile broadened. He was still wearing his long coat, and appeared rather swashbuckling in his narrow jeans and big boots. Jemma found herself smiling back. 'I'd better get on with it. These books won't scan themselves.' He disappeared into the stockroom.

Jemma looked down at the notepad again. She drew a circle, added a dot in the centre, then drew the long and the short hand. *There's no way of knowing yet. I shall watch, and wait, and observe, and hopefully deduce.* On impulse, she went to the box in the back room and peeked inside. Edmund Crispin's *The Moving Toyshop* lay on top of the pile.

Trust you to pick a book I haven't read, she thought, and turned the book over to look at the blurb. Even then, she felt none the wiser.

Chapter 11

Jemma arrived on Monday morning equipped with a notebook and pen to record her observations. She'd even spent some time on Sunday debating precisely what to record. *Anything unusual* had been her first thought. Then she amended that to *Anything unusual for the bookshop*. But should she confine herself to things which definitely involved Luke, or should she record everything? In the end she decided that the latter would be the fairest course of action. After all, she couldn't be sure that Luke was the problem.

Monday passed without incident, and under that day's date Jemma could only write: *Nothing in particular. Must try harder*, she thought to herself. Then again, if there was nothing to observe and record, what was the point of inventing things? That would just be making work for herself, and creating a problem where none existed.

Tuesday started in much the same vein. When Jemma went downstairs for a final check before the shop opened, she found Luke adding to the float in the till. She took a quick tour around the shelves; nothing seemed out of place. Then she remembered that she hadn't mentioned the mis-shelved books to Luke. On

Friday, the priority had been getting him away from the situation, then making sure the customer was dealt with appropriately. 'A customer reported some wrongly shelved books on Friday,' she said, keeping her voice light. 'She found Agatha Christies in Science Fiction.'

Luke frowned. 'That's odd,' he said. 'I'm pretty sure I wouldn't have put them there. Maybe one of the customers put them back in the wrong place.'

'Could be,' said Jemma. *Why didn't I think of that?* she asked herself. *That's obviously what must have happened!* 'I didn't think it was you,' she added.

'I hope I've got enough sense to know where the Agathas go,' Luke replied, and closed the till drawer with a snap. 'All ready.'

'Morning,' said Carl, shrugging off his coat as he walked in. 'Time to pick up the pastries from Big R.' He strolled towards the coat rack. To do so, he had to pass first Luke, then Jemma. And as he did so, he gave Jemma a significant look. She felt as if she were being prompted.

It was so hard not to stare back, or mouth anything. How should she respond? Already she could feel her face heating up. 'Need a hand?' she asked. She thought about adding a friendly grin, but suspected that if she tried it would come out wrong.

'Yeah, if you wouldn't mind,' said Carl. 'Rolando said they'd start sending a few more after we ran out yesterday.' Suddenly he drew himself up, assumed a haughty expression, and declared 'We must keep Little R well-fed and happy,' in a strong Italian accent.

Jemma laughed. 'So our café is Little R now?'

'I guess so,' said Carl, in his normal voice. 'Although at the rate we're going, we could be Medium-Sized R soon.'

'Maybe,' said Jemma. 'But we'd better get a move on if I'm going to be back for opening time. See you later, Luke,' she called, on her way to the door.

'What was that about?' she asked, once the door of the shop

had closed behind them.

'Come on,' said Carl, and she had to hurry to keep up with him as he strode down the road to Rolando's. He pushed open the door and Jemma followed him in. The café was already busy, but two large lidded plastic boxes waited on the counter.

Giulia bustled out of the kitchen. 'Thirty extra today,' she said briskly. 'We see how it goes, yes?'

'Thank you,' said Jemma.

'Is nothing,' said Giulia, and with a quick bob of her head she disappeared again.

Carl glanced around them at the various customers enjoying their drinks and pastries. 'Come on,' he muttered, and walked towards the back of the café. Behind a plain wood door was a corridor, and he opened the first door on the left to reveal a small walk-in cupboard. 'In here.'

'Is this really necessary?' asked Jemma.

'Dunno,' said Carl. 'But I'd rather be too careful than not careful enough.'

'Have you been reading spy novels on your break?' asked Jemma, with a smile.

'Something isn't right,' said Carl. He hesitated, a tentative expression on his face. 'This probably sounds weird, and I don't know what it is, but the shop feels – it feels *heavy*.'

Jemma stared at him. 'How do you mean?' she asked, though she had a fair idea of what he meant.

'You know how it feels when there are dark clouds overhead, and it isn't raining yet, but you know it's going to?'

Jemma's smile faded.

'I see you do,' he said. 'And it's felt like that downstairs pretty much since Luke started.'

'Really?' asked Jemma. 'I must admit, I haven't noticed. It was a bit strange on Friday, but I put that down to it being busy. And having Stella in, of course.'

'Ah,' said Carl. 'And it isn't like that upstairs?'

'No,' said Jemma. 'But it's never as busy.' She frowned. 'Are you absolutely sure?'

Carl moved closer, and lowered his voice. 'At first I thought I was imagining things,' he said. 'It felt odd the first day Luke was downstairs without you, but I thought that was because, well—' He looked down for a moment. 'Because I'm used to having you around.' A sudden, sheepish grin. 'But the feeling has been getting stronger. At first it was just in the back of my mind, like a niggle every so often, but after a couple of days I felt worried. When you or Raphael are downstairs, it goes away. It's only when Luke's down there on his own. And yesterday I walked in after my break and it hit me as soon as I stepped through the door.' Jemma saw fear in his brown eyes. 'I thought about telling you then, but the shop was too busy, and Raphael was out.'

'Oh,' said Jemma. She felt as if Carl had handed her a huge responsibility, wriggly and bulky and awkwardly shaped, and she had absolutely no idea how to manage it. 'Um, why do you think you feel it, and Raphael and I don't?'

'Maybe it's to do with the acting,' said Carl. 'We're trained to feed off the audience's reaction, so you get sensitive to atmosphere. And I spend more time alone with Luke than either of you.'

'That makes sense,' said Jemma. But even as she said the words, she thought, *Is he over-reacting?* 'But what do we do? I can't dismiss Luke on the grounds that he makes you feel a bit funny.'

'I know,' said Carl, looking injured nevertheless. 'That's one of the reasons why I haven't said anything. That, and it being so hard to get a word with you alone.'

'OK,' said Jemma, though she didn't feel OK. She felt uncomfortable, and she wasn't sure whether it was because of what Carl was telling her, or the fact that they were crammed into a cupboard together, and she was very conscious of how close he was. She could smell his aftershave, and if she took a step closer—'Well, um, if I give you my mobile number, we can text each other.' She pulled out her phone and showed him the number.

'We could,' said Carl. He took out his own phone and typed her number into it, sent a text which said *Hi*, then pocketed it. 'I was thinking—' He gazed at his feet.

The pause lengthened, and Jemma checked her watch. 'It's five to nine—'

'We could meet up,' said Carl. 'Outside work, I mean. Somewhere we can't be overheard. We could meet up, and discuss what we've seen, and *felt*.'

Jemma looked into Carl's face, inches from hers. He seemed worried. Worried, and beneath that, upset and trying to hide it. 'You're serious about this, aren't you?'

A slow nod. 'Yes, I am. I don't know what it is, but I don't like it.'

'Then we must sort it out,' said Jemma, with the best brisk managerial air she could summon. 'Today's Tuesday. How is Thursday for you, after work?'

'I can do that,' said Carl. 'We could go to your place, if that's all right?' He gave her a tight little smile. 'Sorry to ask, but it isn't the kind of thing we can discuss in public. And if I take you to ours, you won't get a word in edgeways. Plus my mum would probably want to suss you out.'

'Uh-huh,' said Jemma, trying not to show her alarm. 'Let's say Thursday, and see how we go. We might have nothing to discuss, and in that case, we don't need to meet.'

'I'm not expecting you to cook,' said Carl. 'Or tidy up.'

'That's good, because I wasn't going to,' said Jemma. 'Now, let's get those pastries back to the bookshop before we get in trouble.' She opened the door, and as she did so Carl's expression transformed into a cheeky grin. He strolled out of the stockroom and high-fived one of the shop staff coming the other way, who raised his eyebrows at Jemma, then grinned back.

'Shall I take one of the trays?' she asked, as they approached the counter.

'No need,' said Carl, lifting them both easily. 'You can get the doors for me.'

Jemma looked at him curiously, but Carl appeared his normal happy, positive self, and it was hard to believe that the conversation they'd had moments ago had happened at all. She had a feeling that she wouldn't see any sign of worry on Carl's face again until they were tucked away from prying eyes.

Chapter 12

Jemma kept an eye on Luke that day, but it was not a close eye. While Raphael didn't have any book-buying trips scheduled, he was in and out a lot: nipping next door to Rolando's, taking a long lunch break, and going for a chat with two other bookshop owners in Charing Cross Road.

'Are you doing business with them?' Jemma asked.

'Business? Oh, not exactly,' said Raphael. 'More seeing the lie of the land.' And before Jemma could ask him exactly what that was supposed to mean, he left.

So it was down to Carl. Jemma listened out for her phone in case he texted. She even put it in her pocket, something she never usually did, but after an hour or two she replaced it in her bag. It was too distracting. Every time her phone buzzed her heart leapt, expecting the piece of damning evidence. However, it was always just another social-media notification.

The one exception to this was a notification that the bookshop had been tagged in a post by Stella the Bookworm. Jemma unlocked her phone with trembling hands, and clicked.

She needn't have worried. Stella had written a really nice piece, praising the bookshop's stock and its furnishings. She complimented the coffee which she had barely had a chance to drink. And mercifully, she didn't mention *the incident*. She even, at one point, referred to 'Jemma, the capable bookshop manager'. Jemma could feel her cheeks getting warm, and she couldn't stop herself from grinning. She shared the link on the shop's social-media feeds: *Thank you so much, Stella the Bookworm, for this lovely article about us! Come and visit us again any time!* She sighed out a breath, and only then realised how worried she had been that the shop would get a bad review, and they would be back as the second-worst bookshop in Britain again. Luke was, she felt, at least partly to blame for that.

She showed the post to Raphael on one of his brief returns to the shop. He read it, and as he did his expression resembled that of a proud father. 'That *is* good,' he said. 'Well done, the shop. And you, of course,' he added hastily.

Jemma rolled her eyes, but she was still smiling.

The only text from Carl that day came just after he had left. *Nothing particular to report but weird feeling still there.*

Jemma frowned at the message. What could she say in reply? In the end she settled for: *Fine upstairs. Thanks for watching out.* She hoped Carl didn't find her message dismissive. But what else could she say?

At the end of the day she left slightly after Luke, and as she walked to the station a vague sense of unease prickled at her. Was something going on? Was she perhaps not tuned in enough to the shop to feel it? Then again, Raphael didn't seem bothered, and it was his shop.

Once home, Jemma threw herself into cooking beef stroganoff to take her mind off things. But even as she ate, sitting at the little drop-leaf table, she looked at her flat through a stranger's eyes. The walls could do with a fresh coat of paint; the original pale yellow had lapsed into a sort of jaundiced cream. The curtains and the carpet didn't match. She hadn't folded up the sofa-bed properly, and it appeared lumpy and misshapen. *Not that I'll be inviting him to it*, she thought to herself. Then she almost spat out her mouthful of food. *Not like that!*

Then she sighed. As things were, it looked likely that they wouldn't need to meet on Thursday after all. *So you can stop worrying about that, Jemma*, she said aloud, and silenced herself with more food. But when she had finished dinner, she still went to the little corner cupboard where she kept her clothes, pulled out a casual, pretty floral dress, and checked it for creases before hanging it up, tutting at herself, and closing the door on it.

Wednesday was much the same. The shop was busy enough that Jemma didn't have time to worry about what might be going on downstairs. Indeed, Raphael actually stayed in the shop that afternoon, and Jemma took the opportunity to go downstairs and help in the Fiction section.

She found Luke in a cheerful mood, joking with the customers as he served them or answered their questions, and she felt a little pang of envy that she spent so much time upstairs. Then she told herself that it was her job to manage, not to be on the till all the time. In any case, she got her chance when Luke asked whether he could go and scan books in the stockroom. 'And I'll bring some more down,' he said. 'I labelled the boxes I scanned the other day, so it should be much easier to find stock. For me, at least.' He grinned.

'Yes, you do that,' said Jemma. 'I see our two Golden Age crime ladies are in, so I'll put a request in for that, as they usually buy a fair few between them.'

'Aye aye, Captain,' said Luke, and saluted. At least he wasn't wearing his big coat, in which case the gesture would have seemed more military. She noticed that instead of his usual black ensemble, his shirt was midnight blue.

'That suits you,' Jemma said. 'The shirt, I mean.'

A slow flush crept from Luke's neck to his face. 'Thank you,' he said. 'I'll go and sort out those books.'

Jemma turned her attention to the next customer. But she glanced towards the doorway just as Luke looked back, and their eyes met for a moment before he vanished behind the great oak door.

Now it was Jemma's turn to go a bit pink. She shot a guilty look in Carl's direction, but he was busy at the coffee machine. *In any case*, she thought, as she slipped Dodie Smith novels into a Burns Books bag, *I didn't mean anything like that. I just meant that the blue shirt suited him better than the black ones. It makes him look a bit less washed out.*

She rang up the purchases, and watched the customer count out their change. Working at the bookshop seemed to suit Luke. He definitely seemed less poorly and pale than he had when he arrived. And while he still ate his lunch in the stockroom, he occasionally accepted an offer of tea. He had even brought in some decaf teabags which sat in the kitchen, ignored by everyone else. Perhaps Raphael was right, and it was a matter of the shop and Luke getting used to each other.

And then came Thursday.

It began normally enough, with a journey in on a fairly busy tube train. Jemma couldn't get a seat, so hooked her elbow around the pole by the doors, and took the opportunity to text Carl: *If nothing happens today, we don't need to meet later.*

There was no reply. *He's probably travelling in too.* In any case, she would see him soon, for she was only a couple of stops from work now.

She was surprised to find the lights already on in the shop when she arrived, and Raphael putting his jacket on, accompanied by a volley of meows from Folio. She noted that he was wearing a suit and a coordinating shirt and tie, unlike his usual colourful mishmash of garments, and a stack of unassembled cardboard boxes leaned against the counter. 'Off on a book expedition?' she asked.

'I am,' said Raphael. 'Got a phone call at seven yesterday evening from the widow of Sir Tarquin Golightly.'

'Sir Tarquin Golightly, eh?' said Jemma.

'The very same,' said Raphael. 'Scientist, inventor, and renowned book collector. Lady Golightly, however, can't stand the "dusty old things", as she calls them, and has invited me to Hertfordshire to deal with the problem.' His eyes gleamed blue. 'Obviously I told her I would be more than happy to assist.'

'Do you know what sort of books he has?' asked Jemma.

'I've heard rumours,' said Raphael, rubbing his hands. 'Let's just say this sort of opportunity comes along once in a generation.'

Folio let out another meow, then flung himself on the parquet floor and wriggled at Raphael's feet.

'Stop moaning, Folio, you've had your salmon.' Raphael reached down and tickled his tummy. 'Be careful of him, Jemma, he's in a bit of a funny mood.'

'When do you think you'll be back?' asked Jemma. 'Hertfordshire's not that far away.'

'It isn't,' said Raphael. 'But there will be an awful lot of books to go through. And if Lady Golightly asks me to stay to lunch, then it would be most impolite of me to refuse.'

Jemma eyed his thin figure, and sighed. Given Raphael's enthusiastic consumption of pastries, fast food, and caffeinated beverages, he ought to have been the size of a house and permanently jittery.

'I won't ask what you're thinking,' said Raphael, with a smile. 'Your expression tells me that I don't want to know.'

Jemma grimaced. 'You're probably right,' she said, opening the door. 'Good hunting.'

'The shelves await,' Raphael declared. He hefted his stack of flat boxes, and strode off.

Jemma sighed. That meant another day spent mostly upstairs. Then again, it probably didn't matter. Yesterday had been fine, and the day before, and Carl was more than capable of observing what went on.

Carl turned up, and went to get supplies from Rolando's. When he came back, Luke still hadn't arrived. 'Maybe he's having trouble getting in,' said Jemma. 'The tube was busy this morning. I'm not entirely sure where he's coming from, but there could be trouble on his line.'

'Could be,' said Carl. He glanced at her. 'I got your message.'

'What do you think?' asked Jemma. It felt odd to be talking normally in the empty shop. Almost as if they were doing something forbidden. She caught herself making sure no one was there.

Carl's face was expressionless. 'I don't know,' he said. 'Nothing's happened, but I still think...'

'You still think what?'

'I don't *know*,' he repeated. 'But I don't like it.' A pause. 'I'll go downstairs and get things ready.'

Nine o'clock came, and Luke did not. Jemma opened the shop and found three people waiting outside. 'We're a bit low on staff today,' she said as she ushered them in. 'So can you bring your books to the upstairs till, please.'

All three of them clattered downstairs. *Hurry up, Luke*, Jemma thought. She picked up the walkie-talkie, then remembered that Carl probably wouldn't answer it since it was really for bookshop staff. She fetched her phone, and texted: *Luke still not here, have told customers to use upstairs till. Any questions you can't handle, ask me. Sorry.*

A few more customers came, and a few more, and at nine thirty there was still no sign of Luke. *Should I phone him?* She hunted through the drawers under the counter for his number, but couldn't find it. *Perhaps he's ill.*

208

Even if he is, he should still ring in, her managerial voice nagged. *Or at least text. Everyone knows that's what you do. Or he could get someone to ring for him, if he's too ill.*

But did he have anyone? He'd never mentioned anybody. No partner, or friends, or family. *Anyway,* thought Jemma, *there's nothing I can do but get on with it.* So she got on with doing just that.

Except that there wasn't anything to get on with. The odd customer to serve, of course, but they trooped up obediently with their books, and they all had the right money and no weird questions. She nearly wished for a difficult customer to give her something to do. Then she recalled some of the customers she had dealt with, and thanked her lucky stars.

Jemma made herself a cup of tea at eleven, and even considered popping downstairs for a snack to go with it, but conscientiousness won out, and she stayed behind the counter. *When he gets here—* Then she decided she might as well sit in the armchair and read as it was so quiet, and soon, lost in Narnia, she forgot all about it.

She was so absorbed in her book that she barely glanced up when the shop bell rang. When she did, she couldn't look away.

Chapter 13

Luke stood in the doorway, panting. He was as white as a corpse, his eyes bloodshot. His hand gripped the door as if he might collapse otherwise.

All thoughts of shouting at him disappeared. 'What on earth has happened?' Jemma asked. 'Here, sit down.' She sprang up and led him to the chair, but he resisted when she tried to push him into it.

'I'm late,' he said. 'Something, um, happened. But I'm here now.'

'Should you be here? You look terrible.'

A smile flickered for an instant on his pale lips. 'Thanks. I'm fine.' He took out his drink, swigged from it, then wiped his mouth on the back of his hand. 'I'll get myself downstairs.'

'Take the lift,' said Jemma. 'I'm worried about you.'

'I'm *fine*,' he muttered, and shuffled off, still in his long coat and beanie hat.

As soon as he had gone, Jemma picked up her phone and texted Carl. *He's arrived.* She didn't feel she needed to say any more. Carl would be able to work it out for himself when he saw

Luke.

Two minutes later she got a reply. *What's he been doing? He looks dead.*

He didn't say, Jemma replied. *All OK down there?*

Quiet so far. Serving a lot of cappuccinos ;-)

Jemma's mouth twitched. *Save one for me ;-)* She replaced her phone in her bag. Maybe they *could* meet later, and go out for a drink and a chat. That would be nice. She'd wait a bit, maybe until after lunch so that she didn't seem too keen, then make the suggestion.

Then a customer came in who actually wanted a non-fiction book. Jemma was kept busy bringing books to the counter, only to be told that they were interesting, but not quite right. She succeeded on her tenth try. Then she remembered her wish earlier, and cursed herself.

More customers came, mostly for downstairs, but enough stayed upstairs to keep Jemma occupied. At least now she wouldn't have to deal with all the purchases. She hoped Luke was managing downstairs. *Then again*, she thought, *it isn't difficult. And if he's having problems, he knows he can send them up to me.*

As if on cue, a dapper elderly gentleman approached the counter. 'Excuse me,' he said, 'I'm looking for a book. It wasn't on the shelves downstairs, but the young chap on the till thought you might have a copy in stock.'

'We very well might,' said Jemma. 'What is it called?'

He adjusted his pocket square. '*Ulysses*. By James Joyce.'

Jemma bit back a retort that she knew who had written *Ulysses*, thank you very much, and said, 'If you wait a minute, I'll see what I can find in the stockroom.' *I'm sure we had one downstairs*, she thought, as she opened the stockroom door and switched on the light. *Then again, we might have sold it.* She gazed at the shelves. Luke had labelled the boxes nearest the door. None of those looked likely. 'Pot luck, then,' she said, taking a random box off the shelf and returning to the shop.

'I'll open this and see what's inside,' she said, reaching for the scissors. She cut the tape, and lifted up the flaps.

She lifted out the first book: *Lost Horizon*.

Underneath that was *Lost Empires*.

And beneath that, a guidebook for the Lost Gardens of Heligan.

Jemma lifted out book after book, feeling increasingly worried, but *Ulysses* was not there. 'I can try another box, if you like,' she faltered. In all the time she had worked at the bookshop, she had never failed to find a book that a customer wanted.

'Thanks, but I'm in a bit of a hurry,' said the elderly gentleman. 'I'll leave my number, then you can call me when you have it back in stock.' He wrote his name and number on the notepad, and printed *ULYSSES BY JAMES JOYCE* in neat square capitals. 'Good day to you,' he said, and went out.

Then another customer came forward. 'Have you got a copy of *Whose Body?* It's by Dorothy L Sayers. I looked downstairs, but it wasn't there, and the lad on the till said—'

'I'll try the stockroom,' said Jemma, grimly. She pulled out another box, opened it, saw that the book on top was *Gone Girl*, and shivered. Dutifully, she went through the rest of the box, but had no luck. 'If you leave your name and number, we'll call you when we have it in,' she said, presenting a fresh sheet of the notepad.

Two more unfulfilled queries later, she grabbed the walkie-talkie. 'Jemma to Luke. Please don't send more customers up for books. If they're not on the shelves, I can't help. Over.'

She expected a snarky reply along the lines of: *If you scanned the books when they came in then it wouldn't be a problem.* Instead, Luke's voice sounded exhausted through the crackling. 'Sorry, I didn't know what else to do. Over.'

Jemma sighed. When she had dispensed with the queue, she

went to fetch her phone. *Looks like tonight's meeting is back on,* she thought. *I knew I should have hoovered before I left.*

Her phone screen was full of messages from Carl. The one at the bottom, the first that he had sent, read: *The air is really heavy.* The next: *It's like the air is fizzing.* And finally: *You have to come down, Jemma. Please reply, and I'll come and mind upstairs.*

That message had been sent two minutes before. Jemma pressed *Reply. OK.*

Carl arrived thirty seconds later, and Jemma was shocked at his pallor; his skin had an odd greyish tinge. 'It's not that I'm scared,' he said, as soon as he saw her. 'Well, I am, I guess, but *I* can't do anything about it. I'm hoping the shop will calm itself if you go downstairs.'

Jemma felt the blood drain from her face. 'What's going on?'

Carl shook his head. 'No idea. I felt this chill, and when I looked at Luke he was staring at his phone. Then customers started going up to him and saying they couldn't find the book they wanted, and that the books were in the wrong place, and someone tripped over Folio—'

'Oh heck,' said Jemma. 'Are they all right?'

'Yes, but not best pleased,' said Carl. 'I apologised, and sat them down in a chair with a free drink. And then a light bulb blew.'

'Oh no,' said Jemma.

'And there was a rumble—'

But Jemma was already on her way. As she rushed through the back room she saw Folio standing in front of the stockroom door. He hissed at her, his tail fluffed out with rage. 'No need to do that at me,' she muttered, and ran down the steps.

She heard raised voices, and braced herself as she opened the great oak door. Then she stared at the scene before her.

Close by, two customers were tugging the same book in different directions. Several more customers surrounded Luke at

213

the till, all talking at once. A woman in a tie-dye skirt was standing behind them, saying plaintively to no one in particular, 'I just want to be served, that's all I ask.'

Jemma dashed up to her and took the book gently from her hand. 'I'm so sorry for your wait,' she said. 'That will be two pounds, please. Don't worry, I'll ring it up for you, if you don't need a receipt.'

The woman brightened, and pulled a small purse from her bag. 'Thank you ever so much,' she said. She took the book, put it carefully into her bag, and wandered off.

'Excuse me please,' called Jemma, and moved people aside to get to the till, where she deposited the two-pound coin. 'We can only serve two people at a time, because there are only two of us. Who's next, please?'

Everyone spoke at once, angry expressions on their faces, and Jemma couldn't make any sense of it at all. 'Please, one at a time!' She raised her hands for silence, and didn't get it.

Then the lights went out.

A huge, collective gasp swelled in the pitch blackness. A moment of silence, then people started calling out to each other. Jemma felt along the counter for the walkie-talkie. 'The lights are out down here. Over.'

'Here too,' said Carl, his voice crackling. 'And the card reader. Over.'

What do I do? She blinked, and as her eyes adjusted to the darkness she saw the pale-green glow of the emergency light above the door to the stairs. 'OK, everyone who can reach their phone, please use the light or torch function and make your way to the door. Head for the green light. Please don't use the lift. We think it's a power cut.'

A thud, and someone swore. 'Please don't move until you can see where you're going,' she added. 'I don't believe this,' she muttered under her breath, but Luke didn't reply. She wasn't even sure he was there.

Gradually little beams of light switched on and she saw figures moving towards the exit. 'I'll go and open the door for them,' she said, and made her way over as best she could in the dim, flickering light.

Eventually, as far as she could tell, no one was left downstairs but herself and Luke, who stood motionless, holding his phone at arm's-length, the beam pointed down.

'I guess that's everyone,' she said. 'Come on, let's go upstairs. You first.'

Luke was silent, and she couldn't see his face; it was too dark. What on earth was going on? What had just happened? She had been so busy making sure that everyone was out of the room – and she really hoped they all were, because there was no way she could tell – that she hadn't had time to think about the situation.

'Luke,' she said, as they climbed the stairs, 'it's best that you go home. We won't be able to reopen until we get the power on.'

'Are you sure,' he said. It wasn't a question, more an agreement.

They emerged into the back room, which was almost as dark as downstairs, then into the main shop. Luke winced and put on his sunglasses. Jemma hadn't thought it was possible for him to be any paler, but his skin was greenish white. Carl was behind the counter, his face stricken. And standing in the middle of the room was Raphael. Jemma had never seen him look even mildly angry before, but now his face was twisted with rage.

'What has been going on?' He said it quietly, but Jemma squirmed, and her stomach churned.

'I think it's a power cut—' she said.

'I can see that,' he snapped. 'This whole section of the street is out.' Then his face changed. 'What else has happened?'

'We couldn't find books,' said Jemma. 'Not the ones that customers wanted.' She pointed to the box she had opened earlier, which was still sitting there, *Lost Horizon* on top.

Raphael glanced at the book, and his face looked as if it were carved from stone. 'Out, all of you!' he cried. 'Out, now!'

He marched into the back room, and the stockroom door smacked against the wall. Then he stormed back in. 'Didn't you hear me? I said get out!'

'I'm sorry,' murmured Luke. Without waiting for an answer, he opened the door and left. Jemma saw him jam his beanie hat on his head as he went past the window.

'Come on,' said Carl. He held the door for Jemma. 'Usual time tomorrow?' he asked Raphael.

Raphael stared at him blankly. 'Just *go*.' And as soon as they had stepped outside, he slammed the door and locked it. The sign turned from *Open* to *Closed*, and as Jemma watched, he pulled the blind down.

Chapter 14

'Jemma.'

Jemma was still staring at the door of the bookshop. She jumped as Carl touched her arm.

'We need to go,' he said. '*You* need to go.'

She nodded, but didn't move.

He leaned closer. 'Can I get hold of someone for you?' he murmured.

Jemma looked at him. 'There isn't anyone, really,' she said. 'My family live a long way away, and—' For the first time in weeks, Em came into her mind. Em, who if they were still friends would have told her that she should have listened, and that Em had known this would happen, then probably taken her out to get drunk.

'Shall I take you home? Your home, I mean.'

Jemma thought of her flat, with its lumpy sofa-bed and depressing decor. Somehow, that didn't matter any more. 'Yes, please. If you don't mind—'

'Don't be silly,' said Carl. 'You'll have to tell me where we're going, though, because I've got no idea.'

'Embankment tube station,' said Jemma.

They walked without speaking; not fast, not slow. Occasionally Jemma looked at Carl. Sometimes he looked back, as if he felt her looking. 'We can talk later, if you want,' he said, once. 'There's no rush.'

They didn't really talk on the tube, either, except for Jemma to tell him her stop. And when they got outside and began walking again, everything felt unusual. The light was different, the smells were different. Shops normally open were closed, and the other way round. Jemma checked her watch; it was early afternoon. She told herself that was why things were strange. Carl strolled beside her, his long legs eating up the ground.

They turned into her road, and Jemma fumbled for her keys. 'Here we are,' she said, waving her hand at the once-grand townhouse. 'I'm on the top floor. Sorry.'

'Doesn't matter,' said Carl. 'It's a place of your own.'

'Yes,' said Jemma, and turned the key.

The *B* on her door was still wonky, which Jemma found somehow comforting. She let them in, glad that she had had a quick tidy round that morning, folded the sofa-bed up properly, and done the breakfast dishes. 'Would you like tea, or coffee?'

'Tea, please,' said Carl. 'Three sugars.'

Jemma's eyebrows shot up. 'Three?'

He grinned. 'I need the energy. Especially after today, and you should probably have an extra one, too. Isn't it supposed to be good for shock?'

'I'm not in—' said Jemma. Then she got two mugs out of the cupboard, and put the kettle on. A moment later she reopened the cupboard, reached to the back, and pulled out the untouched packet of emergency Bourbons. She checked the best-before date, grimaced, and put a few on a plate. If this wasn't the time for emergency biscuits, she didn't know when it would be.

'Thanks,' said Carl, when she handed him his mug. 'So...'

Jemma sat down in the opposite corner of the sofa. 'So, what?'

He met her eyes. 'Do you understand what happened today?'

Jemma shook her head, took a biscuit, eased the top off and dunked it in her tea. 'Not really. I mean, I've seen some things, of course I have, but – not like that.'

Carl put his mug down on the coffee table. 'What sort of things have you seen?'

So Jemma told him about the stock's mysterious habit of being exactly what was required, and the occasional changes of temperature and atmosphere, and the casual tricks the shop played on her when it was in the mood. The more she said, the deeper Carl's frown became.

'So you're saying that you think it's magic,' he said. 'The shop . . . is magic.'

Jemma shrugged. 'You have to admit it's the simplest explanation.' She sipped her sweet tea, screwed her mouth up, and reached for another biscuit. Then she caught sight of Carl's expression, and her hand stopped in mid-air. 'What?'

'But it can't be,' said Carl. He drank more tea, then put his mug down on the table with a clack. 'It just can't.'

'Yeah, I used to ignore it, too,' said Jemma. 'I used to tell myself that it was impossible, and that it must be a coincidence.' And then she told him about the underground river and the octopus.

Carl's frown now looked as if it would be permanently etched on his face. 'He came up soaking wet?'

'Yup,' said Jemma. 'He left a puddle on the floor. And when Raphael pulled the carpet back again, it had all disappeared.'

Carl huffed out a breath, shaking his head. 'OK. Fine.' He drank more tea. 'So we'll go along with the bookshop being magic, and possibly the cat, and maybe Raphael as well.' He grimaced as if he couldn't believe what he was saying. 'Even assuming all that, what happened today?'

219

'The shop reacted to Luke,' said Jemma. 'He looked terrible when he arrived, and he was really late. Either he was doing something the shop didn't like before he came to work, or else the shop tried to stop him getting there at all. When he did come in, it started misbehaving.'

'Yes, and it got worse when he pulled his phone out,' said Carl.

Jemma thought. 'Did he phone anyone, or did you see him send a message?'

'If he did, I didn't see him,' said Carl. 'He pulled the phone out, stared at it, then put it back in his pocket. I assume he got a message.'

'Well, short of confiscating his phone, we can't find out what the message was,' said Jemma. 'I doubt he'll tell us.'

'That's if we ever see him again,' said Carl. 'He said sorry when he left, didn't he?'

Jemma stared at Carl. 'Do you think he'd just leave?'

It was Carl's turn to shrug. 'It's possible. And it was obviously him causing the trouble. But what did he do?'

Jemma thought of the missing books, and the box she had pulled out full of books with *Lost* in the title. 'Something's been lost,' she said, 'or taken. The minute Raphael saw what was in that box, he threw us out and went to the stockroom.'

'Which is full of books,' said Carl. 'Are any of them valuable?'

'Some will be,' said Jemma. 'Sometimes antiquarian booksellers visit him to buy books.' She told Carl about the deal he had struck with Brian, and the money that had changed hands. 'But while it's a lot of money for a book, it isn't megabucks. I mean, if you were picking any type of shop to steal from, you'd never choose a bookshop.'

'Not unless you really like books,' said Carl. 'Maybe that's why Raphael was so angry. It isn't that the books are particularly valuable, it's more that someone might have taken one.'

Jemma ran her finger around the rim of her cup. 'Luke likes the stockroom,' she said. 'He eats his lunch in there, and he scans books in there. He doesn't seem to like working upstairs in the shop, but he likes the stockroom.' She sighed. 'Maybe he has taken some books.'

'Could there be anything else in that room?' asked Carl. 'Maybe something you don't know about.'

Jemma managed a smile. 'If I don't know about it, then I wouldn't know.'

Carl grinned sheepishly. 'True. So what we've got is that Raphael is mad at us all, and probably going through everything in the stockroom right now to see what's left. Luke, I assume, won't show his face again, and he'll be sacked if he does.' He gazed into the middle distance, then shifted himself round to look at Jemma. 'Do you think the shop will carry on?'

Jemma stared at him, round-eyed. 'He can't close the shop! It's been there for ever! Raphael's run it for years. He won't close it over a book or two going missing.'

'Sorry,' said Carl. 'It was just – he looked so angry. I mean, no one would be pleased to come back to a power cut, then work out that someone's been helping themselves to stock, but he looked...' He frowned as he searched for the right word. 'Apocalyptic.'

Jemma shivered. She had put her pretty dress on that morning, and going by the weather forecast, hadn't bothered to add a cardigan or jacket. 'Excuse me a moment,' she said. She went to the corner cupboard, took out the first cardigan she saw, a thick cream one, and huddled herself in it. 'He can't close the shop,' she murmured. 'What would I do?'

Carl reached over and patted her woolly arm. 'Don't listen to me, I'm probably talking rubbish. And if he did, it wouldn't matter. You could get a job anywhere. You could manage another bookshop, or even open one of your own—'

'With what, exactly?' Jemma shot back. 'Look at this place.' She waved her hand at the tired walls and drooping curtains. 'If I

221

could afford to set up a bookshop in the middle of London, do you think I'd be living somewhere like this?'

'OK, it was just an idea,' said Carl. 'You could work in another bookshop. Whatever you wanted.'

Jemma stared at him, the lump in her throat growing bigger. 'I was let go,' she muttered.

Carl leaned closer. 'I'm sorry, I didn't catch that.'

'I was let go,' she enunciated very precisely. 'From my previous job. I was an analyst, and they made me redundant. Just me. Nobody else. I came in early, I went home late, and they still got rid of me. Finding the bookshop was a complete accident. And now I've messed that up too.' She hid her face in her hands and tried to stop her shoulders shaking.

She felt Carl shift closer, and with a careful hand he gave her shoulder a tentative rub. That made the floodgates open completely. She found a crumpled tissue in her pocket and did the best she could with it, though wiping her eyes seemed to make them stream even more. Carl continued to rub her shoulder gently, saying nothing.

Eventually Jemma cried herself out, managed to dab at her eyes once more with her soggy tissue, and apart from an occasional sniffle, was silent. 'Raphael doesn't know about that,' she whispered. 'That I was made redundant, I mean. I've never told him.'

'He doesn't need to know,' said Carl. 'And I don't think he'd care if he did. He's not that kind of guy.'

Jemma sighed a long, shuddery sigh. 'But what kind of guy is he? I thought I knew him – well, as much as anyone does – but after today…'

'A couple of things are clear,' said Carl. 'Firstly, there's stuff in that stockroom you don't know about, and Raphael's worried that it's been taken. Secondly, the shop reckons that Luke's been up to no good – maybe stealing stuff, maybe something else – and it wants to get rid of him. And thirdly, Raphael is hopping mad and there's no point trying to talk to him until he's calmed down, which hopefully will be tomorrow.'

Jemma sat for a while, thinking. 'You forgot fourthly,' she said.

Carl raised an eyebrow. 'OK, what's fourthly?'

'Fourthly,' said Jemma, draining her mug and putting it down, 'we haven't had lunch and it's mid-afternoon. I don't know about you, but I'm hungry, and I want to forget all this for as long as I can.' A small smile tugged at the corners of her mouth, and finally succeeded in raising them a centimetre or so. 'So I think we should go out, get food, and watch a big stupid movie.'

Carl raised the other eyebrow. 'So let me get this straight. You're kind of inviting me for lunch and a movie?'

Jemma studied Carl's face. He didn't look horrified at the idea; in fact, he looked rather pleased. 'Yes, I am.'

He grinned. 'Just making sure. And yes, you're right; we definitely should. I can't think why I didn't include that in my summing up. But no scary movies, OK?'

Jemma laughed. 'OK.' And as she got up to wash her face and try and make herself look as if she hadn't been sobbing her heart out a few minutes earlier, she reflected that while the day had been, by anyone's standards, a complete disaster, that was only so far.

Chapter 15

Jemma rode the tube into central London the next morning with a sense of foreboding gnawing at her insides. Would Raphael let her in? Would the shop still be there? And what if Luke showed up?

She had arranged to meet Carl at Embankment tube station, and walk to the shop together. 'I know you could go alone,' Carl had said. 'I could, too. But it's – safer if we go together.'

Lunch had been pizza, at a place where Jemma had a discount card, followed by an early movie at a small cinema. During lunch they had avoided the subject of the shop entirely. Instead Carl had talked a little about his ambitions, the handful of acting jobs he had done, and Rumpus, the small theatre group he and a few ex-student friends had set up. 'But it's not just money that's the problem,' he said. 'Rehearsal space. Time to rehearse, even. We've all got jobs of sorts, and sometimes there's no room for anything else.'

'Maybe you could rehearse downstairs at the bookshop,' Jemma said, without thinking.

'Mmm,' said Carl. 'Anyway, that's enough about me. What do you do, besides work?'

Jemma briefly considered inventing an impressive hobby, like tapestry or wild swimming. Then she looked at Carl's face. *He's genuinely interested in me.*

'Not that much, really, apart from reading,' she said, nudging a pizza crust around her plate. 'My previous job took up a lot of time, and, well, you know what it's like.' She smiled. 'I'm getting into cooking, though.' She told him about the books she had borrowed, and the recipes she'd tried, and a couple of the disasters she'd had.

I probably shouldn't mention this, she thought, even as she was describing the world's driest Victoria sponge. But Carl laughed, and didn't seem bothered at all. 'That's one reason why I still live at home,' he said. 'Apart from not being able to afford my own place, my mum's cooking is awesome. Unlike mine.'

Carl saw her to the tube when the movie was over. 'Did you enjoy it?' he asked, when they were nearing the ticket barrier.

'They could have made more of the ending,' said Jemma. 'I was expecting a bigger explosion, to be honest.'

Carl smiled. 'I meant . . . this afternoon.'

Jemma felt herself flush pink, a sudden burn that shocked her. 'Of course I did! It was – it was just what I needed. Time away from – you know.'

'I know,' said Carl. 'Well, I suppose we should, um...' He bit his lip. 'I'm not very good at this bit.'

'Neither am I,' said Jemma. 'I'll see you tomorrow, about eight thirty. Um, yeah.' And, not quite sure if it was what she ought to be doing, she stepped towards him, stood on tiptoe, and kissed him on the cheek. Then she moved away and busied herself getting her Oyster card out. She hurried to the ticket barrier, head down, and only looked back when she reached the stairs. Carl was watching her, a little smile on his face. Jemma smiled, waved, and disappeared.

***

Carl was waiting outside the tube station, as arranged. 'How are you feeling?' he asked.

'Nervous,' said Jemma. 'You?'

'Same.' He fell into step beside her. 'Mostly, I'm hoping I still have a job.'

We ought to talk tactics, thought Jemma. *I ought to have a plan.* She frowned. *Why don't I have a plan? I always have a plan. You don't have a plan*, said her annoying wiser self, *because when you got home last night you ate toast, watched crap on the telly, and flicked through Hello magazine. How could you plan for this, anyway?*

Thanks for nothing. She pushed her inner voice back into the cupboard and closed the door on her.

When they arrived at the bookshop, the blind was down but the lights were on. Jemma and Carl exchanged glances. 'Guess we'd better knock,' said Jemma. She lifted the knocker a little way, and executed three polite taps.

They waited. Jemma was about to knock again when she heard a key rattle in the lock. A few moments later, the door opened an inch or so and a blue eye blinked at them. 'Um, hello,' said Raphael.

'Hello,' said Jemma.

The door opened a little wider. 'Is it just you two?' asked Raphael.

'Yes,' said Carl.

The door swung open. They stepped in, and he locked the door behind them.

Jemma held her breath as she looked from Raphael to the shop. She had expected carnage; but to her surprise, everything seemed more or less in order. The shelves weren't quite as neat as usual, with some books sticking out a centimetre or two, and the counter could do with a polish, but otherwise... 'Have you had to do a lot of work?'

'I must apologise for yesterday,' said Raphael. 'I was worried about the stock, and I over-reacted. As it turns out, everything is as it should be, but I needed to send you home so that I could make absolutely sure.'

'But there are thousands of books in the stockroom,' said Jemma. 'It must have taken you all night.'

Raphael smiled thinly. 'Not if you know how to look,' he said. 'And luckily, I do. Shall I put the kettle on?'

'Not yet,' said Jemma. 'I'm glad nothing is missing, but what happened? Did you think something had been taken? What have you got in there, Raphael? *Is* it just books?'

She heard a small meow at her feet, glanced down, and gasped. 'What's happened to Folio?'

She crouched down and inspected the cat as she stroked him. Folio seemed a little smaller than usual, his fur rougher, and his usually pristine white paws were dusty. Even his eyes had lost a little of their shine. She tickled him under the chin and looked up at Raphael. 'What's going on?'

Raphael sighed. 'I had a feeling it would come to this.' He went into the back room. They heard running water, and the clack of mugs on the worktop. Raphael reappeared so suddenly that Jemma jumped. 'But you are both sworn to secrecy. Understand?'

'Yes,' they said, together.

Raphael's eyes moved to Carl. 'And the only reason that I'm telling you is because I suspect that if I don't, Jemma will tell you anyway.'

Raphael led them downstairs, and they sat at one of the café tables. 'I should have thought of this earlier,' said Raphael. 'Carl could have made us fancy drinks.'

'Please, Raphael,' said Jemma, shifting uncomfortably in her seat. 'Whatever it is, just tell us.'

Raphael fiddled with his spoon. 'It's not that easy,' he said. 'It isn't the sort of thing you tell people every day.'

227

Jemma looked at his hangdog expression. 'Is it really bad?' she asked. 'Will you get in trouble?'

Raphael stared at her. 'What do you mean? Of course I won't get in trouble. I'm one of the people *stopping* the trouble.'

Jemma stared back. 'What trouble?'

'Please tell us, Raphael,' said Carl. 'After yesterday, we're worried.'

'I understand that,' said Raphael. 'And I appreciate that you did your best. I daresay it would have been a lot worse if you two hadn't been in the shop.' He sat up straight and took a deep breath. 'The shop… The shop is not just a bookshop, but a repository of knowledge.'

Carl frowned. 'Well, yeah.'

Raphael smiled. 'I don't mean that in the usual sense. What I mean is that, as well as being a fairly normal secondhand bookshop, the shop also holds several more interesting volumes. These are sources and reference works for rare and arcane knowledge not available to the general public. Taken as single books, they are extremely valuable. But in certain combinations…' His gaze moved from Jemma to Carl, and back again. 'They are more powerful than you could imagine.'

Jemma picked up her mug and sipped automatically as she tried to comprehend what Raphael was saying. 'Is it secrets?' She considered her next word. 'Spells?'

'It can be anything, and everything,' said Raphael. 'Embargoed knowledge, banned books. Even marginalia; scribbled notes by the finest minds of the centuries.' He looked at their blank faces. 'OK, think of an egg.'

'*What?*' said Carl.

'No, go on, this will help,' said Raphael. 'Think of an egg. It's one thing, but you can combine it with other things in lots of different ways. So you could make an omelette, or a cake. Two very different things, but they both need the egg. So the books, and the pamphlets, and the other things which I keep are like special ingredients. You can combine them in all sorts of ways, and potentially, do all sorts of things. And if my ingredients got into the wrong hands—'

'They could cook up something dangerous,' said Carl. 'OK, but why are the books kept here? Why not in the British Library?'

'That's where people would expect them to be,' said Raphael. 'So obviously you'd never put them there. Let's face it, who'd think this place had anything except for lightly used mass-market books?'

'So the shop is a front,' said Jemma. She drank some more tea. Her head was beginning to swim. 'And when you said you didn't want people coming here and asking questions, and you wanted the shop to stay in balance, that was why.'

'That's exactly it,' said Raphael.

'Oh,' said Jemma. A wave of guilt swept over her, and she blinked. 'So, this thing with Luke yesterday… Do you think he tried to steal something?'

Raphael sighed. 'I don't know. On balance, I think not. The shop thinks he's up to no good, clearly.' He rubbed his nose. 'I wanted to give him a chance, even though I could see there might be problems. But it's backfired.'

'Do you think,' said Jemma, in a small voice, 'that it's happened because – because of things I did? Because the shop's doing better now?'

'No,' said Raphael. 'Well, not directly. The changes to the shop may have accelerated the process, but I'm sure it would have happened anyway. These things do occur every so often, and there's not much I can do about it except stay alert.'

Jemma felt as if a huge weight had been lifted off her. 'So what do you *do*, exactly?'

Raphael considered, stirring his tea absently as he did so. 'Without going into unnecessary detail, I'm a Keeper. I store the knowledge sources I possess in optimum conditions, far enough apart so that no adverse reactions can occur, and occasionally I acquire new ones.'

'But the stockroom isn't even locked,' said Jemma.

'It doesn't need to be,' said Raphael. 'If an unauthorised person tried to take a knowledge source, things would happen.'

'Is that what happened yesterday?' asked Jemma. 'With all the lost and gone and missing books?'

'Not quite, no,' said Raphael. 'But I was worried that someone with strong skills might have bypassed the security somehow. What you saw yesterday was not an alert, but a warning. Throwing you out was a precaution, really.'

'When you say strong skills,' said Carl, 'I take it you don't mean that they're handy with a crowbar, or at picking a lock.'

Raphael smiled. 'No, no. In our line of work, things are different.'

'So there's more than one of you?' asked Jemma.

'Oh yes,' said Raphael. 'It would be a terribly hard job to keep hold of all the powerful writings in the world, wouldn't it? Apart from anything else, you'd need an awful lot of room to store them properly, without repercussions. No, there are people like me in cities all over the world. New York, and Paris, and Athens, and so on.'

'So you're the Keeper for London,' said Jemma. She felt as if she were standing on the point of a pin, on top of the Empire State Building, in a high wind. The world that she thought she knew had changed utterly.

'Sort of,' said Raphael. 'There was talk of moving HQ to somewhere else, like Birmingham or Oxford or Manchester, but everyone agreed that with so many bookshops in London it would be foolish to shift it. So I'm based in London, but I look after England, in general. Not just me, I have Assistant Keepers too. Some here, some in other places.'

'Wow,' said Carl, gazing at Raphael as if he'd never seen him before. 'So you're, like, the Keeper for England?'

Raphael made a rueful face. 'It is a bit ridiculous, isn't it? But yes, that's me.' He drank half his mug of tea in one go. 'That wasn't as bad as I thought it would—'

They jumped at a knock on the door upstairs. 'That's weird,' said Carl. 'I mean, I can't usually hear the door down here.'

'Yes,' said Raphael. Suddenly, his face was stern. 'And the fact that we can still hear it loud and clear means that I know exactly who it is.'

Chapter 16

'What do we do?' asked Jemma. 'It's Luke, isn't it?'

'We go upstairs,' said Raphael, 'and we let him in. And then we ask him what exactly he's been doing.'

Jemma realised as she climbed the steps that she was still clutching her mug as if it would protect her. She put it in the sink as they went through the back room, and wiped her hands on her jeans. She felt shivery at the thought of the confrontation that was about to take place.

Raphael, however, seemed calm; jaunty, even. 'Perhaps he will be able to explain himself,' he said. 'I doubt it, though.' He unlocked the door and flung it open.

Luke stood on the doorstep. His shoulders drooped, his head was bowed, and his hair hung in lank tendrils. He looked as if he had been crying. 'I wasn't sure you'd open the door to me,' he muttered.

Raphael eyed him. 'You don't seem particularly dangerous,' he said. 'Are you coming in, or what?'

'You're letting him come in?' said Jemma. 'After yesterday?'

'Yes, I am,' said Raphael. 'Luke ought to be given a chance to explain, and I for one would like to know more about the possible reasons for yesterday's events.' He motioned towards the interior of the shop, and Luke walked meekly in.

'I'm watching you,' said Jemma. 'Raphael may be prepared to talk to you, but I'm not sure I am.'

Raphael looked at her, an eyebrow raised. 'Jemma, if you could leave this to me.' He turned to Luke. 'What did you do yesterday?' He indicated the armchair. 'Sit down, please, and tell me.'

Luke eyed the chair, and blinked. 'Can we go downstairs?'

Raphael glanced at the window. 'I don't think that's necessary. Sit down, Luke, and explain.'

Luke shrugged. 'I didn't do anything,' he said, and flopped into the armchair. 'I don't know why it all happened.'

'You must have done something,' said Jemma. 'The shop was perfectly normal until you came in, what was it, three hours late?'

'I—' Luke swallowed. 'I got held up.'

Jemma snorted, but at another glance from Raphael she said no more.

'Jemma's right,' said Carl. 'You showed up, and everything turned weird. Even the air was weird. And books went missing, and the customers were fighting, and then there was a power cut.' He gave Luke a hard stare. 'You did something, man.'

Luke raised his hands, and let them fall on the arms of the chair. 'I didn't,' he said. 'I just tried to do my best with the customers, and everything kept going wrong.'

Raphael was staring at him too. 'Let's say, for a moment, that you didn't do anything you shouldn't have yesterday,' he said. 'Why would the shop make things difficult for you? Why might it want to stand in your way?' He caught Jemma's pleading look. 'Luke is an intelligent young man. I'm sure he is perfectly aware that this is not a normal shop, so I won't pretend that it is.' He waited. 'I'll give you one more chance, and that's it.'

Luke's hands tightened on the arms of the chair. 'I didn't do anything yesterday,' he said. 'Or the day before, or the day before that. The only time I did do anything was in the first week. I was on trial, and I figured it didn't matter, because you probably wouldn't keep me on.'

Jemma felt the blood drain from her face, and put a hand on the counter to steady herself. 'What did you do?' she asked, her mouth dry.

'I wish you wouldn't look at me like that,' said Luke, irritably. 'It wasn't anything terrible. It was just – I passed on some information, that was all. To another bookseller.'

Raphael took a step closer. 'Now we're getting somewhere,' he said. 'What sort of information?'

'He wanted to know how the shop was organised – or not organised.' He smiled, briefly. 'And he asked me to find out and tell him what sort of stock you had, and where you were buying books.'

Raphael held his gaze. 'Did you?'

'Not after the first week,' said Luke. 'You were all so nice to me, and I felt as if – as if I belonged. Which I've probably wrecked now.' His pale-green eyes rested on them in turn. 'The bookseller kept badgering me for more information, and after a while I fed him fake stuff. I don't think he guessed.'

Carl frowned. 'When you were looking at your phone yesterday, was it a message from him?'

Luke nodded. 'It was.'

'And who is this mysterious bookseller?' asked Raphael.

Luke took a long time to answer. 'I can't tell you. I'm sorry, but I can't.'

'We could get his phone, maybe, and find out that way,' said Carl, moving forward a little.

Raphael shook his head. 'No, we won't be doing that.'

'All right, let's call the police, then,' said Jemma, eyeing the Bakelite phone nearby.

'Again, that's a no,' said Raphael. 'We can deal with this perfectly well on our own.' He studied Luke. 'I assume this – person has a hold over you, and that's why you won't give me his name.' He checked his watch. 'Well, it's five past nine, and given that we lost most of yesterday afternoon's trading, we should open up.' He walked to the window and threw up the blind. 'I'll run things here. Jemma, please go downstairs with Carl.'

'That's it?' Jemma stared at Luke, who first looked away, then hid his face in his hands. 'You're going to let him stay?'

Raphael glanced at him before replying. 'The shop doesn't seem bothered by him today, so provided he stays somewhere we can keep an eye on him, it shouldn't be a problem.' He smiled. 'And if he's been feeding false information to an enemy, it may even be useful to keep him.'

Jemma was still shaking her head in disbelief as he turned the sign on the front door. 'I give up,' she murmured. Carl reached for her hand, and squeezed it.

They looked up as the door opened. 'Oh, I'm so glad you're open,' said a reedy voice. An elderly lady shuffled in, her stick thunking on the parquet. 'I was here yesterday, but unfortunately you had a power cut and I wasn't able to buy the book I wanted.'

'Yes, sorry about that,' said Jemma. 'Which book was it?'

'*Excellent Women*, by Barbara Pym.' She said the name very precisely. 'I think I put it on one of the little tables.'

'I'll go and see,' said Jemma. 'I shouldn't be long.'

She ran downstairs, and tensed for a moment as she opened the great oak door; but behind it, things appeared normal. The lights were on, and the lower floor was its usual imposing but welcoming self. Jemma took a deep, experimental breath. Yes, the air was fresher. She sighed with relief. Raphael had cleared the tables and re-shelved the books, but *Excellent Women* was shelved under P in General Fiction, just as it should be.

She took the book upstairs and handed it to Raphael. 'Would

235

you mind serving this lady, please? I'll take a couple of boxes down, then we're all set.'

'Good idea,' said Raphael. He looked inside the cover. 'That will be two pounds, please. Would you like a bag?'

Jemma went to the stockroom and chose a box on which Luke had written *CRIME* in neat capitals. *Will it have crime books in it, though? Might he have mislabelled it to confuse us?* She couldn't work out what was most likely. *The easiest way is to open it and see.*

She took the box through to the shop, and hunted for the scissors. Luke turned his head, and at the sight of the box he relaxed.

Jemma snipped at the tape holding the box closed and peeled it off, then lifted the flaps and peered inside. Her brow furrowed. 'That isn't what I expected.'

Raphael leaned over and looked into the box. He glanced at Jemma, then pushed the flaps closed. 'Is that everything for today?' he asked the customer.

She giggled. 'Oh yes, just the one today, but I'm sure you'll see me again.' She beamed at them all, then began to thunk towards the door. Raphael came out from behind the counter, scurried around her, and held the door open. As soon as she had gone, he locked it.

'Mind if I open it now?' asked Jemma, with rather a resentful look. She reached in, took out the first book, and laid it on the counter.

Dracula.

'What the—' cried Luke. 'I put crime books in there, I know I did!'

She reached in again.

Interview with a Vampire.

Twilight.

A *Buffy the Vampire Slayer* novelisation.

'I don't believe it,' Luke whispered, his face pale as death. 'This bloody shop.'

Carl looked at the books, then at Luke, then back at the books. He blinked, several times. Then he stared at Luke. 'You're a vampire?'

Luke gazed at him miserably, and said nothing.

'That's why you don't like working upstairs, isn't it?' said Jemma. 'Because of the light. And that's why you dived under the counter when Stella took a photo of you. And why you don't ever eat lunch with us.' She shook her head. 'I – I don't know what to say.'

Luke's eyes moved from one to the other of them. His bottom lip started to tremble, and he burst into sobs. Apart from his noisy crying, the room was completely silent.

Chapter 17

Jemma looked at Carl, who shrugged, his expression nonplussed. Then she eyed Raphael, who was watching Luke. He didn't appear remotely surprised. 'How did you know?' she asked.

'I wasn't sure at first,' said Raphael. 'I had a suspicion at the interview, and subsequent events bore it out.'

Luke's sobs were beginning to ease a little, and the space between them was growing. Raphael took a large white handkerchief from his trouser pocket and touched Luke's hand with it. Luke grabbed it, buried his face in it, and continued to cry more quietly.

Jemma wasn't sure what to think. *Should I be scared?* But Luke wasn't scary in the slightest. As for biting people – if anything, he seemed to prefer being alone. She thought over his interactions with her, and concluded that maybe she just wasn't his blood type. Or type, full stop. While that was a relief, she had to admit to feeling the tiniest bit offended.

'Erm, would anyone like a cup of tea?' she asked. 'I know we've just had one, but—'

'What a good idea,' said Raphael. 'Why don't you and Carl go and make it?' When he spoke again, his voice was softer. 'Luke, would you like a cup of tea?'

Luke's shoulders stiffened, then he said, through the handkerchief, 'Yes please. Could I have decaf?'

'We'll go and do that, then,' said Jemma. 'Come on, Carl.' He was still gazing at Luke, with an expression that suggested he didn't know what to do with him. She touched his arm, and pointed towards the back room.

'This place is doing my head in,' whispered Carl, as Jemma filled the kettle. 'First magic, now vampires.'

Jemma looked at him. 'Are you scared? I feel as if I should be, but I'm not.'

'I haven't had time to be scared,' said Carl. 'I mean, I thought vampires were meant to be all dramatic and creepy and dangerous, but he's just pale and weedy.' He leaned closer. 'You don't think Raphael is a vampire, do you? I mean, they say it takes one to know one.'

'I doubt it,' said Jemma. 'If he craves anything, it's pastry and caffeine. And then there's his clothes. At least Luke dresses in black.' She smiled. 'Thinking about it now, I can't believe I didn't spot it. But then, everyone knows that vampires aren't real.' She snorted. 'Then again, I didn't believe in magic six months ago.'

'I wonder what Raphael's saying to him,' said Carl.

'Your guess is as good as mine,' said Jemma. She hoped that, whatever it was, Luke would have stopped crying when they went back in. It was awful watching other people cry, particularly when you had a suspicion that you might be partly responsible.

Jemma let the tea brew for quite a while before taking the tray through. When she did, she found Raphael crouching beside Luke's chair, speaking quietly. He saw her, murmured something, then stood up and moved back a little. While Luke looked forlorn and wan, and still let out an occasional hiccup, he appeared much calmer. He accepted the mug that Jemma handed to him, and

239

sipped slowly.

'Luke and I have had a chat,' said Raphael. Jemma and Carl exchanged glances. 'He has assured me that he is a non-practising vampire.'

Jemma frowned. 'Can you do that? I mean, don't you die?'

Luke shot her a pained glance.

'OK, I'm sorry if that's a stupid question,' she said. 'I'm not particularly knowledgeable about vampires. Until now, I haven't needed to be.'

'You're quite safe,' said Luke, with a thin smile. 'I've been clean for over three hundred years. That's the last time I bit a human.'

Carl stared. 'But you look like you're about my age.'

Luke's smile broadened a little. 'That's one of the few benefits, I suppose.'

'So how do you manage without biting people?' asked Jemma.

Luke's eyes narrowed. Then he shrugged. 'You've probably noticed I carry a drinks bottle with me.'

Jemma gasped. 'Don't tell me it's—'

'No it is *not*,' said Luke. 'I drink a blood substitute. It has the same nutrients as blood, and looks and tastes fairly similar, but actually it's vegan.'

'Vegan blood?' said Carl. 'Where do you get that, the health-food shop?'

Luke smiled. 'You can get anything off the internet. I also eat raw meat when it's convenient, which it often isn't. And when I'm absolutely desperate, I go and find a pigeon. Trafalgar Square's handy for that. They're nice and plump because the tourists feed them.'

'So there are probably vampire pigeons in Trafalgar Square?' Jemma grabbed her own mug of tea and drank deep.

Carl grinned. 'Yeah, but have you ever been pecked by a pigeon?'

'Exactly,' said Luke. 'I figured they were less dangerous than rats.'

'But—' Jemma felt as if her brain was overheating. 'But what happens if the pigeon eats a worm? Or half a worm? Would the bit that didn't get eaten be a vampire worm? Then what?'

Raphael laughed. 'Jemma, you may be overthinking things.'

'Maybe,' snapped Jemma. 'But you can't expect me to say fine, my colleague is a vampire, and accept it. I mean, until today I didn't believe vampires were real, and now I'm drinking tea with one.' She looked at Luke, whose head had drooped again, and immediately felt guilty. 'Luke, I'm sorry if I'm not taking this very well. It's just – vampires get a bad press, you know? I've never met one before. To be honest, you're not what I would have expected.'

He gazed up at her, doubt in his eyes.

'I don't mean that in a bad way,' she said hastily. 'I mean, you seem nice. And a good colleague, when the shop isn't messing about. So I suppose I have to get used to the idea that one of my colleagues happens to be a vampire. And if you don't bite people, then I guess that's OK.'

Luke smiled, then blinked, and a tear rolled down his cheek. 'It means a lot to hear you say that,' he said. 'I'd like to be honest with people, course I would, but when you've been hounded and threatened and had people running after you with stakes as much as I have, you learn to keep quiet.' Then his mouth wobbled again. 'I don't think the shop's prepared to accept me, though. I mean, it outed me.'

Raphael's brow furrowed as he thought. 'The thing with the shop,' he said, 'is that it doesn't really consider people's feelings, even though it's quite sensitive itself. In this case, I suspect the shop had seen what you were, and knew what you had been doing, and sensed that the two were linked. So it concluded that the best way to sort things out was to bring into the open the thing it *could* reveal – that you are a vampire – in the hope that the other matter would follow.' He licked a finger and held it up. 'See how calm the shop is now.'

'That doesn't make it right,' said Jemma. 'And in front of a customer, too.'

Raphael seemed to be considering his answer. 'Maybe the shop trusts us to do the right thing,' he said. 'That said, what is the right thing to do?'

'Well, if the shop isn't being weird with Luke, and he isn't stealing stuff or leaking information, then he can stay,' said Jemma. 'If he wants to.' She looked at Luke. 'Do you want to?'

'Of course I want to,' said Luke. 'I love working here. Now you know, and you're OK with it, and—' He spread his hands wide and smiled. 'I'm really happy. No one has a hold over me any more, and you don't know how good that feels.'

'Oh yes!' cried Jemma. 'You can tell us who the bookseller is!'

'Yes, I can,' said Luke, and suddenly he was grave. 'And I'm afraid it's someone you know.'

'I thought as much,' said Raphael. 'How did he find you? And how did he know about you?'

'Family connection,' said Luke. 'He's my great-great-nephew. Obviously he's known me a long time, and known *of* me, and I guess when he needed someone to spy for him, I was the obvious choice. He made me an offer I couldn't refuse. "Do what I ask," he said, "or I'll expose you for what you are, and you'll have to start all over again somewhere else. If they let you live, that is."' The corner of his mouth twisted up. 'For years I've worked on resisting a lot of the usual dangers, like crucifixes and holy water. Sunlight, to a degree, though as you've seen it makes me uncomfortable. I can even eat a clove of garlic, which gives me mild indigestion. Unfortunately, instilling fear and suspicion and hatred in other people still works like a charm. He knows that only too well, and I doubt he hesitated for a second.'

242

Jemma's eyebrows shot up. 'And he's family? What sort of person would do that to you?'

Luke sipped some more tea. 'A man who is on a mission. He has one ambition, and he will stop at nothing to fulfil it. The Assistant Keeper for Westminster, or as I think of him, my great-great-nephew, Brian.'

Chapter 18

'I knew Brian was dodgy!' cried Jemma.

'You didn't say anything,' said Raphael, with a gleam in his eye.

'That's because I thought it was just me,' said Jemma. 'I mean, you can't go accusing people, but that time when he came in and you sold him that book, I could feel that you two didn't get on.' She turned to Luke. 'So what is he trying to do?'

'Take Raphael's job,' said Luke. 'He told me that from the start. He was completely open about it. That's the sort of person he is.'

'But how?' said Jemma. 'I mean, what will he do, walk in and say "I want your job?" Or is he going to, I don't know, accuse you of something and take you to a tribunal or – or what?'

'Your first answer was pretty much right,' said Raphael. 'Appointment to these positions is pretty informal, and one can be challenged at any time. And yes, Brian could walk in here in the next ten minutes, say, "I challenge you," and kick things off. I don't think he will – not yet – but I've sensed something in the air for a little while.'

'But what *happens*?' said Jemma. She felt as if her grip on reality might be slipping. 'I mean, do you play conkers, or joust, or cast spells—'

'What we do,' said Raphael, 'is we put on our ceremonial robes, and stand on adjacent mountain tops, and throw spells at each other.'

Jemma's jaw dropped.

Raphael chuckled. 'I just wanted to see if you'd swallow that. I'm afraid it's much more prosaic. Basically, it's a duel of knowledge. We are each allowed to present three books. The challenger goes first, and we present the books one by one in turn, announcing the name and author. Once the opponent has verified that the book is what its owner says it is, the book is accepted. The strongest set of three books is victorious. That doesn't necessarily mean the strongest three books will win, though. If you remember what I was saying the other day, it's all about the combination; the three books have to work well together. So using our cake analogy, eggs, butter and flour will work better together than eggs, sardines and jam.'

Jemma made a face. 'OK, I get that. So once the winner is decided, what happens then?'

'It's pretty straightforward,' said Raphael. 'If the incumbent, in this case me, wins, then their post is retained. If Brian wins, he takes my job and everything that goes with it. Except Folio. Folio is a personal item.'

Jemma gasped. 'So he'd get the shop?'

'Yes, he would. And depending on what sort of mood he was in, he could choose to keep you on in his employment, or let you go.'

'I'd never work for Brian,' said Jemma. She nudged Carl.

'No, neither would I,' he said, quickly.

'And I definitely wouldn't,' said Luke. 'I managed a week of doing his bidding, and that was only because he forced me into it.'

245

'That's very touching,' said Raphael. 'I am sorry to put you in this position.'

'If he takes your shop,' said Jemma, 'what happens to you?'

'The rules are clear,' said Raphael. 'The loser is banished from their former sphere of influence for ten years. So in my case, that would be England.'

'That's horrible,' said Carl.

'Them's the rules,' said Raphael. 'Anyway, I believe that Llandudno is very nice at this time of year. Perhaps I could open a little bookshop there while I regroup.'

'But this is your life!' cried Jemma. 'This bookshop's been in your family for ages, you said.' A sudden thought occurred to her, and her eyes narrowed as realisation dawned. 'Hang on a minute. If Brian is Luke's great-great-nephew – and I'm ignoring how weird that is – and Luke is at least three hundred years old, then Brian must be pretty old too. Agreed?'

'Agreed,' said Raphael. 'I perceive the cogs are turning.'

'And you said you were selling books before Brian,' said Jemma. 'So how old are you?'

Raphael smiled. 'I'm as old as my tongue, and a little older than my teeth. To be completely honest with you, I've lost count. After the first couple of hundred, birthdays do get a bit samey.'

'I imagine they would,' murmured Carl. 'I mean, there's only so many pairs of socks you can wear.'

'That's true,' said Raphael. 'I won't need any more socks for at least fifty years. Clothes are different, because fashions change, but socks tend to stay with you.'

'Never mind socks, what are we going to do?' said Jemma. 'You can't lose the bookshop, you just can't!'

'I could,' said Raphael. 'How do you think I got it in the first place?'

Jemma's mouth dropped open. 'You didn't,' she said.

'I'm afraid I did,' said Raphael. 'I challenged the previous

Keeper of England in 1812. The Napoleonic Wars were going on, everyone was a bit distracted, and I'm afraid I took advantage of that. He was getting on a bit, though. Very set in his ways. Never liked printed books. He had some lovely illuminated manuscripts, but there's only so far you can go with most of those. Anyway.' He smiled at the three of them. 'I certainly don't intend to go without a fight. Brian is clearly working himself up for a challenge, and I intend to be a little more ready than he thinks.'

'You're absolutely right, Raphael,' said Luke. 'He told me to give him information on any book that looked – what was the word – venerable.'

Raphael chuckled. 'Ever the antiquarian, Brian. It's one of the things I occasionally chide him for, and he always bristles.' Then his smile faded. 'What did you tell him?'

'I didn't see much in the first week that I could tell him about,' said Luke. 'And since I decided I wasn't playing his game any more, I've told him that most of your stock is cheap paperbacks with an occasional modern first edition.'

'Excellent,' said Raphael. He rubbed his hands. 'I'm sure that Brian was heartened by that news, but we can encourage him still further. Would you mind going to the stockroom and taking out – well, any box.'

Luke stared at him. 'Any box?'

'Yes,' said Raphael. 'I'm sure it will have just the thing.'

Luke looked at him for a long moment. 'If you say so,' he said. He pushed himself out of the armchair, and walked into the back room. Then he popped his head round the door. 'It will let me in, won't it? Nothing will . . . happen?'

'I doubt it,' said Raphael. 'I'd watch out for Folio, though, if he's around. I think he's a little upset with his condition. Hopefully that will improve soon.'

'So Folio and the shop are – sort of bound together?' asked Jemma.

'They are,' said Raphael. 'I rescued Folio from a sack in the Thames, and living in the bookshop is all he knows. I don't know what would happen if he left it.' His face darkened. 'But I wouldn't leave him here with Brian.'

Jemma bit her lip and stared hard at the opening to the back room. Carl's hand slipped into hers, and she curled her fingers round his. He drew her a little closer, and she rested her head against his shoulder. She felt a little better, but not much.

Luke reappeared with a box and put it on the counter. 'Shall I open it?' he asked.

'Usually I'd say yes,' said Raphael, 'but on this occasion, perhaps not.' He got the scissors, slit the box open, and brought out a large, black, leather-bound tome. He blew the dust off it, and regarded it critically. 'Yes, lovely. He *will* like this.' He showed them the spine.

'Lyell, *Principles of Geology*, Volume 1,' read Carl.

'That's the one,' said Raphael. 'First edition, published in 1830. But the important thing about this book is that it was read, and at the same time annotated, by Charles Darwin.'

'*The* Charles Darwin?' said Carl. 'Who used to be on the ten-pound note?'

'The very same,' said Raphael. 'Luke, I want you to take a picture of the title page. That will tell Brian what the book is, and...' He opened the book and they saw, at the top right of the page, a small, neat signature. 'That will seal the deal. I'd like you to send Brian the picture, with the message: *You'll never believe what he's got.*'

'Won't that give him an advantage?' said Jemma. 'He'll know you've got it.'

'He will,' said Raphael. 'What he doesn't know is that I have no intention of using it. I have a combination of books in my head, but this is not one of them.'

'So it's a red herring?' asked Carl.

'Precisely,' said Raphael, and smiled a contented smile. 'Jemma, I have a job for you, too.' He reached into the box and brought out another book. This one was slimmer, and bound in maroon cloth. 'Have you ever heard of a place called Sir John Soane's Museum?'

'No, sorry,' said Jemma. 'I'm not a big fan of museums.'

Raphael rolled his eyes. 'I despair of young folk sometimes, I really do,' he said. 'Anyway. Look it up on the internet. It isn't far away, in Holborn. What I want you to do is stroll round – it doesn't open till ten – ask to see the Assistant Curator, and give her this book, along with a note that I shall write for you. She will give you another book in exchange. Put it in your bag, then return as quickly as you can. If at all possible, take a taxi. It is absolutely imperative that you lose no time.'

Jemma swallowed. 'OK.'

'And what about me?' asked Carl. 'Do you have a job for me?'

'Oh yes,' said Raphael. 'We must reopen the shop shortly, as I wish everything to appear as normal as it ever is in this place, and we shall be a shop manager down. During Jemma's hopefully short absence, I shall run things up here. Luke, I shall need you downstairs. And Carl, I shall require you to supply me with strong coffee and items of sugary pastry at regular intervals. I have a lot of thinking to do, and I need to keep my strength up.'

Carl grinned. 'You're on. I don't know much about books, but hot beverages and pastry are absolutely my thing.' Then he looked worried. 'But we haven't got any fresh stuff in yet. Have I got time to go round to Rolando's before Jemma leaves?'

'Of course,' said Raphael. 'Oh, and could you ask Giulia if she could include some cinnamon rolls?'

Jemma frowned. 'Don't you mean Rolando?'

'Not on this occasion,' said Raphael. 'She knows that if I use her name, it's important. Believe me, her cinnamon rolls have powers that you can only dream of.'

Carl's eyes widened. 'You mean they're magical?'

'No.' Raphael grinned. 'But they are exceptionally tasty, and I always do my best thinking with a cinnamon roll in my hand. And today, to get the better of Brian, the very best thinking is required.'

Chapter 19

Jemma stared doubtfully at the Georgian townhouse before her. It didn't look like any museum she'd ever visited. It just looked like a nice big house in a leafy London square.

Carl had returned from Rolando's with two trays of pastries and Giulia herself, who was clutching a brown-paper bag and a book. She burst through the front door and immediately hurled a stream of Italian at Raphael, thrusting the bag and the book at him. He held his hands up, then, after a rapid exchange of Italian, he took her into the back room.

'I'd better go,' said Jemma. 'You two, get ready to open.'

And now she was at her destination. A young man in jeans and an open-necked white shirt stood at the entrance. 'Are you coming in?' he asked.

'Yes, please,' said Jemma. 'Do I need to pay?'

'No, it's free.' He smiled at her. 'But could you switch off your mobile phone' – he eyed the phone in her hand – 'and put your bag in the cloakroom.'

'Ah,' said Jemma. 'There could be a slight problem with that. I have a note and a book for the Assistant Curator.'

A tiny crease appeared between the young man's eyebrows. 'In that case, the best thing to do is to take the book and the note out, and someone in the shop will summon the AC.' He nodded, seemingly pleased with his solution, and handed her a clear plastic bag. Jemma did as she had been told, and proceeded inside.

The shop was to her left past the cloakroom, all art books and curios and pretty jewellery. Jemma explained to the shop assistant, who picked up the telephone. She spoke quietly into the receiver, then listened. 'I'm sorry,' she said to Jemma, 'but who did you say you were?'

'I didn't, but I'm Jemma James, from Burns Books.'

The shop assistant relayed this information, listened once more, then replaced the receiver gently in its cradle. 'She's on her way,' she said. 'If you'd like to go into the next room, she will meet you there.'

Jemma wandered into the next room, which was lined with books. *What a house to live in*, she thought. It was dark, probably to preserve the items within. She was studying a painting on an easel when a small cough made her jump. A few feet away stood a petite woman with a shiny black bob, wearing black trousers and a cream blouse with little blue flowers on. 'Jemma James?' she asked, holding out her hand. 'I am the Assistant Curator. Please come this way.' She took Jemma first down into the kitchen, then into one of the strangest rooms that Jemma had ever seen. If she had thought the gift shop was full of items, it was nothing compared to this. Statues and busts and stone mouldings stood everywhere, and in the middle was a giant sarcophagus.

'He was quite a collector,' said the Assistant Curator.

'I can see that,' said Jemma. From this room they went up a different set of stairs, then into a room which seemed to be a library. To be honest, Jemma wasn't sure what anything was. 'Is this where the book is?' she asked.

The Assistant Curator didn't answer, but went to one of the

bookshelves and pressed a knot in the wood. The bookshelf opened like a cupboard, and she beckoned Jemma through.

On the other side of the door was a small library of perhaps five hundred books. The rest of the room was painted white, and its lack of decoration, in contrast to the rooms Jemma had passed through, made it seem even more bare. In the corner stood a small desk and two chairs. The Assistant Curator waved Jemma to one, and took the other herself. 'May I see your note, please?'

Jemma handed it over. She had thought it odd that Raphael had addressed it to *Assistant Curator*, rather than by name, but now she wondered whether the Assistant Curator had a name at all. Or was she a sort of Keeper, too? The woman picked up a plain silver letter-opener, slit the envelope, and skimmed through the note rapidly. Her expression did not change.

'I see,' she said. 'I'm afraid there is a small problem.'

Jemma's heart plummeted not to her boots, but to the basement kitchen. 'What sort of problem?' she breathed.

'I do apologise,' said the Assistant Curator. 'If I had the book I would gladly give it to you, but it isn't here.'

'Has someone taken it?' Suddenly it was hard to breathe. 'Has an old man visited you? A tall, stooping man with a big white moustache?'

The Assistant Curator regarded her for a long moment. 'It's being restored,' she said. 'We take the best care of the books that we can, but they still deteriorate. It's with a specialist bookbinder in Edinburgh. Well, to be quite honest, it's probably somewhere in the postal system, as we only sent it yesterday.'

If it's in the postal system, thought Jemma, *I doubt even magic can bring it back.* She blinked. 'This is the book Raphael asked me to bring you,' she said, proffering it. 'I don't suppose you have anything similar to the book he asked for?'

The Assistant Curator took the book, inspected it, and re-read the letter. Then she put both on the desk, clasped her hands in front of her, and mused. 'Is everything all right at the bookshop?' she asked.

What should I tell her? What am I allowed to tell her? Jemma wished she had her phone with her, and could consult with Raphael. Then she remembered that Raphael had told her to be quick. 'We think something's going to happen at the bookshop,' she gabbled. 'That's why Raphael wants to swap the books.' She felt even more flustered under the calm gaze of the Assistant Curator.

'I see.' The pause lengthened to a minute. Then the Assistant Curator rose, went to one of the bookshelves, and drew out a curiously shaped book bound in sky blue. It was slim, and much wider than it was tall. 'I'm not sure this will do exactly the same job as the book Raphael wanted,' she said, 'but it may be a good alternative.' She opened the drawer of the desk and drew out a canvas tote bag with the museum's logo on, then slipped the sky-blue book and Jemma's book inside. She pushed it across the desk to Jemma, and got up. 'I'll take you back down,' she said.

'Do I need to sign something?' asked Jemma. 'Or – or fill in a form?'

The Assistant Curator smiled a wintry smile. 'I won't forget. And good luck.'

Jemma hurried through the museum, lingered for a second as she saw some nice earrings in the shop, then reclaimed her bag, put the tote inside it, and stepped out into the not-still air.

A black cab was waiting outside. 'Jemma James?' the driver called.

Jemma nodded. 'Charing Cross Road, please.'

'Don't worry,' said the cabbie. 'I know exactly where you're meant to be.'

London was remarkably quiet, and the journey back to the shop took just a few minutes. Jemma tried to pay the cabbie, who waved her purse away. 'Prepaid, innit,' he said. As soon as she was out of the cab, he drove off.

She turned to the shop and saw Raphael in the doorway. 'Come in, Jemma, quickly. Did you get it?'

Jemma bit her lip, and shook her head. 'It's gone for binding,' she said. 'But the Assistant Curator gave me another book instead, and let me keep yours.' She walked into the shop and found Luke and Carl standing there. She opened her bag and handed the tote to Raphael. He peeped within, then went to the shop door and locked it.

'Why are you both upstairs?' asked Jemma. 'What about the customers?'

'There aren't any,' said Carl. 'We had a couple, early doors, then nothing. It's as if the shop knows.'

'It's as well you came back when you did,' said Raphael. 'I have a feeling that if you'd been five or ten minutes later, you wouldn't have been able to get near.'

'What do you mean?' Jemma shivered, even though the shop didn't seem particularly cold. *It's inside me*, she thought, and tried not to panic.

'You'll probably see later,' said Raphael. 'Now, into the back room with you all. I want to check over this book.'

They followed him in. He laid the tote on the worktop, then took the book out, placed it carefully on top of the canvas, and opened the hard cover. Jemma saw pen-and-ink drawings faded to sepia, and next to them, slanted, reversed writing. Raphael turned another page, and smiled affectionately at it.

'I've seen something like that before,' said Carl. 'This will sound ridiculous, but it was – I think it was on a mouse mat.'

'You're probably right,' said Raphael. 'This is a collection of original drawings bound into a book. They're by someone whose name you probably know: Leonardo da Vinci.'

Jemma, Luke and Carl all goggled at the book. 'This must be worth a fortune,' said Jemma. 'And I've just carried it across

255

London in a canvas bag.' She rubbed her forehead. 'Is there time for a cup of tea?'

A hearty knock at the door made them jump.

'I very much doubt,' said Raphael, 'that there's time for anything.' He closed the book, replaced it in the bag, and walked into the shop. The others followed, and gasped at what they saw. Outside the shop window, London had disappeared. There was only white space; a blank page.

Three more raps.

'Here we go,' said Raphael, and unlocked the door. To no one's surprise, on the doorstep stood Brian.

Chapter 20

'Nice day for it,' said Brian. 'Mind if I come in?' He was carrying a large leather Gladstone bag with shiny brass fastenings.

'I take it this isn't a social call,' said Raphael.

Brian chuckled. 'I'm sure you can work out why I'm here,' he said. He glanced at Luke. 'Still got your new assistant, then?' His eyes twinkled.

'Oh yes,' said Raphael. 'He's doing ever so well. Now, Brian, would you like a cup of tea while I sort myself out?'

'No tea, thank you,' said Brian. He stepped over the threshold and closed the door behind him. His hand stroked the wood as if he already owned it.

'Well, I could do with a cup,' said Raphael. 'And I have fifteen minutes of preparation time.' He strolled into the back room and flicked the kettle on. 'Anyone else want one?'

'Yes, please,' croaked Jemma. Her mouth was dry as a bone.

'And me,' said Carl. 'Here, I'll make it.' He walked into the back room without looking at Brian.

'I'll stick to, um, the usual,' said Luke, getting his drinks bottle from the rucksack which hung on the coat stand. Brian snorted, but turned it into a cough. He sauntered around the shop, peering at the counter, then going behind it and fingering the brown-paper bags on their string. He came out again and ran his finger along a shelf, then inspected it. The only things he didn't inspect were the books. Jemma couldn't take her eyes off him. She felt like a rabbit watching a fox, hoping he hadn't noticed her yet.

'Tea's brewing,' said Raphael. 'I think we'll do this downstairs. I'll join you in a few minutes.'

Brian checked his watch. 'Ten minutes, Raphael. And if you're late, I win by default.' Then he stared as the others walked towards the staircase. 'We're not having *them* in there as well, are we?'

'There's no rule which says that we can't have witnesses,' said Raphael.

'It's hardly fair,' grumbled Brian.

Raphael looked as if he could say many things at this point about what constituted fairness and what did not. But after a second or two he merely replied 'Life isn't fair, is it? Do excuse me.' He opened the stockroom door, and vanished.

Once they had proceeded downstairs with their drinks, Brian surveyed the lower floor of the shop with a professional eye. 'Over there would be best.' He marched to the café area, sat down at a large round table, and stretched his legs out underneath. 'You lot can sit at another table. The last thing we need is you interfering.'

Raphael appeared two minutes later, carrying the now-full tote bag. 'I see you've made yourself comfortable,' he said to Brian.

'Start as you mean to go on,' said Brian. He checked his watch again. 'You cut it a bit fine,' he remarked.

'I'm actually a minute early,' said Raphael. 'Anyone who knows me would tell you that in itself is quite remarkable.'

'Are you ready?' said Brian. He leaned towards the leather bag at his feet, his hand reaching down as he waited for Raphael's answer.

'Oh yes, completely ready,' said Raphael. 'But before we

begin —' He studied Jemma, Carl and Luke, sitting at the adjacent table. 'You three must swear that you will never breathe a word of this to anyone.'

They all nodded, silently.

'I mean it,' said Raphael, looking very serious. 'On Folio's life.'

'Oh man, don't make me say that,' said Carl.

'I wouldn't normally,' said Raphael. 'But it's that important.'

At that moment they heard an angry meow, and a ginger blur streaked across the floor. Folio leapt onto the table and Jemma stared at him. He seemed smaller still, more compact, as if he had somehow condensed himself.

'I'm sorry, Folio,' she said. She stroked him, and he rubbed his cheek against her hand. 'On Folio's life,' she said quietly.

'On Folio's life,' the other two echoed.

Brian sighed. 'It's a ruddy cat,' he said. 'Now, if you've finished messing around, let's get on with it.' He reached down to his bag again. 'I present my first book.' He brought out a large, stout volume bound in ochre leather, and placed it on the table. 'Volume one of Dr Johnson's *Dictionary of the English Language*, 1755. The first dictionary to document the English language properly. I don't think I need to say more.'

Jemma leaned forward. Was she imagining things, or was the book glowing a little?

'A solid opening move,' said Raphael. 'I shall present my first book.' He delved into the canvas bag and brought out the sky-blue book. 'This is a collection of original bound drawings and notes by Leonardo da Vinci.' He set it down in front of him.

'Fancy,' said Brian. 'I take it you won't mind if I verify that.' He opened the book at random, and let page after page fall. A brisk nod. 'Want to check mine?'

Raphael opened the stiff cover of the book, glanced at the title page, and closed it again. 'Looks fine to me.'

Brian exhaled. 'I present book two.' The next book was smaller and clearly ancient; fragile-looking, with uneven yellowish-brown pages. Brian showed a page; writing crosswise over other writing, none of which Jemma could make out. 'May I introduce Archimedes' Palimpsest. You will of course be aware that Archimedes of Syracuse was one of the greatest mathematicians of all time.' Jemma remembered GCSE Maths, and shivered. 'Much of the content of this book was thought to have been lost, and it is centuries ahead of its time.'

'How did you get hold of that?' Raphael asked, quietly.

Brian glared at him. 'Never you mind.'

An eerie glow emanated from the book, and spread to the book beside it. Jemma leaned across to Carl, and whispered as quietly as she could, 'Can you see the books glowing, or is it just me?'

'They're glowing,' he whispered back, his eyes fixed on the books.

Jemma looked at Raphael, her heart in her mouth. What would he bring out next?

Raphael reached into his bag. 'The next one is rather unusual,' he said, and laid a battered book on the table, slightly apart from the first. It had a cover of tooled brown leather, but the design was marred by stains. Raphael opened it, and Jemma saw handwritten pages with occasional spatters and blots. 'This is a recipe book which one of my neighbours has kindly given to me. It contains family recipes handed down through the generations, and is still used in Rolando's café and deli today.'

Jemma's heart sank.

Brian stared at the book, then burst out laughing. 'A recipe book?' he said, grinning. He picked the book up and leafed through it. 'Lasagne? Rigatoni? Tiramisu?' His eyes glinted. 'I suspect you're *trifling* with me.' He let out a hearty guffaw as he threw the book on the table.

'I'll thank you to be careful with that,' said Raphael. 'We

260

respect books, remember?'

'I can't wait to see what you've got for me next,' said Brian. He jerked a thumb at Jemma. 'Her diary, perhaps? Or last week's TV guide?'

'You'll have to wait and see,' said Raphael, very calmly.

He's blown it, thought Jemma. *I could understand the drawings, but – a recipe book?*

Brian looked extremely smug. 'It barely seems worth presenting my third book,' he said, 'but I suppose I'd better.' He brought out one last stout, ancient book, and laid it beside the dictionary. 'This,' he said, 'is a bound collection of writings by Sir Isaac Newton, on a variety of subjects. There.' The book had begun glowing before he laid it with the others, and as Jemma watched the light became brighter still, until nobody, not even the most unbelieving person, could have denied it.

'Nice,' commented Raphael. 'You've been busy.'

'I have,' said Brian. 'I don't go into these things lightly, you know, and I've been preparing for a while.'

'I can see that,' said Raphael. 'Before I present my last book, why did you choose the three books you have?'

Brian raised his eyebrows. 'Isn't that obvious? Words are the foundation of language, and this is one of the best collections of them. Mathematics – well, you can't do a thing without mathematics, and here we have the fresh ideas of a mathematical genius. Followed by the writings of an eminent scientific mind.' He smiled. 'Not even you, Raphael, can deny gravity.'

'I don't propose to,' said Raphael. 'Here is my final book.' He reached into the tote bag for one last time. Then he paused. 'Are you ready?'

Brian's smile widened. 'Are you ready to lose?'

Raphael smiled back. 'I think you'll like this one.' He brought out a book which seemed too large for the bag it had come out of; a thick book bound in plain navy blue, with no writing on the cover. He laid it on the other side of the recipe book.

'What's that?' said Brian, leaning over to look at it.

'This,' said Raphael, 'is a bound set of *Popular Science Ideas*, a magazine which presented difficult concepts in a way both children and adults could understand.' He opened the cover, and Jemma saw that inside, just as he had said, was an A4-sized magazine with a brightly coloured robot on the cover. Jemma read the coverlines: *How does manned space flight work? Could measles become extinct? Did the Universe come from a Big Bang?*

'Care to have a look, Brian?'

'No, I would not,' said Brian, his lip curling into a sneer. 'You really have outdone yourself this time, Raphael. How you've kept your position so long I have no idea. Those cheap paperbacks you peddle have gone to your head. What are you, the People's Champion? You should be a purveyor of the finest that has been thought and said, and instead you present me with this – this *trash*. The book of drawings makes sense. But the rest of it—' His chair scraped back. 'I hope you've made retirement plans, Raphael.'

'Not just yet,' said Raphael, and his voice was deadly serious. 'I see you're surprised at my choice of literature, Brian. To be honest, I never expected anything else. The books you have chosen are wonderful, truly wonderful. They are fine examples of knowledge, and no one could deny that. I knew that would be your approach. That is one of the reasons why I chose to take a different path.'

Jemma swallowed, and leaned forward. She felt Carl do the same beside her.

'My first book,' said Raphael, 'wasn't the one I had in mind. It was even better. I didn't get the book I wanted, but the book I needed. It fulfils the same function, combining artistry, ingenuity, and discovery. The added dimension is that it was chosen for me by a dear colleague, and the transaction was effected by my invaluable shop manager.' He smiled at Jemma, who felt a sudden lump in her throat.

'Who will shortly be out of a job,' said Brian.

'My second book,' said Raphael, 'was again unexpected. It was given to me just this morning. Yes, it is old, it is stained, it has fingerprints all over it, and some of the pages are stuck together. This book of recipes is five generations old. Five generations of culinary knowledge, of improvement, of striving for perfection, all done with care and love. And, moreover, freely given.' He nudged the book across slightly, so that it touched the first, and a gentle, almost imperceptible light appeared. As Jemma watched, it grew stronger.

'My final choice,' said Raphael, 'comes from the library of Sir Tarquin Golightly.'

Brian shook his head in disbelief. 'You had the pick of his library, and you chose *that*?' He pointed an accusing finger at the navy-blue book, and Jemma felt injured on its behalf.

'There are lots of books I could have chosen,' said Raphael. 'But when I went to visit Lady Golightly, she told me that this was the volume that Sir Tarquin kept on his bedside table. He read the magazines when he was a boy – devoured them, in fact – and those magazines inspired him, against the wishes of his family, to embrace a scientific career. That, and the patents he filed in the course of it, made his millions, and enabled him to restore the family home. He never forgot the magazine, and had it bound to preserve it. In his last illness he would ask Lady Golightly to read him an article every so often, and that was one of the few remaining things that gave him pleasure.'

He stroked the plain blue cover of the book. 'So this book stands for education, for science, for making complicated things comprehensible, and for inspiration and growth.' He paused. 'Lady Golightly refused to take any money for this book. She merely asked me to ensure that it would go to a good home where

263

it would be appreciated and cared for.' He moved the book gently across the table to join its fellows.

This time the change in the light was not subtle, but strong. Luke took his sunglasses out of his pocket and put them on. 'What you don't see, Brian,' said Raphael, his face lit from below, 'is that your ambition has narrowed you. You have specialised, and you have excluded, and you have forgotten that books are not just collections of knowledge. They also foster development, and inspiration, and care, and love. You have collected wonderful books, but in the pursuit of that knowledge you have forgotten to be wise. And wisdom, as you should know, is key.' He glanced at the books, which were shooting out rays of white light. Out of the silence a faint hum emerged. It grew louder and louder, until the table vibrated.

A sudden flash made Jemma cover her eyes and turn away. When she looked back, Raphael's books were alone on the table. Brian's books had gone.

Brian stared at the part of the table where his books had been.

'The books will be taken care of, Brian,' said Raphael. He paused, considering his next words. 'It was a good challenge. You did well.' He held out his hand.

'If that's the sort of drivel you have to spout to win this challenge,' said Brian, 'then I'm glad I lost.' He pushed back his chair. 'I know what happens next, you don't have to tell me.' He walked heavily towards the stairs. Then he turned and glared at them all. 'Don't think you've seen the last of me.' He grinned. 'Did you know you've got a vampire on your team? A bloodsucker?' He pointed at Luke. 'Him, he's a plant. He was working for me. Not that he was any good. Won't use him again.'

Luke took his sunglasses off and stepped forward. 'No, you won't use me again,' he said. 'I stopped working for you as soon as I realised what I was doing would harm good people.' He smiled. 'These people know what I am, and they accept me for it.

I'm happier here than I've been for centuries.' He flung up his head. 'Good luck in the outer reaches, Brian. I suspect you'll need it. And don't ever expect my help again.'

Brian snorted. 'Wouldn't want it.' He stomped towards the stairs.

'Better see him out, I suppose,' said Raphael. They got up, and followed.

Brian mounted the stairs, crossed the back room, and walked through the upper bookshop, looking neither right nor left. He paused at the counter, glanced at Raphael, then took out a set of keys and put them down. 'You'll find everything is there,' he said. He opened the door onto the blankness, stepped through, and disappeared.

'You won,' Jemma said, half-dazed. 'Raphael, you won!' She threw her arms around him. 'I can't believe it, and I'm still not sure how you did it, but you won!'

'Yes, yes, I did win,' said Raphael, wriggling as he attempted to free himself. 'I'm very glad that you're pleased. And so am I. I'm not keen on change, as you know.'

'That was intense,' said Carl. He walked over to them, gently removed Jemma, folded her in his own arms, and kissed the top of her head. 'And speaking of change—'

They followed his gaze to where Folio stood in the doorway to the back room. He looked bigger and stronger, like a young lion. He stood proud, his beautiful tawny fur glowing, and his eyes blazed as if they held a light of their own.

Chapter 21

Jemma drifted into consciousness, woken by Elvis Costello on her clock radio singing 'Every Day I Write The Book'. She stretched luxuriously, then jumped as the backs of her hands touched the headboard. *What the—*

Then she remembered. She opened her eyes, and listened to the swishing of traffic in the street below. The traffic on Charing Cross Road.

There had been little time for explanations after Brian's departure. Raphael picked up the keys from the counter, then sent them all downstairs to fetch the three victorious books, maintaining an appropriate distance from each other. When they came upstairs the world outside was just the same as it had always been, and a couple of slightly peevish faces peered in at the window.

'No rest for the wicked,' said Raphael. 'Jemma, would you look after upstairs, and Luke and Carl can go downstairs. As for me—' He picked up the brown-paper bag on the counter and took out the last cinnamon roll. 'If you don't mind, I might go for a nap. I find challenges rather tiring.' For once, Jemma was happy to acknowledge that he had done his bit for the day, and more besides.

Thoughts crashed against each other in her head all through the day, while serving the customers, nipping to the stockroom for books, and fielding questions about Folio's new grooming regime. Folio spent most of the day lounging in the shop window looking mightily pleased with himself, like a predator taking his ease on the plain.

When Raphael came back into the shop, which she noted was five minutes before he usually took his lunch, she checked for nearby customers, then opened her mouth to ask him a question. He held up a hand. 'Not until the end of the day,' he said. And with that Jemma had to be content.

When Raphael had left the shop for lunch, Jemma went to get her phone. Carl had texted: *Are you OK?*

She considered his question. Actually, she felt surprisingly OK, considering that that morning she had fetched a priceless book from a secret library, witnessed an epic battle of knowledge, and also faced losing her job. Typing *Yes, I think so. How about you?* seemed rather mundane, but it was true. Perhaps the more of this sort of thing you did, the more you got used to it.

A reply flashed up on her phone: *It was deeply weird.* Then another text: *Imagine that as a scene in a film or a play. That would be so awesome.*

Jemma smiled. *You'd better get on and write it then!*

It was some time before Carl replied. *Yeah, but would anyone ever believe it?*

Jemma's fingers flew. *Do they have to?* Then she had to put her phone away again, because a customer was waiting at the counter, clutching a book called *Divine Your Future*. 'That looks useful,' she said, and opened the cover. 'Three pounds, please.'

As was always the way with these things, they had a rush of customers at ten to five, and only managed to close the shop at twenty-five past. 'What a day,' groaned Jemma, turning the sign round, locking the door, and leaning firmly against it.

'It was rather, wasn't it?' said Raphael from the armchair, where he had been, he said, thinking for the last hour. Since this involved having his eyes closed and his mouth slightly open, Jemma wasn't entirely sure how much thinking he had managed to get done.

Carl and Luke came upstairs, both worn out. Carl had in fact run out of food at four o'clock, but most of Westminster had needed a late-afternoon caffeine fix. Luke sagged a little, but still looked considerably happier and healthier than he had on several previous occasions. They all gazed at Raphael, who regarded them calmly.

'So…?' said Jemma.

'I've had plenty to think about,' said Raphael. 'I've lost an Assistant Keeper, and gained a bookshop.' He drew Brian's keys out of his waistcoat pocket and jingled them. The keyring glinted: an ancient golden coin.

'Have you made any decisions?' she asked, as casually as she could.

Raphael considered. 'I think we all deserve tomorrow morning off. I don't know about you, but I've had enough for one week.'

Jemma sighed. 'That wasn't quite what I meant.'

'Well, I'll have to recruit a new Assistant Keeper,' said Raphael. 'I may need your help, Jemma.'

'Me?' Jemma stared at him.

'Yes, you. You see, the post has never had a proper job description, or a – what is it?'

'A person specification,' said Jemma. Her head was doing the swimmy thing again, but to be honest that had happened so often lately that she was beginning to get used to it.

'That's the fellow,' said Raphael. 'As you know about these sorts of things, you could help me draw one up.'

268

Jemma giggled. 'For a moment I thought you were asking me to do the job!'

Raphael raised his eyebrows. 'Would you like to?'

'What? But – but – I don't know! I don't know what an Assistant Keeper does, except . . . keep books.' She frowned. 'Anyway,' she added, 'you ought to follow proper recruitment procedure, not just ask the person standing in front of you.' She folded her arms, feeling on considerably safer ground.

'What will you do with the shop?' asked Luke. Jemma shot him a grateful look, glad that he had asked the question occupying her mind.

'I suppose there are two options,' said Raphael. 'Sell it, or keep it. It's a nice little shop, really. I'd take you round, but it's best to let the shop settle first. Let's give it till after the weekend.'

'Is it another magical one?' Jemma asked.

'I expect so,' said Raphael. 'I'm not sure *how* magical, though. For obvious reasons, Brian was never particularly open about the place. It's a bit odd: it's a fairly modern building, but Brian's made it very olde-worlde. All mahogany shelves and brass fittings. It's a bit like being on an old ship, or perhaps in a coffin-maker's.'

Luke's face brightened.

'Yes, it's rather a pleasant shop,' said Raphael. 'And probably pleasanter now that Brian's out of it. So yes, I shall keep it. So long as I can get someone to run it.' He shot Jemma a speculative glance.

She studied him, trying to work out what was behind his expression. 'Do you want me to draw up a job description and help you recruit a bookshop manager?' she said.

Raphael laughed. 'Not this time. I wondered how you'd feel about managing it. I'll still need you here sometimes, obviously, but Brian does have an assistant, and I'm hoping she'll stay on. She is capable, if a little gloomy.'

The pleased expression flickered over Luke's face again.

269

'Really?' exclaimed Jemma. *My own bookshop*, she thought. *Really, actually, mine to run!* Then another thought struck her like a sudden shower of icy water. 'I don't think I can,' she said. 'I don't know anything about antiquarian books.'

'You'll find Maddy very knowledgeable on that front,' said Raphael. 'In any case, it doesn't have to be an antiquarian bookshop. It could be any sort of bookshop.'

Jemma's mouth dropped open, then she nodded frantically. 'Then yes! Yes, I'd love to!'

'Jolly good,' said Raphael. 'If you can get here for say eight o'clock on Monday, we'll go and take a look at things.'

Brian's bookshop, BJF Antiquarian Books, had been much as Jemma imagined: wood, brass, leather-bound books behind glass doors, and no prices on anything. Maddy, Brian's assistant, was a tall, thin, lugubrious woman in capri pants and Birkenstocks, with a long thin plait of dark hair which looked as if she had chewed the end of it. She had taken Brian's departure with equanimity, and Jemma had a feeling that Maddy expected her to be more of the same. She didn't think she would be – she didn't think she *could* be – but for now she was watching, and learning, and inspecting the books in the small stockroom which smelt as old as time.

And she lived above the shop. 'There's no point in not using it,' Raphael had said. And when they went upstairs they found a large, beautifully furnished open-plan living and eating area, and in the eaves of the building, a bedroom with sloping walls and a surprisingly luxurious ensuite bathroom.

'It's beautiful,' said Jemma. 'How much rent will you ask for?' She had a feeling that, given the location and the furnishings, she might need to ask for a pay rise.

Raphael smiled. 'Call it a benefit in kind,' he said.

After some misgivings that the flat and the shop would have malevolent intentions towards her, Jemma eventually plucked up the courage to bring over a sleeping bag and camp out. She spent the first night on the chesterfield sofa in the living room, worried that she would offend the place if she dared to use the bed. She had lain awake flinching at the slightest noise, eyes wide open and darting about the room every time a shadow moved. But she must have slept, for she woke at seven o'clock exactly feeling surprisingly refreshed. She rushed to a mirror to check that she hadn't been turned into a frog or developed a horrendous rash overnight, and only then admitted that perhaps Brian's shop might be a little easier to manage than Raphael's.

After five nights of more or less peaceful slumber, during which she had braved the big double bed, Jemma had given notice on her own flat. She had begun to move her belongings over bit by bit, until Raphael laughed when she came into Burns Books with a toaster, ordered her to pack her things, and turned up on Saturday afternoon in Gertrude. As Jemma carried her last possessions out of the flat and closed the door behind her, she saw that the B on the door wasn't crooked any more. She rolled her eyes and walked away.

And there had been changes at Burns Books, too. She had asked Luke what would help him to work in all areas of the bookshop, and between them they had sourced a clear sunlight-filtering film which Luke said would repel the rays which he found most irritating. Once they had applied a large square to the shop window, his sunglasses only appeared on very sunny days, which were becoming rarer as the year rolled on. They had also installed a table and chair in the stockroom, so that he didn't have to eat standing up. Now Luke looked almost healthy, and Jemma hoped that the pigeons in Trafalgar Square were living easier lives.

Yes, all in all, thought Jemma, *things are going rather well.* And today was her regular morning at Burns Books. She got up, got ready, and started to cook breakfast. Four eggs scrambling in the pan, four slices of toast in the toaster.

At eight fifteen precisely, her doorbell rang. Jemma answered the intercom.

'It's me, Carl. I was, um, passing, and—'

'I'm just making breakfast,' said Jemma. 'Care to join me?'

'Sure,' he said, and she could hear his smile.

This was the third day in a row that he had called in on his way to work. They ate at the round dining table, with proper, heavy cutlery, but Jemma drew the line at damask napkins, and set out the paper ones with watermelons on that she had brought from her flat.

'That was lovely,' said Carl, wiping his mouth. 'Want to walk down with me? You are in our shop this morning, aren't you?'

'I'd love to,' said Jemma. Once they were downstairs and she had locked the door, he held out his hand and she put hers into it.

It was a short walk to the bookshop. Fallen leaves crunched under their feet, and they laughed at their dragon breath in the chilly October street. The lights were already on at Burns Books, and Jemma saw Luke behind the counter, priming the till. Carl stole a quick kiss before diverting to Rolando's for their pastry order. Jemma watched him stroll down the street, then pushed the bookshop door open.

'Morning,' she said. 'All OK?' She could see it was, but she still hadn't got out of the habit of asking.

'Oh, yes,' said Luke, and grinned.

'I'll be down shortly,' called Raphael, from somewhere overhead. 'Just, um…'

Jemma was wondering what strange ensemble Raphael would present himself in today when a stentorian meow jolted her out of her thoughts. 'You're in good voice, Folio,' she said, bending to stroke the cat's luxuriant fur as he weaved in and out of her legs. She wobbled slightly as he pushed between them, and giggled. 'Careful!'

Folio looked up at her, and his amber eyes glowed. Then she

tickled him behind the ear, and he purred with pleasure. *It must be lovely to be a pampered cat in a bookshop*, she thought. *Then again, working in one isn't bad, either.* And as Carl came in with the trays of pastries, she smiled a big, warm, happy smile.

THE MAGICAL BOOKSHOP: 3

Double
BOOKED

LIZ HEDGECOCK

WHITE
RHINO
BOOKS

Chapter 1

Jemma watched the pendulum of the grandfather clock swing backwards and forwards, backwards and forwards. *If I'm not careful*, she thought, *I'll fall asleep right here, at the counter.*

It was almost twelve o'clock, and so far they had had one proper customer. A smart man with a brass-buttoned blazer and a rolled umbrella had strolled in, tipped his hat, and stated precisely what he wanted, down to which edition and bindings he was prepared to accept. Maddy had known exactly what he meant, located the book in the designated area of the stockroom, and brought it out in its protective box for inspection. The customer had pronounced himself satisfied, paid the price asked, and left with the box under his arm. He had not browsed, he had not asked about any other books, and Maddy had not attempted to sell him any.

Apart from that customer, perhaps five people had walked in, gazed blankly at the rows of books behind glass, and left. One couple had whispered, 'It looks expensive, doesn't it?' and scurried out with a fearful glance at the counter, as if Jemma might coerce them into buying something.

'Is it usually this quiet on a Monday?' she asked Maddy.

Maddy tore her gaze from the copy of the *Bookseller's Companion* which she was perusing, and considered. 'This is normal,' she said, eventually. 'This isn't the sort of bookshop where we have lots of casual browsers. People who come to BJF Antiquarian Books tend to know exactly what they want.'

'I can see that,' said Jemma, remembering the man with the umbrella. 'I'm just used to things being busier.'

'You worked in a general bookshop, didn't you?' Maddy asked, with a slightly pitying note in her voice.

'Yes, I managed a general bookshop,' Jemma replied. 'We had people coming in all the time.'

Maddy shuddered visibly. 'Churn,' she said, almost to herself. 'People picking up the books, and putting down the books, and – and *touching* the books.' She rubbed her thumb and forefinger together, then returned to her magazine.

The clock struck twelve like a death knell.

'I think I'll take my lunch,' said Jemma, 'if that's OK.'

'Yes, of course,' said Maddy, without looking up. 'You're the boss.'

Yes, I am, thought Jemma, in an attempt to convince herself. She got her bag, put on her jacket, and set off along the road. She walked quickly, partly because it was chilly out, but also because she didn't want to waste more of her hour away from the shop than she had to. A couple of minutes later she pushed open the familiar door, and walked into Burns Books.

Raphael was reclining in the armchair, his fingertips on his temples, and Luke stood nearby. Folio sat on the counter between two boxes of books, watching them both. 'Let's try again,' said Raphael. 'Visualise horror books. Tell yourself that the shop needs horror books.'

Luke screwed his face up. If anything, he looked constipated. 'All right,' he said, after a minute or so, 'I've got it.' He strode towards the stockroom with purpose and returned with another box of books. But when he opened it, it was full of Harlequin romances. 'I don't believe it!' he cried. 'What am I doing wrong?'

Raphael laughed. 'Jemma, why don't you try.'

'Horror books,' said Jemma. 'We need horror stories.' She walked to the stockroom, selected a random box, and brought it back. But when she opened it, the box was full of books about business management.

'While I regard that as a horror story,' said Raphael, 'I doubt most of our customers would agree.' He looked from Jemma to Luke. 'I suspect you both have something on your mind.' He eyed the box of romance novels, then Luke, who appeared, for him, decidedly pink.

'I'm thinking about – putting myself out there,' he said. 'It's been a long time since I felt – well, in that frame of mind. But now I've got a stable job…'

'You mean dating?' asked Jemma.

Luke fidgeted with a black shirt button. 'I suppose I do,' he said. 'Obviously it's a bit different when you're undead.'

'I imagine it would be,' said Jemma. 'Do you only date other vampires?'

'It would make things easier,' said Luke. 'But I'm open to new experiences.' He fidgeted some more. 'I've downloaded an app.'

Raphael rolled his eyes.

'Don't be like that,' said Luke. 'I haven't opened it yet. I'm waiting for when things . . . you know, feel right.'

'Checking it out can't hurt,' said Jemma. 'I mean, romance is clearly on your mind.' She nodded towards the boxes, and Luke looked rather resentful.

'And what about you?' he asked, indicating the box of business books. 'Trouble in paradise?'

'No,' said Jemma, drawing herself up to her full height, which was still not enough to be remotely on a level with Luke. Then she

279

sighed, and slumped. 'It's just so boring. Hardly anyone comes in, the people who do normally run straight out again because the shop scares them, and Maddy is perfectly capable of dealing with any actual customers. It's barely worth me being there.'

'I did say,' Raphael remarked, mildly, 'that it doesn't have to stay an antiquarian bookshop.'

'I know,' said Jemma. *But I'm worried,* she added to herself. *I'm worried that if I change things it won't work, and I'll have messed up a perfectly good bookshop because I didn't understand it.* 'I guess it's early days,' she said. 'I'm still wondering what to do for the best.'

'That's very cautious of you,' said Raphael. 'Anyway, I'm pleased that your bookshop is quiet at the moment. It means we have more time to think about the Assistant Keeper problem.'

Jemma blinked. 'I actually came over to get lunch,' she said.

'And Carl being downstairs is incidental,' said Raphael, with a twinkle.

Jemma smiled. 'Don't tell him that his cappuccino's the main attraction, will you?' And with that she escaped before any more awkward questions could be asked.

As usual at this time, the large lower bookshop was busy. Customers roamed around the shelves, not quite small enough to be ants in the lofty vaulted space of the shop, but with similar levels of scurrying and industry. Carl himself was dealing with a sizeable queue, making coffees, warming paninis, and exchanging friendly banter with their regulars. It was odd but nice to see him absorbed, not conscious of her. His twists had grown; they stuck straight up from his scalp, maybe an inch and a half now. *Has he redone them? I see him almost every day. Why haven't I noticed?* Then Carl caught sight of her and waved.

Jemma waved back, then walked over to General Fiction and picked up a Wodehouse she hadn't read, *Pigs Have Wings*, to keep her company in the queue. *Not that I'm trying to avoid thinking about the other shop*, she told herself. *I'm being productive and making the best use of my lunch hour.*

When she reached the front of the queue, Carl grinned at her. 'Cappuccino, I presume?'

'Yes please, and a tomato and mozzarella panini.'

'Eat in or take out?' Then his grin narrowed a little. 'You OK?'

She frowned. 'Yes, of course I am. Why wouldn't I be?'

He turned away to put the panini in the warmer, and began making her cappuccino. When he finally put her cup on the counter, he wore the expression of someone walking across ice. 'You just looked a little too pleased to see me.' His gaze moved to the book in her hand. 'And you've got a PG Wodehouse book. You told me once that you read those for escapism.'

Jemma sighed. 'Well done, Sherlock Holmes,' she said. 'It's probably nothing.'

'Doesn't look like nothing,' said Carl. 'I've got rehearsals with Rumpus tonight, but we could go out later, maybe nine? Or I could come round?'

Jemma heard a voice behind her mutter, 'Oh *do* get a move on.'

'No, it's fine,' she said quickly. 'Like I said, it's probably nothing.'

Jemma paid, took her cappuccino and found a small table at the edge of the café area. She opened her book and attempted to lose herself in it, but she had only read two pages when the cry of 'Tomato and mozzarella panini!' brought her back into the café.

The panini was nice, and so was the cappuccino, and the bookshop had just the right soothing background hum; but somehow the image of a bookshop, empty apart from herself and Maddy, and silent apart from the ticking of the grandfather clock, kept getting between her and the Empress of Blandings. Once she had finished her lunch Jemma sighed again, though she wasn't sure exactly why, and took her book upstairs.

'Luke's on his lunch,' said Raphael. He hadn't moved from the armchair, but Folio was sitting on his lap. 'You can serve yourself, can't you?'

Jemma laughed. 'Yeah.' She popped behind the counter, scanned her book with the little scan gun they now had at each till, and held her phone to the card reader. 'All done.'

'Oh yes,' said Raphael. 'I put a book aside for you. I was shelving your boxes and I thought it might be useful.'

Jemma saw a Burns Books paper bag on the counter, with a book inside. She drew it out. *Your Business, Your Way.* 'Oh, um, thanks,' she said. 'Do you think it'll help?'

'Well, you don't seem happy with things as they are,' said Raphael. 'You can always bring it back.'

'I suppose I can,' said Jemma, still gazing at the cover of the book. 'I'll start it tonight. Thanks, Raphael.' She replaced the book in the bag, added the Wodehouse to it, and left the shop.

She still had ten minutes of her lunch hour left, so she stopped in at Nafisa's mini-market and bought a packet of sausages and enough potatoes to make a generous portion of mash for one. *I don't have to impress anyone tonight,* she thought. *And if I'm seriously taking on Brian's bookshop – no, not Brian's bookshop, my bookshop – I need proper food.*

Nafisa frowned at the packet of sausages. 'Are you sure?' she said.

'You're selling them,' said Jemma. 'I assume they're fit for human consumption.'

Nafisa considered her. 'Sausages don't seem very you,' she said. 'You're more chickpeas and lentils these days.'

'Don't forget the quinoa,' said Jemma. 'Yes, I suppose I am. But sometimes you need comfort food.'

Nafisa let out an ominous 'Mmm,' and scanned the sausages. 'May you find comfort in them,' she said, almost as if she were blessing them, and handed them to Jemma. And as Jemma strolled back to BJF Antiquarian Books, opened the door, and saw Maddy sitting just as she had left her an hour before, she really hoped that she would.

Chapter 2

Jemma leaned against the worktop in Brian's – no, *her* – compact but well-appointed kitchen, reading *Your Business, Your Way*. In the background, sausages sizzled. Every so often she would reach across and poke them with a spatula to ensure they cooked evenly. But really, her attention was on the book.

They had closed on the stroke of five, and the afternoon had been as quiet as the morning. They had cashed up at a quarter to five, since Maddy had said with authority that none of their regulars were likely to visit after four thirty anyway, and locked the takings in the safe, ready to go to the bank tomorrow. The takings were fairly respectable, considering the low number of books they had sold. 'Low volume, high profit,' Maddy had said, with a smug air. There was no tidying to do, no books to replace on shelves, and nothing to be said about the day at all. 'See you tomorrow,' said Maddy, and left on the first chime of the clock.

Jemma enjoyed mashing her potatoes. She added plenty of milk and butter, and pretended that she was pummelling the bookshop into shape. *Yes*, she thought, as she mashed, *it's my bookshop, and it is up to me to make the changes*. Perhaps she had mashed the potatoes too thoroughly and added a little too much milk, since she was left with a purée instead of a mash, and when she stuck her three sausages into it at jaunty angles, they immediately sank into the puddle of potato. Jemma refused to derive an insight from this minor cookery fail, adding a dollop of tomato ketchup and telling herself that it would taste fine. Who wanted hard lumpy mash, anyway?

She continued to flick through the book as she ate. It was rather inspiring, with its talk of working out your goals and moulding your business to fit them, and ensuring that the business reflected your values. But while it was heavy on buzzwords, it was extremely light on practicalities. It didn't, for example, tell you what to do if you had taken on a bookshop which was the exact opposite of a shop you would actually want to visit, complete with an assistant who was happy with things the way they were. Jemma laid the book down, and decided to focus on her remaining sausage rather than her values.

She was just chewing the last mouthful, and wishing that Carl was there to laugh over the book with her, when her mobile rang. Jemma's heart leapt. Maybe his rehearsal had finished early and they could go out for that drink after all. But when she got her phone from her jacket pocket the display said *Mum*.

Jemma's heart sank a little, which made her feel guilty, and she pressed *Answer*. 'Hi, Mum.'

'Hello, Jemma. I didn't expect you to answer.' Her mother sounded a little aggrieved that she had. 'I thought you'd still be working. Or on your way home.'

'It's gone half past seven, Mum. Don't forget I live over the bookshop now.'

'Oh yes.' Her mother sniffed. 'I always liked that other flat. Such a nice building. And a nice road, too.'

As far as Jemma could remember, her mother had visited the flat twice, and hadn't been particularly complimentary on either occasion. 'Expensive, though,' she said. 'This one is rent-free. Perk of the job.'

'Probably because the owner can't find a tenant for it,' said her mother. 'Anyway, how are you getting on with your new job?'

Wild horses wouldn't have dragged the truth out of Jemma. 'It's great,' she said. 'The shop has so much potential, and I'm looking forward to making changes.'

'I expect the owner will have things to say about that.'

'Oh no, he supports me fully,' said Jemma.

'Well, it's his money.' Her mother sighed. 'If the bookshop was failing anyway, anything is an improvement.'

'It's only your positive attitude that keeps me going, Mum,' said Jemma.

'I'm sorry, I missed that,' said her mother. 'I wish you'd get a proper phone line. I'm sure phoning your mobile is costing me a fortune. Anyway, your boss. Is he nice?'

Jemma felt on firm ground now. 'Yes, he's very nice.'

'And how old is he, would you say?'

Jemma couldn't help grinning. 'Oh, he's much older than me.' She would have loved to see her mother's face if she had told her *how* much older Raphael was, but sadly it was not to be.

'Oh,' said her mother. 'I suppose at least if you don't have to commute you'll have time to go out and meet people. And I'm sure lots of nice people come into the bookshop.'

'Mum, I'm seeing someone,' said Jemma. 'I did tell you.' She had found more and more, since leaving home, that her mother's brain was like a temperamental sieve. It was good at retaining the things she wanted to remember, and remarkably skilled at letting everything else go.

'Did you? Are you sure? What does he do? I suppose it is a he. Or should I say they? Is that what one says now?'

'He's a he,' said Jemma. 'He works—' She hesitated. But working in the café was nothing to be ashamed of. 'He's working in the main bookshop café at the moment, because he's between jobs. He's an actor.'

'Oh,' said her mother. 'Does he have a name, this actor? Would I have seen him in anything?'

'I doubt it, Mum, he hasn't done any TV work. His name is Carl.'

Her mother sniffed in a way that suggested that if Carl hadn't been on her television, he didn't really exist. 'Amanda and Jake have bought the house they were looking at, in the next village.'

'Oh yes, she texted,' said Jemma. 'I know they really wanted it.' Amanda was two years younger than Jemma, and somehow, since Jemma had left home to go to university and Amanda had decided to live at home and become a primary school teacher, Jemma felt the balance of her mother's affection had distinctly shifted in Amanda's favour. Amanda's career was so rewarding; Amanda's boyfriend Jake had such lovely manners; Amanda came for Sunday lunch every weekend without fail. Jemma probably would have resented her sister if Amanda hadn't been so frank in private about how hard she found teaching some days, and how often their mother praised Jemma to her as an independent woman making her own way in the world.

'Yes,' said her mother. 'I'm so pleased they've been able to get a foot on the property ladder.'

'Oh, absolutely,' said Jemma. 'And with the money I'm saving on rent at the moment, hopefully I can get a deposit together for when I'm ready to buy.'

'Does this Carl have a place of his own?' asked her mother, in a voice which somehow suggested a dragon scenting an addition to her hoard.

Jemma laughed. 'He works in the shop café, Mum, what do you think?'

'I only asked,' said her mother. 'Anyway, I'd better go; *EastEnders* is on soon.' Jemma had a distinct suspicion that, though her mother must have visited London several times, she still thought *EastEnders* was an entirely accurate representation of the whole of London life. She considered asking if she had seen *Notting Hill*, then decided that would just bring a whole new range of assumptions to deal with.

'It's been nice talking to you, Mum,' she said. 'Are you all right? And how about Dad?'

'Oh yes, we're both fine,' said her mother. 'Your father is building the Millennium Falcon at the moment. It's all over the dining-room table.'

Jemma grinned. Dad had always been a Lego fanatic, building things for them when they were tiny, then with them, and when Jemma and Amanda reached their teenage years and preferred hanging around the local shopping centre, without them. 'I'm sure it won't take him long to finish it,' she said.

'You haven't seen it,' her mother said, darkly. 'Anyway, it's five to eight and I've just got time to make a cup of tea, so I must go. I'll phone you next week, Jemma.'

'OK. Bye, Mum,' said Jemma. And as always, her mother managed to put the phone down first.

Jemma looked at the phone in her hand. As usual, her mother had said nothing about her own life. Jemma occasionally wondered whether her mother could be a secret operative for MI5, or engaged in a string of glamorous affairs. She was certainly good at gathering information while managing to divulge only select snippets of her own.

Jemma sighed. *Even if she did have an amazing secret life*, she thought, *I still wouldn't want to be my mum. She's so – so determined to be disappointed. Particularly in me.* She knew full well that even if she made the bookshop into the most high-profile, successful bookshop in London – no, the world – and earned a six-figure salary, and married Carl, who then landed a leading role in *EastEnders*, her mother would find something to be disappointed about. But she still wanted to please her.

I'll make a go of this bookshop, she thought, and her hand tightened on the phone. *I'll work out my goals, and my vision, and my values, and I'll make that shop into a place where I'm proud and happy to work. And if Maddy doesn't like it, well—* She shrugged. *She can put up, or shut up.*

Jemma nodded, to bed in her resolve more deeply, fetched her laptop, and went into the kitchen to make tea and raid the emergency biscuits. Perhaps, if she could transform the bookshop into the shop of her dreams, everything else would follow. At any rate, it was worth a try.

Chapter 3

Jemma's resolve to take the bookshop in hand was still firm when she woke in the morning. She had created a new spreadsheet the previous evening: colour-coded, with goals, milestones, and dependencies. That had made her feel much better. When Carl texted at nine o'clock, she had replied: *Yes, I'm fine, I've got a plan.* She hadn't even read herself to sleep with *Pigs Have Wings*, because she had no need to escape any more.

When getting ready, she selected comparatively businesslike attire: black trousers, a smart top, and a jacket instead of her usual cardigan. She thought of Maddy's Birkenstocks, and added a pair of shoes with a slight heel. After all, now that she spent most of her time sitting, baseball boots weren't required. Thus armoured, she made herself a strong coffee, tucked her laptop under her arm, and went downstairs.

She almost jumped out of her skin when Maddy arrived five minutes later, and only just managed to swallow her mouthful of coffee. 'You're . . . early,' she said, and felt her resolve trickling away. She put her mug down and sat up straight.

'Not really,' said Maddy, hanging up her coat and beret. Jemma eyed her feet and wondered whether the Birkenstocks would persist throughout the winter, and what Maddy would do if it snowed. 'I always come in early on the third Tuesday of the month. It's stocktake day.'

'Stocktake day?' said Jemma, feeling like an inadequate echo.

'Yes, Brian and I always went through the stock and checked that our flagship books were in good condition, and then he would review his acquisition plan,' said Maddy.

'Oh,' said Jemma. 'I see. Um . . . is there a system?'

'Oh yes,' said Maddy. 'We developed it together. It is quite complicated, but I can explain it to you if you like.' Her expression was kind.

'That would be . . . great,' said Jemma. She cast an imploring look at her laptop, begging her action plan to save her, and saw the little power light blink off. With that, the last of her resolve dribbled from the toes of her modestly heeled shoes.

'I'll make myself a drink,' said Maddy, 'then we can get started.'

At that moment Jemma's phone rang. The display said *Burns Books*. 'I have to take this,' she said. 'Hello, Jemma James speaking.'

'Oh, hello Jemma,' said Raphael, sounding surprised. 'I don't suppose you could pop round? I'm having a spot of trouble and I'd welcome your advice.'

Jemma could have kissed the phone. 'Of course, I'll come now.' She ended the call. 'I'm sorry, Maddy, but something's come up at Burns Books. I'm afraid I'll have to leave you to it.' A sudden evil impulse led her to add, 'Will you be able to manage on your own?'

Maddy's face was absolutely expressionless. 'Oh yes,' she said.

'In that case,' said Jemma, 'I'll get going.' And she shrugged into her jacket with a distinct sense of being let off the hook.

Jemma was almost at the bookshop when she began to wonder

what the trouble might be. Had Folio gone on the rampage? Was the shop throwing a tantrum? At least it was too early to be customer-related. She found lights on when she arrived, and Luke sitting behind the counter, engrossed in *The Rules Of Dating*. 'Oh, hi,' he said. 'Raphael's downstairs. Everything's in hand.'

'Is it?' Jemma glanced about her for signs of trouble, but none were apparent. The only difference from usual was that Luke had had a haircut, and his normally shaggy hair was neatly combed. It made him look as if he were in his late teens. 'Doing research?'

Luke lowered the book. 'Yes, I am,' he said. 'I'm going to a – a thing tonight, and I thought it best to be prepared.'

'A thing?' said Jemma. 'What sort of thing?'

'Speed dating,' said Luke. 'Downstairs at the Rat and Compasses. It starts quite early, so I'm going straight from work.'

'Oh,' said Jemma. 'Well, good luck.' All sorts of questions were on the tip of her tongue, but she suspected she might not want to know the answers. 'I'd better go and see what Raphael wants.'

Downstairs, Raphael was sitting at one of the café tables, with a takeaway coffee cup from Rolando's and a large notepad in front of him. 'I need help,' he said. 'I'm stuck.'

Jemma sat opposite him and turned the notepad to see what he had written. At the top were the words *Assistant Keeper: Westminster* in Raphael's beautiful copperplate hand, and the rest of the page was blank.

'I see,' she said. 'Let's start at the beginning. Is the role permanent, or temporary?'

Raphael frowned. 'It's sort of both. It's permanent if you can manage to hold on to it, and temporary if you can't.'

Jemma sighed. 'Maybe put "to be confirmed". Who does the role report to?'

'Oh, that's easy,' said Raphael, looking much happier. 'The role reports to me. Keeper of England.' He passed Jemma his pen.

'OK,' said Jemma, writing it down. 'Salary?'

'Ooooh, I know this!' cried Raphael. 'One thousand guineas per annum.'

Jemma's pen froze above the paper, and she stared at him. 'A thousand guineas?'

'Yes,' said Raphael. 'It's a nice round sum, that's why I remembered it.'

'Is that all?' asked Jemma.

'There are some special allowances,' said Raphael. 'One's expenses are paid, for example.'

'What sort of expenses?'

'Well, you know.' Raphael shifted in his seat. 'Expenses incurred in the course of performing one's duty. So if one happened to be at a meeting, and one required sustenance...'

Jemma grinned. 'So all those coffees and pastries from Rolando's go on expenses?'

Raphael shrugged. 'Completely necessary,' he said. 'I've never had any trouble getting them signed off. And of course there is the book budget, which in the case of agreed acquisitions is unlimited.'

'I see.' Jemma thought for a moment. 'And Gertrude?'

'Company car,' said Raphael.

Jemma wrote: *Plus generous expenses including subsistence and company car.* 'Pension?'

'Nooooo,' said Raphael, as if the idea were ridiculous. And now that Jemma thought about it, a pension scheme for staff who were presumably immortal *was* rather unrealistic.

'OK, got that,' she said. 'What about hours?'

'Flexible,' said Raphael. 'But on call for twenty-four hours, seven days a week.'

'Really?' said Jemma.

'Oh yes,' said Raphael. 'Keepers never sleep. Well, obviously we do, but in an emergency—'

'I get it.' Jemma considered the sheet of paper. 'How would you summarise the job?'

Raphael drank some coffee, then sat back in his chair and closed his eyes. Jemma was just debating whether to poke him when he sat bolt upright. 'The Assistant Keeper of Westminster,' he declared, 'is responsible for maintaining the knowledge sources in their care in good condition, and for acquiring new assets with the agreement of their superiors. They are also responsible for preventing any knowledge-related emergencies in the borough of Westminster, and if any do occur, containing same without involving outside agencies or the media.'

'Hang on a minute,' muttered Jemma, busy scribbling. 'You're asking them to do that for a thousand pounds a year?'

'Guineas,' Raphael corrected. 'Plus allowances.'

'Good luck with that,' said Jemma. 'OK, let's go to qualifications and experience.'

'Hmm,' said Raphael, stretching his legs out beneath the table. 'The most important is that they must be able to read.'

Jemma laughed. 'I would have thought that went without saying.'

'Ah, someone got past me in 1850,' said Raphael. 'He lasted a good three months. Oh yes, and they need to be able to write, too.'

'What about actual qualifications?' said Jemma.

Raphael looked nonplussed. 'That's a bit tricky,' he said. 'You see, not all of us have had what you might call a formal education.'

Jemma decided not to ask for clarification. 'All right, what about experience?'

'We don't ask for too much at this level,' said Raphael. 'This is a relatively junior position, so we'd be looking for a minimum of ten years running a book-heavy environment with no major incidents. We'd also be prepared to consider people with twenty years experience and one successfully contained major incident.'

He smiled. 'In some ways those candidates are better, because they've had firsthand experience of disaster management. Oh yes, you can put that. Non-accountable involvement in one disaster or three minor incidents, with no loss of assets. Oh, or life.'

Jemma sighed, and wrote. 'Anything else? Business experience?'

Raphael laughed. 'You've worked with me, Jemma, what do you think?'

Jemma put her pen down. 'If you can fill in the basic duties of the post, that's more or less it for the job description,' she said. 'And you can work out the experience and the qualities you want.'

'Oh yes,' said Raphael. 'Not like Brian. That's mainly why I'm doing this, so that I don't end up with another one of him.'

'So how does the recruitment process work?' said Jemma.

'Oh, we always have lots of candidates,' said Raphael. 'I normally tell them to bring three books, shove them in a room together, and see who's left at the end.'

Jemma remembered the graduate scheme recruitment processes she had gone through, and revised her opinion of them to actually quite humane. 'What about the people who don't make it?'

'Oh, they can always try again,' said Raphael. 'They generally find a home somewhere. Many of them end up working in normal bookshops. Mostly, you see, they just like books, and the rest of it is a bit of an add-on.'

'As opposed to the people who think they'll be working in a normal bookshop, then find out that isn't the case,' said Jemma. 'OK, so once you've added the duties and written the person spec, you advertise the job somewhere appropriate. I'd suggest for a role like this that you should have a closing date of three weeks to a month from the date you post the advert—'

'A month?' Raphael's eyebrows were almost in his hairline.

'Yes,' said Jemma.

'And where do I advertise?' said Raphael. 'I was planning to mention it to my staff and see who was up for it.'

'And then put them all in a room, I suppose,' said Jemma.

'Of course,' said Raphael. 'How else am I meant to pick someone?'

'You remember when I made you interview me?' said Jemma.

'But that was different,' said Raphael. 'That was for the bookshop.'

'You could write competency-based questions that would show you how people cope with emergencies, what sort of books they would want to acquire, and what knowledge they have of storing books appropriately,' said Jemma. 'Or you could give them an emergency scenario and ask what they would do.'

Raphael picked up his coffee cup and drained it. 'This is much more work than I thought it would be,' he said. 'Why don't you just take the job?'

Jemma goggled at him. 'Don't be ridiculous, Raphael,' she snapped. 'I have no idea how to look after valuable books, I don't know what I'd do in a knowledge-related emergency, and I've spent less than six months working in a bookshop.' She felt heat creep up her neck. 'I'm not qualified, according to your criteria, and apart from anything else, you can't afford me.'

'Oh,' said Raphael. 'Is that your final word on the subject?'

'Yes, it is,' said Jemma. 'I'm surprised at you, Raphael. The system you've got at the moment is why you ended up with someone like Brian working for you. There's no job security, the pay is terrible, and I sincerely doubt that this is a family-friendly job. Frankly, I'm disappointed.' She stood up, and pushed her chair in.

As Jemma turned to go she saw Carl framed in the great oak doorway, staring at her. 'Excuse me,' she said, marching towards him, 'I have a bookshop to run.' And still staring, he got out of her way.

Chapter 4

Jemma arrived back at her own bookshop to find a small note hanging from the knocker. *Stocktake in progress: please knock or ring for admission.* She let herself in and, as ever, was surprised when no bell rang. There was no bell. She imagined Brian's face at being summoned by a bell, like a grocer, or a vendor of something he would consider less classy than books.

'I'm back,' she called, removing her jacket. 'Are you in the stockroom?'

There was no answer, but presently Maddy appeared with not a hair out of place. 'Sorry, I was in the middle of something,' she said. She looked Jemma up and down, taking in her slightly increased smartness. 'You were quick.'

'Yes, it turned out to be recruitment advice, so it didn't take long.'

Maddy's eyes opened a little wider. 'Recruitment advice?'

'That's right,' said Jemma. How much did Maddy know? She couldn't be sure, but she could see that Maddy was interested. 'Seeing as I'm back, would you mind showing me the ropes? Of the stocktaking, I mean.'

Maddy smoothed her hair. 'I, um – yes, of course. Come this way.' She smiled, but it lasted only a moment before it flickered and went out.

Over the next half hour, Jemma was inducted into the mysteries of book care. Maddy showed her the special boxes that the most valuable books were kept in, often made to measure, and the thermostat in the stockroom. 'I always check it when I come in, and when I leave for the day,' she said. 'If it's colder than nineteen degrees or warmer than twenty-one, I take action. And if it's a particularly hot or cold day, I check it at lunchtime as well. It only takes a second, but it's essential for peace of mind.'

'And how do you know where everything is?' asked Jemma.

Maddy laughed. 'Oh, that's easy. Each set of shelves has a letter, and each individual shelf, a number. We arrange books by subject, so botany goes here' – she pointed – 'and art here.' She twisted round and pointed the other way. 'So when we bring in a new book we type its details into the computer, add the shelf code, and that's it. If it has its own box, of course, we label that. There's a label maker under the counter.'

'I see,' said Jemma, gazing about her. Brian's stockroom was perhaps a sixth of the size of Raphael's, if that, and meticulously organised. 'Do you find that the books stay where you put them?'

'I'm not sure what you mean,' said Maddy. 'The shelves are very sturdy, so we've never had any collapses.'

'I'm sure you haven't,' said Jemma. She ran a finger along the nearest shelf when Maddy wasn't looking, and it came away clean. 'I mean, have you ever come in here for a book and found it wasn't where you expected it to be?'

Maddy shook her head. 'No, never. The system is agreed. So long as everyone knows what's going on, nothing should go astray.'

'And you've never... You've never found a book in your stockroom that you didn't expect to be there?'

298

Maddy's head-shaking became more vigorous. 'We keep track of everything,' she said. 'If we found something unexpected in the stockroom, that would mean it hadn't been catalogued.' She frowned as if this possibility had never occurred to her. Then she gazed at Jemma. 'Would you mind me asking,' she said, 'what the position is that you were advising on?'

'I'm not sure I can,' said Jemma. 'I haven't been sworn to secrecy exactly, but it isn't my job to discuss.'

'So it isn't a job here,' said Maddy.

Jemma smiled. 'No, it isn't,' she said. 'It's nothing to do with me.'

'Oh,' said Maddy. 'I see. Would you like a cup of tea? We're just about finished.'

'Yes, please, if you don't mind,' said Jemma. 'That would be lovely.'

While Maddy was making tea Jemma took the opportunity to nip upstairs and fetch her laptop cable. *Hmmm,* she thought as she came back downstairs. Maddy was clearly relieved that the recruitment wasn't for their shop. *Perhaps she's worried I'll replace her.* Jemma heaved a sigh. *She really shouldn't be. I wouldn't have the first clue how to run this place.*

But you can run a bookshop, said a surprisingly encouraging inner voice. *You've done it, remember? And Raphael still relies on you.*

That's different, she told it as she opened the door into the bookshop, cable in hand. *I run a general bookshop, not a bookshop like this.*

But you don't want it to be a bookshop like this, the little voice insisted. *You want it to be different. What about that book you read last night? And your plan?*

You be quiet and let me think things over, Jemma told it, as Maddy handed her a mug of tea. The mugs here were all bone china. 'Thank you, Maddy.'

And anyway, the voice piped up, *it should be much easier here, because it doesn't look as if this bookshop is magical. It just does what it's told.*

'You could be right,' said Jemma.

Maddy turned surprised eyes on her. 'Excuse me?'

'I, um, I said that I hope Luke has a good night,' said Jemma. 'You know, Luke who works at the other bookshop. He's going speed dating tonight.'

Maddy looked at her feet. 'Luke's the – the young man in black, isn't he?'

'That's right,' said Jemma. She had once, in a moment of managerial enthusiasm, brought Luke and Carl to say hello to Maddy, hoping that they would get along and perhaps be able to work between the bookshops. The experience had been five minutes of embarrassed shuffling and one-word responses which she never wanted to repeat.

'Oh,' said Maddy. She took the teabag out of her cup of camomile tea and put it neatly in the bin.

'I thought you usually left it in,' said Jemma.

'What?' Maddy followed Jemma's gaze to her mug. 'Oh. I don't like it too strong, though.' She paused. 'Have you considered new acquisitions?'

'I can't say that I have, yet,' said Jemma. 'I mean, I feel as if I've only been here five minutes.'

'Oh yes, I understand that,' said Maddy. 'But with Brian's, um, departure, it's important that people still have a reason to come to the shop. He was known for his select but interesting stock.'

'I gathered,' said Jemma. 'What did he specialise in?' She noted, in passing, that this was the first time Maddy had referred to the fact that Brian was no longer there.

'Rare antiquarian books,' said Maddy. 'For preference, nineteenth century or earlier, and always non-fiction.' She giggled. It was rather an odd sound, as if she wasn't used to doing it. 'He always said that novels were a pack of lies.'

'Did he,' said Jemma. She hadn't thought it possible, but Brian went down another notch in her estimation.

'Yes, he said—' Maddy winced and put a hand to her head. 'Oh dear,' she said. 'I think I have a headache coming on.'

'Why don't you sit quietly for a bit,' said Jemma. 'Do you need to take something?' She looked under the back-room sink for the first-aid kit, but of course it wasn't there. *Definitely not a magical shop*, the little voice muttered.

'No, no, I'm sure I'll be fine in a minute,' said Maddy. 'Perhaps it's dust from the stockroom.'

'I doubt it,' said Jemma. 'It's absolutely spotless in there.'

'I think I need peace and quiet,' said Maddy. She sat down, put her camomile tea on the table, and rested her head in her hands, massaging her temples gently. 'Would you mind switching off the lights?'

'Of course,' said Jemma. 'I'll go through and mind the shop.'

She went through and took the sign off the door, then plugged in her laptop and typed in her password. Immediately her action plan filled the screen, in all its multicoloured glory. Jemma scrolled through it, then sipped her tea and put it out of harm's way. She scrolled left, so that the more ambitious milestones exited stage right. Then she looked at her initial goals.

- *Learn more about the stock*. She pursed her lips and changed the cell colour to light green. There was still work to be done, but she had a much better idea of what she was dealing with.

- *Find out if the shop is magic, and if so, how much*. Jemma selected a neon-bright green for this one, and in the notes column, typed: *Not at all. It's a completely normal bookshop.*

- *Get to know Maddy better and find out what drives her.*

Jemma frowned. From what she had seen, Maddy was devoted to the bookshop. She seemed genuinely relieved to learn that

Jemma wasn't planning to recruit new staff for her shop, and she might even have accepted that Brian wasn't coming back. At least, not for another ten years. It was definitely progress of sorts, so Jemma coloured the cell light green.

The cursor winked in the comments field. Jemma thought for a moment, and typed: *Continue to talk to Maddy. Find out what, if anything, she does outside work. Be nice to her.*

I'm never not nice to her, she thought indignantly. Then she remembered her little snipe earlier that morning, and felt herself going pink. *OK, I'll try.*

The door to the back room opened and Maddy stood there, looking rather pale. 'I've had a rest, and I feel much better,' she said, walking into the shop.

It can't be easy for Maddy, Jemma thought. *She's probably worked here for years, and she's used to having things just so. This must all have been a shock. Be kind,* Jemma added in the comments box, then closed the laptop and smiled at her. But Maddy, who almost appeared to be sleepwalking, didn't smile back.

Chapter 5

Jemma was doing the stocktake in the bookshop, but it was taking a lot longer than when Maddy did it. For one thing, several of the books weren't where they were supposed to be. Some weren't even in their protective boxes. And when Maddy checked the thermostat, it was a full two degrees higher than it should have been. 'The books will spoil,' she said, fixing Jemma with a stern eye. 'And that will be your fault. I suggest that you go to bed.'

'What a good idea,' said Jemma. 'I'll see you in the morning, then.'

'Oh no, you can't leave the stockroom,' said Maddy. 'You have to mind the books. Here, I've made up a bed for you.' She pointed to a large wooden box with a blanket in it. 'You'll be fine in there. You fit perfectly, I've checked. So if you'll just climb in, I'll put the lid on—'

'I don't think that's a good idea,' said Jemma, taking a step back.

'Why's that?' asked Maddy, advancing. 'Don't you like the way we do things in the shop?' Her hand shot out and grabbed Jemma's wrist. 'Come along, you'll like it when you get used to it.' Then somehow Jemma was in the box and trying to get out, but her hands slipped on its smooth sides. Now the lid was closing— 'Help!' she yelled, and thrust upwards with all her strength.

Her eyes opened. It was pitch black, possibly because she had managed to pull the throw she kept on the chesterfield sofa over her face. But when she struggled free, it was still dark outside. Something was digging into her back. She felt around carefully and retrieved *Pigs Have Wings*, which looked slightly the worse for its experience.

Oh dear. She glanced at her phone: a quarter past four. She sighed, padded upstairs to her bedroom, and lay down as she was. After all, she'd have to get up in three hours.

It's been ages since I had a nightmare, she thought, but she didn't bother to interrogate the cause. She knew perfectly well.

Jemma had tried her best to honour her new action point to be kind to Maddy, but somehow, it wasn't bearing the fruit she had hoped for. Far from the glimpses of possible companionship, and a future for the bookshop without Brian in it, Maddy had grown even more set in her ways. When Jemma had suggested gently that perhaps the bookshop could widen its remit and introduce a shelf of classic novels, plays, and poetry, Maddy's head had pulled back and her nostrils had flared, as if she were a warhorse ready to charge.

'I'm not sure what our customers would make of that,' she said, fetching a cloth and wiping an invisible smear from the counter. When a customer came in, she asked him – after she had fulfilled his requirements, of course. 'While you're here, Mr De Vere,' she had said, 'Jemma wonders whether we should present classic fiction in addition to our current offer.'

Mr De Vere, a lean man in a tweed jacket, snorted. 'Not for me, thank you,' he said, regarding Jemma as if she were a slug on his salad. 'The shop is fine as it is. I wouldn't want it – diluted – with fiction.' He leaned forward and murmured something to

Maddy which Jemma was too far away to catch.

Maddy considered, and as she did so, Jemma moved closer. The pair of them eyed her, then Maddy said, 'I really couldn't say.'

'Since you're here, Mr De Vere,' said Jemma, feeling that as she was already in his bad books it couldn't hurt to sink any lower, 'are there any other books you might be interested in? I'm thinking of compiling a database of customers' interests.'

Mr De Vere ignored her while he put his purchase into the large leather satchel he had brought for the purpose. Only then did he respond. 'When I want a book, my dear, I shall come in and ask for it. Good day to you.'

'That went well,' said Jemma, once the door had closed behind him.

Maddy turned, and Jemma almost recoiled at her forbidding expression. 'We do not solicit the customers in the shop,' she said.

'Why not?' said Jemma. 'Usually people like being asked what their interests are.'

'Our relationships with our clients go back years,' said Maddy. 'You can't expect to get chummy with them in a matter of days.'

'Then maybe we need friendlier customers,' said Jemma. 'Meanwhile, I need tea.' And she stomped to the back room in high dudgeon.

The rest of the afternoon had been no better. They had two more serious customers who also rejected the idea that the shop might stock even Folio Society editions of appropriate fiction. In between, a sprinkling of browsers were scared off either by the books or by Maddy, who had told one customer with great contempt that they did not stock chick lit.

'If that's what you're looking for,' said Jemma, 'why don't you try Burns Books? It's just down the road that way. They have lots of fiction, including chick lit, and a café.'

'Oh, right,' said the woman, slinging her handbag more firmly over her shoulder. 'Thanks for that, I'll go there now. I could just fancy a coffee.'

Maddy was silent until the customer had left. Then she rounded on Jemma. 'What did you do that for?'

Jemma shrugged. 'If we don't have what she wants, it's only reasonable to send her to a shop that does. Perhaps they'll send people our way, too.'

Maddy muttered something.

'I didn't quite catch that,' said Jemma.

'I said,' Maddy declared, clear as a bell, 'that left up to you, the shop would be run into the ground within a fortnight. Sending people to our competitors?'

'They aren't our competitors,' said Jemma. 'In case you've forgotten, I work for both shops, and I don't see why they can't complement each other. Perhaps you should stop being so narrow-minded.'

Maddy muttered again at that, and Jemma decided that, whatever she was saying, she couldn't be bothered to listen to it. They had spent the rest of the afternoon in different parts of the shop.

They closed bang on five o'clock, as usual. *So much for kindness*, thought Jemma. She gazed around the beautiful, cold shop, and sighed. Then she texted Carl. *Just finished here. Want to come round? I'll cook.*

It took longer for him to reply than usual. Jemma sat at the shop counter, waiting. It wasn't as if she needed to go anywhere. *Sorry, not tonight. I'm meeting up with Rumpus. Will you be in the shop tomorrow?*

Jemma's eyebrows rose. *I thought rehearsals were yesterday*, she replied.

His response was quicker this time. *They were. This is something else.*

Jemma rolled her eyes. He really wasn't getting the message. *When are you meeting them?* she texted.

7.30, but I've got stuff to do first. Can we talk tomorrow?
~~No, I want to talk now!~~
~~I've had a rotten day and I want someone to be nice to me.~~
~~My plan isn't working and I don't know what to do.~~

Sure, see you tomorrow. Jemma had debated putting a kiss on the end of her message, but decided he didn't deserve it. And now, huddled in a cold bed in the dead of night, she still felt exactly the same.

***

Jemma woke the next morning sticky-eyed and grumpy. Everything still rankled. What annoyed her most was that she had succumbed to the lure of a Snacking Cross Road double-pepperoni pizza and two cans of full-fat Coke. No wonder she hadn't slept well. 'Bad choices, Jemma,' she groaned as she peeled herself out of bed.

At least I don't have to face Maddy this morning, she thought, staring at her doleful reflection in the bathroom mirror.

But you do have to face Raphael.

She winced, and turned the shower on.

Two slices of toast and a strong coffee later, she felt slightly more human. *I suppose I should apologise*, she thought, as she put mascara on.

'Yes, you should,' said a voice rather like her mother's. 'He thinks you're capable. Let's face it, you need people like that.'

Jemma had an almost overriding impulse to put her mascara away and slam the cabinet door on that annoying little voice, but remembered just in time that she had only done one eye. So she endured more nagging, her mouth half-open so that she couldn't even retort, then took great pleasure in shutting it in for the day.

At least once she got to the shop Luke looked his normal, slightly scruffy self. 'How did it go?' she asked.

Luke glanced up from *The Language of Film*. 'Good, thanks,' he said.

'And…?' she prompted.

The book lowered. 'I'm going on a date tonight,' he said. 'Drinks, then a movie. I'm finishing early so that I can get ready.'

'Oh, right,' said Jemma. 'Hope it goes well.'

'Raphael isn't in yet,' said Luke. 'Carl is setting up.'

Jemma checked her watch. 'He's early,' she said.

'Yeah, he's finishing a bit early tonight too,' said Luke. 'Something about a project.'

Everyone but me's got stuff going on, thought Jemma, pushing her hair out of her eyes. But she merely said 'Uh-huh,' and headed downstairs.

She heard whistling as she pushed open the oak door. Carl was sweeping the floor. 'Oh, hi,' he said, leaning on his broom.

'Hi,' said Jemma. 'Have you got time for a cappuccino?'

He hesitated. 'Yeah, go on then. The machine's on.'

Jemma sat at one of the café tables and watched him make her drink. 'Luke says you've got a project on,' she said, as he sprinkled cocoa powder on top.

His shoulders stiffened a fraction. Then he picked up the cup and brought it over. 'Here you go,' he said. Then he took a seat opposite her. 'I've been working on something.'

'With Rumpus? Is that what yesterday's meeting was about?'

Carl smiled. 'Yeah.' He leaned back in his chair. 'That night we didn't go out, I had an idea for a play. And I had a go at writing it.'

'Oh.' Jemma stared at him. 'But you don't—'

'I know,' said Carl. 'It was weird. I got some paper, I thought about the characters, a line came into my head, and I wrote it down. The rest just sort of happened. I wasn't going to say anything, but then I mentioned to Josie that I'd written a play. She made me tell her about it, then said I should tell everyone. So I did, and last night we did a read-through. And they want to do it.'

'Do it?' Jemma echoed. 'You mean—'

'Put it on. I mean, it needs work, I know it needs work, but we could workshop it and then maybe ask Raphael. It's set in a bookshop, you see.' He grinned. 'Write what you know, and all that.'

'Wow,' said Jemma. 'That's great. No, that's brilliant. It really is. I'm so pleased for you.' She reached out and squeezed his hand, but the gesture felt inadequate.

'Thanks,' said Carl. 'How did your plan go?'

Jemma drank her cappuccino while she considered her answer. There was so much she wanted to tell him, and she sensed that pouring her heart out would get the poison out of her system. But she couldn't do it. She couldn't dump that negativity on him, not when he was doing such a cool new thing. 'Early days,' she said. 'I'm working on things.' She took a deep draught of her coffee. 'Anyway, I'd better leave you to it if you've got things to do.' She got up.

Carl studied her. 'OK,' he said, eventually. Then he got up, took her cup, and slotted it into the dishwasher. 'Maybe see you later?'

Jemma forced a smile. 'Sure,' she said. 'See you later.'

She walked slowly back upstairs, undecided whether she would be more miserable in Carl's company or Luke's. *If ever there was a day not to be around people...* 'I'm just nipping into the stockroom,' she called to Luke. 'Let me know when Raphael comes down.'

She switched the light on and wandered along the aisles, looking at the rows of book-filled boxes and seeing nothing. *Of course Maddy would have a label maker*, she thought sourly. Then she stopped, turned to a shelf, and rested her forehead on the nearest box. *What am I going to do? I have no authority in my own shop. My. Own. Shop.*

'Then take it,' whispered a little voice.

Jemma jumped, and stared at the box as if it had spoken to her. 'How?'

'Maddy sees you as an inferior,' the whisper came, a little louder this time. 'But if you were Assistant Keeper...'

'But what if I don't want to be Assistant Keeper?' Jemma rubbed her forehead. *I'm talking to a box. This is ridiculous.*

'But I'm giving you answers,' the little voice said. 'Think about it. It doesn't have to be for ever.'

Possibilities swam in Jemma's mind. If she were busy learning Assistant Keeper duties, no one could expect her to make sweeping changes in the bookshop. With that added authority, she would feel more able to give orders to Maddy. And as it was only temporary, then assuming no major disasters occurred, no one could blame her if she didn't get things exactly right.

A gentle tap at the door. 'Anyone home?' called Raphael.

'Sshh,' Jemma told the box, then clapped her hand over her mouth. 'I'm in here,' she said. 'Have you got new stock in?'

Raphael entered, resplendent in a maroon velvet smoking jacket, teal-coloured trousers, and a pale-grey shirt with a teal silk cravat. 'Yes, I have,' he said. 'I've been thinking, and perhaps you are right.'

'I've been thinking too,' said Jemma, 'and I agree. I wouldn't be suited to the permanent job, but if you like, I could take it on while you recruit somebody. So long as you teach me the basics.'

'Oh,' said Raphael. He studied her for perhaps a minute. 'I hadn't expected that. You were rather—'

'I've slept on it,' said Jemma, 'and I need a challenge.'

'Well,' said Raphael, 'if we're recruiting in the, er, approved manner, it would help to have somebody holding the fort in the meantime.'

'Good,' said Jemma. 'So that's settled, then.' She walked towards Raphael and stuck out a hand. 'Pleasure to work with you, boss,' she said, plastering a wide, confident smile on her face. And as Raphael, looking bewildered, shook it, she wished with all her heart that she felt even a tenth as confident beneath.

Chapter 6

'As luck would have it,' said Raphael, 'we are in exactly the right place to begin.' He swept a hand round the stockroom.

Jemma swallowed. She hadn't expected her instruction to commence quite so soon. 'W – where is the thermostat?' she asked.

Raphael's hand was arrested mid-gesture. 'The which?'

'The thermostat,' said Jemma. 'To keep the books at the right temperature.'

Comprehension dawned. 'Oh,' said Raphael. 'You've been listening to Maddy, haven't you?' He smiled. 'The shop does that.'

'Is that why our books aren't in special boxes?' said Jemma.

'Exactly. The stockroom preserves the books for me.'

'But how does it know?' asked Jemma.

They heard a meow outside the door. Raphael raised an eyebrow. 'I suspect Folio wishes to be involved.' He opened the door and let the cat in. Folio strolled towards the table and chair which Luke used, jumped on the chair, and sat watching them.

'In answer to your question,' said Raphael, 'the shop is enchanted. Various powerful charms protect any book that comes in here. Allow me to demonstrate.' He reached for the nearest box and took out a book. 'This is one of my favourites,' he said. 'It's a book of cures, lotions and poultices, compiled by a woman called Sukey Nobbs in the fifteenth century. There is more practical wisdom in this than in many a modern textbook. Jemma, could you go to the far end of that aisle, pull out any box, and take out the first book you find.'

Jemma did as she was told. '*On Life and Death*,' she read. '*Essays.*'

'That'll do nicely,' said Raphael. He took two steps forward. 'Now walk towards me. Oh, and hold the book out.'

Jemma did as she was told, feeling exceptionally silly. 'I really don't understand what this is—'

She stopped, not of her own volition. She felt as if she had walked into an invisible wall.

'That's it,' said Raphael. 'Have another go.'

Jemma's foot moved forward, then stopped. She tried to hold the book out, but her arm just wouldn't stretch.

'As you can see, we have a slight problem,' said Raphael. 'However, it is easily solved. I want you to tell the book that you are an Assistant Keeper.'

Jemma looked at the book, then at Raphael, and shrugged. 'I'm an assistant keeper,' she mumbled.

'Not like that,' said Raphael. 'As if you believe it. Come on, stand tall.'

Jemma stared at him. 'Is this necessary?'

'Oh, absolutely,' said Raphael. 'Come on, have a try.'

Jemma took a deep breath. 'I am an Assistant Keeper,' she said, louder.

The book vibrated in her hand.

'That's better,' said Raphael. 'Once more. Imagine you want Maddy to hear you.'

That did it. Jemma filled her lungs and shouted 'I am an

Assistant Keeper!'

'There,' said Raphael. 'Try moving now.'

Jemma took a step forward, then another, until she was perhaps two feet away from Raphael. 'That will do,' he said.

'It works,' said Jemma. 'It really works.' She gazed at the book in her hand, which resonated with a gentle hum. Then she peered closer. 'Is it glowing?'

'It is,' said Raphael. 'Probably best that you take a step back. No point in wasting the power. Now you can see why I keep books like these well apart.'

'So do you actually know where all the important books are in the stockroom?' asked Jemma. This was a level of organisation she would never have suspected of Raphael.

'Not as such,' Raphael replied. 'I tend to assume that this room, given the enchantments it has, will keep things apart that need to be kept apart.'

'But how does that work in – in *my* shop?' asked Jemma. 'It isn't magical.'

'Don't be too sure,' said Raphael. 'It may not be as magical as this shop, but few places are.'

'But if it were,' said Jemma, 'then why would it need the thermostat, and the special boxes, and the cataloguing system?'

'Maybe it does need some of those things,' said Raphael. 'Or maybe that's just smoke and mirrors to keep Maddy happy. Who knows?' He smiled. 'What you *could* do is look for the more – interesting – resources, and see if you can bring them together. If you can do that without telling the books that you're an Assistant Keeper, then yes, it probably is a normal shop.' He sighed. 'I do hope for your sake that it isn't, Jemma. That would be remarkably dull.'

'So should I assume that everything is stored correctly?' said Jemma.

'Have there been any fires?' asked Raphael.

'Of course not,' said Jemma. 'What do you take me for?'

'Floods? Plagues of insects? Things or people disappearing?'

Jemma shook her head.

'In that case,' said Raphael, 'you're probably fine. But maybe check, to be on the safe side.'

'How did you learn all this?' asked Jemma.

'I spent a lot of time in my uncle's bookshop when I was a boy,' said Raphael. 'He taught me to read. I don't remember him telling me anything, as such, but I sort of absorbed it.'

'Is he still alive?' asked Jemma, wide-eyed.

'Good heavens, no,' said Raphael. 'Unfortunately the plague got him.'

'The – the Great Plague?' asked Jemma.

'That's the one,' said Raphael. 'And then the fire finished off the bookshop. Not a great decade, I think you'll agree.'

'No,' said Jemma, faintly. 'I don't suppose it was.' She felt her mind reaching for something to grasp hold of, something that made sense. 'So if there is an incident,' she said, 'what should I do?'

'If books are too close together,' said Raphael, 'the best thing to do is to move them apart, taking care that in doing so you don't move them towards another book they might react with.'

'OK,' said Jemma. 'Move books apart, keeping clear of other books.'

'If a book is damaged, then in the first instance bring it to me for inspection,' said Raphael. 'Obviously, in this shop we have some stock which is in, shall we say, not the best condition. But if it's a standard volume, carefully applied sticky tape will probably do the trick.'

'And if it isn't?' Jemma imagined torn parchment, accidentally dogeared pages, cracked spines. Now she understood the reason for all that glass.

'Bring it to me,' said Raphael, 'and we shall decide what is best to do given the age, value, and importance of the item.' He paused, considering. 'Your shop's stock is different from mine. You have far fewer books, but on average they are more valuable.' He grinned. 'I have to admit I was rather impressed when he brought out Archimedes' Palimpsest. I wasn't expecting that.'

'But wouldn't he have had to clear that with you first?' asked Jemma. 'You said in the job description—'

'Ah, but when it's for a challenge,' said Raphael, 'all bets are off. Anything goes, pretty much.' He frowned. 'I should probably have a chat with its previous owners, and find out what he gave them in exchange.'

Folio jumped down from his chair and wound himself round Jemma's legs. Jemma bent to stroke him, then remembered the book in her hand. 'Is it all right to—' She mimed stroking.

'Oh yes, of course,' said Raphael. 'Folio is very much attuned to the books. He won't damage them.'

'Good,' said Jemma, crouching and giving him a proper fuss. 'With everything else going on, I need to be able to stroke my favourite cat.' Folio let out an extremely loud purr.

'Mmm,' said Raphael. 'What else is going on?'

Drat, thought Jemma. 'I meant with Luke dating,' she said, 'and Carl's play.'

'And...?' Raphael's blue eyes were sympathetic, but Jemma felt them boring into her.

She sighed. 'I'm having a hard time with Maddy,' she said. 'She's resistant to change. Of any kind. Even adding fiction to the stock. And the customers share her views.'

'That must be frustrating,' said Raphael.

'Just slightly,' said Jemma. She looked around the stockroom and sighed again. 'What was the shop like when you took it on?'

'Sparse,' said Raphael. 'Specialist. A collector's shop.'

'So you've been through this too!' cried Jemma. 'What did you do?'

'Well,' said Raphael, 'as I won with a combination of three printed books, I decided that print was the way to go, and the more modern the better. It took until the late nineteenth century to pay off, though. Admittedly one of my printed books was Shakespeare's First Folio, but it's all relative.'

Jemma looked at the cat. 'Is that where Folio got his name?'

Folio sauntered over to Raphael and gazed at him expectantly. Raphael pulled a packet of cat treats from his pocket and gave him a couple. 'That's right,' he said, 'although I got Folio slightly before I took on the shop.'

'So he's immortal too?' Jemma gazed at Folio, who narrowed his eyes and gave her a sharp meow.

'Not immortal,' said Raphael. 'Neither of us are. Just – lucky. And certain, um, protections come with the job.'

'Oh,' said Jemma. She thought for a moment. 'Does that apply to all these sorts of jobs?'

'Not to the same degree,' said Raphael. 'But yes.'

'So if I took the job, permanently,' Jemma said slowly, 'I wouldn't die?'

'Not unless there was a major major incident,' said Raphael. 'You wouldn't get any older, either.'

Jemma had a sudden vision of Carl in thirty years' time: maybe grey-haired, maybe balding, and herself looking just the same. 'Oh,' she said.

'Indeed,' said Raphael. 'It's a blessing, and a curse. It's – difficult to form relationships with outsiders, since you know they won't be around for long. Comparatively speaking.'

'Oh dear,' said Jemma. Suddenly she felt more sorry for the ageless, powerful man in front of her than she would ever have thought possible. 'That doesn't apply to temporary staff, does it?'

Raphael laughed. 'No, Jemma, you're quite safe. Though some people see it as a perk.'

Jemma remembered the Assistant Curator at Sir John Soane's

Museum, and wondered.

'That's enough for now,' Raphael said gently. 'You've taken in a lot of information, and I don't want to overload you on your first day. Let's go downstairs and get a drink, and you can help me finish the job description. If we're doing this thing, we should get on with it. Then you can head over to your shop and check your own assets.'

'Yes,' said Jemma, dreamily. 'Yes, I can. I can check the assets in my shop.' She smiled. 'Come on then,' she said, 'I could murder a brew.'

They tidied the stockroom, let Folio out, then left. Jemma popped her head into the main shop, where Luke was buried in his book. 'Sorry about the noise,' she said.

Luke looked up. 'What noise?'

'You know,' said Jemma. 'The shouting.'

Luke considered this, then shrugged. 'Didn't hear anything.'

Jemma scrutinised as much of him as she could see, but he didn't appear to be making fun of her. Reflecting that the day couldn't get much stranger, she walked downstairs to join Raphael. 'I am an Assistant Keeper,' she whispered, very quietly, and felt the thrum of thousands of books, listening.

Chapter 7

Jemma returned to her shop armed with new knowledge and a cheese and Parma ham panini. When she reached it, she stepped back and surveyed it critically. *Would I want to shop in here?*

The answer was a resounding no.

Why, exactly?

The bookshop looks boring, she thought. *All that black paintwork. I don't like the name; all it tells me is that someone with the initials BJF sells old books. I don't know if they're interesting, just old. And as there's only one book in the window and I can't see what it's called, there's no way for me to tell if I'd like it or not.*

Well, I can't do anything about the name of the shop or the paintwork just yet. But I can deal with that display.

She opened the silent door. Maddy, as usual, was alone. 'Hi, Maddy,' she called. 'Busy morning?' She kept her face neutral as she said it.

Maddy glanced up from an auction catalogue. 'Nice and quiet, thank you. Just two customers, and we had what they wanted.'

'I've been thinking,' said Jemma. 'I'd like to encourage more customers into the shop.'

Maddy opened her mouth to reply, but Jemma held up a hand. 'Please let me finish. I know you don't want to broaden the bookshop's stock and our existing customers don't either, but I can't help thinking that if we put affordable books in the window, it might encourage more people in to buy what we already have. With a greater range of customers, we may find that they have different needs.'

Maddy sniffed. 'The bookshop does make a profit,' she said.

'Based on a few customers who have the money to buy our more expensive items,' said Jemma. 'If we lost even one or two of those customers we'd feel it, wouldn't we?'

Maddy said nothing.

'So what I would like you to do, Maddy,' said Jemma, 'is go through our stock and find me eight or nine attractive books priced at less than fifty pounds. Preferably less than twenty-five. How much is that book in the window?'

Maddy told her.

'Better make that nine,' said Jemma. 'It's not surprising that people don't come in. Now, have you had your lunch? If you'd like to go out, I can eat mine here.'

'I haven't,' said Maddy. 'And yes, I think I will go out today.' She closed the auction catalogue, picked up her hessian shopper, and slipped it inside. She did this without looking at Jemma. 'Bye,' she muttered, and made for the door.

Jemma sat in Maddy's still-warm seat. She was halfway through her panini and a re-read of Appendix 2 of *Your Business, Your Way* when a cough alerted her to the presence of a customer.

She swallowed her mouthful hurriedly. 'I'm terribly sorry, I didn't hear you come in,' she said. *I'm getting a bell put on that door*, she thought. *I don't care whether Brian would approve.*

The customer, a woman with expensive blonde highlights, wearing something tailored and obviously designer, raised an eyebrow. 'Is Brian in, please?'

Jemma considered how to answer. 'He doesn't work here at present,' she said.

'Maddy, then.'

'She's on her lunch break,' said Jemma, 'so I'm afraid you'll have to make do with me.' She stood up and extended a hand. 'I'm Jemma, the new manager of the shop.'

The woman looked at the hand. 'Are you,' she said. 'In that case, I want an early edition of Darwin's *Origin of Species*. First edition and original binding if possible, but I don't mind so long as it is in excellent condition. It's a present.'

'I'll check our database,' said Jemma. She moved to the computer and typed in search terms. 'We have one first edition in reasonable condition, and a fourth edition described as being "as new". Would you like to see them both?'

The woman studied Jemma as if she were a talking dog. 'Um, yes please,' she said.

The fourth edition was shelved in the main shop, while the other was in the stockroom. 'I shouldn't be long,' said Jemma, hoping fervently that she wouldn't. *B7*, she repeated in her head as she scanned the shelves.

The book was exactly where it should be, in a labelled case. Jemma felt a rush of unexpected warmth towards Maddy. 'Thank you,' she whispered, and picked up the case. She laid it on the counter, then unlocked a glass door in the main shop and brought out the second book. Both were green, both had gilt decoration on the spine. 'Here we are,' she said. 'There's quite a difference in price—'

The woman flapped an impatient hand. 'That one,' she said, pointing at the fourth edition. 'I'd prefer the other, but there isn't time to get it restored.' She sighed. 'These last-minute birthday invitations are so tiresome.'

'I'm sure whoever receives it will love it,' said Jemma. 'It's a very generous gift.'

The woman smiled for the first time since she had entered the shop. Her teeth were white and even, and there was a tiny gap between each. 'It's a convenient gift,' she said. She opened her bag, extracted a small purse, and took out a plain black card.

'Well, if you need any more last-minute book presents,' said Jemma, 'you know where we are.' She took payment and handed over the receipt. 'Would you like a bag?'

The customer considered. 'It's probably best,' she concluded. 'Excuse me a moment.' She went to the door, beckoned, and presently a uniformed man came in and bore the book away. 'Thank you, er—'

'Jemma,' said Jemma.

The woman seemed to be considering whether that could possibly be her name. Eventually, she nodded. 'Thank you, Jemma.' And she sailed out.

As soon as the door closed, Jemma slumped on the counter with a huge sigh of relief. Then she started laughing. *I made a sale! I made a sale, on my own, and nothing bad happened!* It was only when she straightened up that she realised her half-eaten panini had been sitting next to her on the counter all along.

***

'Quiet, I suppose,' said Maddy, when she returned.

'Just one customer,' said Jemma. She had considered whether to swap her business book for *Pigs Have Wings* before Maddy got back, but decided that what she chose to read was up to her.

Maddy hung up her jacket and bag, and removed the auction catalogue. 'Will you be going out?'

'No thanks, I'm fine,' said Jemma. 'Oh yes, and we have a gap on that shelf.' She pointed to the empty space where *Origin of Species* had been.

Maddy gaped. 'You sold one?'

'I did,' said Jemma, trying not to puff up. 'For the price listed

321

on the database. And I've updated the record.'

'Oh,' said Maddy, still gazing at the empty space. 'Um, good.'

'Actually,' said Jemma, 'why don't you make yourself a drink, then look for cheaper stock for the window? Maybe pick out fifteen to twenty books, so we can choose the ones that complement each other for the display.' She beamed at Maddy, then returned to her book.

'Would you – would you like a drink too?' asked Maddy. Her voice was slightly thick and hoarse, as if she were having trouble forming the words.

'Oh, yes please,' said Jemma. 'Tea with milk and one sugar, if you would.'

Maddy said no more, but went into the back room. Jemma noted that her usually beautiful posture was slightly off; her upper back curved, her shoulders slightly forward, her head down. She bit her lip. *Am I being mean?*

Give over, said a little voice which Jemma thought of as coming from the book. *You're setting the direction for your business. It's a perfectly normal request. And you asked nicely.*

I did, didn't I? thought Jemma. *And I'm including her in the choosing process, so I'm empowering her.* Feeling almost unbearably smug, she returned to her book.

'It's no good,' said Maddy, ten minutes later. 'Only six books in the shop cost less than fifty pounds, and three of those are in poor condition.'

Jemma sighed. 'Then we should review our stock,' she said. 'I don't want the shop to be a place for rich people only.'

Maddy shot a glance at her. 'But if that's what the books cost...'

'I'm not saying that we can't sell expensive books,' said Jemma. 'But we should sell affordable ones, too. I mean, could you afford to buy most of the books we sell?'

'Well, no,' said Maddy, 'but that isn't the point—'

'What do you like to read?' Jemma asked.

Maddy recoiled as if she had asked a very personal question. 'I read – I read auction catalogues, and the *Bookseller*, and the *Bookseller's Companion*, of course—'

'I asked you what you *like* to read,' said Jemma. 'I like reading novels, usually contemporary ones with a bit of humour, but I'll try most things.' She went to her bag, pulled out *Pigs Have Wings*, and held it up.

Maddy stared at the book in Jemma's hand. 'I—' She swallowed. 'I like Gothic fiction,' she said. 'Classic Gothic fiction, like Ann Radcliffe.' She looked as if she were confessing a secret shame.

'Like *The Mysteries of Udolpho*?' said Jemma. 'I've seen that in Burns Books, but I don't know what else she wrote.'

'She wrote six novels,' said Maddy, 'but they're hard to get hold of. Some of them—' She paused as if what she were about to say might shock Jemma. 'They're only available *online*.'

'Oh yes, I've got a reading app on my phone,' said Jemma. 'It's great for holidays, but I do prefer a paperback.' She grinned. 'I'm probably Brian's most un-ideal reader.'

A small smile lifted the corner of Maddy's mouth. She leaned forward. 'He doesn't know about the novels,' she whispered. 'I've never told him. But I do like reading auction catalogues,' she said in her normal voice. 'Very interesting.'

'Like reading store catalogues when you were a kid, and picking out the things you wanted?' said Jemma.

Maddy giggled. 'Kind of.'

'Right,' said Jemma, 'what we'll do is put any cheap books in good condition in the window, and add some between fifty and a hundred pounds. Popular names that people recognise, not obscure stuff. The customer who came in earlier wanted *Origin of Species* for a birthday present, which goes to show. With the money from the sale, what I propose to do is buy good-quality cheaper stock.

Agreed?'

'Agreed,' said Maddy. And while Jemma wasn't entirely sure how she had got Maddy on her side, or how on earth she would acquire the new stock that she had spoken of so lightly, she was still pleased with the outcome. *It's remarkable what a bit of confidence can do*, she thought, as Maddy arranged a rainbow of books in the window.

Chapter 8

Jemma monitored customer numbers for the next few days. More people were coming in, certainly, and they were making more sales; but she couldn't be sure that her new strategy was paying off.

The new customers were a little less certain of what they wanted, and more inclined to chat. She could see that Maddy found this unnerving, and looked to her for help. Which was fine, because the regular customers made a beeline for Maddy, and to be honest, Jemma preferred it that way.

One morning Jemma took a tour around the bookshop. There were gaps, undeniable gaps.

'We have a problem,' she said to Maddy.

Maddy's eyes opened wide. 'What sort of problem?'

Jemma grinned. 'We need more books! It's a good problem, Maddy. Only I'm not sure how to go about getting more stock.'

Maddy, eyebrows raised, pointed at the little stack of auction catalogues on the counter.

'We've got more than enough of that sort of thing,' said Jemma. 'We need entry-level books.' She thought for a moment.

'You know what, I'll ask Raphael.' She picked up the phone, and dialled.

Luke answered. 'Hello, Burns Books.'

'Hi Luke, it's Jemma. Is Raphael around? Or could you pass on a message?'

'He's in,' said Luke. 'Hang on a minute, and I'll transfer the call.' His voice was replaced by hold music; for some reason it reminded Jemma of skeletons waltzing in a ballroom.

A few seconds later Jemma heard fumbling, and a cautious 'Hello?'

'Hi, Raphael, it's Jemma. Can I ask you about stock?'

'Um, yes, I suppose you may,' said Raphael. 'What do you want to know?'

Jemma frowned. 'Are you all right? You sound a bit – I don't know, a bit down.'

'I thought you wanted to talk about stock, not psychoanalyse me,' Raphael said tersely.

'OK, well can I come over?'

A pause. 'I'm not sure it's a good time.'

'Why, is the shop busy?'

Silence.

'I'll see you in five minutes, then,' said Jemma, and put the phone down before he could object. Something was clearly not right with Raphael, and while her desire to learn more about the mysteries of acquiring stock was keen, her desire to know exactly what was going on was keener.

***

'It may have begun with the job description.' Raphael dropped a lump of sugar in his coffee and stirred it, then looked sadly at the Danish pastry glistening on its white plate. 'But I can't be sure.'

They were in Rolando's. That in itself worried Jemma. She had had several bookshop-related conversations with Raphael, but never in Rolando's. They had always managed with careful substitutions of words, or even mouthing them when necessary. So as this was an outside-the-bookshop conversation, it must concern a matter more serious than they had ever discussed.

'What began with the job description?' Jemma sipped the Americano she had decided she would need, and put her cup down.

'The dissent,' said Raphael. 'I let it be known that I was considering handling recruitment a different way, and apparently people aren't happy.'

'Why not?' said Jemma. 'I thought it was pretty robust.'

Of course you did, you fool, said her ever-present inner voice. *You wrote a lot of it.*

'I'm sure it is,' said Raphael, 'but having a job description at all was a bone of contention. And while the job itself hasn't changed, your idea of making provision for ousted Keepers annoyed several people.'

'Oh,' said Jemma. That had been the bit she was proudest of. 'Your current system is merciless,' she had told Raphael, her eyes flashing. 'At any time someone could find themselves out of a job and forced to leave their home, since they're banished. What happens if they have kids? What are they supposed to do then, move them to a new school? Get themselves a flat in the adjoining region? And what if they're caring for an elderly relative?' She paused briefly for breath. 'It's an equal opportunities nightmare, Raphael.'

'I thought you might say that,' Raphael had remarked, faintly. 'All right then, tell me what you'd do.'

So Jemma had. To a reasonable extent, it had been included. Banishment would not be complete, but confined to running a similar business or occupying a similar post in the same borough. Moreover, efforts would be made to slot a displaced Keeper into a similar post nearby whenever appropriate. 'So why didn't they like that?' she demanded. 'Less upheaval, and at least it offers some security.'

'As it turns out,' said Raphael, 'everyone who expressed an opinion said they were perfectly happy with things just the way they are.'

'Because it's self-selecting,' said Jemma. 'Only the sort of people who are comfortable with those conditions will apply for those jobs.' In a huff of indignation she looked across at him, and softened immediately. 'I'm sorry,' she said. 'What did they say?'

'Oh, there was grumbling about this being the thin end of the wedge, and that I was likely to get applications from all sorts of people wanting an easy ride.' He grimaced. 'That isn't what bothers me, though. It's the whispers. Nothing direct, of course, but lots of little messages from colleagues of mine, saying they've heard on the grapevine that people are saying I've lost my edge. That I'm softening. Even that my recent victory over Brian was a fluke, and technically ought not to have been allowed.'

'Rubbish,' said Jemma.

'Oh, I'm sorry,' snapped Raphael. 'I forgot how experienced you are in these matters.' Then it was his turn to look guilty. 'I apologise, Jemma. I wasn't expecting such a backlash, and it has shaken me rather. Usually when one wins a challenge it enhances one's reputation and standing, but this time, apparently not.'

'Why do you think that is?' asked Jemma. 'What's different?'

'It's hard to say.' Raphael sipped his coffee, and thought. 'It's been a while since anyone challenged me. Perhaps the fact that Brian dared to do so has made more people consider the possibility. And it has to be said that the books I won with were pretty unconventional.'

'But isn't that a strength?' said Jemma.

'In some ways,' said Raphael. 'But your challenges and the books you chose go on record, so in a sense I showed my hand. Some people, seeing what I chose, may think that's the best I've got. It was, to defeat Brian, but the books have to suit the challenger, and also the circumstances.'

'So you're safe, then,' said Jemma.

'One is never safe in this job,' Raphael replied. 'Someone could walk through the door of the bookshop and challenge me this afternoon, and someone else tomorrow morning, and again the morning after, and I would have to step up every single time.' He sighed. 'I'm not as young as I once was.'

'But if you never get any older—'

'That doesn't mean you don't get tired,' said Raphael. He looked up as a coffee jug refilled his cup. Giulia put a hand on his shoulder, and muttered something in his ear that made him smile. Then she bustled off.

Jemma shifted in her seat. 'I don't like hearing you talk like this,' she said. 'It worries me.'

'I can't say it's my favourite topic of conversation, either,' said Raphael. 'Anyway, you wanted to talk about stock.'

Jemma studied him. 'I do,' she said. 'But if I can help in any way—'

'I'll think about it,' said Raphael. 'Thank you. It's nice to talk to someone who understands. I mean, I'm sure many of my Assistant Keepers would, but there's always that niggling feeling that they might use that knowledge against me.'

Jemma shivered at the thought of an army of subordinates gunning for him. 'I don't know how you can bear it,' she said.

'Mostly, I put it aside,' said Raphael. 'Besides, I'm a wily old fox, and I do find that it helps to be a bumbling idiot.'

'You mean pretend to be a bumbling idiot,' said Jemma.

'Oh no,' said Raphael. 'I really am. Just not in everything.' He took a large bite of his danish pastry, and apart from appreciative noises, was silent for a good minute. 'So, stock,' he said, eventually. 'We *are* going to talk about this.'

Jemma grinned. 'Yes, we are. We're starting to sell more lower-price books, but the catch is that we don't have many left. So I'm after good-quality books that won't break the bank. If possible' – she leaned forward – 'I'd like to get fiction in there.'

'Oooh,' said Raphael. 'So what do you need to know?'

'Firstly,' said Jemma, 'do you have any stock like that which we could put into the shop? Most of your customers want paperbacks. If you had any nice hardbacks, though...'

'I take your point,' said Raphael. 'Although this will probably mean making an arrangement about inventory—'

'Such language, Raphael,' said Jemma reprovingly. 'When I'm looking to strengthen both our respective niches, too.'

'Oh well,' said Raphael, 'if you're strengthening our niches...' He grinned back at her. 'Come and pull a couple of boxes out of the stockroom, and we'll see what turns up. You may have them on a sale-or-return basis.'

'Thank you,' said Jemma. 'But I can't pinch your stock all the time. I need to buy books myself, and I haven't a clue where to begin.'

'Oh, I can talk you through that,' said Raphael. 'But take a couple of boxes from me for now, and see how you get on. Time enough to think about your own book-buying expeditions when you've seen if you can make this *expanded niche* work.' He sipped his coffee. 'Ugh. I need to wash my mouth out.'

A brief foray into the stockroom yielded three boxes of books. Among the spoils were hardback sets of Jane Austen, Thackeray, and Henry Fielding, a complete Wordsworth, a beautiful edition of *London Labour and the London Poor*, and a book of Aubrey Beardsley drawings which made Jemma blush. The stockroom also yielded rather a dusty Folio, who jumped on the counter and shook himself, releasing a fine mist of particles which made Jemma sneeze. 'What have you been doing?' she asked him.

Folio gazed steadily at her, his eyes golden with a tiny black pupil slit. 'Meow,' he offered.

'Silly cat,' she told him, and concentrated on loading her boxes onto a small wheeled trolley, to transport them to her own shop. But once she had thanked Raphael and left, a fine dust of concern settled on her too. What would happen if Raphael were challenged again, and this time he didn't win? Would he lose both shops? And what would happen to him?

Never mind him, a little voice nagged. *What about you?*

Never mind me, Jemma told it crossly. *I'll be fine. What about Raphael?* And the seeds of that particular worry were far harder to remove than dust from a cat's fur.

Chapter 9

Jemma towed the trolley of books carefully behind her, making sure to keep it level and avoid any bumps in the pavement. She stopped dead when she got to the door of her shop. The trolley, due to momentum, bumped into her hip, and Jemma bit back a swearword.

The swearword wasn't entirely for the trolley.

In the window of BJF Antiquarian Books, the rainbow of books had gone. One book, one expensive-looking book, was spotlighted.

Jemma blinked, then looked again. *After all I said... I thought Maddy was finally on board, and the minute I leave the shop—*

She rattled up to the door and pushed it open, fully on the warpath. But inside, Maddy was laughing with Mr De Vere, and a large leather-bound book hunkered smugly on the counter in its protective box.

'I'm back,' she announced to nobody, and squeaked her way into the stockroom. Once there, she parked the little trolley against the wall and stared at the boxes of books morosely.

There's no point even unpacking them, she thought. *I can't get to the computer, so I can't put them on the system, so I don't know where to shelve them.* Instead, she went and made herself a cup of tea. *The minute he's gone–*

But as Mr De Vere was leaving, another customer greeted Maddy like an old friend. Jemma seethed until she wondered whether she might actually whistle like an old kettle, to let off steam.

Eventually the customer left – without buying, Jemma noted – and she stormed back into the shop. 'Why did you change the display?' she demanded, pointing at the book in the window as if it were the lone contender in an identity parade.

Maddy drew herself up and her lips tightened. 'It was a business decision.'

'What do you mean, business decision? I make the business decisions. I'm in charge of the shop.'

Maddy stood firm. 'I reviewed our sales,' she said. 'We've sold more books since your display went up, but unfortunately, as they're low in value, we've made half what we usually would. Within half an hour of me changing it back we've had two sales. Two *good* sales.'

'Right,' said Jemma, 'show me.' But when Maddy did, she had to admit that the figures were right. If anything, Maddy had been generous in saying that the shop had made half as much.

Oops, said her inner voice. *Maybe that change of direction wasn't such a good idea.*

'I'm still not happy about this,' Jemma said, eyeing Maddy. 'It's been less than a week. You haven't given people time to get used to the change.'

'Mmm,' said Maddy, straightening the card reader on the counter.

'You had no right to do that without asking,' Jemma chided. 'I've a good mind to put that display back exactly as it was.'

Maddy gave the tiniest shrug. 'Unfortunately, you weren't here to ask,' she said. 'You're the boss. But I wouldn't advise it.'

Jemma spent the rest of the day in a fairly even split between annoyance, indecision and resentment towards Maddy for being right. Every so often she glanced at the window, and the sight of the book, lit up as if it had won an award, made her hackles rise.

Mid-afternoon, as an act of mutiny against the shop, she brought her new acquisitions through and put them on the database. But there was no place for fiction in the shop, and no category for it in the database. In the end, Jemma entered them under Z9, an empty shelf in the far corner of the stockroom, to give them a home of sorts. *I ought to fight*, she thought, *but I haven't the energy. I'm worried about Raphael, and sad that I was wrong about the shop, and I honestly don't know if I'm doing harm or good.* So she packed the books away out of sight, closed the stockroom door on them, and got *Pigs Have Wings* out of her bag.

Maddy sold two more books that afternoon, and every time the shop door opened Jemma's heart sank a little lower, as her folly was driven further home. *I really don't know what I'm doing; I'm completely out of my depth. I may as well let Maddy get on with it, because I'm worse than useless.* She studied the clock, willing the hands to move faster and get Maddy out of the shop so that she could mourn her great mistaken idea in peace.

She didn't even look up when Maddy said hello to somebody. Then the person replied, and she almost pulled a muscle as her head shot up.

Carl stood there, an odd expression on his face. 'Hi, Jemma,' he said.

'Um, hi,' said Jemma. *Why is he here?* She couldn't quite take him in.

'I wondered if you fancied going for a quick drink,' he said. 'I can wait while you close the shop.'

Of all the days to invite me out, thought Jemma. She checked the clock. Five to five. 'We may as well close up,' she said. 'It won't take long.' She cashed up quickly, noting that there wasn't much actual money in the till. The sales had all been paid for with credit cards.

'I'll head off, if you don't mind,' said Maddy, on the first stroke of five.

'Yes, see you tomorrow,' said Jemma, unable to put any feeling into her voice. Once Maddy had gone she looked at Carl. 'I don't want to go for a drink,' she said. 'I'm not in the mood. I'm sorry to make you wait, but I didn't want to say it in front of Maddy.'

'What's up?' said Carl. 'You seem really down.'

'I can't run this place,' said Jemma. 'I'm not making the right decisions. It isn't working. I put the wrong books in the window. Maddy knows what to do, and I don't, but I'm stuck with it. And I'm worried about—' She stopped herself just in time. Raphael wouldn't want her to discuss his problems. 'I'm worried,' she finished.

'I'm worried too,' said Carl. 'About you. You haven't given me the time of day for the last week or so.'

'That isn't my fault,' Jemma retorted. 'You've been busy.' *And so have I*, she thought. *Though I might as well not have bothered.*

'There you go again,' said Carl. 'Why are you being so negative? And why haven't you answered my texts?'

'What texts?' said Jemma. 'I wasn't aware that you'd sent any.'

'Course I have,' said Carl. 'Look.' He pulled his phone out of his jeans pocket and brought up a stream of messages. 'See?'

Jemma looked.

Monday, 7.55 am: Room for one more for breakfast?

Monday, 5.15 pm: Fancy a coffee? I know a place :-)

Tuesday, 8.30 am: I miss scrambled eggs :-(

Wednesday, 4.30 pm: You could come and watch us rehearse. If you like.

Jemma reached for her own phone, and showed him. 'I haven't

had a text from you all week,' she said. 'Not since Saturday. I thought you were busy.'

'I was,' said Carl, 'but not that busy.' He frowned. 'That's weird. What network are you on?'

Jemma checked his phone. 'Same as you,' she said. 'I don't get it. I'm sure I searched for stuff on the internet, and that worked fine.'

Carl's mouth curled in a wry smile. 'At least now I know you weren't ignoring me.' A sidelong glance. 'Unless you would have anyway.'

'Of course I wouldn't,' cried Jemma. She felt the unfairness of it welling up inside her. 'It's not my fault. At least that's one thing that isn't my fault—'

Then she was in Carl's arms, and weeping as if she would never stop.

'Come on,' whispered Carl, after a minute or two. 'Let's lock the shop and go upstairs, and you can tell me all about it.' And Jemma was too exhausted to do anything but agree.

***

'It wasn't the drink I had in mind,' said Carl, as Jemma handed him a mug of tea with three sugars. 'But it's lovely,' he added hastily, as her lower lip wobbled. 'It's just nice to see you. I mean, I've seen you in the bookshop but you've been all stridey-about and managerial.'

'Not that it helps,' said Jemma. She sat down on the chesterfield sofa and sipped her tea reflectively. 'I've been swanning around as if I know what I'm doing, and obviously I don't.'

'But you do,' said Carl. 'Look at what you've done at Burns Books. Raphael is full of praise for you.'

Jemma snorted. 'I got lucky,' she said.

'Oh come on,' said Carl. 'No one is that lucky for that long. Please, Jemma. Please tell me what's up.'

He paused, then reached out a hand to her. 'I know you don't want to talk about it, but it might help.' He smiled. 'How many acting jobs do you think I haven't got? How many times do you think I've been turned away because I'm too tall, or too young, or my hair is wrong, or I'm not what they're looking for? Believe me, I know all about rejection.'

After her initial resistance, Jemma told him. It was over so quickly that she wondered whether she'd left anything out.

'That's . . . kind of interesting,' said Carl.

'I don't need a critique of my business strategy,' Jemma snapped. 'I've had quite enough of that from my assistant, thanks.'

Carl grinned. 'I'm hardly qualified to comment on that,' he said, 'but I can comment on the words you used. Everything is about what you *don't* want. Almost every verb you use suggests conflict. You're fighting, you're struggling, you're losing. You keep telling me that you're wrong, you're mistaken, you don't know, you don't understand.'

Jemma hung her head. 'I don't understand,' she muttered.

'But you do,' said Carl. 'You understand how you want the shop to work. You know how you want the shop to be. And instead of going for it you're changing little things here and there: just enough to wind Maddy up, but not enough to achieve what you want. Stop thinking about the customers you don't want, and the books you'd rather not sell. Think about the people you do want to sell to, and the books they'll like.'

'I'm wading through treacle the whole time,' said Jemma. 'I thought I was getting somewhere with Maddy and she was finally coming round to my point of view. Then she pulls a stunt like this morning's, changing my display the minute I go out.'

'So tell her that's unacceptable,' said Carl. 'She can't do that. It's your shop.'

'But it doesn't feel as if it is,' said Jemma, shifting uncomfortably on the firm leather. 'I try to tell myself it is, but it still feels like Brian's. I'm just making a mess of it until he comes back.'

'So do something about it,' said Carl. 'Do something to make it yours.' He gazed around the beautiful, elegant room. 'To be honest, Jemma, lovely as this flat is, it doesn't feel like your home. It feels as if you're flat-sitting.'

Jemma sighed out a breath. Then she picked up a cushion with a sunburst on, which she had brought from her own flat, and hugged it. 'I thought I'd get used to it,' she said quietly. 'I thought it was just a bit more sophisticated than I was used to, and I'd grow into it. But it isn't me, not at all.'

Carl reached for the pink fleecy throw and draped it over the sofa. 'It's a start.'

Jemma managed a shaky smile. 'It is,' she said. Then she glanced at the carriage clock that she'd never liked. 'Aren't you rehearsing tonight?'

Carl looked at her. 'I'm supposed to be,' he said. 'They've got scripts, they can manage without me. If you want me to stay—'

'To be honest,' said Jemma, 'what I'd really like is to get out of this flat, and the shop. Could I come and watch?'

Carl beamed. 'Sure you can,' he said. 'Now we're getting somewhere with it, I'd love to see what you think.' A sudden, shy smile. 'I thought you weren't interested.'

'Of course I'm interested,' said Jemma, 'it's your thing. Come on, let's get out of here.' She got up from the sofa and held out her hand. 'Have we got time for food first?'

Carl grinned. 'You're definitely feeling better.'

It's amazing what a difference someone else's view makes, thought Jemma, as they strolled down Charing Cross Road hand-in-hand. Now she was bursting with things to get on with, both in the shop and in her flat. But all that could wait until tomorrow. First, she had something far more pressing to do.

Chapter 10

Jemma woke with a pleasing sense of anticipation. *Today's the day.* She reached out and smoothed the duvet cover. It wasn't one of the superfine Egyptian cotton duvet covers which Brian favoured, but a slightly faded Indian sari-print one she had bought in the sales years ago, when she was getting things for her first flat. *It may not be posh,* she thought, stroking the soft, slightly pilled fabric, *but it's mine.*

Watching Rumpus the night before had been a strange, out-of-body experience. She had known beforehand that Carl's play was set in a bookshop, and she had also known that they were rehearsing downstairs at Burns Books. But seeing it, seeing characters move around the shop being customers or staff, and handling the books as if they worked there, was bizarre. *Almost as if I'm a ghost haunting the place. I really should develop some outside interests.*

She had worried that the setting would remind her of the day's events; but Carl's small cast of characters was so well-drawn, so real, and so different from herself, Maddy and Raphael that she had no difficulty in sinking into the drama, to the extent that she was cross when one of the actors fluffed their lines, or when Carl, who was directing, stopped the action to give notes.

'Did you enjoy it?' Carl asked her afterwards, when the rest of Rumpus had dispersed and he was making his usual checks before locking up. He asked the question when he was busy locking the toilet door.

'Don't be silly,' she said, from the front-row armchair where she had acted as their audience. 'Of course I did. I'm not just saying that because I'm – you know.' The word *girlfriend* stuck in her throat. *Partner*, too. 'Because we go out,' she finished.

He turned to her then, and smiled. 'We do,' he said. 'I'm glad you liked it. I was – a bit worried.'

'Why wouldn't I have liked it?' said Jemma. 'It was funny, it was moving—'

Carl raised his hands, palms upwards, then let them fall. 'The others say the same, but I still worry. Call it imposter syndrome. It's the first time I've written a whole actual play. We improvised sketches at uni, but this is different. This feels big: serious. The idea of putting on an actual thing that I wrote—'

Jemma grinned. 'The play what I wrote,' she said.

Carl grinned back at her. 'This play is like my shop window. I'm putting my work out there and worrying that people will decide it's not their thing, and I'm no good—'

Jemma walked over, touched his arm, and kissed him. 'Let's go for that drink,' she said.

***

They had made it one drink then parted company, since Jemma had plans for what was left of the evening. As soon as she got home she changed the bed. *I can't bear to sleep in his sheets any more.* Then she went to the big cupboard where she had stored everything she had brought from her previous flat which didn't fit with the new one. Big bright towels that looked incongruous in the tasteful bathroom. Framed posters, some from her student days, which had seemed unsophisticated compared to Brian's art prints and watercolours. The scented candles in glass holders she had bought from IKEA, and the bundle of postcards which she had stuck to her fridge with souvenir magnets. She brought it all out, and stared at it.

Not everything, she thought, picking up a particularly horrible pottery rabbit which her mother had brought back from somewhere or other. *But this, and this—*

She moved around the flat, taking down pictures and replacing them with her own. A couple, which she liked, she moved to a different room. Brian's placemats, featuring scenes from Renaissance Italy, were replaced with her multicoloured woven straw ones. The abstract ceramic figures on the mantelpiece, which unnerved her every time she looked at them, were boxed and put away. And the deep-pile pale-beige rug in the sitting room, which she never walked on for fear of making it dirty, was rolled up, and a more colourful and forgiving rag rug laid in its place.

Jemma picked up the carriage clock; the hands said it was a quarter to midnight. *I'd better stop there*, she thought, carrying the clock to the cupboard and swaddling it in a pillowcase to muffle it until it wound down. She closed the door and locked it, and suddenly she could have floated away, she felt so light. As if she could do anything she wanted.

***

Jemma moved easily around the flat, getting breakfast. She smothered her guilt that she was scrambling her eggs in Brian's heavy copper saucepan instead of one of her own cheap ones. *That's my choice*, she thought. *Maybe when I'm earning more money I'll replace this with one of my own.* That made her smile.

She even managed a smile for Maddy when she came into the shop. 'Good morning, Maddy,' she said.

'Good morning,' said Maddy warily, her eyes searching Jemma's face for signs of trouble.

'Let's get on with things, shall we?' said Jemma.

'Yes,' said Maddy, and bit her lip. 'We are a little low on stock —'

'Oh, because you've been selling so many books,' said Jemma. Maddy gave her a quick glance, as if trying to winkle out a hidden, sarcastic meaning. 'Well, I'm planning to go and see Raphael today, and that's on my list.'

'Oh,' said Maddy. She picked up a couple of auction catalogues and handed them to Jemma. 'Brian used to go to these regularly, and some other dealers. I can give you their addresses if you want.'

'Yes please, that would be helpful,' said Jemma. Maddy drew out a small black book from the drawer under the counter, and began leafing through it. 'I'll go and put the kettle on,' Jemma continued. 'I might wait until Raphael's got a good amount of caffeine inside him before I head over.'

An odd sort of bark shot out of Maddy and made Jemma jump. Then she realised it was a laugh. Maddy looked as surprised as she felt. 'What will you ask him?' she said.

'I'd like his advice about buying books,' Jemma replied. 'I'm a bit worried that otherwise I'll get fleeced.'

'Oh yes, very wise,' said Maddy. 'Always good to consult an expert. Although the names I've given you should help a lot.'

'I'm sure they will,' said Jemma. 'And there are a couple of other things I want to ask him. Anyway, tea.' She went into the kitchen and filled the kettle. She felt guilty that she had no intention of using the information that Maddy had vouchsafed to her. But not very.

***

She found Raphael upstairs doing the crossword, while Folio snoozed in a patch of bright autumn sunlight. 'How are things?' she asked.

Raphael considered. 'The bookshop's doing well,' he said.

'I know it is,' said Jemma automatically. Then she noted his emphasis on the word *bookshop*. 'How about you?'

Raphael sighed. 'Still fielding criticism of my, what was it, namby-pamby people-pleasing gone-to-the-dogs recruitment process.'

'Oh dear,' said Jemma.

'Yes dear,' said Raphael. He waved a hand. 'Anyway, what brings you here?'

'I want to repaint the exterior of the shop,' said Jemma. 'And give it a new name, and buy plenty of books for it.'

'I see,' said Raphael. 'So the new stock's selling well, then?'

'I haven't put it out yet,' Jemma confessed, and explained the reason why. 'Carl made me see that I should make a proper change, not just tinker round the edges.'

'I see,' said Raphael. 'Carl, eh?'

'He's smart,' said Jemma, indignantly.

'I never said he wasn't,' said Raphael. 'So are you telling me, or asking me?'

'I'm asking you,' said Jemma. 'I wouldn't presume to rename and repaint your shop without your permission.'

'And if I said no,' said Raphael, 'what would you do?'

Jemma studied him, but his words seemed hypothetical. She could feel a smile trying to get out. 'I'd attempt to talk you round.'

'Of course you would,' said Raphael. 'And for the record, you're doing the right thing. What I would suggest is that you don't pick a colour or a name that you're likely to get tired of.' He paused. 'Do you have something in mind?'

'Not yet,' admitted Jemma. 'I was just thinking not black and not BJF Antiquarian Books.' She slapped her forehead. 'Which is exactly what Carl told me I was doing. Being negative.' Then she looked at Raphael. 'Actually, that might help you,' she said.

'Might it?' said Raphael.

'Yes,' said Jemma. 'You're firefighting at the moment, aren't

343

you? Dealing with people's negative feedback and what they don't want, and *you* don't want that either. Maybe if you focused on telling them what you hope to get out of making the changes, they'd understand.'

'Oh,' said Raphael. 'I did say I was doing this so that I didn't hire another Brian.' He mused. 'Good heavens.'

'We both need to reframe our narratives,' said Jemma.

Raphael winced. 'What I need is a nice cappuccino.'

'You know what,' said Jemma, 'you could be right.'

***

Over cappuccinos and a biscotti each at Rolando's, Raphael outlined the dos and don'ts of buying stock, and gave her three names. One was a house-clearance man with a warehouse in Putney; one was a secondhand book dealer in Colindale; and the third, according to Raphael, had no profession. 'I would call her a snapper-up of unconsidered trifles,' he said. 'She is more expensive, but if you're seeking a particular volume she's sure to have it. Very important when you're making a set.' He sat back. 'What sort of stock are you looking for, anyway?'

'Books I want to read,' said Jemma. 'Not necessarily books that I have read, but books I'd like to read someday. And books that look nice on the shelves. It's hard to explain, but I'll know it when I see it.'

'You'll know it when you feel it,' said Raphael. He drained his cappuccino and Giulia appeared at his elbow. 'Un altro?' she asked.

'Sì, grazie,' said Raphael, and smiled at her. She laid a hand on his shoulder briefly, then picked up his cup and was gone.

Jemma frowned. 'Are you two…?'

'She is a lovely person,' said Raphael, 'and smart as a whip. Under different circumstances…' He muttered something and Jemma caught the last few words: 'couldn't go through it again.'

'But would you make each other happy?' she asked, very

344

quietly and very gently.

Raphael shrugged. 'Probably. For a little while.' And then he looked sad, until Giulia reappeared with another cappuccino with two little Gianduja chocolates tucked into the saucer. 'One for you,' she said to Jemma, pointing at the chocolates, then at her. 'Don't let him eat both.' And with a chuckle, she was gone.

'I'm saying nothing,' said Jemma, helping herself to a chocolate. 'You know what I think.' She unwrapped it and took a bite.

'Everything is so simple when you're young,' said Raphael, wistfully. 'Even now I can remember it.' He took a sip of his cappuccino. 'But I think you're right about my problem.' He smiled. 'So, thank you.'

Jemma took a convoluted route back to her shop, which passed the hardware store. There she grabbed all the paint catalogues she could lay hands on, and popped them in her bag. *I'll look at them over lunch and pick out some colours. And I can think about a name while Maddy serves the customers.* A secret naughty thrill ran through her, as if she were planning to get something past a teacher, or possibly her mother. *I should just do it,* she thought. *Openly, in front of Maddy, so that she knows what's going to happen.*

Then she considered, and grinned. *Actually*, she admitted to herself, *I like the idea that I'm sneaking this in under Maddy's nose. Maybe it's because it feels as if I'm outwitting Brian.* Outwitting Brian, she had to admit, was a delightful thought. Almost as delightful as the thought that soon, very soon, she would have a bookshop arranged exactly the way she wanted it.

Chapter 11

'Are you sure you don't want me to come?' said Raphael.

'I'll be fine,' said Jemma. 'Driving is like riding a bike; you never forget how. I promise I'll look after Gertrude.' She jingled the keys, hoping she appeared less apprehensive than she felt. She was a good driver – no accidents, no speeding tickets – though an infrequent one. And she had never driven a vehicle as big as Gertrude. However, she was unlikely to have to parallel park or do a three-point turn in a narrow road. 'Slow and steady wins the race,' she added.

'I was thinking more of the book-buying aspect of the expedition,' said Raphael. 'As you know, I do like a trip out.' He sighed. 'I suppose you must start sometime. One's first solo book-buying trip is a rite of passage.'

'Don't make me more nervous than I already am,' said Jemma. 'Now, I've got the addresses, my phone is fully charged, and you're sure they'll send the bill to the shop?'

'As you said approximately two minutes ago, Jemma, it'll be fine,' said Raphael. 'Off you go, and enjoy yourself.'

'And if you bring back any copies of *Fifty Shades of Grey*, we won't let you in,' said Luke, grinning.

Jemma rolled her eyes. 'You're cheerful,' she said. 'And rather smart.' The midnight-blue shirt had made a reappearance, teamed with snazzy black trousers with a thin black satin stripe down the side. 'Another date tonight?'

Luke looked away, then gave her a little sidelong glance. 'Might be.'

'Are you leaving today or tomorrow?' asked Raphael. Just then, the shop bell rang. 'Good, a customer. Off you go, and stop disrupting my shop. I expect to hear all about it when you get back.'

'You will,' said Jemma. 'And thank you.' She smiled at the customer and hurried out. Gertrude was waiting, her bright orange paint shining in the mellow autumn sunlight as if she were a giant pumpkin.

Jemma had popped downstairs earlier and asked Carl to stay there when she left the shop. 'I know you want to see me off,' she said. 'But you'll say something encouraging or motivational, and I don't want to cry in front of the others.'

'Who, me?' said Carl, with a cheesy grin. 'Motivational? All right then, I guess I'll just have to do it now.' He folded her in a big hug, and whispered, 'Go do your thing, and be awesome.'

'Aargh!' cried Jemma, but it was too late; she could already feel tears welling up, and his hug squeezed them out of her even faster. 'I'm happy, really I am,' she hiccuped.

And here she was, bowling along in Gertrude, with the maps app on her phone set to Putney. *The roads seem quiet.* She had expected to crawl out of the city, but somehow all the traffic lights changed to green as she approached them, and the bits of road coloured red on her map faded to orange, then their usual colour as she drove along them. *Hmmm,* she thought, and rubbed Gertrude's steering wheel.

Her mood was further improved by the knowledge that the

painters would arrive that afternoon. Having obtained three quotes, Jemma had gone with the cheapest, from the firm that Raphael used. 'They've been in business for two hundred years,' he had said. 'They know what they're doing.'

On one hand, Jemma hoped that she would be out when they arrived, so that she wouldn't face the initial wrath of Maddy. Then again, she didn't want to miss seeing the look on Maddy's face when they arrived and started unpacking their equipment. After much thought she had gone for a deep, rich burgundy which was still bookshop-ish and classy, but much warmer and brighter than the current dull black. As for a name – unable to settle on anything, she had booked a signwriter for two days' time, on the grounds that that would make her come to a decision.

Almost before she knew it, she was in Putney. Gertrude rolled down quiet leafy streets until eventually they came to a long, low warehouse, nothing special to look at. 'You have arrived at your destination,' the phone declared.

A tall, skinny, balding man in faded jeans and a voluminous shirt sauntered outside. 'Hello, Gertrude,' he said, rubbing her wing mirror. 'Jemma James, I presume,' he said, extending a hand to her. 'I'm Dave Huddart. I gather you're after books.'

'I am,' said Jemma. She dismounted from Gertrude and pulled a long list out of her bag.

Dave took the list and scanned it rapidly. 'Yep,' he said. 'Got boxes?'

'Oh yes,' said Jemma. 'And the trolley.'

'All prepared, then.' He twinkled at her. 'First time?'

'Is it that obvious?' said Jemma, fighting the urge to take a step back.

'Nah,' said Dave. 'You've just got that look about you. If you get your things and come this way, I'll take you to the book department.'

He led Jemma through an Aladdin's cave. To the left bristled a forest of chairs. To her right, a small army of mannequin heads wearing elaborate hats stared with sightless eyes. Then lamps and lights of all descriptions, some lit but most not, gleamed in their dark home.

'I'm afraid things aren't in order,' said Dave. 'I've split the fiction and non-fiction, but that's about it.'

Don't go mad, Jemma cautioned herself, as she gazed at the shelves. *This is your first shop. Only choose things you're sure will sell.*

'I'll come back in ten minutes and see how you're getting on,' said Dave.

Jemma undropped her jaw long enough to say thank you, then continued to gawp at the shelves.

You've seen a lot of books before, she told herself. *There probably aren't as many here as there are in the stockroom at Burns Books. Or on the lower floor, come to that.* But somehow these books, crammed into shelves, on top of shelves, in piles at the foot of shelves, had an impact all their own. 'Folio would love this,' she said aloud. Timidly, she reached out for a hardback copy of Hans Christian Andersen's fairy tales. When she held the book in her hand, she knew she would buy it. 'This is so tempting,' she whispered, putting the book on a small table which stood nearby. 'And so dangerous.'

Jemma decided to limit herself to five boxes. She chose carefully, visualising the book on her shelves, or turned so that its cover faced the customer, and considering how it would complement her other selections. Even so, she had amassed a good four boxes' worth when Dave reappeared. 'Found some stuff, then,' he said.

'Could I have two more minutes?' asked Jemma.

He laughed. 'I think that's safe. Any more than that, and I suspect you'd buy the whole shop.' He stood by as she chose twenty more books, her hands shooting out confidently, stroking

349

the books as she laid them down. 'Want me to price that lot up?'

Jemma blinked. 'I'm not sure.' She blinked. Now that she had been brought back to reality, she did seem to have chosen an awful lot of books. Very nice books. 'Um, can I put some back if I'm over budget?'

Dave frowned, then laughed. 'Course you can. Give me a minute.' He crooked his forefinger and waggled it as he scrutinised the spines of the books, muttering to himself all the while. Jemma heard numbers, and words like *original slipcase* and *colour plates*, and her heart sank. What if she had to put half of them back? She felt as if it would break her heart.

Then Dave said a number, and she stared at him. 'Excuse me?'

He said it again.

'Are you sure? For all these books?'

'Yep,' said Dave. 'I've got books coming out of my ears and you'll be a good customer. And you're a referral from Raphael, which counts for something.' He grinned at her. 'I take it you're happy with that?'

'Are you kidding me?' said Jemma, grinning from ear to ear. She held out her hand. 'Let's shake on it, before you change your mind.'

Dave helped her pack the boxes, and she wheeled her new acquisitions over to Gertrude with a spring in her step. *I can see why Raphael enjoys this part of his job. It's like being a kid in a sweet shop, only less fattening.*

She selected another three boxes' worth at the secondhand bookshop in Colindale. Here the prices were keener, though the owner was as nice and as welcoming as Dave, in his own way. At first sight he had looked rather forbidding: like the first Doctor Who, in fact. But he made her tea in a china cup, and his melodious, slightly cracked voice rose and fell like a gentle sea as he told tales of authors he had met while Jemma chose her books. She felt as if she were bobbing in a small boat, surrounded by soft cushions.

She was in two minds whether or not to bother with the third name on Raphael's list. 'I have plenty of books already,' she argued as she drove towards the city. 'Raphael did say she was expensive.'

But it wouldn't hurt to look, said an eager voice in her head. *It's on the way back. You won't even be going out of your way.*

If Jemma could have stared at herself, she would. She was so used to her inner voice being critical and negative that this was something entirely new. As such, she ought to encourage it. So she pulled over at the next opportunity, and put the final address into her phone.

To her surprise, she drew up at an ordinary semi-detached house. She gazed doubtfully at the phone, which looked reasonably sure of itself. And the number on the white PVC front door was correct. Slightly deflated, Jemma got out of Gertrude and walked up the neat garden path.

The door was answered by a middle-aged woman slightly smaller than Jemma. She was plump, and dressed in a pale-blue top, a beige skirt, and fluffy pink slippers. 'Good afternoon,' she said, in an unexpectedly deep voice. 'I take it you're here about books.'

Jemma made a couple of fishlike motions with her mouth before managing to form words. 'Yes, that's right.'

'Anything in particular?'

'I'm relaunching my bookshop and adding fiction,' said Jemma. Inwardly, she frowned. That wasn't what she had meant to say.

'Oh, so you want a book which says exactly what your new bookshop will be about.' The woman's gaze wandered for a moment, then refocused on Jemma. 'If you wait in the hall, I believe I have what you're looking for.' She paused. 'Who am I speaking to, by the way?'

'Jemma James,' Jemma stammered.

The woman inclined her head and opened the door wider. 'I am Elinor Dashwood. Yes, I know.' She stepped back, showing Jemma a completely unexceptional hall with laminate flooring and a waiting-room type chair. 'If you'll take a seat.'

It took Jemma perhaps thirty seconds to take in her surroundings. A dark-wood telephone table, a barometer on the wall, Constable prints, and pale striped wallpaper. In its own way, it was by far the strangest of the three establishments she had visited that day.

'Here we are,' said Elinor Dashwood, emerging from what looked like a dining room. 'Rather nice, if I do say so myself.' She put the book into Jemma's hands. 'Preowned, of course, but in mint condition.'

Jemma gazed at it. The book was a hardback, bound in beautiful blue silk that made you want to stroke it. Set into the cover, in swirling silver script, was the book's title: *Jane Eyre*. The first book she had ever sold. She opened it and found marbled endpapers, a blue silk ribbon bookmark, and delicate engravings.

'It's absolutely beautiful,' she said. 'How much is it?'

'It is beautiful,' said Elinor Dashwood. 'But it isn't a first edition, it isn't by a famous binder, and it was published by a little-known company. It is also a duplicate; I have two of these. So I could let you have it for fifteen pounds.'

Jemma fumbled for her purse. 'Done.' She could already see it in the shop window. *Her* shop window. 'I'll be back,' she said, as Elinor opened the drawer of the telephone table and brought out a sheet of tissue paper.

'I know you will,' said Elinor.

Jemma drove the few miles to Charing Cross Road almost in a trance. *What a day it's been, and it isn't even over yet.* It was one o'clock, she had visited three booksellers and bought books from all of them, and she was still, just about, within her budget. And she would have time for lunch before the painters arrived.

Or so she thought. For when she pulled up outside BJF Antiquarian Books, the painters' van was already there. More worryingly, the painters were getting into it. She switched Gertrude's engine off, and as if on cue, the engine of the van coughed into life.

'Wait! No!' she shouted. Then, realising that was no use, she jumped out of Gertrude, ran to the driver's side of the van, heedless of traffic, and knocked on the window. She could see the frown on the driver's face even before he wound it down. *What's been going on?*

Chapter 12

'Got our marching orders, didn't we,' said the driver, putting the van into gear.

'No you didn't,' said Jemma, with desperation. 'I'm the manager.'

'The woman we spoke to in there made it clear that we weren't expected or welcome,' snapped the driver. 'To be honest with you, after what she said I wouldn't stay.'

'Please stay,' said Jemma. 'I don't know what Maddy said to you, but I shall make sure she apologises.'

The driver muttered something which sounded like 'She'd ruddy better,' put the van into neutral, and switched off the engine.

'Thank you,' said Jemma. 'I'm sorry I wasn't here to welcome you, but I thought you were coming at two o'clock.'

'Job before finished early,' put in the man next to the driver. 'Thought we'd get a jump on this one.' He peered out of the window at the shop, and turned back with a critical expression on his face. 'We'll need to.' He got out of the van and looked up at the building, wrinkling his nose.

The driver sighed and leaned out of his window. 'You could at least unload the stuff,' he said.

'Thank you so much,' said Jemma. 'Would you like some tea?'

She had to jump back as the door opened. The driver got out and slammed it. 'Haven't done anything yet,' he said, shielding his eyes as he scrutinised the building. 'Burgundy, was it?'

'That's it,' said Jemma, feeling rather in the way. 'I'll, um, go and talk to Maddy.'

She had expected Maddy to be deep in conversation with a favourite customer, but when she entered, the shop was empty. Maddy was sitting at the counter, flicking through an auction catalogue and eating something worthy-looking in a box. She glanced up when Jemma closed the door. 'Oh, hello.'

'Would you mind telling me,' said Jemma, putting her hands on her hips, 'why you sent the painters away, and what exactly you said to them? It's lucky I got here when I did, otherwise they would have taken off.'

Maddy waved her fork while she chewed. 'The shop's fine as it is.'

Her offhand tone stung Jemma. 'Well, I say that it isn't. I'm in charge and I have Raphael's backing, so what I say goes, whatever your opinion is.' She stalked up to the counter. 'What did you say to them?'

Maddy shrugged. 'I told the head one that the shop didn't need painting, and that as far as I was concerned they were a bunch of crooks looking to swindle an inexperienced shop manager.'

'You what?' cried Jemma. 'How dare you!'

Maddy put down her fork, a cold glint in her eyes. 'Do you think that under your management the shop is earning enough for an expensive makeover? Do you really?'

'Maybe if I had an assistant who supported me, instead of sticking to the ways of her former and now departed boss, we might get somewhere.' Jemma could feel herself swelling with rage. 'Firstly, you will go and apologise to the painters for calling them crooks, and tell them that you were wrong. Then you will help me unload the new books I have bought for the shop. And finally, you will accept the changes I make in the shop, or else hand in your notice. I'm not having any more of this.' She gazed around her. 'I've a good mind to rip out this shelving and put in something a bit less dark and depressing.'

Maddy gasped and hurried outside. Jemma followed, and stood in the doorway while Maddy choked an apology out, 'I'm-sorry-for-calling-you-crooks-I-was-wrong.' That done, she dashed inside so quickly that Jemma had to step out of the way, and bolted for the staff toilet.

Five minutes later she still hadn't emerged. *Was I too harsh?* thought Jemma, as she stood in the middle of the shop and waited.

She insulted people who came to do a job for you, and managed to be dismissive of you in the process. She's lucky you didn't give her a warning.

Don't tempt me, thought Jemma. But she still watched the door.

Maddy reappeared ten more minutes later. Her eyes were red-rimmed, and she wore a slight, perplexed frown. 'I don't feel well,' she said.

'Mmm,' said Jemma. 'You'll excuse me if I'm not particularly sympathetic towards you at the moment, Maddy.' Then she relented, as Maddy did look genuinely confused. 'What is it?' she said.

'I'm not myself.' Maddy put a hand to her head.

'Why don't you take your lunch break and go out for some fresh air,' said Jemma. 'Maybe that will help.'

'Thank you,' said Maddy, quietly. She fetched her bag and hurried across the shop floor, stumbling in her haste to leave.

The door closed behind her, and Jemma pondered. Was it a not-very-cunning ploy to get out of unloading the books? Somehow, she didn't think so. To be honest, she would have been perfectly happy to send Maddy out of the shop for an hour after a much less convincing performance, simply to recover her own composure. Perhaps Maddy's anger had brought on a headache; it was perfectly possible to feel sick with nerves, wasn't it? But Maddy's expression – bewildered, helpless, lost – had struck at Jemma in a completely unexpected way. *I'll try to be kinder when she comes back*, she thought. *I don't want to fall out with her if I can help it. I don't want to be that kind of manager.* Instead, she spent the next half an hour unloading boxes of books from the van and stacking them beside the counter. She had no idea where they would go yet, but she intended to enjoy every minute of sorting, organising, and shelving her new acquisitions.

***

Jemma felt a stab of misgiving even as she handed Gertrude's keys to Raphael. Had she done the right thing? Could she trust Maddy?

'Did it go well?' asked Raphael. 'You seem rather burdened with care, if I may say so.'

'What? Oh, sorry. Yes, it went really well. I bought eight boxes of books and they were actually much less expensive than I thought they would be. I got a beautiful copy of *Jane Eyre* from Elinor Dashwood.'

Raphael smiled knowingly. 'So you haven't been too scarred by the experience?'

'No, not at all. Um, would you mind if I went back there now? It's just that I've left Maddy in charge of the shop, and I'd like to get things organised for tomorrow if I can. I'll tell you more about it once I've got the shop straightened up.'

'Make sure you do,' said Raphael. 'Did you meet Dave's parrot?'

'Dave's parrot? No, I definitely didn't see a parrot.'

'Just checking. Off you go then.'

As Jemma hurried out of Burns Books she wondered at the

expression in his eyes. Pride? Wistfulness? She couldn't tell. Anyway, she needed to check on Maddy. She had only been away for ten minutes at the most, but ten minutes with Maddy in charge of the shop was a very long time indeed.

When Maddy had returned from her break her face seemed less drawn, she had colour in her cheeks, and she looked thoroughly ashamed of herself. 'I'm sorry,' she said, advancing to the counter and meeting Jemma's eyes. 'I don't know what came over me to speak as I did. Unless it's all the change. I didn't think it would affect me so much, but obviously it has.'

'Change can be difficult to get used to,' said Jemma, with the wisdom acquired from hours of diligent study and course attendance. 'I should have warned you that they were coming. It wasn't fair of me to spring it on you like that. I'll do better in future.'

Maddy managed a wan smile. 'Are we friends again?'

Jemma's first thought was that their relationship was one of manager and employee, not friends, but Maddy looked so pathetic with her little hopeful smile that she dismissed the thought as unworthy. 'Sure,' she said. 'Shall we make a drink, and think about where these books will go?'

She had already redone the window display, which to be honest was a matter of taking the expensive spotlighted book out of the window and replacing it with a mix of attractive and reasonably priced offerings, with the beautiful hardback *Jane Eyre* at the centre. To appease Maddy, she had included some non-fiction in the mix.

'I'll go and put the kettle on,' said Maddy. On her way into the back, she hesitated. 'I like the window. And the painters are getting on well with the prep work.'

'Good, I thought they would,' said Jemma. 'They did come recommended.'

While Maddy was making drinks, Jemma considered the

shelves. To emphasise the shop's change of direction, the new books ought to be at the front. She unlocked the doors of the first bookcase and began clearing the shelves. She should probably alphabetise the new books, but that could wait; she was too eager to make the change. By the time Maddy returned bearing drinks, Jemma had filled two shelves of the bookcase and was beginning the third. 'I've started,' she said. 'I haven't put them in order. It's just for now.'

Maddy's left hand trembled a fraction, but she didn't look angry. If anything, she looked enquiring, as if she were trying to make sense of it. She opened her mouth, and closed it again. Eventually, she spoke. 'I don't suppose . . . I don't suppose you found any Ann Radcliffe?'

'I didn't,' said Jemma. 'I did keep an eye out.' That was a little white lie, but she was fairly confident that she had seen no Radcliffe novels that morning, which was almost the same thing.

Maddy put the mugs on the counter. 'Shall I clear the next bookcase?'

Jemma tried not to stare at her. 'Yes please, that would be helpful,' she said. 'I guess I'm doing this the wrong way round, but I can't wait to see the new books in the shop.' She crossed to the counter and took a sip of her tea, regarding the shelves. Already it was more colourful. And she wouldn't lock the doors when she'd finished. Maybe she would even get the glass removed.

Half an hour later two bookcases were full of new books, and the previous inhabitants were packed and heading for the stockroom. 'I'll update the database, I promise,' said Jemma. 'Um, would you mind if I nipped upstairs and got myself some toast? I haven't eaten since breakfast.'

'Oh no, that's fine,' said Maddy. 'If you like, I can get on with putting the new books into the database.'

Jemma took the stairs two at a time, wondering at Maddy's sudden turnaround. She had been prepared for hostility and possibly hard words, but instead Maddy had taken it more or less in her stride. She hadn't looked mutinous, which pleased Jemma. She had wanted to help, and shown interest in Jemma's plans.

'I give up,' said Jemma, and put two slices of bread into the toaster. She only hoped that when she went downstairs she wouldn't find that Maddy had flipped and begun feeding her new prized possessions into the shredder.

When she did re-enter the shop she found Maddy listening to a customer, an elderly gentleman with a monocle whom Jemma was convinced she had never seen in the shop before. 'So this is your new manager,' he said to Maddy, scrutinising Jemma through the monocle, which made his eye look alarmingly large. 'Making changes, I see. I don't believe in change for change's sake, but it's interesting. How much is that *Jane Eyre* in the window?'

Jemma was tempted to tell him that the book wasn't for sale, but fought her urge to keep it. 'I haven't priced it yet. How much would you be prepared to pay for a book like that?'

'If you fetch it out of the window, I'll tell you.' He rocked on his heels while he waited.

Jemma laid the book on the counter. She couldn't work out whether she wanted him to snap it up or say that it wasn't quite what he was looking for. If he rejected it—

He adjusted his monocle so that his eye grew even bigger, and opened the cover. Then he leafed through a few pages, opened the book gently to the middle, and examined the binding and the ribbon. 'I'd expect to see this in a bookshop for about fifty pounds,' he said. 'As I've done you the favour of assessing it for you, perhaps you would accept forty.'

Jemma blinked.

Maddy gazed at the gentleman. 'Shall we split the difference, and say forty-five?'

He frowned, and for a moment Jemma feared the monocle would crack. Then he chuckled, said, 'I suppose we have to make a living,' and drew an ancient leather wallet from his trouser pocket.

Once he had left, Maddy said, 'Which book should we put into the display?'

'Why don't you choose,' said Jemma. And as Maddy advanced to the new books, slowly Jemma shook her head. One day she would understand people; but today was not that day.

Chapter 13

'May I go for lunch?' asked Maddy.

Jemma glanced at the clock. Was it really only a quarter past twelve? She felt as if she had been working for at least six hours. 'Sure.'

'Thanks,' said Maddy. She collected her bag and her coat, a short, stone-coloured mac, and made for the door.

Before she could reach it, it opened and Luke stepped in. 'Hello, Maddy,' he said, pausing as they came face to face.

'Hello, Luke,' said Maddy, and looked quickly away.

Luke stepped aside and held the door open for her. 'Thank you,' murmured Maddy, and scurried off, head down. Was Jemma mistaken, or were her normally pale cheeks rather pink?

'Hi, Jemma,' said Luke. 'How's it going?'

Jemma had maintained the same erect, straight-backed posture all morning. She found she could hold it no longer, and slumped over the counter. 'I'm knackered,' she said.

'Business is booming, then?' Luke advanced to the counter and leaned on it, facing her.

'I'm doing my best,' said Jemma.

A week ago, Jemma had gone on her book-buying expedition and returned to find Maddy banishing the painters. Since then, the shop had been repainted and she had chosen a name.

It had taken many sheets of A4 paper, filled with evocative words and synonyms which eventually were all scored through. Some were too ambitious, some too ambiguous, some too specific. Sitting at the dining table in her flat upstairs, Jemma heard the grandfather clock strike midnight as she crumpled another sheet of paper and threw it in the bin. Finally, at her wits' end, she had scrawled *The Friendly Bookshop* and gone to bed. The signwriter was due the next day, so she had ten hours to go with it or think of something better. When she woke the next morning no brainwaves had occurred, but when she looked at the piece of paper it didn't seem such a bad choice. After all, what was wrong with wanting your bookshop to be friendly?

In her new spirit of openness, she had informed Maddy of the change the next morning. Maddy had said nothing, but her shoulders stiffened beneath her boat-necked Breton top. The signwriter, when he arrived, had accepted the name without comment, merely asking what sort of lettering she would like. Jemma chose a rounded, reasonably conservative style, and he set up his ladder and got to work.

And now there was no going back, Jemma had worked harder than ever to make sure that The Friendly Bookshop was a success. She created themed window displays with autumn leaves, pumpkins, and books draped in woollen scarves, or wearing bobble hats. She wrote book recommendations on little cards and attached them to the shelves. She opened an online shop, and listed stock there. Lunch hours became a hasty slice of toast and jam at the counter, or a banana eaten on the fly, and dinner was often delivered by Snacking Cross Road, because Jemma had neither the time nor the inclination to cook once she had closed her laptop.

'You look knackered,' said Luke, snapping her back to the present.

'Thank you so much,' said Jemma. *I'm not even sure if it's all worth it.* Her efforts were achieving something – she could see that from her accounts – but while the shop was now making as much as it had when she took it over, she couldn't help reflecting that it would have been much less bother to put her feet up and let Maddy step into Brian's shoes. She stretched her arms above her head and felt her shoulders click. 'How are things at Burns Books?' she asked, more out of politeness than concern.

'That's why I'm here,' said Luke. 'I'm worried.'

Jemma frowned. 'In what way? Is the shop misbehaving?'

'No, the shop's fine.' Luke pushed his hair back and Jemma noticed that he was rather pale. Of course; he had left the shop in broad daylight to visit her.

'You'd better tell me,' she said. 'Would you mind if I made a cup of tea first?'

They sat at the counter, Jemma with her tea and Luke with his drinks bottle. He took a pull at it before speaking. 'The shop is absolutely fine. Business is great: books are flying off the shelves. No, it's Raphael. He doesn't seem himself. For one thing, I haven't seen much of him.'

'That's hardly unusual,' Jemma commented.

'But he isn't out buying books or sneaking into Rolando's. He's upstairs in his flat. I don't know what he's doing up there, but when he does come downstairs he looks worried. I've tried asking if he's OK, but he just brushes me off and goes out. I'd follow him, but obviously I can't leave the shop.' His eyes darted around guiltily. 'I shouldn't be here now, but I asked Carl to mind the till upstairs for a few minutes while I came to see you. Raphael went out at eleven, and he hadn't returned by the time I left. I checked Rolando's, but he wasn't there.'

'What does Carl think?' asked Jemma.

364

Luke stared. 'Don't you know?'

'We've barely seen each other,' said Jemma. 'He's been busy with his play, I've been busy here, and our phones are playing up.'

'Well, he's downstairs, so he doesn't see as much of Raphael anyway,' said Luke. 'But he agrees he isn't his usual self.' He paused. 'Could you come and talk to Raphael when Maddy returns from lunch? He's more likely to tell you.'

Jemma's first impulse was to say no, she couldn't possibly, she was far too busy with running her own place. Then all the support that Raphael had given her rushed in like a determined wave. 'Of course I will,' she said. 'I don't know if it will do any good, but I'll pop down as soon as Maddy gets back. Maybe I can loosen his tongue.'

'I hope so,' said Luke. 'It will be nice to see you in the shop for a change. You've been quite a stranger this last week.'

'I know,' said Jemma. She sighed. 'I'm starting to think running my own bookshop isn't as easy as I thought it would be.'

'It looks great,' said Luke. 'And I like the new name. It does seem a lot friendlier.'

'Despite Maddy's best efforts,' said Jemma. She had done her best to be nice to Maddy and make her feel appreciated, but her behaviour varied with the weather. Some days she was willing and helpful; others she was uncommunicative and sulky. It didn't seem to relate to the books she sold, the customers who came in, or anything in particular. Jemma had been forced to conclude that she was moody and a bit unpredictable.

'I'm sure it'll all work out,' said Luke, and Jemma recognised his tone as a soothing one. 'I really had better go. Hope to see you later.' And with that he whisked through the door, wincing as he stepped over the threshold.

***

In the end, Jemma didn't leave The Friendly Bookshop until nearly two o'clock. Maddy had taken her full lunch hour, which of course she was perfectly entitled to do, but Jemma couldn't help thinking that it was typical of her to do that when Jemma needed to be somewhere else. Then Jemma had to explain that she was popping out to Burns Books and wasn't sure when she would be back, and leave Maddy a list of things to get on with, since she had found herself unable to concentrate for wondering about Raphael. And as Jemma was winding that up she had realised how hungry she was, and nipped upstairs for a fortifying helping of cheese on toast. It wasn't that she was delaying her visit; more that she wanted to be fully prepared for any eventuality.

Perhaps he's worried about another challenge, she thought, as she hurried down Charing Cross Road. *Maybe he's going out and researching books. Or maybe he is going on book-buying trips, and he hasn't mentioned it to Luke.*

She pushed open the door of Burns Books and found Luke at the till, dealing expertly with a line of customers holding piles of books. He smiled at Jemma before he registered who she was, and then the smile vanished as if someone had wiped it away.

'Is the boss in?' asked Jemma, a cold hand clutching at her heart.

'He's upstairs in his rooms,' said Luke. 'A letter came, and he said he needed time to read it.' The smile reappeared. 'Cash or card, madam?'

Jemma walked towards the back of the shop and knocked at the door which led to Raphael's quarters.

There was no response.

She knocked again. Nothing.

'Raphael?' she called. 'It's me, Jemma.'

Silence.

Then she heard a yowl from upstairs. *Folio.* She tried the handle of the door, and to her surprise, it opened.

Could it be an anonymous letter? she thought as she climbed the stairs. *A threatening letter, like the ones we got before?* But

366

that had been dealt with, and she was pretty sure that neither of the perpetrators would try that again. Certainly not with Raphael.

At the top of the stairs was another closed door. Jemma knocked. 'Raphael, it's Jemma. I've come to see you.'

He is there, isn't he? Then something worse occurred to her. *He hasn't . . . done anything?*

Folio yowled and scratched at the door. Jemma swallowed the hard lump of terror that had lodged in her throat, and opened it.

Inside, it was dark. All the curtains were drawn. Folio rubbed against her shin and meowed, and she reached down carefully to stroke him. He seemed the same size as usual, but his fur was a mess of tangles and burrs. 'Poor Folio,' she said, and Folio purred in agreement.

'Is Raphael here?' she asked the cat.

Folio answered with a short meow and dashed towards the left-hand door, which Jemma was pretty sure led to Raphael's sitting room, though she had never actually been upstairs. She knocked, then entered.

Jemma didn't often think about how Raphael lived, but if ever she did, she imagined good-quality furnishings worn with age, possibly with an air of decayed grandeur. Once her eyes had grown accustomed to the dim room, she saw that if anything, it was spartan. A threadbare high-backed armchair; a small side table with a reading lamp; an old-style television on a rickety-looking unit. The floorboards were covered with a large, worn rug. The most luxurious thing about the room was the wall of shelves that faced her, filled with books and occasional devices which looked as if they might well be either magical, dangerous, or both.

But the focal point of the room was Raphael. He was sitting in the armchair, one hand supporting his forehead, the other clutching a letter with what looked like an official seal at the top. His eyes were squeezed tight shut. Folio hopped onto the other arm of the chair and butted Raphael's arm, but he didn't seem to notice.

'Raphael, what's up?' Jemma advanced into the room, then crouched beside the armchair. 'Is there anything I can do to help?'

Folio meowed again and rubbed his head on Raphael's upper arm. And Raphael ignored him. Jemma had never, ever, seen him fail to respond to Folio.

Suddenly she had an idea. 'I'll be back in a moment,' she said, and ran first down to the ground floor, then to the lower bookshop, where Carl was leaning against the café counter, enjoying a brief lull in customers.

'A double espresso and a cinnamon roll please, as quickly as you can,' she said.

Carl raised his eyebrows.

'Don't ask questions,' Jemma said. 'It's urgent. This could be a matter of life and death.'

Once she was equipped, Jemma hurried back up to Raphael and shoved the coffee and the cinnamon roll under his nose. He sniffed, then an eye opened and swivelled round to the cinnamon roll. 'Is that for me?' he asked.

'Of course it is,' said Jemma. 'Please, Raphael, tell me what's wrong.'

'You can read it for yourself,' he said, and reached out his free hand for the coffee. Jemma relieved him of the letter and replaced it with the cinnamon roll, which he looked at with curiosity, as if he ought to know what to do with it.

Jemma skimmed the letter. The text beneath the seal said *From the European Head of the Keepers' Guild*. Words and phrases jumped out at her:

Following several complaints...

...unbecoming conduct...

...neglect of duty...

...failure to manage effectively...

...formal written warning...

Jemma looked up from the letter. 'What does it mean?' she said. 'I can tell it isn't good, but what is it saying?'

A bark of something like laughter erupted from Raphael. 'What it means, Jemma, is that I've been reprimanded by my boss. What that means, in layperson's terms, is that it's over. It's all over.'

Chapter 14

'Over? What do you mean, over?' Sick dread filled the pit of Jemma's stomach. Whatever the answer was, she didn't think she would like it.

'I shouldn't be sad,' said Raphael. 'I've had a good run. Two hundred years is quite something, when you think about it.'

'But the letter says it's a warning,' said Jemma.

Raphael looked up, then downed half of his espresso in one go. 'I know it says that, but in practice, once you've had a warning, that's it. Your card is marked. You're on borrowed time.'

'But I don't understand this letter,' said Jemma. 'What unbecoming conduct, exactly?'

'That's not so much me as the others,' said Raphael. 'The accusation is that I haven't been sufficiently in control of them.' The corner of his mouth twisted in a wry smile. 'It isn't exactly a fair system, but it's what we're used to.'

Jemma blinked. She had a horrible feeling that her push for equal opportunities and better employment rights had directly caused Raphael's warning, not to mention the anger and resentment of the people it was meant to help. 'It's all gone so very wrong,' she murmured, and buried her head in her hands. She felt if she were in a black hole of despair, and wanted nothing more than to be buried in it and left alone. *This is my fault. I thought I was helping, but obviously not. I didn't even understand what I was dealing with.*

A few moments later a tentative hand touched her shoulder. 'It's not the end of the world,' said Raphael. 'I'm sure there are other things I could do. I mean, I could just run the bookshop. It could be a sort of retirement.'

Jemma removed her hands and stared at him. 'But – but you'd *die*,' she said.

'Most people do,' said Raphael. 'That wouldn't happen immediately. At least, I hope not.'

'No,' said Jemma, looking about her as if she might spot something in the room that could help. 'There has to be a way. There has to.'

'I don't think there is,' said Raphael. Then he sighed. 'I must admit that I didn't expect the reaction I got. Dissent or disagreement, perhaps, but not such anger. I did indicate that I was happy to discuss the matter, but not one person has taken me up on that.' He ran a hand through his hair. 'I should probably prepare for a challenge. That will be the next thing.'

'Well, it shouldn't be,' said Jemma. 'The system shouldn't work like that.'

'Ah, but it does,' said Raphael, and bit into his cinnamon roll for consolation.

'I'll try and think of something,' said Jemma. 'I'll do whatever I can to help. This is my fault, and if I can fix it, I will.'

Raphael patted her arm. 'I do appreciate it, Jemma, but I'm not sure what you can do. I don't mean that as a slight, not at all; I don't see what anybody could do.'

Jemma sensed the conversation could go round in circles for hours if she let it. 'I'm going back to my shop,' she said. 'But I'll keep thinking about it, and if I have any ideas I'll be in touch.' She got up and studied him. 'Are you sure you'll be all right?'

'Of course,' said Raphael. 'Folio is here.' He tickled the cat under the chin and received a purr in return. 'I'll go downstairs in a bit and look after the ground floor. It'll probably do me good to think about something else.'

'I think you're right,' said Jemma. 'One of the customers might give you an idea. Or maybe a book. I'm sure I saw some employment law textbooks—'

Raphael laughed. 'I'm no expert on employment law, but I'd hazard a guess that the Keepers' Guild runs on an entirely different legal system,' he said. 'Anyway, you get back to your bookshop. Books to sell, people to serve.'

Luke raised his eyebrows when Jemma emerged into the main shop, but she shook her head. It was too big and too horrible to explain. 'I'll do the best I can to help,' she said. 'Hopefully I'll have a brainwave.'

'I hope you do,' said Luke. 'I miss Raphael, you know. While he's not in the shop that much, at the moment he's not here in a completely different way.'

Jemma nodded, and the tinkle of the shop bell as she left sounded like a death knell.

***

Jemma's feet dragged as she walked down Charing Cross Road to The Friendly Bookshop. When she arrived, though, she found it looking far from friendly. The window was completely empty, the spotlight shining on an absence.

'What's going on?' she said, as she opened the door.

Maddy stood behind the counter, packing books into a box. The former window display, if Jemma wasn't mistaken.

'What on earth are you doing?' A couple of customers were browsing, but Jemma had reached the point where she didn't care what the customers thought. 'Why are there no books in the window?' Then she saw that the shelves at the front of the shop, the shelves she had filled with her lovely new books, were also completely bare.

'It isn't working,' said Maddy. 'The fiction isn't working.'

'Yes it is,' said Jemma. 'We're selling more books, and making the same money as the bookshop did before.'

'But what about the expense?' said Maddy. 'What about the cost of all those books, and the redecoration? I doubt you've taken *that* into account. I suspect you've been looking at the profits and ignoring the costs.'

'Don't be ridiculous,' snapped Jemma, and a woman nearby, flicking through *A Brief History of Time*, jumped. 'I've lost count of how often you've made changes without asking me first, and as far as I'm concerned, this is the last time.'

Maddy came out from behind the counter and faced her. She stood tall, and two spots of colour burned on her cheekbones. 'And what will you do, exactly?'

The words *Fire you* were on Jemma's lips, but she couldn't bring herself to say them. What if she were in the wrong and Maddy sued her for unfair dismissal? Or what if she went through the accounts and found that Maddy was right, and she *had* overspent, and she had made a mess of things yet again? But she drew herself up too and glared at Maddy. 'I'm sending you home,' she said. 'I'm not prepared to tolerate an employee who constantly undermines me. I suggest you think about that before you come in tomorrow. *If* you do.'

Maddy flung up her chin. 'I shall most certainly think that over,' she said. She pushed the box of books away from her as if it were contaminated, got her bag and coat, and clumped out of the shop.

Jemma exhaled, closed her eyes, and pinched the bridge of her nose. When she opened her eyes she found that everyone left in the shop was staring at her.

'But isn't *she* the manager?' said the woman who had jumped earlier, laying her book on the counter. 'I thought she was.'

'No, she isn't,' said Jemma, 'but she clearly thinks she is.' She processed the sale, then opened the box of books on the counter and began putting them back in the window, possibly with less than her usual care. 'If any of you were looking for fiction,' she said, when she had finished, 'tell me what you'd like and I'll check on the database. It appears that while I was in a meeting with the owner, my assistant has taken it upon herself to rearrange the shop.' The customers stared. 'Do carry on,' she said. 'Don't mind me.'

Jemma found her books boxed neatly and stacked in the far corner of the stockroom. *I trusted her alone for what, an hour, and look what happened.* Re-shelving the books ought to have been restful and calming, but Jemma found herself pushing them firmly into their places on the shelf in a way that she wished she could do with Maddy. *What is wrong with her? Why won't she accept my authority? Is there something wrong with me? Am I a bad manager?*

By the time the shop closed for the day, though she had fully restocked the shelves and even sold a reasonable amount of books, Jemma was thoroughly convinced that she was, quite possibly, the worst bookshop manager in the entire world. *So much for helping Raphael,* she thought, as she locked the shop door, set the alarm, and stomped upstairs to her flat. *I'm a complete failure. Everything I touch turns to crap.* She kept up a constant stream of angry muttering as she slammed around the flat, turning the TV up loud enough to give herself a headache, breaking the teabag as she made a drink, and, devastatingly, discovering that she was out of emergency biscuits. That was when she broke down in tears and huddled in the corner of the sofa, rocking and worrying about Raphael, and the terrible things she had done.

Chapter 15

After a while Jemma's sniffling got on her own nerves, so she surfed mindlessly between channels, staring at local news, then a brightly coloured cartoon, then a consumer programme, then a house-renovation show. She didn't care about any of it; she just felt numb. *There's nothing left.*

She could hear someone knocking at the door downstairs: three light taps, a pause, then persistent, harder knocking. Whoever it was, she didn't want to know. Then a voice shouted 'Jemma! Jemma, are you there?'

It was Carl's voice.

Jemma debated whether or not to let him in. On one hand, she didn't feel like talking to anybody. On the other, it was Carl, and she hadn't seen him for days. Then her phone solved the problem by ringing. She glanced at the display: *Mum.*

'I'm coming,' she yelled, opened the door of the flat, and clattered downstairs.

Carl looked rather confused when he saw her face. 'What's up?'

Jemma shrugged. 'Everything.' She felt as if that ought to be her cue to weep on his shoulder, but it seemed pointless.

'Can I come up? Or would you rather come out?'

Jemma eyed him. He was still in his barista uniform of black polo shirt and jeans. 'Aren't you supposed to be rehearsing?'

Carl exhaled, and seemed to deflate in the process. 'I was worried about you,' he said. 'Luke told me that you'd been in and spoken to Raphael, and that you wouldn't tell him what was wrong. And you didn't come and see me.'

'I had to get back to the shop,' said Jemma. 'And when I did, I found that Maddy had rearranged everything again, so I sent her home for the day.' She leaned on the doorframe, looking at him. 'You can come up if you like, but I'm not sure why you'd want to. I'm not very good company right now.' She led the way upstairs. *In fact, I probably haven't been good company for weeks.* A shiver came out of nowhere. 'You haven't come round to dump me, have you?' She said it lightly, but kept climbing the stairs, not wanting to turn and see his face.

Carl said nothing, but she heard his feet behind her. A part of her wanted to press him for an answer – *You have, haven't you?* – while she also wanted to kick herself for potentially putting the idea into his head. She reached the landing and waved her hand at the sitting room. 'Would you like a drink?'

'I want to talk to you,' said Carl. 'I'm not happy with the way things are at the moment. Before you say anything, that doesn't mean I want to break up with you. But we aren't really going out at the moment, are we? We don't text because of the weird phone thing, and you're too busy to meet up after work, and I'm busy with rehearsals now we've scheduled the shows—'

'Wait a minute,' said Jemma. 'You're putting on the play?'

'Yes,' said Carl. 'Raphael said we could put on a couple of performances downstairs at the end of November.' He walked into the sitting room and sat on the sofa. 'I would have told you, but—'

'I know, there wasn't an opportunity,' said Jemma. She

376

remembered when she and Raphael had discovered the crypt in the basement, and her suggestion that they could put on events. *They've done it without me.* 'I'm sorry, but everything's been so busy.'

'Everything is always so busy,' said Carl.

'Yes, but this is different,' said Jemma. 'Maddy is undermining me at every turn, and that's nothing compared to what's going on with Raphael—' She clapped a hand over her mouth.

Carl stared at her. 'What's going on with Raphael?'

Jemma sighed, walked into the sitting room, and flopped in the opposite corner of the sofa. She looked at Carl. 'He could lose his job,' she said. 'His boss has given him a warning.'

'He's got a boss?'

Jemma nodded. Then, judging that she might as well let the whole cat out of the bag, she told him the rest of it.

'That's bizarre,' said Carl. 'Why would people want their jobs to be insecure? Why wouldn't they want better terms and conditions? Obviously they're not in any sort of union – or if they are, it's the strangest one I ever heard of.'

'I can't get my head round it either,' said Jemma. 'Apparently people have been complaining over Raphael's head. They must think that will do them some good, and apparently it has.' She frowned. 'Maybe Raphael's boss wants a quiet life and he doesn't care who's right.'

'Maybe,' said Carl. 'What's going on with Maddy? I thought you two were getting on better.'

'We were,' said Jemma. 'Then we weren't again, and I don't know why. I thought maybe she was just moody, but sometimes it feels as if she is – almost a different person.'

'Do you think… Not that I know anything about this, but could she have some sort of personality disorder?'

'If she has,' said Jemma, 'it's come on very recently; Raphael has never mentioned anything. And Brian wouldn't have put up with it. I'd like to have seen his face if Maddy started moving his displays around and telling him that things weren't working.'

'True,' said Carl. 'She'd get her marching orders.' He studied Jemma. 'So why do you think she's doing it with you?'

'Maybe she thinks she can get away with it,' said Jemma. 'Maybe she thinks I'm a pushover. Or maybe I just really, really wind her up, and she can't stop herself. But afterwards, she's so very sorry. Sometimes I call her out over something, and she apologises, and she's even helpful. I mean, more than she needs to be. For all I know, she'll come in tomorrow morning and be full of apologies and nice as pie, then rearrange everything after lunch.'

Carl leaned over and touched her arm. 'Would you fire her?'

Jemma considered the question. 'Not without speaking to Raphael first, and I don't want to bother him right now. He's got enough going on, never mind me coming to him with personnel issues.' She giggled at the idea of knocking on Raphael's door to request employment law advice. Then she found that she couldn't stop.

Carl gave her a sharp look. 'Stop that, Jemma,' he said, quietly and firmly.

Jemma, shocked, stopped immediately. 'Thank you,' she said. 'I don't know why I did that.'

He shuffled along the sofa and put an arm round her. 'You're worried and upset,' he said. He gave her a squeeze. 'I don't like seeing you like this, Jemma, but I don't know what to do. I'm not even sure I can help you.' His hold loosened, and he looked away. 'I feel a bit useless.'

'Don't be daft, of course you're not useless,' said Jemma. 'Talking to you is helping, it really is.' She smiled. 'And you turning up meant I could ignore a phone call from my mum.'

'Oh, so I'm the slightly better option, am I?' said Carl. Then he grinned. 'Well, if I helped…' Then he grew serious. 'Why didn't you want to talk to your mum?'

378

'Oh, nothing's ever right,' said Jemma. 'If it isn't perfect, then it wasn't good enough. If it is perfect, then I'm either aiming too low or doing the wrong thing. Anyway. Do you want a drink?'

'I wouldn't mind,' said Carl. 'I take it you don't want to go for a bite to eat.'

'I know it's unlike me to be uninterested in food,' said Jemma, 'but I'm not that fussed.' Carl was scrutinising her. 'Why are you looking at me like that?'

'When did you last cook a meal?' he said. 'I mean properly, from scratch. Not putting something in the microwave, or doing pasta with a jar of sauce. Not that there's anything wrong with that,' he added.

She frowned. 'Why do you want to know?'

'I'm not sure,' he said. 'It seems important, somehow.'

Jemma thought. Not that week – that had mostly been toast, occasionally cheese on toast, and at least one pizza. She couldn't really answer for the week before, either. 'I'm not entirely sure,' she admitted. Then she grimaced. 'That isn't good, is it?'

'It isn't like you,' said Carl. 'I remember when I brought you home that first time, and we went out to lunch, and you were talking about how you'd started cooking and you were really into it.'

'It's not that I've gone off it or anything,' said Jemma. 'I've just been busy.'

'But you're often busy,' said Carl. 'And it hasn't stopped you cooking before. In fact, you said you found it relaxing. So why don't you cook now?'

Jemma thought – or tried to think, because nothing came to mind. She could remember cooking, certainly, and enjoying it. But somehow it seemed as if someone else had done that, a long time ago, not her. And the idea of finding a recipe, assembling ingredients, and methodically working through the steps to produce a meal seemed very remote indeed. 'I don't know,' she said, in a small, uncertain voice.

'I wonder…' said Carl. 'Tell me what Raphael was like when you went up to his flat.'

'But I already said—'

'Humour me.'

Jemma's brow furrowed. 'He was sitting in the armchair with his head in his hand, clutching the letter. He didn't answer me when I called him, and he didn't pay any attention to Folio.' She looked at Carl. 'I managed to bring him round with a cinnamon roll, but even then…'

'And Maddy's behaving oddly, and you – well, something's stopping you from doing things you'd normally do, like cooking —'

'I'm so tired,' said Jemma. 'And Raphael's had all this bother to deal with. It's no wonder he isn't himself—'

'There it is again,' said Carl. '*Not himself. Sometimes she seems like a different person.* And you aren't yourself, either.'

A chill ran down Jemma's spine. 'What do you mean?'

'I'm not entirely sure,' said Carl. 'But something's going on with all three of you, and I intend to get to the bottom of it.' He paused, his face set and determined. 'You know what?'

'What?'

'A cup of tea would really help.'

Chapter 16

The next day Jemma was in the bookshop by eight o'clock, waiting to see which Maddy would come in. Despite a long chat with Carl the previous evening, they had come up with no better plan of action than keeping their eyes open and, if possible, teasing more information out of Raphael and Maddy.

Jemma got her answer when she heard a tap at the door at twenty-five minutes past eight, and Maddy shuffled in, thoroughly hangdog. 'I'll understand if you tell me to go away,' she said. 'I don't know what came over me.'

'Neither do I,' said Jemma. 'And we should discuss it.'

Maddy winced. 'Could I apologise, and then we can draw a line under it?'

'We've tried that,' said Jemma. 'Everything is fine for a few days, but the minute I leave the shop you start messing around again.' She wanted to look Maddy in the eye, but Maddy wasn't letting her, keeping her gaze firmly on her twisting hands. 'Why do you do it, Maddy? You must know all that happens is that I get cross with you and put it back as it was.'

'I do know,' said Maddy. 'I – I suppose I'm not as ready for change as I thought I was.'

'I'm sure you've said that before,' said Jemma. 'But why keep doing something if you know it doesn't work?'

Maddy said nothing, peeping at Jemma from under her eyelashes.

'Maddy, you would let me know if you were feeling ill, wouldn't you?' said Jemma.

'I'm perfectly well, thank you,' said Maddy, looking Jemma full in the face for the first time. 'There is absolutely nothing wrong with me.'

'Good,' said Jemma. 'I'm glad to hear it.'

'I haven't had a day off sick in ten years,' Maddy continued. 'That's how long I've been working here.'

'That's a long time,' said Jemma. 'What did you do before?'

The corner of Maddy's mouth moved upwards a tiny bit. 'I worked in an antiquarian bookshop just down the road. But I'd always been interested in this shop – I used to pop over in my lunch hour – and when a job came up—'

'I see,' said Jemma. 'So antiquarian books are in your blood, sort of.'

Maddy actually giggled. 'I suppose they are.'

The letterbox rattled, and a few envelopes dropped onto the mat. 'Post's here,' said Jemma, walking to the door. Out of the corner of her eye she caught a quick, nervous glance from Maddy, whose expression seemed to have frozen. She flicked through the pile. 'Utility bill . . . letter . . . might be a card . . . oh, and one for you.' She passed it to Maddy. 'You'll have to let your correspondent know we've had a name change.'

'Thank you,' said Maddy, taking the letter and thrusting it into her bag unopened. 'Yes, I shall.'

'It must be nice to get a personal letter,' said Jemma. 'Handwritten, too. I don't think I've ever seen ink that colour.'

'Isn't it your morning to go to Burns Books?' said Maddy. 'Not

382

that I'm trying to get rid of you—'

'Yes, it is,' said Jemma. She gave Maddy what she hoped was a moderately stern look. 'Can I trust you not to do anything to the shop while I'm gone?'

Maddy gazed past Jemma, a faraway expression on her face.

'Maddy?'

Maddy snapped to attention. 'Everything will be fine,' she said.

'Good,' said Jemma. 'Then I'll head out. The till's primed, and we have plenty of bags. If anything happens, you can always phone me at the shop.' She frowned. *Why did I say that?*

'Yes, Jemma,' said Maddy.

Jemma got her coat, slung her bag over her shoulder, and left. She had gone a few steps when she realised she hadn't turned the shop sign round. She was about to open the door and do it when she glimpsed Maddy, standing where Jemma had left her, devouring the letter which had arrived a few minutes before.

Whatever, thought Jemma, and hurried away.

***

She was startled to find Raphael on the ground floor of the bookshop, dressed in a conventional dark-blue suit with a white shirt and red bow tie, humming to himself as he fed the till with bank bags of change. Folio sat on the counter, supervising the process and occasionally patting an empty bag. 'Hello,' said Jemma. 'You look happier, if you don't mind me saying.'

'I am,' said Raphael. 'I've decided on a course of action, and you can help.'

'Oh good,' said Jemma. 'I think. What would you like me to do?'

'I'm calling a meeting,' Raphael replied. 'Actually, I've already called it and sent the invitations.'

'Gosh,' said Jemma. 'That's . . . dynamic. Who have you invited?'

'Everyone,' said Raphael. 'Well, not everyone, but all my staff

383

and associates. And if you wouldn't mind, I'd like you to explain how you influenced the recruitment process.'

'I see,' said Jemma, quailing inwardly. 'Um, when is it?'

'Ten o'clock,' said Raphael.

'*Today?*'

'Yes, today. Seize the day. Strike while the iron is hot. Seize the opportunity with both hands – well, as long as it isn't a hot iron. You get my drift.'

Jemma gazed at Raphael, bewildered. On one hand, the thought of addressing a meeting full of strangers was terrifying. On the other, Raphael seemed more enthusiastic than he had for a long time, and utterly convinced that his plan would work. 'Where will the meeting be?' she asked. 'Are you closing the bookshop?'

'No need,' said Raphael. 'We can do it upstairs.'

'What?'

'It's a virtual meeting,' said Raphael, as if speaking to a small child. 'We can do it on my laptop.'

'You have a laptop?'

'Of course I— Um, yes, I do,' said Raphael. 'Though I don't use it often.'

'I figured,' said Jemma. *All this time I thought he was a complete technophobe, and here he is running a virtual meeting.* She remembered all the times she had scrolled slowly through spreadsheets for him and explained formulas. 'I suppose you emailed the invites?'

'Oh yes,' said Raphael. 'I sent a brief agenda to my mailing list.'

'Good grief,' said Jemma. 'Would you mind if I put the kettle on? I have a sudden urge for tea.'

'What a good idea,' said Raphael. 'In fact, I'll put the kettle on, and you can go and say hello to Luke and Carl.'

Jemma descended the stairs slowly, her mind whirling. *Whatever next*, she thought. *In fact, I don't want to know.*

'How's it going?' they both said in a ragged chorus, as she pushed open the great oak door.

'Fine, I think,' she said.

'Raphael seems happy today,' said Carl, in an encouraging voice.

'Yes, he does,' Jemma replied. 'Luke, you'll be on the upstairs till this morning. Raphael and I will be busy.'

'Uh-huh,' said Luke.

Jemma looked at him more closely. Luke was back in head-to-toe black, his hair straggling from under his beanie hat, and he hadn't shaved that morning. 'How are you?' she asked.

'Oh, fine,' said Luke, continuing to look glum. 'Well, no, not really. I've been ghosted.' He sighed. 'If she didn't want to see me again, she could've texted. Although come to think of it, I'm not sure she can.'

'I'm not even going to ask,' said Jemma. 'But I'm sorry.'

'It's OK,' said Luke. 'We were a bit of an odd couple anyway. And we only went out twice. Better now than later, I guess.'

'How was Maddy?' Carl asked.

'Apologetic,' said Jemma. 'We had a chat. She's promised not to change the shop around while I'm gone. I'll have to trust her, otherwise I won't be able to go anywhere. Anyway, she was reading a letter when I left. Hopefully that will take her mind off making changes.'

'Jemma!' called Raphael. 'Tea's ready.'

'That's my cue,' said Jemma. 'Hopefully I'll see you guys later and we can catch up properly.' She surveyed the lower floor of the shop, which was in impeccable order yet still managed to look cosy. *I wish I could come down here and read*, she thought. *A good book, and a cappuccino, and maybe Folio next to me.* The pull was so strong that she took a step towards the nearest armchair before shaking the thought off and galloping upstairs.

***

'Are you ready?' said Raphael, at five minutes to ten.

'I think so.' Jemma had already visited the staff bathroom to brush her hair and put lipstick on. She flicked through the bullet points she had scribbled on a couple of index cards, muttering them to herself. 'Do you promise I won't have to talk for more than five minutes?'

'And take questions,' said Raphael, in a reasonable tone. He had fetched an extra chair and placed it beside the armchair, and put the little table in front of both. 'Time to set up.' He went to a corner cupboard that Jemma hadn't noticed, opened it, and brought out a laptop. A slim, impressive-looking laptop.

'You are full of surprises, Raphael Burns,' said Jemma, as he opened it and began clicking on icons.

'Here we go.' A window opened, and in the middle was a countdown clock captioned *Time to Meeting*. 'Webcam on.' He clicked and their faces filled the screen.

'Do I really look that pale?' said Jemma, eyeing herself with distaste.

'Yes,' said Raphael. 'You need to get out more. Now, I'll keep the sound off until people start joining. I've had a few apologies, but I'm expecting around a hundred and fifty people to show up.'

'A hundred and fifty?' Jemma blurted. 'You didn't mention that.'

'Oh, and I'm recording it,' said Raphael. 'That way I can send the meeting to everyone who missed it.'

'Ugh.' Jemma slumped in her chair.

'They can see you, you know,' said Raphael, waving a hand at the screen. Jemma saw two impassive faces sharing the screen with them, sat up straight, and stuck a smile on her face. 'I'm *so* going to get you back for this, Raphael,' she said, out of the side of her mouth.

More and more faces popped up. 'Interesting,' commented Raphael. 'Most of the people here so far are pretty moderate. I was expecting the rabble-rousers to turn up early, to psych me out. If and when they join, I'll point them out to you.'

'Thank you so much,' said Jemma.

'One minute,' said Raphael. 'Sound on.' He waved at the camera, and a few hands waved back.

Jemma crossed her fingers. 'Good luck,' she whispered. The clock ticked down.

'Right, good morning everyone,' said Raphael. 'I expect you're wondering why I've called this meeting today, although those of you who were present at our last update will no doubt have a good idea.'

Two more faces appeared on the screen. 'Ah, good morning,' said Raphael. 'We've just started, so you haven't missed anything.' He glanced at Jemma, then pointed at the faces in the two new windows.

Jemma gasped. *It's them!* She nudged Raphael, who ignored her. 'So if we're all quite ready,' he said, pointedly not looking at the two latecomers, 'let's begin.'

Chapter 17

Jemma did her best to keep a smile on her face as her brain worked furiously. *It is them, isn't it?* She leaned forward slightly to examine their two windows. She remembered those blonde highlights, the tailored designer outfit, the icy demeanour. And she recognised both De Vere's tweed jacket and his superciliousness. *I'm absolutely sure of it. But what can I do?*

She tuned into what Raphael was saying. 'Some of you may be surprised to hear that I received a letter from Armand Dupont, the European Head of the Guild. It was not a pleasant letter, and he indicated that he had received complaints about me. No one has contacted me to discuss the proposed recruitment changes. I was not so foolish as to assume that meant you were all happy, but I hoped that you would seek a meeting rather than go over my head.'

Even in the tiny window, Jemma saw the posh woman's nostrils flare, while Mr De Vere appeared to be looking down his nose from a great height.

'At the last meeting there was an – atmosphere, and a few people dominated the discussion,' said Raphael. 'Indeed, some of you tried to talk over me. I explained that my change of heart regarding our recruitment process was based on feedback from a potential candidate. However, I'm not sure many of you heard.'

Angry buzzing came from the screen, like a colony of wasps about to strike.

'So I have invited my contact to speak to you herself.' Raphael turned to Jemma.

'And what credentials does she have?' demanded an exceedingly well-bred voice.

'The same as all of us, Drusilla,' Raphael replied. 'Experience and knowledge, though in a somewhat different field. I'll mute everybody so that Jemma can speak.'

Jemma picked up her index cards. She felt as if she ought to stand, but that was impossible. She also felt desperate for a glass of water. She swallowed, looked at the tessellation of faces, and tried to smile. 'Hello everyone,' she said. *Don't wave. Whatever you do, don't wave.* She could actually feel her hand lifting. She grabbed her wrist with the other hand, and forced it down.

'My name is Jemma James, and until a few months ago I had no idea such a thing as the Keepers' Guild existed.' *I can imagine what they're thinking.*

'While working at Burns Books, and managing The Friendly Bookshop, I have gained experience. However, before joining the bookshop I worked as an analyst, and I have a keen interest in management theory and business strategy. Your current recruitment model encourages you to attack your colleagues to gain promotion, or defend your own position against attack. At any moment your job and your home could be in jeopardy; that isn't a healthy way to live. I'm sure some of you don't want change. But talented people who don't want to take such an unstable job will either leave the Guild, or never join it.'

She glanced at Raphael. 'Go on, Jemma,' he said.

'Raphael invited me to apply for the position of Assistant

389

Keeper; however, I could not consider it. For people with families and caring responsibilities, the risk of having either to leave them, or move everyone to a new area without a job to fund it, isn't worth taking.' Jemma paused, saw no obvious hostility on the faces before her, and ploughed on.

'If no new people come into your organisation, eventually no new thoughts will enter the organisation either, and it will grow stale. Then how will you perform your great task of preserving, managing, and protecting knowledge? The threats out there may change, but what if you can't?'

She considered stopping there, but it seemed a very negative way to leave things.

'I don't want to sound negative,' she said hastily. 'But what a way to spend your working life; either plotting to overthrow your colleagues, or watching your juniors for signs of aggression. Wouldn't it be better if you could concentrate on your work, instead of having that constant distraction? And wouldn't you rather enjoy your home life without worrying that it could be taken away from you in an instant?'

She gathered herself for a conclusion. 'I hope that what I have said makes sense, and I urge you to consider it, both for yourselves and for the future of the Guild. Thank you.'

Raphael smiled at her. 'Well said, Jemma. Does anyone have a question? If so, please raise your hand, either by pushing the button or by the antiquated method of actually moving your arm, and I'll unmute you one at a time.'

Please don't unmute those two, Jemma thought. *At least, not yet.*

'Percy, I see your hand is up,' said Raphael, and reached towards the trackpad. Jemma crossed her fingers.

One of the squares filled the screen, and she recognised the elderly man with a monocle who had bought *Jane Eyre*.

'I enjoyed your speech, Jemma, though it doesn't apply to me,' he said. 'I am an old man, and I have no plans to take over the world.' He chortled at his own joke. 'Where was I? Oh yes. Based as I am in a suburban backwater, I doubt any young thrusting individuals will challenge me any time soon. Yet I am not getting any younger, even if I am getting no older.' He bestowed a beatific smile on his listeners.

'One day in the not too distant future, I may wish to relinquish my position and retire. I am not particularly keen on the idea of watching a gaggle of aspiring Assistant Keepers fighting over my role as if they were dogs scrapping for a bone; I would like my replacement to be appointed with dignity. And that is how I wish to leave my position, rather than fearing I shall be thrust out of my library and made to leave the place I have called home for so long. I have seen the changes Jemma is making at her bookshop, and I for one am in favour of them. We need to move with the times.'

'Thank you, Percy; those were relevant and heartfelt words,' said Raphael. He nudged Jemma, and pointed to the chat window at the side of the display. It was scrolling quickly. Jemma saw comments like *Good point*, and *Yes, what am I supposed to do with the children?* and *This sounds too good to be true*. She sighed. Of course, you had to accept some scepticism.

'Ah, Drusilla, I thought you might have something to say.' Raphael reached towards the trackpad and the blonde woman's face filled the screen. She was almost all glare.

'Thank you so much for your speech, my dear,' she said. 'Would you mind telling me how many years you worked as an analyst?'

OK, thought Jemma. *I can handle this.* 'After graduating I joined a management training scheme, where I both worked and learnt management and analytical skills,' she said. 'I was in the scheme for two years, then transitioned into a full-time analytical role which I held for two more years.'

'So, four years then,' said Drusilla. 'If we're feeling generous.'

She paused just long enough for Jemma to feel that she ought to respond, then continued. 'You do realise, dear, that most of us have been part of the Keepers' Guild for well over a hundred years. What you're proposing is nothing more than a passing fad.'

'What about equal rights?' said Jemma. 'What about human rights, in fact?'

Drusilla said nothing, merely looking amused. 'Really, this is like any occupation,' she said. 'There is work to be done, and occasionally, sacrifices to be made. The organisation is paramount. I'm sure that your keen business intelligence would be in agreement with that.'

'Actually, no,' said Jemma. 'Research shows that employees who have a good work-life balance perform better.'

'Oh, research,' scoffed Priscilla. 'You can make numbers do whatever you want. Of course, as an analyst, you know that. You've probably faked statistics in your time.'

'I most certainly have not,' said Jemma. 'And if you have to rely on criticising my youth and resorting to personal attacks, then I don't think your argument is worth much.'

Drusilla recoiled slightly, then recovered her composure and lifted her chin. 'If you can't keep your temper under pressure, dear, then this isn't the career for you.'

Raphael, looking pained, leaned towards the screen. 'Does anyone else have any useful or relevant comments to make?'

Jemma regarded the sea of faces. Comments were still scrolling down the right-hand side of the screen.

I'm not sure I want new people coming in and telling us what to do.

Maybe we should do a six-month trial and monitor it.

Does anyone know when this finishes?

She swallowed, and wished again for a glass of water. *Well, I said my piece, although I have no idea if it was any use.* Then she remembered what she had wanted to tell Raphael. She flipped over an index card and grabbed the pen she had used to make notes. She scribbled: *Drusilla, De Vere and Percy have all visited my shop.* She nudged Raphael and pushed the card towards him. He read it and pursed his lips, considering for a moment.

'I see plenty of comments, but no one appears to have any burning questions. I have delayed advertising the post in the hope of reaching a consensus, but it is not fair to delay further. My door is still open for discussion, and I ask that anyone wishing to speak to me does so by the end of next week. Pending any necessary changes, I aim to recruit a new Assistant Keeper for Westminster by Christmas.' He paused, but no one spoke. 'Speaking of Christmas, we have to finalise this year's festivities. I believe you are leading on this, Nina?'

A small blonde woman with winged glasses and an Alice band took over the screen. 'As ever, we have three choices for this year's theme, and I would like to present them to you.'

Jemma nudged Raphael and pointed to the mute button. He pressed it. 'Can I go and get a drink?' she asked. 'I'm gasping.'

'Of course,' said Raphael.

'A desert island theme would be new, but it doesn't feel very Christmassy...'

'What do you think about' – Jemma mouthed the next words, even though they were muted – 'those three?' She tapped the index card.

'Interesting,' said Raphael. 'And not unexpected. I know Drusilla and De Vere are friends with Brian. Same university. And no, don't ask me which.'

'Or an Australian beach theme...'

'Percy's a bit of an oddity,' said Raphael. 'A nice oddity, though. And he's impressed with you.'

'And there's always traditional Dickensian, but we've done that so often.'

'I have to talk to you when this meeting finishes,' said Jemma.

'How much more of it is there?'

'Maybe ten, fifteen minutes?'

'So if you type A, B, or C in the chat window, I shall collect your votes and we'll go with the majority.'

Raphael unmuted himself. 'Most concisely done, Nina. Shall we say five minutes to make your decision, then we'll reconvene.' He clicked the mute button. 'Jemma, why don't you see if Carl can rustle up some drinks? I feel the need for a strong coffee.'

A few minutes later they were both supplied with caffeine, and Nina, her mouth turned down, announced the festive result. 'I can't say I'm surprised,' she began. 'Perhaps Desert Island and Australian Beach Christmas were a little too similar; they have scored 31% and 33% of the votes respectively. Three people abstained. Therefore the winning option, yet again, is a Dickensian Christmas celebration with 35% of the vote.'

'Thank you, Nina,' said Raphael. 'That concludes our short agenda, but does anyone have any other business? Any relevant business, I should add.' He surveyed the sea of faces. 'I see no raised hands. In that case, if you wish to speak to me privately, my door is always open. I shall communicate with you again before I advertise the post, and inform you of any changes. Until then, I hope you have a safe and knowledgeable week.' He beamed at them, and ended the meeting.

He turned to Jemma. 'How do you think that went?'

'It was OK,' said Jemma. 'To be honest, I thought they'd be much meaner to me.'

'You probably surprised a lot of them,' said Raphael. 'They won't be used to hearing views from someone who isn't, so to speak, one of us. I suspect many of them, though they kept quiet, agreed with what you said. It does actually make sense.'

'You're so kind,' said Jemma. She took a gulp of her cappuccino, which she felt she had earned approximately ten times over. 'Anyway, why do you think they came to my shop?'

Raphael considered. 'Did they buy books?'

'Well, yes, but I'm sure they could have got them elsewhere at trade prices.'

'True,' said Raphael. 'In that case, they probably wanted to see what you were doing with Brian's shop. Unless they were checking up on Maddy.'

'Do you think they reported back to Brian?' asked Jemma.

'I wouldn't be surprised,' said Raphael. 'Certainly not in the case of De Vere and Drusilla. Percy may have come out of curiosity. He likes a trip to the city once in a while.'

Report back... Suddenly Jemma's blood ran cold, and the hand holding her cappuccino shook. She put it down before she spilt it on the laptop. 'Maddy was reading a letter when I left,' she said. 'Do you think she's in touch with Brian? Could that explain her behaviour?'

Raphael laughed. 'Maddy is a very sensible woman.' He frowned. 'But what you've described doesn't sound like Maddy. Did you see the letter?'

'It was addressed to Maddy, so I didn't open it,' said Jemma. 'The handwriting was old-fashioned and shaky, and it slanted backwards. I could just make out Maddy's name. But the strangest thing was the colour of the ink.'

'Can you describe it?' asked Raphael.

'Yes, it was blue. Not navy blue, and not electric blue, and not bright blue—'

'Wait a minute.' Raphael opened Google and typed rapidly, then clicked on the first result before Jemma had a chance to read it. The screen loaded, and showed a hexagonal ink bottle of exactly the right colour.

'That's it,' said Jemma. 'Mysterious Blue.' She gazed at Raphael. 'How did you know?'

He rolled his eyes. 'Brian never uses anything else. I should have realised he was up to something, but I never thought he'd move so quickly.'

Jemma turned to him, eyes wide. 'What do you think he's told Maddy to do?'

'I have no idea,' said Raphael. 'But we should go to your bookshop right away, and find out.'

Chapter 18

Jemma scurried down Charing Cross Road alongside Raphael. What might Maddy have done this time? What *could* she have done? She peered ahead. She couldn't see flames or smoke, which was something.

'Jemma, I can feel you worrying,' said Raphael, not breaking stride. 'Please don't.'

'I'm trying,' said Jemma. 'Strangely, my corporate training didn't cover what to do when your deadly rival has put a spy in your shop. There wasn't a module on undercover espionage.'

'Call that an education,' said Raphael. 'Anyway, here we are.' He waved his hand at the shop. 'Things don't seem too bad.'

'Let's wait until we get inside, shall we?' said Jemma, and pushed open the door.

She glanced at the front shelves. As she expected, her books had been removed and Brian's books, as she thought of them, put in their place. 'What did I say?' she cried.

There was no answer.

'I knew it,' she said to Raphael. 'She's probably messing about in the stockroom right now.' She looked around the shop and spied the letter, lying on the counter. 'There it is!' She sprang across the room and seized it, scanning the lines.

Then she turned to Raphael. 'I don't understand. It's just . . . a letter.' She handed it to him.

'*Dear Maddy*,' Raphael read aloud, '*I hope this letter finds you well—*'

Maddy erupted into the room. 'How did you come– Oh.' She pulled up, staring.

'I begin to see,' said Raphael. He continued to read. '*I am very well, and finding my new surroundings most stimulating.*'

Maddy ran to the front shelves and began removing books, stacking them on the floor.

'*I hope you are upholding the standards of the bookshop while I am away.*'

Maddy jumped to her feet and ran into the stockroom.

Raphael followed her. '*Finding my new surroundings most stimulating,*' he repeated.

Maddy passed him on her way to the shelves, and continued emptying them.

'What's wrong with her?' said Jemma. 'Is she under a spell?'

'In a way,' said Raphael. 'Jemma, call her by her name.'

'Maddy,' said Jemma, 'please stop doing that.'

Maddy's arms dropped to her sides. She turned, saw Jemma, and blinked. 'Hello, Jemma,' she said, uncertainly. 'You haven't been gone long.' Her gaze settled on Raphael. 'You brought Mr Burns.'

'We wondered how you were getting on,' said Raphael, 'so I decided to pay the bookshop a visit. Maddy, would you mind making tea?'

'Yes, of course, Mr Burns,' said Maddy, and hurried to the back room.

'OK, that's weird,' said Jemma, as soon as Maddy had disappeared. 'What's going on?'

'I'm no expert,' said Raphael, 'but I suspect Brian has hypnotised her. When we used her name, she obeyed unquestioningly. And when I read certain phrases from the letter she performed certain actions. They must be cues.'

'But is it possible to hypnotise someone by letter?' asked Jemma.

'I doubt it,' said Raphael. 'I suspect Brian hypnotised Maddy in person before he left to challenge me. If he lost, that was his last chance to influence the bookshop. If I lost, it would be easy for him to return and bring Maddy round.'

Jemma gasped. 'That's so sneaky,' she said. 'But it's an awful lot of trouble to take, just to inconvenience us.'

'I don't think it's that,' said Raphael. 'As he's been sending his friends round to spy, I think there's more to it. I'm hoping Maddy will tell us.'

Maddy returned with a tray full of mugs a few minutes later. 'Thank you, Maddy,' said Raphael. 'Please take a seat. I'd like to talk to you, if I may.'

'Of course,' she said, sitting down.

'Maddy, sleep,' said Raphael, making a movement with his hand.

Maddy stared at him. 'I'm sorry, what did you say?'

'I just wondered if there were any biscuits, Maddy,' said Raphael.

'I'll go and see,' said Maddy. Her chair scraped back.

'She's resisting me,' said Raphael, when she had gone. 'I don't know if Brian has built that in, or if she doesn't trust me. She doesn't know me very well.'

'She probably doesn't trust me either,' said Jemma. She thought for a moment. 'I might be able to help. Hold the fort, I'll fetch Luke.'

'Luke?' said Raphael. 'Really?'

Jemma turned to him. 'Have you got any better ideas?'

'Well, no, but who will run the shop? Carl will be on his own.'
Then Raphael's face cleared. 'Got it.'

They jumped to their feet just as Maddy returned with a biscuit
barrel. 'Maddy, stay put,' Raphael said. 'We'll be back in a couple
of minutes.' They ran out of the shop as Maddy, still clutching the
biscuits, gazed after them.

'You get Luke,' Raphael panted, as they jogged down the road.
'I have something to do first.' He stopped, straightened his tie, and
opened the door to Rolando's.

Jemma stopped dead. 'Raphael, we don't have time for coffee!'

'I'll see you in two minutes,' shouted Raphael. 'Don't worry.'

Jemma sighed, and hurried on.

***

'What's up?' said Luke. 'You two dashed out of here as if the
police were after you.'

'Not this time,' said Jemma. 'We need you.'

'Me? What about the shop?'

'Raphael's sorting it,' Jemma said. 'Don't ask how.'

'OK,' said Luke, 'but what do you need me for?'

'Tell you when we get there,' said Jemma. 'Actually, can you go
downstairs and tell Carl you're coming with us? And – and give
him my love.'

Luke raised his eyebrows. 'Isn't that your job?'

'Oh, for heaven's sake,' said Jemma. 'If you want anything
done properly—' She scowled at him and ran downstairs.

The queue at the café counter was long; early birds were
already ordering lunch. Carl saw her and waved. Jemma ran
straight towards him, and he looked rather alarmed. 'I'm a bit
busy—'

'I don't care,' said Jemma, and threw her arms round him.
'Brian's messing about again. Raphael and I need to deal with
him, and I don't even know what that means yet. But I love you,
and I had to tell you.' And she kissed him. From behind her came

400

whistles and cheers, along with comments about jumping the queue, but she didn't let it interrupt her very important business.

Finally she had to come up for air. She looked at Carl, embarrassed, but not at all sorry.

'If this is what happens when Brian messes about,' Carl murmured, 'I kind of wish he'd do it more often.' And then it was his turn to kiss her.

They broke off at an extremely loud throat-clearing and found Giulia watching them, arms folded, and managing somehow to combine a glare and a twinkle. 'Business first, Carl,' she said, 'fun afterwards.'

'Quite,' said Raphael. 'I've explained to Luke, and while we're gone Giulia will be in charge.'

Carl saluted both of them. 'Yes, boss.' He gave Jemma a final squeeze, then let her go. 'I'll see you later,' he said.

'Yes,' said Jemma, 'you will.' She wished she felt as confident as she sounded.

***

They found Maddy where they had left her, still holding the biscuit barrel. 'Maddy,' said Raphael, 'you may put the biscuits down now.'

Maddy put the biscuits on the counter.

'She's exhausted,' said Luke.

Jemma glanced at him, then at Maddy. 'You're right,' she said. 'Now you've said that, it's so obvious.'

'Take a seat, Maddy,' said Raphael. 'You may sit next to Luke.'

She eyed Luke, then looked away.

'Please, Maddy,' said Luke. 'I'd like you to sit next to me.'

The faintest flush of pink appeared in Maddy's pale cheeks. Slowly, she walked towards him and sat down.

'That's right,' said Luke, and patted her arm.

'Are you tired, Maddy?' asked Raphael.

She gazed at him. 'Yes,' she murmured.

'Would you like to sleep, Maddy?' He made a pass with his hand. Her eyelids flickered, then opened.

'It's all right, Maddy,' said Luke. He put his hand on hers. 'You're safe. You can sleep.'

She looked at him, and Jemma saw the hint of a smile on her face. Raphael made the gesture again, and her eyes slowly closed. 'Tell me about Brian, Maddy.'

'I knew he would challenge you,' she said, dreamily. 'He spoke of practically nothing else. He said that if you won you would ruin the bookshop, and he would arrange insurance just in case. Then one day he came out of the stockroom, where he'd been rearranging books – I don't know why, everything was in order – and told me I had to listen carefully. The next thing I knew he was gone, and he didn't come back. Ever since, I haven't felt quite myself. I stop in the middle of doing something and can't remember why I'm doing it. I don't sleep well; I wake in the night worrying about the shop. And Jemma's angry with me so often. I try my best, but sometimes I do the wrong things. I think it's because I'm not concentrating.'

Raphael and Jemma exchanged glances. 'Maddy, Brian writes to you, doesn't he?'

'Yes, Mr Burns,' said Maddy. 'Only short letters, but it's nice to hear from him. He writes quite often.'

'So that's how he's doing it,' said Jemma. 'He's prompting her behaviour by letter.' Her fists clenched.

'Maddy, can you remember which books Brian moved?' asked Raphael.

'I can't,' said Maddy. 'But he told me that if I found a book out of place in the stockroom, I was to leave it where it was and update the database.'

'Jemma, can you get into the database?' said Raphael.

'Yes,' said Jemma. 'I'll take a look.' She moved to the counter, typed in the password, and began scrolling.

'Maddy, listen,' said Raphael. 'None of this is your fault. Do you understand?'

Maddy smiled, her eyes still closed. 'Is that true?'

'Yes, it is,' said Raphael.

'Of course it is,' added Luke, and squeezed her hand.

'I've found something,' said Jemma. 'Three books about technical interference, and three about signal jamming, shelved on either side of the communication section.' She took her phone out of her pocket and looked at it. 'My phone hasn't picked up messages for ages...'

'See what happens if you put them back in the right place,' said Raphael. 'I'll keep talking to Maddy.'

'I can go, if you want,' said Luke.

'You're busy here,' said Raphael. 'Besides, this is a job for an Assistant Keeper.'

Jemma went into the stockroom. For the first time she was pleased it was so much smaller than the one at Burns Books; it made everything easier to find. She found the first three books easily. They were slightly pulled out, as if Brian dared her to move them.

Jemma took a step towards the books, and tried to take another, but her foot wouldn't move. *Let me do this.* 'I am an Assistant Keeper,' she said aloud. She took a step, and her hand closed on the first book. A shock like static ran through her and she yelped, but she managed to pull it out. She took it to its rightful place, and couldn't help sighing with relief as she pushed it home. The second book was less painful, and the third felt like moving any book between any pair of shelves. And as Jemma moved the second trio of books, she noted how the closeness in the stockroom had lifted.

As Jemma pulled the last book from the shelf, her phone buzzed and buzzed. She took it from her pocket, and as the screen filled with the messages that had been held back for so long, her

403

eyes filled with tears. She blinked hard, and put her phone away. *I can catch up with it all later.*

'Did it work?' asked Raphael, when she returned.

'Yes,' she said, sitting at the computer. 'I'll keep looking.'

Raphael turned back to Maddy. 'You're sure there's nothing else you can tell us, Maddy?'

'I don't think so,' said Maddy. 'Except that Brian invited his friends here in the evenings, and he was always very smug and energetic the next day. He'd say bookselling ought to be more strictly regulated, and we needed more rules. I generally humoured him.'

'I don't believe it,' murmured Jemma. 'I've just found loads of books on financial mismanagement sandwiching the business section. No wonder it's been so hard to get the shop to make a decent profit.' She stood up.

'Wait,' said Raphael. 'Maddy, do you know where Brian is?'

'No,' said Maddy. 'Sorry.'

'You're sure?'

'Yes, I'm sure. His letters aren't postmarked, and he said before he went that if he had to leave, he'd go where no one could find him.'

Raphael sighed. 'Thank you, Maddy.' He looked at the others. 'I'm going to bring Maddy round. Keep holding her hand, Luke.' He leaned forward. 'Maddy,' he said, gently. 'You've helped us a great deal, and I know you've done your best. When I wake you up, that will end Brian's hold over you. If you ever receive another letter from him, don't open it. Give it to Jemma, or me. Do you understand?'

'I understand.'

'And will you do as I ask?'

'Yes.'

'Good,' said Raphael. 'Maddy, Brian is no longer your employer, and he has no hold over you.' He paused. 'It's time for you to wake up.'

Maddy's eyes pinged open. She stared at Raphael, then at her surroundings, and her eyes grew rounder and rounder. She took in the piles of books by the door and put a hand to her mouth. 'Did I do that?' she asked, in a shocked whisper.

'Yes,' said Jemma, 'but you couldn't help it. I understand now. I'm so sorry, Maddy.'

Maddy blinked at her. Her shoulders tensed, then suddenly she was shaking with sobs. 'It was him, wasn't it?' she cried, between gulps and wails. 'He said you'd lower the bookshop's standards and corrupt me, and that he'd stop you if it was the last thing he did! He said that the happiest day of his life would be when he read your obituary in the *Bookseller's Companion*. I told him how wrong those thoughts were, but—'

Luke moved closer and put his arms around her. 'Don't worry, Maddy, it's all right,' he murmured. 'You're free of him now. We'll make sure he can never do this to you or anyone else ever again.' He looked at Raphael. 'Won't we?'

'Yes,' said Raphael, rather uncertainly. 'Yes, we shall.'

'But how?' said Jemma. 'We don't know where he is.'

'I can guess,' said Raphael. 'He's barred from Westminster, and he won't be able to bear being far from books.' He sat up straight. 'Luke, stay here, look after Maddy, and mind the bookshop until we get back. Jemma and I must track Brian down and finish this.'

'Where are we going?' said Jemma. 'Do I need to pack?'

Raphael grinned. 'Perhaps a coat. We're going to the town of books: Hay-on-Wye.'

Chapter 19

'This will take hours,' said Jemma, gazing at the maps app on her phone. 'I know London was quiet, but it's such a long way to the Welsh border. The bookshops will probably be closed by the time we get there.'

'Don't you worry about that,' said Raphael. 'Gertrude's got a good turn of speed when she puts her mind to it.'

'Yes,' said Jemma, 'I gathered.' She had found herself clinging to the handle above the passenger door as Raphael navigated the back streets of London, twisting this way and that until she felt dizzy and nauseous. No hairpin was too tight for Gertrude, no alley too narrow. 'Out of interest, Raphael, have you ever been stopped by the police when you're out in Gertrude?'

'Nope,' said Raphael. 'But if you distract me by talking too much, there's always a first time.'

Jemma subsided into silence, and tried to relax as Raphael took the slip road to the motorway. *I do hope he'll observe the speed limit.* That was a minor worry compared to what would happen once they got to Hay-on-Wye. Would they be able to find Brian? And if so, what then?

She had thought Raphael would at least pack books for the journey, in case of another battle of knowledge. However, all he had brought was an overcoat, a multicoloured stripy scarf, a flask of coffee, and a bag of cinnamon buns. 'The essentials,' he said, passing the flask and the buns to Jemma. 'We may not be able to stop for lunch.'

At the last minute he had run up to his flat, and come out holding a small, strange contraption which Jemma thought she had seen on his shelves. It was made of metal, covered in black enamel, and featured several intersecting cogs and a handle. Jemma had no idea what it was for, and she really didn't want to ask. She remembered Raphael and Brian's previous confrontation, when she had been convinced that Raphael had lost, and fretted. What if Brian's powers had grown? What if his enchantments had affected Raphael's powers?

Suddenly Gertrude shot forward, and Jemma's back pressed into her seat. Jolted out of her thoughts, she stared at the road ahead, which was advancing at a ridiculous speed. 'Slow down, Raphael!' she cried. 'We'll get pulled over! Or we could die!'

'Don't know what you mean,' said Raphael. 'I'm doing a steady seventy, and the conditions are perfect.'

'I know what seventy miles an hour feels like,' said Jemma, through gritted teeth, 'and this is not it.' A police car pulled alongside. 'See, I told you.'

Raphael raised a hand to the police officer in the passenger seat, who waved back. The police car pulled ahead of them, indicated, and moved into the exit slip road. 'See? Nothing to worry about,' said Raphael.

'Have we got any cinnamon rolls left?' asked Jemma.

'Yes, plenty,' said Raphael. 'Would you like one? It might take your mind off things.'

'Not right now,' said Jemma. 'But I may need the bag.' She pointed at the speedometer, whose needle pointed at the number

70. 'Is that thing working?'

'Oh yes,' said Raphael. 'We are doing seventy. It's just that the motorway happens to be doing sixty-five in the opposite direction.'

Jemma closed her eyes. 'That makes me feel so much better.'

'Oh good,' said Raphael. 'If you don't mind, we'd better stop chatting so that I can concentrate on the road.'

Jemma fell silent, and lapsed into an uneasy mixture of looking at the road ahead, wishing she hadn't, and pondering what might happen. 'Can I ask you something?'

'You may,' said Raphael, his eyes on the road, 'but I don't guarantee an answer.'

'How come we haven't brought the others with us?' asked Jemma. 'Last time you and Brian faced off, Carl and Luke were there too.'

'They were,' said Raphael. 'This is different. For one thing, there's Maddy to consider. I couldn't possibly bring her anywhere near Brian.'

Jemma gasped. 'You mean that Brian might harm her?'

'There is that,' said Raphael. 'But I'm also worried that she might harm Brian. I have a feeling that the extreme upset and disgust that Maddy experienced when we brought her round could easily turn into rage. And anyway, it isn't her job to deal with Brian. In the first instance, it's mine.'

'Yes, but we could have sent her home,' said Jemma. 'Or Luke could have looked after her, and Carl could have come with us. I know it would mean closing the bookshop, but—'

'That isn't the reason,' said Raphael. 'The challenge you observed has strict rules. This is entirely different, and I would never risk bringing anyone ranked lower than Assistant Keeper to assist at a confrontation such as this.'

'But I'm only acting,' said Jemma. 'I'm not qualified!'

'You were qualified enough to remove Brian's enchantments

from your shop,' said Raphael. 'You undid the work of an Assistant Keeper, as he was when he undertook it. You are more than qualified, and I have every faith in you.'

'I don't,' mumbled Jemma.

'Well, I do,' said Raphael, 'and that's the end of it. Now do be quiet; we are coming off the motorway, and I always take the wrong road at this point if I'm not careful.'

Gertrude slowed to something approaching normal speed, then picked up the pace as they took an A road. Another motorway followed; Jemma had given up even trying to navigate. Eventually Raphael turned onto a narrower country road, and Jemma breathed a sigh of relief as Gertrude's engine modulated from a roar to a purr. She looked at the clock set into Gertrude's dashboard. Ten past one. 'We've made good time,' she said, weakly.

'We have,' said Raphael.

They drove on, and Gertrude seemed to crawl along. More houses appeared and they eased into a town. A sign read first *Y GELLI: tref y llyfrau*, then *HAY-ON-WYE: town of books*. Jemma felt a little pull at her heart, as if someone had plucked it like the string on a guitar. She shivered.

Raphael glanced across. 'You can feel it too,' he said. 'Never tell me that you're not qualified again.'

They drove on, and came to a fork in the road. 'Left or right?' asked Raphael.

'Left,' said Jemma, though she could not have said why. Her heart trembled, and she couldn't tell if it were from anticipation or fear.

They joined a queue of traffic. 'Let's find a car park,' said Raphael. 'The rest will be easier on foot. Here we are.' He indicated, manoeuvred Gertrude under the barrier, and parked. 'I'll get a ticket.'

Jemma held up her right hand, which trembled slightly. Her left did, too. She was about to rub her face when she remembered she was still wearing the make-up she had put on for the meeting. *Maybe I can scare Brian into submission*, she thought, with a wry smile. Then she looked around. To the left seemed fine; to the right, that twanging feeling.

Her door opened. 'I've got two hours,' said Raphael, 'that ought to be enough. Let's go and get this over with. Oh, wait a minute—' He reached into the inner pocket of his jacket and brought out two pencils, one of which he handed to Jemma. Then he fished out the small metal contraption and put it on Gertrude's dashboard. 'Excuse the mess.' He inserted his pencil into the device, turned the handle, and wooden shavings spilled out.

Jemma stared. 'You brought a *pencil sharpener*?'

Raphael drew out the pencil, now very sharp, and regarded it critically. 'I hope we won't need these, but it's always best to be prepared.' He held his hand out, and Jemma passed him her pencil.

'What am I supposed to do with this?' she asked, when he passed it back.

'If you need to use it,' said Raphael, 'you'll know. Which way?'

'Right,' said Jemma.

She led the way, following the feeling, turning left, then left again. The feeling pulsed inside her, then strengthened suddenly as they approached an alley. Jemma swallowed.

'Take deep breaths if you're worried,' said Raphael. 'Don't let it get the better of you.'

Jemma did as Raphael instructed, taking slow, deep breaths as she walked along. Eventually they came out of the alley, and without hesitation Jemma turned right. She stopped outside a small, ramshackle shop, whose sign said *Curious Books and Antiquities*. 'I think this is it,' she said.

'I think you're right,' said Raphael. 'Got your pencil?'

Jemma rummaged in her pocket and held it up.

'Good. Then in we go.' And he pushed open the door.

A bell jangled, and Jemma felt almost reassured. The shop was dim, shabby, quaint. She could see why Brian had been drawn to it. But the cheerful young man who materialised from behind a curtain to greet them was not Brian. 'Hello, how may I help you?' he asked.

'I wondered if I might speak to your assistant,' said Raphael. 'Is he about?'

'Yes, and no,' said the young man. 'He is in, but he's having his lunch. I can see if he's free, if you like.'

'That would be most helpful,' said Raphael.

The young man vanished and they heard the murmur of voices in the back room. Raphael delved into his pocket and pulled out, of all things, a mobile phone. 'Ten to two,' he commented, peering at it. 'Hopefully we can get things sorted in time for a late lunch.' He pushed a button on the phone and put it in his pocket. 'If we don't, I doubt that either of us will want lunch anyway.'

'Don't cheer me up with too much positivity, will you,' said Jemma. She was still trying to take deep, slow breaths, but finding it difficult. She gazed around her to calm herself, and jumped at the sight of a familiar book; hardback, green cloth, with gilt detailing. 'The *Origin of Species*!' she cried, clutching Raphael's arm. 'Drusilla bought it for him!' Then her heart leapt into her throat as the curtain twitched, and a familiar figure appeared.

Chapter 20

A familiar figure, and yet not. In the few months since she had last seen him, Brian's stoop had become more pronounced. His hair was thinner, his face more deeply lined. *He's grown older*, she thought, trying not to stare. *Much, much older.*

'Ah, there you are, Brian,' said Raphael, as if Brian had popped into the back half an hour ago. 'How are you enjoying your new employment?'

'It keeps me busy,' said Brian. He struggled to look Raphael in the eye now, but his eyes were the same bold, defiant blue. *Mysterious blue*, thought Jemma.

'I wasn't referring to your work in this bookshop,' said Raphael. 'I meant your extra-curricular activities. Specifically, sending your cronies to spy on Jemma here, booby-trapping her bookshop, and last but not least, putting your poor ex-assistant under a hypnotic enchantment. What do you have to say for yourself?'

'The Keepers' Guild always upholds the rights of the individual,' said Brian, drawing himself up as tall as he could. 'The right of the individual member to challenge whomever he likes; the right of an individual member to maintain his bookshop as he sees fit. How I arrange the books in my shop is my concern. How I manage my staff is my concern. And if people who may know me choose to visit a bookshop, that's hardly unusual. If that's all you've come for, I suggest you browse in the shop, see if there's anything you wish to buy, then return to London. I have nothing to say to you.' He shuffled towards the curtain.

'Wait a moment,' said Raphael. He pulled out his pencil, and pointed it at Brian's back.

Brian stopped dead.

Raphael drew a slow circle in the air, and Brian began to turn. He resisted every movement, but despite his struggles, in a few seconds he was facing Raphael again.

Raphael advanced to the counter and rested the point of his pencil on it. 'It isn't very nice to feel as if you're out of your own control, is it, Brian?' he said.

Brian glared at him but did not move, and Jemma realised that he couldn't.

'Jemma, take out your pencil,' said Raphael.

She looked at him doubtfully, but obeyed.

'Brian, if I were cruel, I would instruct Jemma to make you dance to her tune,' said Raphael. 'However, luckily for you, I am not a cruel man, and I have no wish to wear out your old bones any more than necessary.' He pointed with the pencil to a chair. 'Sit.'

Brian shambled over to the chair and sat, glowering. 'You'll get nothing out of me,' he said.

'You have already told me that, Brian,' said Raphael. 'There is no point in repeating it. Jemma, would you mind doing something for me? There is a notepad by the cash register. I would like you to write, as concisely as you can, what Brian has done to hamper your management of the Friendly Bookshop.'

Brian winced. 'I tell you I've done nothing—'

413

Jemma pointed her pencil at Brian and he was immediately silent. She glanced at Raphael. 'Please, write,' he said.

And Jemma wrote.

Brian, former Assistant Keeper for Westminster, hypnotised Maddy Shenton, assistant at the Friendly Bookshop. He did this with the intention of controlling her, and forcing her to perform actions which would impede the bookshop's business. After the initial hypnosis, he controlled her by means of regular letters. We know this both from Maddy's testimony and our own observations.

Brian also arranged books in the stockroom to thwart the business and block communications: specifically, texts and calls. I removed these arrangements, and communications were restored immediately.

It is also likely that Brian instructed friends of his to visit the bookshop, report back, and acquire books from it. These friends are known sympathisers of Brian, and they have stirred up trouble and disrupted Raphael's work. I cannot confirm this without further investigation.

She showed Raphael. 'Will that do?'

Raphael scanned the page. 'That seems fair-minded and well-evidenced,' he said. 'Your penmanship needs improvement, but you can't have everything.' He pushed the notepad back to her. 'Please sign it and add the date and your title, and then I have a little to add.'

Jemma signed her name, with the little flourish that she always added, and printed it underneath. She added the date, then wrote *Assistant Keeper*. After it she drew a bracket, then began to write the A of *Acting*, but a tiny piece of the pencil lead broke off. 'Darn,' she said.

'Don't worry about it,' said Raphael, 'just rub out the bracket. It will do as it is.'

'But—'

414

'Trust me.' Raphael took the notepad and wrote rapidly beneath Jemma's script. *I certify that this is a true account, evidenced, and written moreover with a Pencil of Truth, as is this statement. Raphael Burns, Keeper of England.* He held the notepad up for Brian to see. 'Can you deny any of this?'

'No,' said Brian, 'and I don't wish to.'

'Oh dear,' said Raphael. 'Never mind, eh?'

Brian grinned, showing crooked teeth with one missing from the bottom row. 'Is that all you've got? Some scribbles with a so-called magic pencil?'

'I also have this.' Raphael held up his mobile phone. 'Nifty, isn't it?'

Brian's grin broadened. 'What will you do, dial 999?'

'Oh, I can do better than that,' said Raphael. He pressed a button and took a picture first of the notepad, then of Brian. His fingers moved over the screen, and they heard a whoosh.

'Aren't you supposed to ask permission before you take pictures of people?' said Brian, frowning.

'Usually, yes,' said Raphael. 'But I'm pretty sure there's an exception when you're either investigating or preventing crime. Isn't there?' he asked the phone.

'Indeed there is,' the phone replied, and Jemma jumped. There, filling the screen, was the face of a man who seemed middle-aged, but for a shock of white hair. His expression appeared neutral, but every so often a ripple of anger disturbed it.

'Jemma, may I introduce Armand Dupont, Head of European Operations for the Keepers' Guild,' said Raphael. 'Armand, this is Jemma James, Assistant Keeper for Westminster until the vacancy is filled.'

'Delighted,' said Armand Dupont. He spoke in perfect, unaccented English. 'Thank you for dialling me in earlier, Raphael. It has been a most interesting conversation. Could you turn me to face Brian, please.'

415

Brian's lower lip trembled and he edged backwards, seeming to shrink into his chair. 'Please... I did nothing wrong.'

'Oh, but you did,' said Armand Dupont. 'You are correct in that you may arrange your bookshop as you like, and manage your assistant as you see fit. However, those rights end from the moment the bookshop ceases to be yours. By deliberately putting those precautions in place, you were violating the rights which you spoke of so self-righteously earlier. And by hypnotising your assistant, who is also an associate of the Guild, you violated *her* rights. Impeding the operations of a bookshop under the auspices of the Guild is absolutely forbidden, and carries a heavy punishment.'

'I'm sorry!' cried Brian. 'I didn't know!'

'In your heart, you knew,' the remorseless voice continued. 'But you chose to misinterpret the rules; to observe the letter and ignore the spirit. You chose to remain wilfully ignorant. In doing so, you disrupted the work of one of the highest-ranking officials of the Guild, and you also caused me inconvenience. I can't decide which of these things displeases me more. But I digress. Raphael, could you turn me back to your Assistant Keeper, please?'

As Raphael did so, they heard a low mutter, 'Why couldn't the man use a laptop, for heaven's sake? Or even a tablet.' Jemma straightened her face hastily as the phone found her. 'As a member of the Guild, you of all of us have suffered the most severe injury from Brian's actions. What do you think would be an appropriate punishment?'

'Oh, um, I don't know,' said Jemma. 'I mean, he's already banished.' Then a thought occurred to her. 'Hang on, is he a member of the Guild any more? Can you punish him?'

'Once a member, always a member,' said Armand Dupont. 'What do you feel is appropriate?'

Jemma bit her lip. *That applies to me, too. I'll always be a member of the Guild.* She wasn't sure whether to be pleased or worried. 'His punishment should stop him doing things like this,' she said. 'He is very old.' She remembered how he had been silenced by her pencil. 'And quite weak,' she added.

'That is true,' said Armand Dupont. 'But as we can see, still capable of venom. Raphael, what do you think?'

'I agree with Jemma,' said Raphael, giving Brian a pitying look. 'When Brian had power, he used it to attempt to overthrow and destroy. He acted in his own interests, not those of the Guild. But I believe we should be as merciful as we possibly can.'

'I concur,' said the phone. 'Brian, this is my decision. You may no longer approach or speak to another Guild member or associate, whether face to face or by means of technology. I shall also prevent you from handling books or communications technology with any malign intent. If you attempt it, you will suffer. Do I make myself clear?'

Already Brian seemed smaller, more wizened and shrunken. 'Yes,' he croaked.

'Good,' said Armand Dupont. 'Those measures are in force as of *now*.' He snapped his fingers.

Brian shrieked and hid his face. He peeped at Raphael and Jemma, screamed, and hobbled into the back room as fast as his legs could carry him. The curtain rippled for a moment, and then the folds settled and became motionless, as if Brian had been swallowed by a merciless sea.

Jemma and Raphael looked at each other, then at the phone. 'That seems to have worked,' said Raphael.

'Yes,' said Armand Dupont. 'I apologise for that letter, by the way. I was dealing with an incident in a library in Paris, you see, and you caught me at a bad time. Now I see what has been going on, I completely understand. Skulduggery is absolutely a tactic of the Guild, but not when it undermines our own business.'

'Quite,' said Raphael. 'Well, now that's all settled, Jemma and I might have lunch.'

For the first time, Armand Dupont's face showed strong emotion. 'You haven't had lunch? What were you thinking of? How could you even contemplate undertaking tasks such as this on an empty stomach? Go and remedy this matter immediately. Oh yes, and it was nice to meet you . . . Jemma, was it?'

'That's right,' said Jemma. 'Jemma James.'

'Jemma James. I shall remember. Go and have a nice lunch, and don't forget to charge it to expenses.' His brow furrowed. 'Are you in Hay-on-Wye?'

'Yes,' said Jemma, 'we are.'

'Ah, Hay-on-Wye...' A dreamy expression came over his face. 'Oh, to be browsing, free from care.' He smiled, and suddenly looked younger still. 'Enjoy your afternoon. Au revoir.' His face disappeared, replaced by a blank screen.

Jemma stared at Raphael. 'Is that it? We've done it?'

'No,' said Raphael. 'We haven't done it. *You've* done it. You did pretty much all of it. You noted unusual phenomena, alerted your manager, and detected and removed misused knowledge sources without personal protective equipment.' He held up his pencil, and a faint wail came from the back room. 'You tracked down a felon, bore effective witness using a Pencil of Truth, and recommended mercy, as an Assistant Keeper should.' He sighed. 'You do realise this means I shall have to write a report, don't you.'

'But not yet,' said Jemma. 'Come on, let's get out of here.' She noticed, with great relief, that the fear and apprehension she had felt earlier had completely vanished. 'I feel better than I have in weeks.'

'You know what,' said Raphael, 'so do I.'

'We must tell the others,' said Jemma, as they walked along the main street, looking for restaurants.

'Oh yes,' said Raphael. 'But not until we've ordered.'

Chapter 21

Carl appeared from behind one of the screens which was acting as the wings, and faced the applauding audience. 'We will now have a half-hour interval. Refreshments are available from the café.' He waved a hand at the café counter, towards which Giulia was hurrying. 'The bathrooms are in the corner. I'll come out again and give you a five-minute warning to resume your seats. Thank you for your attention.'

'It's going well, isn't it?' Raphael murmured to Jemma.

She beamed with pride. 'Yes, it is. I'll nip backstage and check on Carl. I don't suppose you could get me a cappuccino?'

Raphael stood up and stretched. 'On it,' he said, and ambled over to the forming queue.

Jemma nudged Luke, who was sitting on her other side. 'What do you think?' she whispered.

'What? Oh yes, it's very good. Isn't it, Maddy?'

Maddy looked enraptured, although Jemma suspected that was more to do with sitting next to Luke than the premiere of Carl's play. 'Oh yes, it's delightful.'

'I'll pass that on to Carl,' said Jemma. 'See you after the

interval.'

Maddy's right, she thought. *It's really, really good. And thoroughly deserved; they've worked so hard on it.*

Now that things were running more smoothly at the Friendly Bookshop, she had attended a few rehearsals as an 'average spectator'. 'I want this to be the sort of play that anyone could enjoy,' Carl had said. 'Not just people who go to the theatre all the time and know what to expect. I want someone who maybe goes once a year or less to get something out of this play.' He looked rather fierce as he said it.

'Well, that's me,' Jemma had replied. 'I can't remember the last time I went to the theatre.' She thought for a moment. 'That ought to change. Now the bookshop is behaving more or less as it should, I can have hobbies. I can go out in the evening and enjoy myself.' She gave him a playful nudge. 'That's if I can get you to come with me, of course, when you're not rehearsing.'

Carl had laughed. 'I daresay I'll be at a loose end soon enough. We're only doing three performances, then we'll probably be hustling again.' But somehow, Jemma suspected he wouldn't have to hustle too hard.

She walked to the screen and stuck her head round it. 'Is it OK to come in?'

Carl turned. 'Do you think it's going all right?'

Jemma spread her hands. 'Didn't you hear the applause? Didn't you hear them laughing in all the places you wanted them to?'

Carl looked slightly less anxious. 'I suppose. But I worry.'

'Of course,' said Jemma, 'and that's normal, but everyone's enjoying it.' She moved closer and wrapped her arms around him. 'You've done such a brilliant job. Your first play, and the audience love it.'

'There's the second half yet,' said Carl, still appearing a little uneasy. 'Don't jinx it.'

'I won't,' she said, and kissed him.

A couple of cast members wandered over. 'Sorry to interrupt, Carl, but have you got any notes for us?' said one.

'Sure, give me two seconds,' said Carl. He looked at Jemma. 'Sorry.'

'Don't apologise,' said Jemma. 'You're doing your job.' She stroked his cheek. 'I'll see you afterwards.'

As Carl beckoned to the rest of the cast, Jemma lingered behind the screen, gazing at the lower floor of the bookshop. They had sold out the venue, a hundred seats, and they were packed to capacity. In the third row – 'we don't want to be too conspicuous' – were her mum and dad. Even from this distance she could hear her mother talking to someone in the second row. 'It's excellent, isn't it? My daughter is the playwright's partner—' She spotted Jemma and waved, then stuck two thumbs up. 'And Debra is his mum...' Debra, sitting next to her, smiled politely, but underneath Jemma could tell that she was bursting with pride.

Some of the audience would be friends and family of the cast, of course, but she could also see a few bookshop regulars. The two Golden Age crime ladies were there, and Mohammed, in the third row, studying his programme. And was she mistaken, or were Felicity and Jerome whispering together at the back?

Speaking of together, Luke and Maddy seemed very happy. They weren't going out exactly, but Luke had expressed an interest in spending time at the Friendly Bookshop to learn more about antiquarian books from Maddy. Since this freed Jemma to spend more time at Burns Books with Raphael and Carl, she had ordered more sunlight-filtering window film and been only too happy to agree.

Once Maddy had recovered from her anger and distress at the ordeal she had been through, with Luke acting as a sort of unofficial therapist, she had made a proposition to Jemma. 'We have all these valuable books in the stockroom,' she said, waving a hand at it in a dismissive way that Jemma could not have imagined a few weeks ago. 'Now that – things have changed, and the fiction section is doing so well, it makes sense to extend it. But at the same time, it's silly to ignore the stuff we have. Why don't we sort of split the bookshop in half? You put more of your books out, and I work with the existing books.' She gazed at Jemma, her anxiety visible on her face.

'That's a really good idea,' said Jemma. 'Let's draw up a plan, try it for a month, and see how things go.'

Already, the idea was bearing fruit. The people who wanted non-fiction in posh bindings flocked to Maddy, and those seeking good-quality fiction made a beeline for Jemma – or Luke, if he was in. Often Jemma would return from lunch, or from the other shop, and find Luke and Maddy having an animated discussion about *Seven Gothic Tales*, or which was the best film version of *Dracula*.

'Don't you find the age difference a problem?' she asked Luke once, when they were in the back room making tea.

Luke considered for a moment, then shook his head. 'I know I'm a lot older than Maddy,' he said, 'but she is so wise when you get past her shy exterior. I don't see it as a problem at all.'

Jemma looked at the café counter, where Raphael was laughing with Giulia as she made his drinks. They had arrived together, too. She wasn't sure if that meant anything, or if it would continue, but she hoped it did. *He deserves happiness as much as anyone.*

A chirrup made her look down. Folio, wearing a smart collar for the occasion, was rubbing against her leg. She scratched him behind the ears. 'Are you enjoying the play?' Folio had been allocated his own seat in the front row, and when she glanced at him from time to time, he was paying attention, his head moving as the different actors spoke. She had been slightly worried that he might attempt to become part of the proceedings, but so far he had behaved very well.

Folio chirruped again, which she presumed was a yes, then ran towards the café area, pulling up next to Raphael. Raphael murmured something to Giulia, who laughed.

'I thought it was you!'

Jemma jumped. A small pink-haired woman had materialised beside her. 'Stella!' she exclaimed. 'You came!'

'Oh yes,' said Stella. 'I've never attended a first night before, and it's ever so good. Do you think I could maybe speak to some of the cast? I want to write this up on my blog.'

'I'm sure that would be fine,' said Jemma. 'You know Carl, don't you? He's the writer and director.' She pointed to where Carl was talking with the cast, gesturing occasionally. Just then his hands fell to his sides, and the cast began to drift away. 'Now looks like a good time, if you're quick.'

'I shall be quick,' said Stella, and bustled away. A couple of minutes later, a tall man with an interesting beard, wearing jeans, a fisherman's sweater, and an artfully-draped scarf, wandered over to join them. 'Promising first half,' he declared, extending a hand and at the same time holding up a card. 'Henry Sims, drama critic at the *Evening Clarion*.'

Carl's face lit up, and Jemma's heart filled on his behalf.

And what about me? Well, I have Carl, and there's the flat to redecorate, and the bookshop is flying–

And the other thing? her inner voice prompted.

Yes, my mum finally understands that I'm serious about the bookshop, and she's happy–

You know exactly what I mean.

Jemma smiled. She had applied for the post of Assistant Keeper, on the grounds that it wouldn't hurt, and the closing date was tomorrow. She had handed her application to Raphael herself. 'Although now I know how tech-savvy you are,' she said, 'I could have emailed it, couldn't I?'

Raphael looked shamefaced. 'Sometimes it pays to have a little in reserve,' he said. 'Anyway, I'm glad you've applied.'

'Have you had much interest?' asked Jemma.

'Are you fishing, Jemma?' Raphael laughed. 'Not a great deal. Those in the know are aware that there is a very strong candidate in the field whom they don't want to go up against.'

Jemma grimaced. 'It isn't Drusilla, is it? I don't think I could bear her being any closer than she is.'

Raphael gazed at her with something like affection. 'For someone so smart and talented, Jemma James, you really can be an absolute chump. I mean you.'

'Me?' said Jemma. 'But I—'

'Remember in Hay-on-Wye—'

'I know, I helped with sorting out Brian,' said Jemma.

'If you'll let me finish,' said Raphael. 'Remember when your pencil broke?'

Jemma frowned. 'Yes, but I was probably pressing too hard.'

'What were you writing?'

It was like yesterday. Jemma could see it in her mind's eye: printing her name, writing *Assistant Keeper*, opening the bracket... 'I was about to write *Acting*.'

'Yes, and your lead broke, because a Pencil of Truth can only write truth. You weren't *acting* as an Assistant Keeper; you were *being* an Assistant Keeper. There is an important distinction, and the Pencil of Truth never lies.' For a moment he looked like a wise old owl. 'That is all I shall say on the subject for now.'

Jemma remembered the flood of pride she had felt; but she also remembered her nausea when they were searching for Brian, and the shock that had gone through her when she removed that first enchanted book. *Can I really do it?* she thought. *Can I face that fear, possibly every day, and master it?*

'But wouldn't it be an adventure?' whispered her inner voice. 'Wouldn't it be an incredible adventure?'

Carl walked out of the wings and faced the audience, and Jemma strolled back to her front-row seat. Tonight there was the

424

rest of the play to enjoy, and dinner with her family and Carl's. But then— She closed her eyes and imagined a strange and wonderful future rolling out ahead of her like a magic carpet. *Do I dare?* Her toes tingled with anticipation, and she smiled to herself.

Acknowledgements

My first thanks go to my marvellous beta readers – Carol Bissett, Ruth Cunliffe, Paula Harmon, and Stephen Lenhardt – and to my excellent proofreader, John Croall. Thank you with your help with all three books!

A huge additional thank you goes to my husband Stephen for his continued support and encouragement, which has been more valued than ever in these interesting times.

Another big thank you to Audrey Cowie, who first gave me the idea for a story set in a bookshop.

My final thanks are for you, the reader. Thank you for reading, and I hope you've enjoyed Jemma and Raphael's adventures. If you did, a short review or rating on Amazon or Goodreads would be very much appreciated. Ratings and reviews, however short, help readers to discover books.

FONT AND IMAGE CREDITS

Cover and heading fonts: Alyssum Blossom and Alyssum Blossom Sans by Bombastype

Stars: Night free icon by flaticon at freepik.com: https://www.freepik.com/free-icon/night_914336.htm

Chapter vignette: Opened books in hand drawn style Free Vector by freepik at freepik.com: https://www.freepik.com/free-vector/opened-books-hand-drawn-style_765567.htm

Cover created using GIMP image editor: https://www.gimp.org

About the Author

Liz Hedgecock grew up in London, England, did an English degree, and then took forever to start writing. After several years working in the National Health Service, some short stories crept into the world. A few even won prizes. Then the stories started to grow longer...

Now Liz travels between the nineteenth and twenty-first centuries, murdering people. To be fair, she does usually clean up after herself.

Liz's reimaginings of Sherlock Holmes, her Pippa Parker cozy mystery series, the Caster & Fleet Victorian mystery series (written with Paula Harmon), and the Maisie Frobisher Mysteries are available in ebook and paperback.

Liz lives in Cheshire with her husband and two sons, and when she's not writing or child-wrangling you can usually find her reading, messing about on Twitter, or cooing over stuff in museums and art galleries. That's her story, anyway, and she's sticking to it.

Website/blog: http://lizhedgecock.wordpress.com
Facebook: http://www.facebook.com/lizhedgecockwrites
Twitter: http://twitter.com/lizhedgecock
Goodreads: https://www.goodreads.com/lizhedgecock
Amazon author page: http://author.to/LizH

Books by Liz Hedgecock

Short stories
The Secret Notebook of Sherlock Holmes
Bitesize
The Adventure of the Scarlet Rosebud
The Case of the Peculiar Pantomime (a Caster & Fleet short mystery)

Halloween Sherlock series (novelettes)
The Case of the Snow-White Lady
Sherlock Holmes and the Deathly Fog
The Case of the Curious Cabinet

Sherlock & Jack series (novellas)
A Jar Of Thursday
Something Blue
A Phoenix Rises

Mrs Hudson & Sherlock Holmes series (novels)
A House Of Mirrors
In Sherlock's Shadow

Pippa Parker Mysteries (novels)
Murder At The Playgroup
Murder In The Choir
A Fete Worse Than Death
Murder in the Meadow
The QWERTY Murders
Past Tense

Caster & Fleet Mysteries (with Paula Harmon)
The Case of the Black Tulips
The Case of the Runaway Client
The Case of the Deceased Clerk
The Case of the Masquerade Mob
The Case of the Fateful Legacy
The Case of the Crystal Kisses

Maisie Frobisher Mysteries (novels)
All At Sea
Off The Map
Gone To Ground
In Plain Sight

The Magic Bookshop (short novels)
Every Trick in the Book
Brought to Book
Double Booked
By The Book

For children (with Zoe Harmon)
A Christmas Carrot

WHITE
RHINO
BOOKS

429

Printed in Great Britain
by Amazon

18023570R00253